YOU'RE THE CREAM IN MY COFFEE

You're the cat's meow!

Jennifer Lamont Leo

Jennifer Lamont Leo

Smitten
Historical Romance

YOU'RE THE CREAM IN MY COFFEE BY JENNIFER LAMONT LEO
Published by Smitten Historical Romance
An imprint of Lighthouse Publishing of the Carolinas
2333 Barton Oaks Dr., Raleigh, NC, 27614

ISBN: 9781938499074
Copyright © 2016 by Jennifer Lamont Leo
Cover design by Elaina Lee
Interior design by AtriTex
Author photo by Cary Burnett

Available in print from your local bookstore, online, or from the publisher at:
www.lighthousepublishingofthecarolinas.com

For more information on this book and the author, visit: www.jenniferlamontleo.com

Scripture quotations are taken from the King James Version (KJV).

Brought to you by the creative team at Lighthouse Publishing of the Carolinas:
Eddie Jones, Kathryn Davis, Shonda Savage, Lucie Winborne, and Christy Distler

Library of Congress Cataloging-in-Publication Data
Leo, Jennifer Lamont
You're the Cream in My Coffee / Jennifer Lamont Leo 1st ed.

Printed in the United States of America

Praise for *You're the Cream in My Coffee*

The cat's pajamas! Rich in jazzy details of 1920s Chicago, *You're the Cream in My Coffee* is a sparkling debut novel. With an adventurous heroine, intriguing side characters, and a thought-provoking message, this story will keep you riveted. Jennifer Lamont Leo is a name to watch for in historical fiction!

~ **Sarah Sundin**
Award-winning author of *Anchor in the Storm*

Every single inch of this novel is delightful. From the start, Marjorie Corrigan felt like a friend, one I was glad to see each time I returned to her story. With charming characters and a plot that keeps moving, this is a novel you don't want to miss. Jennifer Lamont Leo is a fresh voice in Christian fiction. I can't wait to read more of her work.

~**Susie Finkbeiner**
Author of *A Cup of Dust: A Novel of the Dust Bowl*

For Patricia and Donald

CHAPTER ONE

First off, I need to set the record straight. In a town the size of Kerryville, Illinois, rumors have a way of catching fire and burning a hole straight through the truth.

Despite what you may have heard down at Madge's Cut 'n' Curl, the fact that I, Marjorie Corrigan, fainted in the balcony at the Orpheum during the Sunday matinee had nothing to do with the movie's intense Great War battle scenes. Or the steamy romance between an American soldier and a French farm girl. Or the scandalous appearance of a curse word right there in black and white for the whole world to see. It had nothing to do with Myrtle Jamison's off-tune piano accompaniment, or the refreshment stand running out of Coca-Cola even before the feature started.

Above all, it had nothing—absolutely nothing—to do with my being in the "family way," a rumor as mortifying as it was untrue. Honestly! I realized the good ladies of Kerryville thought my engagement to Dr. Richard Brownlee had dragged on entirely too long, but spreading malicious rumors was not the way to speed things along.

Here's how it all began. On an unseasonably warm April afternoon, the theater grew close and stuffy, especially up in the balcony where my kid sister, Helen, and I were seated. The new air-cooling systems, all the rage in city theaters, had not yet made it to little Kerryville. I pressed my handkerchief to my face and debated whether to sneak down to the lobby for a cold drink. I knew the picture by heart, anyway. Helen and I had already watched John Gilbert in *The Big Parade* several times. The feature selection at the Orpheum changed with glacial slowness, and the owner swapped in an old favorite now and then when new reels were slow to arrive. Still, I hated to annoy people by crawling over their legs in the dark, so I stayed put and watched a favorite scene in which the soldier and the French girl first meet in the village near her family's farm.

As the doughboy and farm girl flirted onscreen, I mentally recast the scene. The French village became Kerryville, the farm our family's dry goods store, and the French girl was me, stocking thread and cutting fabric on an ordinary day, when in walks a handsome soldier, ready to change my life forever. What would it be like to have my whole world turned upside down by this soldier, his dazzling smile hinting at adventure and mystery? What if he invited me to run away with him? What if he held out his hand to me and said—

"Stop hogging all the Jujubes." Helen reached over and snatched the candy from my hand. With a start I snapped back to reality, guilty I'd been caught daydreaming, especially since the soldier in my fantasy clearly bore a face other than that of my fiancé, Richard. With a sigh I relinquished the sweets. Real life wasn't anything like the movies.

Helen had begged to see *The Big Parade* yet again, but playing around the misty edges of my mind lurked the real reason I had given in. In John Gilbert's soulful expression, in his strong jaw and khaki uniform, I saw Jack. Jack, the sweetheart lost to me forever on some battlefield in France. And for just a little while, in the dark, I could think back and remember.

For heaven's sake, Marjorie, snap out of it. I straightened my spine against the velvet cushion. *It's been ten years. You're engaged to someone else. Move on with your life. Forward, march.*

Sternly I directed my mind to imagine Richard in the soldier role, but it didn't quite work. For one thing, Richard hadn't served in the war. For another, he was not prone to impulsive romantic gestures. Our courtship proceeded on a steady course, free of drama. Silently I recited his good qualities, a habit I'd acquired of late. Richard was kind. Generous. Faithful. Prosperous. Toss in thrifty, brave, and clean and he'd make the perfect Boy Scout. In fact, he made perfect husband and father material. Everyone said so. If together we seemed to lack a certain, well, *spark*, then so what? A girl can't build a future on castles in the air.

At sixteen, Helen still firmly believed in air castles. Beside me she mused, "I wonder if our brother fell in love with any French girls during the war."

Or if Jack did, I wondered against my will, then chased that thought straight out of my head. Remembering my old flame invariably brought on useless comparisons between *then* and *now*.

"Not likely," I whispered to Helen. "Charlie's never mentioned any girls."

"Not that he'd tell us, of course. You don't tell that sort of thing to your sisters."

"Shhh! Watch the picture."

Helen fell silent, but she'd seen the movie too many times to become engrossed. Minutes later she whispered, "I wish you and I could travel to France."

"Maybe we will. Someday."

She snorted. "You say that now. But once you're married, we'll never get to go anywhere or do anything fun, ever again."

This time the "Shhh!" came from the row behind us.

My sister's words echoed in my head. *Never do anything fun again.* Suddenly, in spite of the heat, shivers that had nothing to do with John Gilbert's dreamy dark eyes raised goose bumps on my arms. The screen blurred. The flocked-velvet walls closed in on me. My pulse pounded. I needed air.

I nudged my sister. "Come on. We have to leave."

Helen gaped at me in the flickering light. "What's the matter?"

The rows of seats rearranged themselves in dizzying patterns.

"Now, please. I'm—I'm not feeling well."

"What's wrong?"

"I don't know. I just feel—strange."

She gestured toward the screen. "But the soldier and the French girl—"

"Oh, for heaven's sake, Helen," I hissed, gripping her arm. "How many times have we seen it? War happens, he leaves, he comes back, they kiss, end of story."

"Ow. Stop it!" Helen yanked her arm away, swatting the man in front of us. He turned and glared. "Sorry," she whispered, then to me, "See what you made me do."

The theater dipped and spun. "I mean it, Helen. I have to leave. Now."

She peered at me. "Jeepers, Marjorie, you don't look so hot."

I stood and lurched over legs and handbags toward the exit. "Sorry. Sorry."

And the next thing I knew, I was lying flat in the aisle, Helen rubbing my wrist, a pockmarked usher shining his flashlight in my face, and Eugenia Wardlow, the town's biggest gossip, leaning over me with a look of delighted concern.

"If you wouldn't attend those ghastly pictures, this never would have happened," my father's wife, Frances, scolded that evening, after getting an earful from Sadie Miller, who heard it from Penelope Blake, who got it straight from Eugenia Wardlow herself. "I'm mortified. Simply mortified."

"*You're* mortified?"

Feeling more like an obstinate youngster than a woman of twenty-six, I avoided her gaze and watched her hands tense and flex as she kneaded bread dough.

"'Family way,' indeed," she sputtered. "That woman is a—a—" She gave the dough an extra-vigorous punch—whether on Eugenia Wardlow's behalf or mine was unclear. "Well, being a Christian woman, I can't say what she is. But she spreads a nasty rumor quicker than 'one if by land, two if by sea.' I'll be on the telephone all evening, trying to set things right." She straightened up and blew a strand of hair out of her face. "Honestly, if Eugenia weren't the only florist in town, I'd order your wedding flowers elsewhere, just to spite her."

"That's what I hate about small-town life," I said. "Everybody's always poking their noses into everyone else's business and offering up their own skewed versions of things. Since when is fainting a sign of the stork, anyway?"

"Since busybody spinsters like Eugenia decided to liven up the gossip mill." Frances glanced at the wall calendar, where Phillips' Milk of Magnesia and the Kerryville Pharmacy wished us a healthy 1928. "I suppose we could move the wedding earlier."

My heart lurched. "Earlier! That would only make matters worse."

She sighed. "We'd never be able to pull it off, anyway. So much remains to be done: the guest list, the invitations . . ." She paused.

"You ought to see Dr. Perkins. Best make sure you're not coming down with something."

"I'm fine, really. The theater was simply roasting, and I . . ."

"Yes, Helen told me all about it." Frances returned to kneading. "Marjorie, you're a grown woman. I can't stop you from going to the pictures, but I can at least insist you stop taking Helen with you. At her age she doesn't need to see all that romantic folderol and get strange ideas in her head."

Strange ideas like there's room for a little romance and adventure in a person's life. Like there's a world beyond Kerryville. Anyway, at sixteen, Helen practically knew more about the birds and the bees than I did. But all I said out loud was, "Yes, ma'am."

The back door swung open and my older brother, Charlie, shuffled in. "Hi, all. When's supper? I'm starving." He reached around Frances to pinch a bit of bread dough, but she playfully slapped him away and covered the bread pan with a cloth. "That's for tomorrow. We'll eat early tonight since your father's out of town."

"Hey, sis, you all right? I heard you made quite a scene at the Orpheum. Swooning over some love scene?" He batted his eyelashes.

"Very funny. *The Big Parade* is a good war story. Which you would know if you'd ever seen it."

"'Good' and 'war' don't belong in the same sentence." His face darkened. "I lived it. Why would I want to watch it?"

I changed the subject. "Where did you hear I fainted?"

"Some fellows were talking about it over at Riley's."

"Oh, that's just swell," I mumbled, embarrassed to be the object of gossip but secretly relieved not to detect any alcohol on my brother's breath. When he returned from the war, broken in body and spirit, he too often drowned his pain in whiskey. Prohibition or no Prohibition, he was always able to get his hands on some. Knew the right people. With Frances active in the Women's Christian Temperance Union, those were some tense years in the Corrigan household. Thankfully, as far as I knew, he'd remained sober for the last year or so. He'd gone back to church, too. Still, I couldn't break the habit of expecting a whiff of alcohol on his breath and felt relieved when there was none.

"Don't worry, I set them straight." Charlie raised his good arm. "I'll pummel any goon who gets out of line. I'll go wash up. Glad you're okay, sis." He limped out of the room.

Frances pulled a pitcher from the icebox and set it on the table. "I do wish he wouldn't hang around a tavern on Sunday with all that riffraff. It's not seemly."

I set out plates. "It's not a tavern, it's a soda fountain. And they're hardly riffraff. Just friends he grew up with."

"It *was* a tavern before Prohibition. I don't trust that Riley not to keep a bottle stashed under the counter." Frances frowned. "Charlie would get further in life if he chose a better class of companions. You don't see the Cavendishes wasting Sunday afternoons at Riley's—or at the Orpheum, for that matter."

"Who cares what the Cavendishes do?" I muttered, knowing full well that at least one of the two of us cared deeply. The Cavendishes were Kerryville aristocracy. Dr. Cavendish ran Kerryville General Hospital. Mrs. Cavendish ran the Hospital Auxiliary, the WCTU, and practically everything else. Frances, anxious for the Corrigans to rise in society, coveted the Cavendish seal of approval on everything from how we spent our Sundays to who our friends were. My engagement to Dr. Richard Brownlee was a jewel in her crown.

"I dread to think what your father will say," Frances continued. "Fortunately he knows Eugenia Wardlow's a ninny. What about Richard? You'd better telephone him right away, before he hears it from somebody else."

"I'm seeing him tonight for dinner. Speaking of which, I'd better freshen up." I stood, bone-weary and not of a mind to discuss any more of my personal business with Frances.

She crossed her arms. "You know, you two would already be married by now, if only—"

"If only I hadn't dragged my feet on setting a date," I finished, sparing her the trouble of repeating herself for the thousandth time.

"He's wanted to marry you for ages, and you keep putting him off. It's no wonder people have started . . . speculating."

Heat rose in my chest. "Let them speculate. Anyway, I'm not putting him off any longer." September fifteenth, my wedding day, loomed just on the other side of summer.

"He's a real catch, Marjorie," Frances admonished, "and you're not getting any younger."

"Thanks." I made tracks for the door, desperate to escape the conversation.

"Marrying Richard is the wisest decision you've ever made. You'll be set for life," she called after me, "if you don't spoil your chance."

On the staircase I bumped into the eavesdropping Helen.

"Was she sore?"

"A little. She'll get over it. But no more pictures for you for a while."

"Aw." She trailed into my room. "Have you finished my dress for Spring Fling?"

Helen would be making her dramatic debut at the high school's end-of-the-year program, reciting "The Wreck of the Hesperus" to a packed, and likely sweltering, auditorium. I was her wardrobe mistress for the event, but I'd promised Frances that as soon as Helen's dress was out of the way, I'd get busy on my own wedding gown.

"Not yet, Miss Impatience. I've been a little preoccupied with creating a town scandal."

"Will you finish it soon?"

"Not if you don't stop pestering me. Besides, you don't need it until Spring Fling."

"Can I at least see it?"

"Helen."

"Please?"

I surrendered and opened my sewing basket. "Oh, all right. Here. Mind the pins."

She held up the pale violet frock—an old one of mine that I was altering to fit her—and swayed to and fro in front of the pier glass, glowing. "Oh, Marjie, it's the cat's meow."

"That shade suits you. Brings out your eye color."

"Am I pretty, Marjie?"

"Pretty is as pretty does."

She wrinkled her nose. "Now you sound like Frances."

I cringed. Sounding like Frances was not one of my goals in life.

"You might be pretty," I teased. "Maybe the tiniest little bit. When your horns aren't showing."

She stuck out her tongue. "Oh, you're a hot sketch. Be serious."

I smiled. "You look like our mother."

Her eyes widened. "I do? Honest?"

"Honest. And she was stunning."

Helen was silent a moment as she absorbed that thought.

"But remember what the Bible says," I said. "'Favor is deceitful, and beauty is vain . . .'"

"'. . . but the woman who feareth the Lord, she shall be praised,'" we finished together.

"That's Scripture," I added. "Not Frances."

"I know. Mrs. Varney had us memorize it in Phoebe Circle. That reminds me. She wants to know if you'll help out next fall."

"Help out with what?"

"Phoebe Circle. After you're back from your honeymoon, of course. She says the group is getting too large for her to handle all by herself. I overheard her tell Superintendent Lewis that we're quite a handful," she added with pride.

"I can imagine."

"Aw, she's just getting old. Anyway, she said you used to love Phoebe Circle, and she's hoping you'll come back and help lead it. She said she's been planning to speak to you about it at church, but you always disappear right after the service. Which is true." She tossed me an accusatory look.

I made no reply. Mrs. Varney was right. As a girl I'd been active in Phoebe Circle and other church activities. But that was before the Lord chose to take away everything that mattered most to me. His prerogative, of course. "Thy will be done," said the prayer I still dutifully recited. But for the past few years, as my Bible gathered dust on my bedside table, I'd found it hard to pay Him much more than a perfunctory visit on Sunday morning. And even that was largely due to Frances's insistence that "nice people" go to church.

"I'm sure she'll ask you about it herself," Helen concluded. "I only said I'd mention it."

"Thanks for the warning."

"It'd be fun, having you for a leader."

"You just think I'd let you get away with more high jinks than Mrs. Varney does," I teased. "You'd be surprised what a tough old bird your sister can be."

She took one last twirl and handed me the dress.

"I don't know about that. But you sure are a whiz with a needle and thread."

She whirled out of the room. As I opened the sewing basket, I caught sight of something half-hidden in its depths. My heart squeezed. I lifted the photograph, worn around the edges from much handling. Jack in his army uniform, smiling and confident.

I turned it over. "I'll be home before you know it," he'd written on the back in his strong, black cursive. "You won't even have time to miss me."

Oh, Jack, how wrong you were. I rubbed my thumb over the sepia image. *I've had plenty of time to miss you. Ten years, and I'm just getting started.*

Gently I replaced the photograph and covered it with Helen's half-sewn dress. If only a heart could be restitched as neatly as the seams of a dress after it's been torn apart.

CHAPTER TWO

The misty evening enveloped Richard and me as we sat on the front porch swing after we returned from dinner at the Tick-Tock Café. A light breeze cooled the air, and I shivered slightly in my pale blue sweater and skirt, in spite of the weight of Richard's arm around my shoulders. Nonetheless, it was easier to talk on the porch than to move indoors, with inquisitive ears around every corner.

Richard had taken Eugenia's rumor remarkably well under the circumstances.

"Time will prove her wrong, of course," he said with his usual faultless logic. "Someday we'll look back on this and laugh."

But at the moment he wasn't laughing. Neither was I. The harsh social consequences of an out-of-wedlock birth, even a mere rumor of one, cast a dim light on our (mostly my) virtue. Still, there was nothing we could do except wait it out.

"Good thing the Hospital Auxiliary tea is coming up on Tuesday." Richard gave the swing a push with his legs. "That'll give the other doctors' wives a chance to meet you and see for themselves how sweet you are."

"Oh, Richard, do I have to go?" I blurted before thinking. Unfortunately I did that a lot.

He adjusted his spectacles, something *he* did a lot, particularly when annoyed. "What do you mean, do you have to? I should think you'd be pleased. A personal invitation from Mrs. Cavendish doesn't come along every day."

I shifted on the hard seat. "I know. Of course I'll go. I understand how important it is to you that I make a good impression. I just feel so . . . I don't know. Like I'm being interviewed for a position. Like they'll cross-examine me to see if I qualify as your wife. I'm sure some would have liked to match you up with their own daughters."

Richard chuckled. "You've nothing to worry about. I only have eyes for you. Once they meet you, they'll understand why you're the perfect match for me."

"Will they?" Breathing in his familiar scent of bay rum and cloves, I wished I shared his confidence.

"They will. Trust me." He lifted my chin so I could see my face reflected in his spectacles. I readied myself for his kiss, but instead he said, "Of course, I don't like it one bit that you fainted in public. I don't detect any other symptoms, but I wish you'd see Doc Perkins, just to rule out anything I might be overlooking."

"My goodness, I feel like one of your patients." I turned away from his gaze. "Everyone is making too big a fuss over this."

"You've been under a strain. You're working too hard, that's all. Maybe it's time to give up your job at the store."

I sat up straight. "Give up my job? You mean—now?"

He touched his spectacles. "Why not? You'll be quitting soon anyway. The wedding's only a few months away."

I squirmed, my blouse sticking damply to the back of the seat. "Well, yes, but I didn't think I'd stop working right away. Maybe when we start our family . . ."

Richard rocked the swing. "You'll have plenty to keep you busy, even before children come. Ask the other doctors' wives. They'll tell you. Committee meetings, socials, volunteer work." His voice took on a certain stiffness, and a little vein throbbed in his temple. "Besides, you won't *have* to work. I'm fully prepared to support my wife."

"Of course you are, but Pop needs me at the store."

He patted my knee. "I'm sure he'll manage fine, sweetheart. Helen's old enough to help out after school. Isn't it almost time for summer break anyway? She'll need something to do besides loafing around reading movie magazines."

"Helen can't replace me. She doesn't have my experience."

He smiled. "Really, darling, how much experience does it take to measure out fabric and choose some buttons to go with it?"

I braced my legs to stop the rocking, which was making me sea-sick. "There's more to the job than that."

"Now, sweetheart, don't take it the wrong way. I know you're good at what you do. But you oughtn't to keep working if your health is compromised. And the only way Helen will get any experience is by actually doing the job."

"I suppose she'd appreciate the pocket money," I said. "But I won't have her taking over because of my health. My health is just fine, thank you."

We sat in silence for a while, listening to the crickets. The air felt thick, hard to breathe. Suddenly exhausted, I leaned back against Richard's arm. Maybe he was right. Maybe I did need a rest. But how would Pop and Charlie manage the store without me?

Finally Richard yawned. "Ah, well, sweetheart, this will be your last summer as a single girl. Enjoy it while you can. Before you know it, you'll be Mrs. Richard Brownlee."

"Mrs. Richard Brownlee." The words felt strange on my tongue. "Marjorie Brownlee." There was security in becoming Mrs. Richard Brownlee. A bright future stretched before me. A prosperous husband. A fine house. Pretty clothes. A shiny automobile. Children.

So why did I feel reluctant to stop being Marjorie Corrigan?

His arm tightened around my shoulder. Scads of girls would kill to be in my place. What difference would it really make if I had to give up my little job, when I was blessed in so many other ways?

I looked up at his even profile and said, "I'm the luckiest girl in the world." Wasn't that the sort of thing leading ladies said to leading men as they sat on porch swings in the moonlight?

Richard smiled. "No, sweetheart, I'm the lucky one." At last he kissed me.

But as he did, the same weariness I'd felt earlier settled over me again. Where was the delicious shiver I'd savored so long ago with Jack? Was this what grown-up love was like? Sensible and practical? *I'm the luckiest girl in the world*, I repeated silently. *I'm the luckiest girl in the world.*

Somehow I could not imagine the French farm girl, in the arms of John Gilbert, needing to remind herself how lucky she was.

CHAPTER THREE

The morning sun slanted through the display window of Corrigan's Dry Goods and Sundries, making me squint as I wrestled a white cotton voile tea dress onto a dressmaker's dummy. I'd designed the dress myself to showcase some new summer fabric. In my youth, poring over the public library's copy of *Vogue*, I'd dreamed of becoming a great *couturière* like Coco Chanel, but that wasn't the sort of thing Kerryville girls could pronounce, much less become. Besides, there wasn't an art or design school within hundreds of miles. Even so, I sought to bring a bit of artistry to the shop—no easy task where Pop was concerned.

For example, I'd been nagging him for months to order one of the new modern mannequins—the kind that looked like a real woman, with a head and face, arms and legs. The sort used in Meyer's Department Store down the street, our fiercest competitor. But he insisted on keeping the old-fashioned dressmaker's dummy. A conservative shopkeeper of the old school, he was not quick to adopt what he called newfangled ideas. Charlie had a fight on his hands even to update the inventory system.

As I climbed out of the display window, Charlie appeared from the stockroom and surveyed the sales floor with a dubious eye. "We're supposed to receive that shipment of seersucker this morning. Any place to put it?"

"I'll make room. This pale blue wool can go on the markdown table. With the weather turning warm, it'll never sell."

Charlie squinted. "You call that blue? More like battleship gray. No wonder it didn't sell." He gave a mischievous grin. "Speaking of dull, how was your date with Dr. Darling last night? I'll bet he was sore when he heard about the crazy rumor going around town."

"As a matter of fact, he was not. And I'll thank you to mind your own business."

Charlie lifted his hand. "Hey, just making conversation. Anyway, I meant what I said about pounding anybody who says a word against you."

"I appreciate that."

"'Cause I bet the dear doctor can't risk getting his delicate surgeon hands dirty in a fistfight."

I crossed my arms. "You're right. Richard is too much of a gentleman to resort to barroom brawls."

"Too refined to fight for his country, too," Charlie grumbled.

I groaned. "Charlie, we've gone over this. It's not his fault that by the time he enlisted, the war was practically over."

"Doesn't change the facts. He was lounging at some fancy college while Jack and I were over there doing the dirty work."

"I'd hardly call medical school 'lounging.' And Dr. Perkins was mighty glad to have his help when the influenza came to town."

"Face it, sis. You wouldn't be giving Richard a second glance right now if Jack were still around."

I reeled as if he'd slapped me across the face. "Leave Jack out of this. Look, I don't know what you have against Richard, but whatever it is, it has nothing whatsoever to do with Jack."

Charlie's eyes took on a faraway look. "But what if someday he comes back? He's still officially classified as missing, presumed dead. They've never actually found—"

"—his body." I held up a silencing hand. "Don't you think I know that? Don't you think I've thought of that, *wished* for that, a thousand million times? For Pete's sake, Charlie, Jack was my sweetheart."

"He was my best friend."

Our gazes locked.

Finally I said, "It's been ten years. I need to move on with my life."

"I know." Charlie rubbed the back of his neck. Ironically, it was a gesture Jack used to make whenever he was perplexed or worried about something. Seeing it brought a pang to my heart.

"Sorry I said anything," Charlie continued. "At least you'd have welcomed home your soldier. Not like . . . some people." He tilted his head away, his expression stony.

He meant Catherine, the sweetheart who'd jilted him when he returned from Europe with a bum leg, a damaged arm, and screaming nightmares that woke the entire household. I appreciated Charlie's faith in my loyalty, his certainty that I would have happily married Jack if he'd come back from the war alive, no matter his condition. But in my deepest heart of hearts I honestly did not know if I deserved Charlie's faith in me, or whether I'd have behaved any better than Catherine, had Jack returned broken and crippled. Maybe no woman knows for sure how she'd react until she's in that situation. At least Catherine was honest about her feelings. But poor Charlie had never gotten over her rejection. Nor had he dared to court any other girl. He assumed his injuries made him a pariah where romance was concerned. Which was a shame, because my handsome, charming brother would make a first-rate catch for any girl. Except when he drank.

Or when he was being stubborn and annoying. Like now.

"My life would be very different if Jack had returned," I admitted. "But he didn't, so there's no sense dwelling on it. Besides, think of the grief Frances would have given us. She didn't even want us to date."

"You were very young."

"I was old enough to know my own heart. Frances hated Jack, but she adores Richard."

Charlie snorted. "That's because Frances is a social-climbing schemer. She thinks your marriage to Richard is her ticket into Kerryville society, such as it is."

"A little harsh, don't you think?" I said, although he had a point.

"Come on, we both know it's true. Frances married Pop thinking she was landing some tycoon-in-the-rough, only to discover he's perfectly content as a small-town shopkeeper. She's never recovered from taking a step down socially. So you're her only hope, see? Richard's a college-educated doctor from a well-to-do family, while Jack was facing a lifetime on the factory floor. He never measured up, in her estimation."

"Maybe. But you never give Richard credit for his many fine qualities." *Thrifty, brave, clean* . . . "He treats me well."

Charlie smirked. "If you say so. It'd just be nice to hear you say that *you* love Richard, instead of rattling on about how much Frances loves him."

"Nonsense. Just because I don't gush doesn't mean I don't have deep feelings for Richard."

"Doesn't mean you *do* have them, either."

Touché.

I avoided Charlie's gaze. He rested a hand on my shoulder. "Marjie, don't get sore. I hope you're doing the right thing by marrying Richard, that's all. He's all right, I guess. I just don't know if he's right for *you.*"

"Thank you for your concern, but that's not your call to make." I cocked my head. "Is that a truck I hear pulling up in the alley?" Charlie limped back to the stockroom and out of my hair, just as the bell over the door jingled, announcing a customer. I shoved Charlie's comments to the back of my mind and pasted on my best salesgirl smile for the customers, a neighbor and her daughter.

"Good morning, Mrs. Calloway. How can I help you today?"

The sturdy matron peered at me with a mixture of curiosity and sympathy. "Oh, my *dear*," she breathed. "I should be asking how I can help *you.*"

"I beg your pardon?"

She clucked her tongue. "So shocked to hear the news. Shocked."

"What news?"

"You know, dear," she murmured with a sidelong glance at her daughter. "The *stork*." She took my hand and patted it. "After all, these things do happen."

"The *stork*?" My face burned. "Mrs. Calloway, I assure you, there is no stork. But there is the most awful falsehood going around town. Perhaps you've heard it."

Mrs. Calloway stepped back. "Oh. Well, glad to hear it's a falsehood. As I was just telling Sadie Miller—" She stopped short at the look on my face, then briskly changed the subject. "My Daisy here needs a graduation dress. I'm thinking white cotton lawn with a rose-colored sash. Not exactly rose, a rosy sort of coral, but not *too* coral . . ."

By the time I deciphered what Mrs. Calloway meant by not-exactly-rose, measured and cut the goods, rang up the purchase, and sent her on her way, Charlie reappeared, carrying a large box.

"Is that the seersucker? Don't bring it out yet. I have to make room."

Charlie grinned. "I think you'll want to see this." He set the box on the counter and opened it with a flourish. Inside lay a shimmering bolt of white satin alongside a froth of matching tulle.

Wedding dress fabric.

My wedding dress fabric.

My breath caught as I gingerly touched it, light and silky under my fingertips, like a waterfall of the richest cream. My throat convulsed in a swallow.

Charlie looked at me with concern. "What's wrong? It's what you ordered, right?"

"Yes," I breathed. "It's perfect. Absolutely per—"

The fabric swam before my eyes. The wooden floor tilted. From a far distance I heard Charlie say, "Sis? You all right?"

Then all was blackness.

"How long has this been going on?" Charlie demanded, jaw clenched, when I'd recovered enough to sit on the stool behind the counter. "First you pass out in the middle of a movie theater, for Pete's sake, and now this. How many other times has it happened?"

"None. Don't yell at me." Mercifully the shop was empty of customers.

"You've been keeping secrets."

My stomach clenched. "Don't look at me that way. It isn't my fault."

"It is your fault that you haven't seen a doctor. Jeepers, Marjorie, something could be seriously wrong with you. What in blazes are you waiting for?"

"It seems like a silly thing to bother a doctor about. Ladies faint all the time."

Charlie slapped his palm on the counter. "Who faints? Name one person we know."

I squirmed. "I don't know . . . *Ladies* do."

"Well, *you* don't. This isn't some Victorian novel, or one of your blasted movies." He rubbed his forehead. "Wait here."

He shuffled off. Outside the front window, two women stopped to admire the dress on display. *Please don't come in*, I pleaded silently. *Please, just move along and come back later, after my brother has finished raking me over the coals.*

He returned with a glass of water, which I accepted with shaky hands.

"Charlie, you can't tell Pop or Frances. They'll worry needlessly."

"I'll tell anybody I want to. If you're too stubborn to go get yourself checked out, then—"

The doorbell jangled, interrupting Charlie's tirade.

"Morning, ladies," he mumbled. Then he leaned toward me and hissed, "Dr. Perkins. Today."

"I promise. Just don't tell the folks."

His eyes bored into mine. "Today." He nodded toward the customers and retreated as I glued on a smile, praying that my ghostly pallor wouldn't frighten away the customers. Later I used the telephone in Pop's office to call Dr. Perkins, partly out of concern for my health, but mostly to keep Charlie from yelling at me.

CHAPTER FOUR

"What's this about fainting, then? Sounds like it's becoming something of a habit with you." Kindly Dr. Perkins had been our family physician since I was a child. The comfortable examination room had a familiar smell of camphor and rubbing alcohol. I supposed I was too old to earn a lollipop by not crying.

"Only twice," I said. "I think it's the heat. I feel perfectly well otherwise."

"Hmm." He tapped my knee, checking my reflexes. "I hear wedding bells will be ringing soon. I believe Dr. Brownlee is the lucky fellow?"

"Yes. We're to be married in September."

"Ah. Are you feeling anxious about the wedding? About marriage in general?"

"I suppose I am a wee bit apprehensive," I admitted. "My stepmother's idea of a wedding is much more elaborate than mine. However, she's taken on most of the preparations, so I can't complain. As for marriage in general, well, I couldn't hope for a better match." That's what everyone said. Who was I to contradict them?

"That's good news, my dear." Dr. Perkins pressed his fingers behind my ears and along my throat. "The life of a doctor's wife has its challenges, as my Gretchen says, but also its rewards." He pressed the cold steel stethoscope against my chest. "Breathe in. Now out."

At last he straightened up and removed the stethoscope from his ears. "Well, Miss Marjorie, the good news is I can't find anything wrong. Your blood pressure's good, your lungs sound fine. You appear to be in perfect health."

"Just as I thought." I gathered up my handbag and gloves. "Thank you for your time, Doctor."

He held up a hand. "Not so fast. I'm recommending further testing."

I blanched. "Why? You just said I'm in perfect health."

"I said you *seem* healthy. But I can't dismiss these random faint-ing spells of yours." His eyes narrowed. "Your mother suffered from a congenital heart condition."

I deflated. "Yes, I know."

"As I recall, her condition, too, went undetected until—"

"Yes." My throat tightened, willing him not to continue. I was ten years old when my mother died of sudden heart failure immediately after Helen's birth. Until then, no one had known she had a weak heart, not even she.

"These things can be hereditary," Dr. Perkins's gentle voice con-tinued. "Given your family history, we must rule out any hidden problems. There are some new, more sophisticated tests available now that detect problems early. But I'm not equipped to perform them here in this office." He pulled a pad of paper from his desk drawer and jotted something on it. "Dr. Cragin is one of the best cardiologists in the Middle West. You'll be in excellent hands with him. See Mrs. McLean at the front desk on your way out. She'll make the arrangements."

"I'm not familiar with the name. Is he at Kerryville General?"

"Oh, no, dear." The doctor ripped the paper from the pad. "He's at the big university hospital in Chicago."

"Chicago?" Frances said when I broke the news after dinner that evening. She set aside her knitting project—a white tennis sweat-er intended for Richard. "Dr. Perkins is sending you all the way to Chicago?" It might as well have been Timbuktu, the way she said it.

"I don't have to go," I replied, though secretly the idea thrilled me. The Chicago part, not the medical part.

"Don't be a goose. Of course you're going. If the doctor says you need tests, then you need tests. What if something's seriously wrong with your heart? Mercy, that's the last thing we need right now." She resumed knitting, needles clicking with a vengeance.

"You make it sound as if I did it on purpose. Anyway, Dr. Perkins himself said the tests are merely a precaution. I'll end up traveling all the way to Chicago only to have this Cragin fellow confirm I'm in perfect health."

Frances clutched her knitting to her chest as if it were her heart causing all the trouble. "I don't understand you, Marjorie. One minute you're moping around, complaining that Kerryville is small and boring. And now you have a chance to go to Chicago, and you're balking?"

"I'm not balking. Just being practical."

"If you were so healthy, you wouldn't have fainted at the Orpheum." Thankfully it appeared Charlie had not mentioned the second incident at the store. "It's best to get a clean bill of health now, well before the wedding. Charlie and Helen will manage fine while we're gone."

"We?" I hadn't pictured Frances going along for the ride.

Her face brightened. "We'll do some shopping while we're there. We need gifts for the bridesmaids. The selection in the Kerryville shops is simply dismal."

The weight of wedding chores settled on my shoulders. "When will I have time to shop? I'll be at the *hospital*, remember? Getting tests done on my *heart*."

"Don't be melodramatic, Marjorie. We can take an extra day or two. I'm sure your father won't mind."

"I'm sure he'll mind it when the he sees the hotel bill, on top of the medical bills."

"Oh, for heaven's sake," Frances muttered. But on that point she didn't disagree.

"Besides," I said, "the wedding is still months and months away."

"Four months, two weeks, and two days." She jabbed a knitting needle in my direction. "The sooner, the better."

Richard unexpectedly presented a solution to the money problem a few days later, when we went on a riverside picnic. "No need for a hotel," he assured me as he poured coffee from a vacuum flask. "You and Frances can stay with my father's aunt, Gloria Brownlee. She lives just a short distance from the university hospital."

"I'm sure your great-aunt wouldn't appreciate complete strangers landing on her doorstep," I protested, reaching for a cookie.

"You're hardly strangers," he said. "You'll be a Brownlee soon. Besides, she lives alone in a big house, except for a nurse. She'd appreciate the company, and you'll all have a chance to become better acquainted before the wedding."

I squirmed. "I don't know, Richard. I don't want to impose."

"Nonsense. You need to have those tests done. Why not kill two birds with one stone and visit Aunt Gloria as well?"

"I wish you could go with me instead of Frances."

Richard reached across the plaid horsehair blanket and touched my hand. "If I could get away from the hospital, sweetheart, you know I would. But we're terribly short-staffed and—"

"I know. I'm being silly."

We sat in silence for a while, listening to the chirping of sparrows. The truth was, I didn't want Richard to go with me, either. I wanted to travel to the city alone and savor the sights and sounds, enjoy one last fling of independence before married life. But few things sounded less appealing than going to Chicago with Frances to take care of medical tests and wedding chores.

"Here's the deal," I said, after some thought. "If I don't have any more fainting spells, then I won't go to Chicago. But if I have another one—even one—I'll go willingly. I'll even stay with your great-aunt, if she'll have me."

Richard frowned and adjusted his spectacles. "If Doc Perkins said—"

"He said I'm *fine*. The tests are just a precaution."

His lips tightened. "One more episode and you'll go willingly?"

"Willingly."

"No arguments?"

"No arguments."

"Even once? Even just a tiny dizzy spell? Even just a—a loud sneeze?"

"I promise."

He sighed, but I knew I'd won. I leaned back onto the blanket and nibbled on the cookie. There'd be no more "episodes," I felt sure of it. So there'd be no way in blazes I'd be going to Chicago. No way in blazes.

CHAPTER FIVE

"All aboard for Chicago." The conductor leaned out of the car and swung his lantern in the midday drizzle.

At the last minute, Frances had been laid low with a bad cold. So I was on my own after all. "Don't talk to strangers," she'd rasped from her bed. "Telephone the very minute you get to Miss Brownlee's. And mind you make a good impression. You'll be joining her family soon."

While Charlie paid for my ticket, Helen clung to me like a barnacle. "I'll miss you so much."

I peeled her arms from around my neck. "I'll be back before you know it." My confidence was pure bravado. I'd never traveled to a city alone, and had only the vaguest notion of what I'd do when I got there.

"Thanks for finishing my dress," Helen said. "I'll be the prettiest girl at Spring Fling. I hope you get home in time to do my hair."

"I will," I promised.

"Richard should have come to see you off."

"He can't miss his morning rounds, goose. His patients need him."

"Still," she said, "he should have tried."

I playfully tugged her braid, not wanting to admit I'd been thinking the same thing.

Charlie walked up and handed me my ticket. "Don't take any wooden nickels," he instructed. "I'll be praying for you."

I gave him a peck on the cheek, then climbed aboard for the two-hour train ride to Chicago.

The train lurched and I lurched with it, nearly sprawling in the lap of a startled gentleman huddled behind a newspaper. "Beg your pardon," I stammered. He peered at me over the top of his spectacles, then snapped his newspaper back into place.

I found a seat next to a woman wearing a dove-gray traveling suit and matching fedora. Something about her appearance sparked a cringe-inducing memory of the Hospital Auxiliary tea a few days earlier. Richard had been remarkably sanguine about the matter, under the circumstances, but I wondered if Frances would ever forgive me for disgracing myself, and therefore her, in front of the esteemed Mrs. Cavendish.

That fateful Tuesday, after burnt toast, a torn stocking, and a futile attempt to wrestle my long, thick, wavy brown hair into something resembling a style, I felt defeated from the get-go. Then a sudden thundershower had caught me without an umbrella en route to the tea.

The Cavendish home, in what Frances called the "better" part of Kerryville, loomed in half-timbered glory behind a circular driveway. A maid swung open the heavy door, accepted my dripping wrap, and directed me through an arched doorway into a parlor filled with impeccably dressed women. Thick carpeting and velvet draperies gave the room a hushed quality in spite of the crowd. Mrs. Cavendish, whom I'd only briefly met once before, glided toward me.

"My dear, how lovely of you to come all this way on such a beastly afternoon. Do come in." To the assembled flock she announced, "Ladies, may I introduce Miss Marjorie Corrigan. Miss Corrigan is the bride-elect of our fine young Dr. Brownlee." A low-pitched hum ensued. Several ladies nodded coolly in what I hoped meant approval. Dampness formed under the arms of my white cotton voile frock, snatched from the front-window display at Pop's store after every other dress in my closet had been considered and rejected by me or by Frances, who'd hovered all morning as if I were headed for tea at the White House with Grace Coolidge herself.

Mrs. Cavendish steered me toward a white-clothed table spread with silver platters bearing delicate crustless sandwiches and dainty pastries. I didn't think I could swallow a bite, but placed a teacake on a plate. A woman standing near a gleaming teapot produced a porcelain cup and saucer.

"Lemon?"

"Yes, please." Balancing cup and saucer, plate, fork, and lace-edged napkin, I made my way to a brocade armchair in a quiet corner. Too late I realized the armchair sat next to an enormous palmetto plant that thrust its annoying fronds in my face.

"So you're the future Mrs. Brownlee," crowed a large woman with a *pince-nez* as she settled herself on a nearby sofa. "How pleased we were to hear of Dr. Brownlee's engagement. Such a fine young doctor." I nodded, mouth full of dry cake. She continued, "I'm Eleanor Steiglitz. My husband, Dr. Herman Steiglitz, is head of podiatry at Kerryville General. Perhaps you've met my daughter, Constance. She's away at Bryn Mawr now."

I swallowed the cake with some difficulty and dabbed at my lips with the napkin. "How do you do."

"And this is Mavis Gleener, wife of Dr. William Gleener. Obstetrics." She gestured to a thin, rabbit-faced woman who joined her on the sofa.

"We're so looking forward to having your help with the bazaar," Mrs. Steiglitz continued.

My teacup halted in mid-air. "Bazaar?"

"The Hospital Auxiliary Spring Bazaar. Surely Dr. Brownlee has mentioned it."

"Oh . . . yes. The bazaar." I wracked my brain for any mention of such an event and made a mental note to ask the Fine Young Doctor about it later. "I'll check my calendar and see if I'll be available."

"My dear, *all* of the doctors' wives help with the bazaar," Mrs. Steiglitz pronounced in ringing tones. "It's our major fund-raiser of the year."

"We'll be setting up all week. Do you prefer pricing or folding?" Mrs. Gleener cut in.

"Well, you see, I have a job," was my feeble answer. "So I'm not usually available during the day."

"A job? How inconvenient." Mrs. Gleener and Mrs. Steiglitz exchanged a glance. "Well, there's always the summer cotillion. I'll introduce you to the chairman. Diantha, darling," she called discreetly across the room. "Come meet your new recruit."

"Cotillion? Oh, I don't think—Ow!" I turned my head too quickly and was poked in the eye by a palmetto frond. Tea sloshed into my lap.

"Oh, dear, Miss Corrigan, do be careful," said Mrs. Steiglitz.

"I'm all right," I stammered. "It isn't too hot." I patted my skirt with the napkin.

"I meant, be careful of the *plant*," she clarified. "That's Lucille Cavendish's prize-winning palmetto. It won first place at the county horticultural exhibition three years in a row."

I eyed the offending plant and leaned away from its menacing green tentacles.

Mrs. Cavendish suddenly materialized. "Ah. I see you're admiring my *Ravenia rivularis*." She lovingly stroked a frond. "Dr. Cavendish and I brought it back from our travels. I'm told it's a very rare specimen." She beamed at me. "Have you an interest in horticulture, Miss Corrigan?"

"Then you simply must join the Garden Committee," Mrs. Gleener broke in before I could answer. "We donate all of the flowers on the hospital grounds. This year we're doing zinnias. Simply *acres* of zinnias."

"Where is my new cotillion recruit?" asked the tall, fair-haired woman called Diantha.

"She's right here. She's engaged to marry our young Dr. Brownlee."

"Marvelous. How is your quadrille?"

"But I never said . . ." I faltered. Suddenly a clear vision of life as a Kerryville doctor's wife panned across my mind: an endless round of committees and teas and teas to plan the committees and committees to plan the teas. The doctors' wives circled me like a pack of well-dressed wolves eyeing fresh prey.

Mrs. Cavendish turned to me with wide eyes. "Oh, by the way, Miss Corrigan. Eugenia Wardlow and I were speaking just the other day, and your name came up."

My stomach lurched. My cheeks flamed.

Eugenia Wardlow. That gossip! She'd been spreading her awful rumors. To Mrs. Cavendish, of all people. Heat rose up my neck.

"So tell us, dear," Mrs. Cavendish said in a kindly way. "When is the big event?"

"Oh," I rushed to explain, "there is no big event."

Mrs. Steiglitz looked confused. "Whatever do you mean, dear?"

In my panic I blurted, "I mean, that's just a silly rumor going around town. I'm not . . . in a family way."

Silence reverberated. Every eye in the room was trained on me, or more precisely, my midsection.

After an interminable moment, Mrs. Cavendish recovered. "Well, of course not, my dear. I don't believe anyone said you were."

Floor, swallow me now. "But you—you said—Eugenia Wardlow, and a big event, and so I thought—"

Someone said, "My word." And someone else said, "Who is she again?"

"The *wedding*, Miss Corrigan," Mrs. Cavendish said. "By big event, I meant your *wedding*. Eugenia was discussing your flowers."

Feeling sick, I squeaked, "September fifteenth."

"Have you considered zinnias?" Mrs. Gleener chirped in an overly bright tone.

"Will you excuse me, please?" As gracefully as I could, I rose from the armchair and set my cup and saucer on an end table. I ached to run from the room, but my legs suddenly wouldn't carry me. I shot up a quick and desperate prayer. *Dear Lord, whatever You do, please don't let me throw up in front of all these ladies!*

The Lord obliged. I did not throw up.

But before I knew what was happening, I keeled over face-first, straight into Mrs. Cavendish's prize palmetto.

And faster than you could say "social pariah," I found myself bundled onto a train hurtling its way to Chicago.

CHAPTER SIX

As the miles clattered past, I scratched around in my brain to ferret out some common thread among the fainting spells that had overtaken me at the theater, the dry goods store, and the tea. I could recall no specific food that would have made me ill. No certain time of day, no circumstance I could pinpoint. When I wasn't passing out cold, I felt fine. Vertigo? Dr. Perkins had ruled that out. Maybe he was correct in his suspicion of some heart problem, some congenital weakness passed down to me from my mother like an unwanted inheritance. Maybe I, too, was doomed to die young.

I stared out the rain-spattered window at the passing horizon, wishing I still shared Helen's, and lately Charlie's, firm conviction in the power of prayer. Church felt like a duty, something decent people did on Sundays and didn't think much about during the rest of the week. Even Frances, for all her talk about what Christian ladies do and don't do, seemed to care more about appearances and how things looked than in actually living out her faith.

Charlie's faith had helped him overcome his battle with the bottle. And Helen—under the influence of the devout Mrs. Varney— sought God at every opportunity. I used to feel the same way when I was her age, even younger. But that was before God saw fit to take away both my mother and Jack, in spite of my fervent prayers to keep them safe. Gradually I'd stopped trusting Him with anything important, lest He see fit to yank it away from me. I figured that if today I turned my health situation over to God, tomorrow I'd wake up with bubonic plague. So while I admired Helen's deep faith, I chose to stumble along without the comfort of prayer, except about the most trivial matters.

With such discomforting thoughts swirling in my head, I lapsed into a fitful doze laced with strange dreams involving John Gilbert and Eugenia Wardlow and a gigantic wedding cake. When I awoke with a crick in my neck, we were nearing the city. Through the grimy window, the farms and small towns gave way to neat suburbs, then belching factories, and finally the clanging, clattering, smoky cavern of Chicago's Union Station. I gathered my things, followed the other passengers off the train, and became engulfed in the flood of humanity pouring into the terminal. The air smelled thick with axle grease, popcorn, and bus fumes. My ears rang with the din, punctuated by announcements crackling over the loud speaker and cheery greetings directed toward other passengers. I longed for a friendly face in the crowd but knew it was pointless to look. Richard's elderly great-aunt was too frail to come down to the station. I'd assured Richard I'd manage fine on my own, but now, faced with multiple staircases and exits, I didn't know which way to turn. I must have looked lost because after several terrifying moments a kind female voice called, "May I help you, miss?"

I followed the voice to see a neatly dressed lady standing behind a desk under a sign reading "Traveler's Aid." That was me: a traveler in need of aid. I scurried over and gratefully handed her the piece of paper on which Richard had scribbled Miss Brownlee's address. The woman unfolded a map of the city and mapped out a route to Miss Brownlee's house. Then she directed me through the maze of a station.

At last I stood outdoors with my suitcase, trying to get my bearings. The Windy City earned its nickname with warm powerful gusts that threatened to blow my hat straight into the murky river. The rain had subsided and brilliant bands of pink and orange glowed to the west where the sun was burning down. Towering iron-gray buildings cast gloomy shadows over noisy streets, where more automobiles than I'd ever seen in one place honked and jockeyed for position in a sort of endless road rally. A billboard caught my eye: "Marshall Field & Company . . . Give the lady what she wants."

What the lady wants right this minute is to turn around and go home.

But there was no turning back. After two streetcar rides, one of them in entirely the wrong direction, I found myself standing in front of a narrow brick building on a leafy street. I paused to check my face in a pocket mirror and collect my courage. I'd never met any of Richard's family, other than his parents, who lived in a tony section of Des

Moines. I'd dined with them exactly once—a starched-linen affair in an atmosphere as chilly as the ice cubes clinking in the silver pitcher. It was not an experience I was eager to repeat, although of course I would embrace them as my parents-in-law once Richard and I married. I'd dwell on that another time. Right now I had a great-aunt to impress.

In response to the bell, the door was opened by a woman who looked younger than I expected. I offered my hand. "Good afternoon. Miss Brownlee?"

"I'm Miss Jessop, Miss Brownlee's nurse." She scanned me with a cool, appraising eye. "You must be Miss Corrigan. Miss Brownlee is expecting you."

I picked up my bag and followed her into a gloomy parlor that looked like a stage set for a Victorian play. She took my raincoat and excused herself from the room. While waiting, I took stock of my surroundings. Photographs of unsmiling relatives peered down from ornate frames. A stiff horsehair sofa sat against one wall, flanked by two upholstered chairs. A spinet piano, a fringed rug, and a table bearing a lamp and two china shepherdesses completed the decor. Limp lace curtains hung at the window facing the street.

A stooped woman with gray, marcelled hair shuffled into the room, leaning on a cane and assisted by Miss Jessop, who announced, "Miss Brownlee, this is Miss Corrigan, Richard's fiancée."

Pale blue eyes peered up at me through thick spectacles.

"Miss Corrigan," the elderly woman said in a quivery voice. "How do you do." She held out a gnarled hand and I took it.

"Very well, thank you."

She smiled. "I've been looking forward to meeting Richard's bride. I only wish it were under better circumstances than medical tests. I do hope they find nothing wrong." I was about to thank her when she added, "The Brownlees have never had any health problems of any sort. Goodness knows it's best not to introduce any now. Do sit down."

I perched on the horsehair sofa as Miss Jessop eased Miss Brownlee into a chair. Then she said, "I'll fetch our tea," and left Miss Brownlee and me to regard each other with polite curiosity. I wracked my brain for something clever to say but came up blank. Eventually she spoke.

"How was your journey, dear?"

"Fine, thank you."

"Oh, lovely." The mantle clock ticked off the seconds. "How is dear Richard these days? He hasn't paid me a visit in ever so long."

"He's well," I replied. "As you know, he's practicing medicine in Kerryville."

"Kerryville?"

"It's a small town in western Illinois. He's on staff at the hospital there."

She shook her gray head. "I'll never understand why he chose to serve in the middle of nowhere when he could have had his pick of positions here in the city."

"I wouldn't say Kerryville is the middle of nowhere." In truth I *had* said that, many times, but felt prickly about a stranger saying so.

Miss Jessop returned with tea and crumbly shortbread cookies. The conversation jerked along for another half hour or so until Miss Jessop interrupted, explaining Miss Brownlee needed a rest. She wasn't the only one. Miss Jessop showed me to my room and said, "Dinner's at seven. I believe Cook is making beef stew this evening." As I unpacked my belongings, the growling of my stomach was the only thing that kept me from dreading the next grueling round of sociability.

The next morning, once I'd located the correct building at the sprawling university hospital, a brisk and efficient clerk guided me through a confusing labyrinth of hallways to the cardiology wing.

Gruff and abrupt, Dr. Cragin wasted no words and asked only the most necessary questions as he conducted his examination. He drew blood, listened to my heart, checked my pulse. Later I was thoroughly poked and pinched by an unsmiling nurse. It was impossible to tell from anyone's facial expression, or lack thereof, whether my diagnosis was excellent or dire. I was told to come back on Friday for the results. Until then, I had three days to ponder whatever problem the tests might reveal. I needed to find a distraction.

In the May sunshine, the city seemed friendlier than it had the evening before. Skyscrapers that had looked scary and forbidding at dusk now stood majestic and proud. Shop windows beckoned with glittering temptations. Delicious smells wafted from café doorways. Eager to put off the gloom of Miss Brownlee's house as long as possible, I decided to go exploring.

Vast Lake Michigan sparkled azure blue in the sunshine, dotted with crisp white sailboats. Enthralled, I strolled along Michigan Avenue, past the gleaming white Wrigley Building. A warm wind whipped off the lake, blowing my hat brim and ruffling the hem of my skirt. From the bridge over the murky Chicago River I watched a flat brown barge glide past, bound for some mysterious port of call. All around me, men in suits and hats and women in bright summer dresses rushed past on their way to somewhere important. The only one without a clear destination, it seemed, was me.

A seawall of skyscrapers towered to the west, while to the east stretched the green lawns of Grant Park and the shimmering lake beyond. At the south end of the park stood the neoclassical façade and wide staircase of the Art Institute, flanked by two majestic bronze lions. Carved high into the limestone walls were the names of famous artists. *Botticelli. Rafael. Titian.* My breath hitched as I recognized some old friends from art class at Kerryville High. I went inside, and didn't emerge until closing time. After wandering the spacious galleries for a while, I'd sat captivated in front of a painting of people at a picnic. The longer I looked at it, the more deeply it drew me in.

A Sunday Afternoon on the Island of Grande Jatte, the label read. I called upon my high school French to pronounce the artist's name. *Seurat.*

Passersby voiced mixed reactions. "Why, it's just a bunch of dots," complained one woman. "Let's go back to the statues."

But to me it was an explosion of color and light that touched something deep inside of me, something aching and hopeful, like a long-dormant storybook fairy stretching her fragile wings.

At the bottom of the grand staircase near the exit, a rack of literature caught my eye. I scanned it, searching for a pretty postcard for

Helen. Instead I spotted a brochure titled "Art Classes" and picked it up. A guard called out, "Please move along." I folded the brochure and jammed it in my handbag.

Even as I stepped out onto the sunbaked boulevard, my mind still swam with vivid color. On board the streetcar, I unfolded the brochure. "Beginning Art Classes for Adults," it read. "Evenings and Saturdays." My eyes trailed down the list of offerings. Sculpture. Oil painting. Textiles.

Textiles. The word rolled deliciously on my tongue as I gazed out the streetcar window at the lake, envisioning the expanse of water as a bolt of silk moiré, gleaming sapphire and azure and sky-blue, depending on the way the light hit the waves.

My reverie ended when a grandmotherly-looking woman laden with shopping bags sat down next to me.

"My land, it feels good to sit down," she said to no one in particular. I smiled.

The streetcar lurched forward. "Warm one today," the woman said, mopping her brow with a handkerchief.

"Yes, it is."

"Are you an artist?" she asked, gesturing to the brochure in my lap.

"Oh, no," I said, blushing. I folded the brochure and stuffed it in my handbag. "I'm—I'm getting married."

If the woman was taken aback by the abrupt change of topic, she didn't show it. "Oh. Well, that's nice," she said. "Best of luck to you."

"Thank you."

I looked out at the cityscape without really seeing it as thoughts jumbled around in my mind.

An art student. Me. What a scream. I can't take an art class. I have to go home. I'm getting married. I'm not meant to be an artist. I'll be a doctor's wife. A doctor's wife.

The streetcar felt stuffy and airless. I tugged the grimy window open for a breath of fresh air. A crowded streetcar was no place to faint.

Pull yourself together, girl. I needed to be practical. *How silly, getting so riled up over a few paintings.*

Which was exactly what Frances would say.

And the thing deep inside my soul—the dreamy sprite that awakened from her slumber when she laid eyes on those paintings—whispered, *Frances isn't here.*

I sat up straighter. Maybe I did not have forever, but I had tomorrow. Maybe I could not enroll in an art class, but I'd be staying in the city for a few more days and could visit the museum whenever I wanted. With nobody to stop me, or accuse me of wasting time.

As quickly as it had come, the dizziness subsided. I glanced up to see my seatmate peering at me.

"Are you feeling all right, dear?"

"Fine, thank you."

"You looked a bit peaked for a moment there."

"I'm all right."

When I reached Miss Brownlee's, Miss Jessop was seated in the parlor, working a piece of needlepoint while Miss Brownlee napped. "What did the doctor say?" she asked politely.

I shrugged. "Nothing yet. He did some tests and told me to come back on Friday for the results."

"Friday?" She sniffed daintily. "How tedious for you."

"Oh, I don't mind. It will give me a chance to explore the city."

Lines deepened around Miss Jessop's mouth. "I don't know how appropriate it is for a lady to be traipsing about the city unchaperoned."

"I feel perfectly safe. I'm beginning to understand how the streetcars work, and I've already been to the Art Institute. What a magnificent place."

"Magnificent?" she spat. "You wouldn't catch *me* there. All of those naked statues." She shuddered. "Why, everyone knows all of those artists have loose morals."

She shook her head as she bent over her needlework. "Not that it's any of my business, but I don't think the Art Institute is a respectable place for Christian ladies to be seen."

I suspected Miss Jessop didn't think nice Christian ladies belonged anywhere outside of their own parlors. "Excuse me. I'll wash up for dinner."

"By the way, Miss Corrigan," Miss Jessop called as I climbed the stairs, "please be so kind as to limit the length of your baths. We are not running a hot springs resort."

Up in my room, as I pulled a comb from my handbag, the brochure fell to the floor. I picked it up and glared at it, and then at my reflection. What a harebrained idea. My student days were far behind me. I was on track for a different future entirely. I dropped the pamphlet in the wastebasket. Only later, after another tiresome meal with my hosts, did I fish it out and tuck it into my suitcase.

CHAPTER SEVEN

Mindful of the promise I'd made to Frances to look for bridesmaids' gifts, the next day I took the streetcar to the downtown intersection where the giant Marshall Field & Company clock loomed over the corner. Although I was pretty sure I wouldn't be able to afford to buy so much as a pencil at the famously luxurious emporium, it had been recommended by Richard's mother as the last word in retail. I thought I could pick up a few merchandising pointers for Corrigan's Dry Goods, if nothing else.

I pushed open the heavy revolving door. The main floor took my breath away. Fanning out in all directions were glorious displays: delicate chiffon scarves in brilliant peacock colors, snowy linen handkerchiefs, glittering crystal perfume bottles, glossy leather handbags. Deferential clerks and well-heeled customers spoke in hushed tones, in contrast to Meyer's Department Store back home, where Mabel Meyer screeched at the clerks in a voice that could peel paint off the walls.

I stood disoriented for several moments, breathing in the scent of luxury. A gentleman sporting a boutonniere in his lapel approached and asked if he could help me. Had my well-worn shoes and unfashionable hat signaled I wasn't a regular customer? I explained my errand.

"I see. You'll want Bridal, on six. The elevator is to your right." He gestured with a sweep of his arm.

I thanked him and headed for the elevator. I stepped into the gilded box.

"What floor?" asked the uniformed attendant.

"Six, I think. The bridal section."

He nodded and shifted a lever. The elevator rose smoothly at breakneck speed, a vast improvement over the only elevator in Kerryville, a menacing contraption at the hospital that lurched and shuddered with a great rattling of chains. I could not suppress a grin.

This was better than a ride at the county fair. Tempted as I was to ride up and down a few more times, just for the thrill of it, the operator called out "Six," and I felt compelled to hustle out.

The bridal area was resplendent in Wedgwood blue and creamy white. Chandeliers dangled from ornate plaster medallions. Snowy gowns hung behind glass, softly spot-lit like museum exhibits. I felt torn between stepping onto the pale blue carpet and running for my life.

A young woman with the glossy good looks of a North Shore socialite examined a gown critically in the three-way mirror, flanked by a fawning saleswoman. Her eyes caught mine in the glass. She raised an eyebrow and I hastily looked away, caught in the act of staring.

Just then another black-garbed saleswoman, practically a duplicate of the first, materialized at my side. I hadn't heard her approach. At Field's, clerks apparently glided rather than walked.

"Good afternoon," she said. "Have you an appointment?"

"I'm afraid not. Do I need one?"

The saleswoman smiled with her mouth, if not her eyes. "I happen to have an opening." She produced a clipboard from behind her back and took up a pencil. "Are you the bride?"

"Yes."

She made a notation on the clipboard. "And what is the date of your nuptials?"

"September fifteenth."

Her forehead creased. "Of this year?"

I nodded.

"I'm afraid a custom gown requires many weeks to—"

"Oh, no," I interjected. "I don't need a gown. I'm sewing my own."

Her smile stiffened. "What a courageous undertaking." She cocked her head. "How may I help you, then?" She glanced down at her clipboard. "Headpiece? Veil? Shoes?"

"Gifts for the wedding party."

She brightened. "Ah. Such a thoughtful tradition. We have a lovely selection. Step this way, please." She led me to a fancy desk adorned with white-and-gold curlicues, where she produced a brochure titled

"Special Gift Ideas for Your Special Day." She opened it to a two-page spread of merchandise. "Any of these would make delightful attendants' gifts. Will it be a large wedding party?"

"Not large." I glanced over the brochure. Crystal bud vases. Jewel-backed compacts. Sterling silver cigarette cases. I chuckled, trying to picture what Helen would do with a cigarette case—probably use it to hold her baseball cards. My chuckle turned to choking when I read the prices. I handed the brochure back to the saleswoman. "Thank you, but I'm looking for something . . . simpler."

"I see," she sniffed. "Well, perhaps you'll find something more suitable in Housewares. Here's a list that might help you."

I thanked her, and she bustled off to assist her colleague with the glossy bride-to-be. I glanced over the list. The possibilities in forks alone were staggering. Fish forks. Pickle forks. Dessert forks. Meat forks. Strawberry forks.

If I'd been able to marry Jack Lund, we would have lived happily ever after with forks and knives from Meyer's Department Store. But as the future Mrs. Richard Brownlee, I knew I would be called upon to host many dinners for the likes of Mrs. Cavendish, for whom only the best would do. My anxiety over this was only heightened by the knowledge that there were such things as strawberry forks to worry about. Chastened, I set the list down on the fancy desk and made tracks for the elevator. I could only tolerate wedding chores for so long before panic threatened. What kind of a bride was I?

I was ready to abandon the quest and return to Miss Brownlee's in defeat. But when the elevator operator called out, "Fifth floor. Millinery," the perfect solution to my gloomy mood suddenly became apparent.

What I needed to lift my spirits, more than anything, was a new hat.

CHAPTER EIGHT

I stepped off the elevator like Alice through the looking glass. Before me lay rows and rows of hats of every description: cloches, toques, derbies, picture hats, knit caps, riding hats. I touched a soft brown felt hat with a jaunty feather, perched on a mannequin's stylish head. Brown was my usual choice, a practical nondescript color, but the feather gave it an extra kick. A saleswoman floated forth in the Field's manner.

"Good afternoon, miss. Have you been helped?"

"Just looking," I replied.

This clerk looked different from those presiding over Bridal. For one thing, she was younger, closer to my own age. And even though she wore a similar plain black dress, the dress was form-fitting and startlingly short, almost revealing her knees. She wore her shiny dark hair in a stylish chin-length bob ("chopped off like a boy's," Frances would have sneered), charcoal pencil around her dark eyes, two spots of rouge, and dark red lipstick. Against all the strong colors, her skin looked alarmingly white. She might have looked almost ghoulish, if she hadn't been so pretty.

She gazed back at me and smiled. "What lovely blue eyes you have. Wait here. I have the perfect thing for you. Please take a seat."

I did as I was told. Knowing I wasn't likely to make a purchase, I hesitated to waste her time. On the other hand, the department wasn't busy, and it would be fun to try on a few hats.

The clerk, whose nametag read "D. Rodgers," produced a fashionable cloche in a brilliant shade of yellow, trimmed with a navy grosgrain ribbon. I removed my own hat and set it on my lap. She handed me the cloche and I gingerly placed it on my head.

"No, no. Not like that. You wear it *down* like this." She grabbed the hat on each side and firmly tugged it down until it rested low on my forehead, shading my eyes. "There. That's better. What do you think?"

I gazed at the three-way mirror. I almost didn't recognize the sophisticated woman who looked back. I examined my head from all angles. "It's lovely," I admitted.

"It's amazing what a difference the right *chapeau* can make," Miss Rodgers exclaimed. "Just look what it does for your coloring." My complexion did indeed look brighter—what I could see of it beneath the lowered brim. "It's a darling hat," she continued. "And so classy. You know what the great fashion designer Coco Chanel says: 'A girl should be two things: classy and fabulous.'"

I hadn't known, but I doubted Kerryville was ready for both classy *and* fabulous. Reluctantly I pulled off the hat and smoothed my flyaway hair. "I'm not sure. It might be a little *too* fashionable. I live in a small town, you see."

"Then be a fashion leader. *Someone* has to set the standard."

I doubted I'd be setting a standard in Kerryville anytime soon, for fashion or anything else. "I love it, but the brown suede would be more practical."

"Oh, piffle. Who needs practical? That dull brown makes you fade into the woodwork. I should think you'd be tired of it and want a change."

If she only knew how much I wanted a change—and not just of my hat.

Under other circumstances I might have found the clerk's forthright manner offensive. But strangely, talking with Miss Rodgers felt like an amicable argument between friends.

"It's not the same hat at all," I protested. "The one on the mannequin has a feather."

"Feather, *schmeather*," she said. "Don't you want something entirely new, something fresh and exciting?"

I glanced down at my old hat, which was looking sorrier by the minute.

But canary yellow! In such a daring, modern style. Every head on Main Street would swivel my way if I wore a hat like that. Did I dare?

The clerk sensed my waffling and winked at me in the mirror. "Come on, doll," she coaxed. "Live a little."

"Miss, may we have your help?" called a voice from a small clutch of ladies gathered around a display of wide-brimmed sunhats.

"I'll be with you in a moment," Miss Rodgers caroled back. To me she whispered, "Meat packers' wives."

I glanced at the women. "How can you tell?"

"By their hats, of course. Will you excuse me a moment?"

As Miss Rodgers sailed off to attend to the customers, I checked the price tag on the yellow cloche and swallowed hard. It would take most of the money I'd earmarked for bridesmaids' gifts to buy it.

Yet it was such a darling hat . . . a smart, summery, sunshiny hat. A sophisticated city hat, infused with the power to transform even me into a sophisticated city girl. When would I ever find one like it again? Certainly not at Meyer's Department Store.

Suddenly Frances's voice popped into my head. *Yellow is such an impractical color. You'll never be able to keep it clean. Isn't that style a little bold for you?*

That settled my decision. "I'll take it," I blurted when Miss Rodgers returned.

"Now you're cooking with gas!" Miss Rodgers cocked her head and gently grasped the thick coil of hair pinned at the nape of my neck, weighing it in her hand. "If I may make a suggestion, this style of hat would look even better if your hair were bobbed. Have you thought of having that done? There's a beauty salon upstairs that'll fix you right up."

I recoiled. "Oh, no. My fiancé says girls who bob their hair look like . . . well, let's just say he wouldn't approve. This hat will be about as much 'modern' as he can stand."

Miss Rodgers laughed. "Oh, men don't know *what* they like." She swept the hat out of my hands. "We'll wrap this up and get you on your way. Unless, of course, you'd like to see more hats. We have an adorable little sailor number, just the thing for yachting."

"I'd better not. I've done enough damage to my budget as it is. But if you don't mind, I'd like to wear it home."

"Why, sure, doll. I'll wrap up your old one. Maybe you can donate it to some worthy cause."

I set the Darling Yellow Hat on my head and tugged it down the way she'd shown me. "Like this?"

"Like that." She grinned. "Perfect. Now there's a girl who's ready for an adventure."

As I left the store in the Darling Yellow Hat, I did indeed feel ready for an adventure, but couldn't think of anything particularly adventurous to do. I came upon a theater showing a matinee of *Love*, a John Gilbert film I hadn't yet seen, and I went inside.

Two hours later, though, I wished I hadn't, as the Gilbert/Garbo retelling of Tolstoy's tragic love story cast a pall over the lovely evening. I left the theater with a vague hollow yearning in my heart. Perhaps I was just lonely for Richard, as any good fiancée would be.

Before bed I scribbled a few lines to him on a postcard I'd bought at the Art Institute. Richard wasn't a big fan of art, but I thought he might find this one amusing. It had a dog on it; he liked dogs. I did my best to drum up enthusiasm for going home to Kerryville, and to think happy thoughts of marital bliss.

But later that night, the face haunting my dreams belonged not to Richard, but to the young man who never came home.

CHAPTER NINE

"Darling, I've missed you." Richard's smile beamed across the telephone wire. I felt unaccountably irritated at his cheerfulness. "Just one more appointment with Dr. Cragin and you'll be on your way home."

"Yes, that's right." I tried to match his enthusiasm, but frankly, I hated leaving the city I'd only just begun to discover. The thought of returning to Kerryville so soon depressed me. How could I explain this to Richard?

"I've cleared my schedule on Saturday and told your folks I'll meet you at the station," he continued.

I shifted the receiver to my other ear, drew a deep breath, and plunged ahead. "Actually, I am thinking of staying in the city a little while longer."

Surprise tinged his voice. "How *much* longer?"

I twisted a piece of fringe on the arm of Miss Brownlee's horsehair sofa, half listening for Miss Jessop's footsteps in the hall. "I'm not sure. A few more days, I guess."

"You guess?" He sounded perplexed. I couldn't really blame him. I felt pretty perplexed myself. "Why?"

"I want to see the sights. I've been so busy." This was at least partially true. I hadn't seen many of the sights because I'd spent most of my time at the Art Institute, soaking up the beauty and peace of the galleries.

But the real reason was that this was my last taste of freedom, to do what I wanted to do, no matter how silly or time-wasting it seemed to others, before returning home to Kerryville and married life. It sounded so selfish to say it out loud. I wanted to wear a yellow hat, and eat real Italian food, and go to a movie in the middle of the afternoon without feeling guilty. Was that too much to ask?

"You want to see the sights?" Richard parroted. "What sights?"

"Oh, you know. Museums. Lincoln Park Zoo. The opera."

"The *opera*?" A strong note of disbelief crept into his voice. "Since when do you like opera?"

"Since . . . I don't know. How do I know if I like it if I've never been there?"

Richard sighed. "I don't understand. I should think you'd be eager to come home."

My words tumbled in a rush. "I thought so too, but—well, I don't feel quite ready to come home. After all, soon we'll be married, and I might not have the opportunity to come back, ever."

He sounded amused. "Sweetheart, it's not as if we'll never set foot in Chicago ever again. I attend medical conferences there on occasion. Now that I know you'd enjoy it, I'll bring you along. Right now, though, you need to come home."

A vision flashed before my eyes of Richard and me, some day in the future, the respectable Dr. and Mrs. Brownlee. We'd check into one of the nicer hotels, the Conrad Hilton or the Drake. While he attended meetings, I'd join the other wives for shopping, perhaps an afternoon concert at Orchestra Hall or a matinee at one of the glittering theaters. We'd attend ladies' luncheons, with chicken salad in a pastry shell and dainty portions of raspberry sherbet in little glass dishes. We'd visit the museums, maybe even the Art Institute. The other wives would murmur politely about this or that painting or piece of sculpture, how this one was divine, and that one (perhaps some artfully disrobed Greek athlete) shocking and appalling. This they would linger at the longest, shaking their heads in disgust to reinforce how shocked and appalled they were, while their eyes remained glued to the statue's rippling torso. Then we would all return to Kerryville and committee work and the endless planting of zinnias.

"Hello? Marjorie? Are you still there?"

"I'm here." The vision made me feel frantic. But I didn't know how to convey that to Richard over the telephone, so all I said was, "I'd like to stay."

"Darling, you don't sound at all like yourself." His voice oozed concern. "Are you not feeling well?"

"I'm fine, Richard. No dizziness whatsoever." This realization startled me. Was there something about being away from home, away from Richard, that kept the dizziness at bay?

"Has Dr. Cragin told you anything you're not telling me?" he pressed.

I felt like a child accused of fibbing by a teacher. "Honestly, Richard, I fully expect him to give me a perfectly clean bill of health tomorrow." I fought to keep my tone pleasant. "You mustn't worry. I'll be home in a few days."

When we hung up, I felt proud of my negotiating skills. But he must have immediately relayed the news to Frances, because when Miss Brownlee's telephone rang fifteen minutes later I could practically see steam rising from the receiver.

"What's all this nonsense about your staying in the city?" Frances asked. "Of course you'll come home Saturday, as planned. Your father needs you at the store, and we have endless wedding tasks to do. Or have you forgotten? Will I have to do all the preparations myself?"

I saw my excuse and grabbed it. "That's one reason I need a few more days." I tried my best to sound apologetic. "I haven't bought the bridesmaids' gifts yet." Thanks to my Darling Yellow Hat, I no longer had much money to do so, either, but that was beside the point.

I pictured Frances standing at the other end of the line, one fist gripping the receiver, the other firmly planted on her aproned hip. "For heaven's sake, Marjorie. I asked you to do one simple thing . . ."

"I know. I'm sorry. Say, is Pop there? May I speak to him?"

She ignored me. "Marjorie, I'm not going to argue. You mustn't impose any longer on Miss Brownlee's hospitality. As for the attendants' gifts, well, we'll just have to make do."

"Please put Pop on the line."

But she had already hung up.

I resigned myself to going home as planned. It didn't seem worth the trouble of upsetting everyone by remaining in the city, especially with no clear idea what I would do if I stayed, or where I would live, or how I would pay for such an adventure. Pop wasn't likely to lend money to cover my expenses if Frances vehemently opposed the idea.

At the hospital on Friday, I was prepared for Dr. Cragin's brusque, dismissive manner. The last time I was in his office, he'd avoided all eye contact. So I was alarmed when he sat down and looked intently into my face.

"Miss Corrigan," he began. "I've carefully gone over the results of your tests."

"And?"

"I believe there's a case for having further tests done."

I went cold all over. "I'm that ill? Is it serious?" A dozen possibilities raced through my mind. Seizures. Epilepsy. A brain tumor.

"No, no, nothing like that," the doctor soothed. "I believe you have what used to be called a bad case of nerves."

Relief flooded my body. "Nerves! That's it?" I gathered up my handbag and gloves and stood. "I'm sorry to have taken up your time, doctor."

"Now, Miss Corrigan," he said. "Your tests show you to be healthy. Physically, that is. But I still have some concerns."

I sat back down. "Go on."

"It isn't normal for a healthy young woman to faint with such frequency." The doctor leaned back in his chair, holding his fingertips in a V formation. "Have you been under any unusual strain recently? Any problems of a mental or emotional nature?"

I shrugged. "Nothing I can think of."

"At our first appointment you mentioned you're getting married soon. Are you feeling anxious about that?"

"No, of course not."

"I see," he said in that doctorly way that means nothing and everything. My glance strayed to a calendar on his desk, where "May 18, 1928" glowed in red type. Less than four months to my wedding day.

"Not anxious at all."

But at those words, my insides gave a lurch. If I'd been Pinocchio, my nose would have grown an inch. My mind flashed back over my fainting spells. That day in the theater, mooning over John Gilbert's portrayal of wartime romance. The day my wedding dress fabric arrived. The day of the Hospital Auxiliary tea. The visit to Field's bridal department.

Suddenly I realized with lightning clarity that every dizzy episode had happened when I was contemplating my upcoming marriage. No wonder I didn't like to think about it or talk about it. I was allergic to my own wedding.

A strange sort of horror mixed with hilarity gripped my chest, and I nearly burst out laughing at the ridiculousness of it all.

Dr. Cragin's forehead creased. "Miss Corrigan? Are you all right?"

I had no desire to discuss my premarital misgivings with Dr. Cragin. I needed time and space to sort things out. I swallowed hard and tried to speak normally. "You—you said you wanted to run more tests."

"I do, but not on your heart." He tapped a pen on his desk. "When tests come back clear, as yours did, we start looking for other possible sources of the problem." He pressed a little box on his desk. "Nurse, please summon Dr. Finkelburg. I believe he's waiting for us." He turned back to me. "Dr. Finkelburg is one of my esteemed colleagues. He's a doctor of psychoanalysis. I'd like to have him run some tests to determine your mental state."

"Psychoanalysis?" I sputtered, staring at Dr. Cragin in disbelief. "I don't need a psychoanalyst. I'm not crazy."

"Of course you're not," he soothed. "But since I can find nothing wrong with you physically, I believe your attacks must have some psychological cause. Dr. Finkelburg will help us find out what that is. Ah, here he is now."

A kind-looking older gentleman in a white lab coat stepped into the room, but before he could say a word, I gathered my belongings and stood, struggling once again to suppress a wave of inappropriate laughter that bubbled up from my chest.

"I believe there's been a mistake, Dr. Cragin. I don't need a psychoanalyst."

"Now, Miss Corrigan, be reasonable."

"I came here to discover whether I had a heart problem, and you've verified that I do not. Thank you, and good day."

Dr. Cragin's face reddened. "But I've spoken to Dr. Brownlee about it and he agrees that a psychiatric evaluation would—"

My blood chilled. "Wait a minute. You spoke to Dr. Brownlee about me? But Dr. *Perkins* is my doctor."

He nodded. "Yes, Dr. Perkins and I did discuss your heart condition. But then just yesterday Dr. Brownlee called me. He said he was concerned—"

I lifted my chin and fought to keep my voice even. "He called you? Dr. Richard Brownlee? To discuss me?"

Dr. Cragin scowled. "Who else? He and I discussed the possibility that you might be undergoing some kind of nervous—"

I didn't hear the rest of what he said. I was already halfway down the stairs. I burst out onto the sidewalk, panting with exertion and rage.

One thought kept swirling across my steaming brain. *Richard thinks I've lost my marbles.* He'd been discussing my situation. With Dr. Cragin. Behind my back. I had not known he was capable of such betrayal.

No wonder I was allergic to the idea of marriage. How could I possibly marry a man I couldn't trust?

I pounded up and down city sidewalks, no destination in mind other than to delay going back to Miss Brownlee's. After some time, I found myself in the Loop, sweaty and spent. The roar of the elevated train overhead matched my turmoil. To calm my roiling spirit, I sought out the cool, serene galleries of the Art Institute. I passed the bronze lions, paid the fee, and wandered aimlessly before folding myself onto a bench in front of one of my favorite paintings, *The Song of the Lark.*

I loved it because the girl in the picture—a peasant girl standing in a field—reminded me of the French girl in *The Big Parade.* Secretly I imagined her waiting for her man to return—from the front, perhaps, or from some distant journey. The painting brought me joy as I saw the radiance of her face. But now my gloomy mood cast it in a different light. *What if her man lets her down? What if he turns out not to be the man she thought he was?*

Or worse. *What if he simply never comes back, ever? What if she waits and hopes and he never returns?*

With an aching heart, I realized Charlie was right all along. If Jack had come back from the war, I'd never have given Richard a second glance. And I would not be in this mess now. My whole life would be different, if only Jack had come home.

Grateful for the seclusion of the empty gallery, I groped in my bag for a handkerchief and let my sadness pour out in great, gulping waves, until my heart lightened and the waterfall trickled to a mere sniffle. After a while I sensed someone joining me on the bench. A gentle voice spoke.

"Young lady, excuse me, but you seem distraught. May I help you?"

I glanced up through watery eyes to see an older woman, silver-haired and neatly dressed in a rose-colored suit. Her lined face bore a kindly expression.

"Oh, no, thank you," I stammered, gathering my thoughts from the dark corners where they'd skittered. "I've just received a bit of a shock, I'm afraid."

"Oh, dear. Bad news?"

"Yes. I suppose it is bad news." Bad news indeed to discover that one's future husband can't be trusted. Bad news to still be mourning, after ten long years, a true love who would never return.

"Is there something I can do?" the woman asked. "Shall I summon a guard? Perhaps he could call you a taxicab."

"Oh, no." I straightened up and dabbed my eyes with the handkerchief, embarrassed to be making an emotional scene in front of a stranger. "I'll be fine. I just—I have to make a difficult decision. That's all."

"I see."

The woman continued to sit beside me. Although we were strangers, I found her presence comforting, almost motherly. But I didn't think to introduce myself, nor did she do so. Eventually she said, "You know, I've always loved this piece, *The Song of the Lark*."

I glanced at the painting and nodded.

"Do you know the story behind it?" she asked. "The artist was walking in the field early one morning when he heard the song of a lark singing high overhead. As he looked around, he noticed a peasant girl also listening raptly to the beautiful sound. Thus he felt inspired to paint the scene."

"Yes." I could read the description in the museum guide as easily as she could.

"But you know, I like to think the girl is listening to more than a lovely birdsong," the woman continued. "From the expression on her face, I like to think that, working alone in the field in the early morning quiet, she might have prayed to the Father about some concern that lay on her heart. And now, her face turned toward heaven, she is expecting His answer."

Oh, swell, I thought. *A proselytizer.* I braced myself to be called "Sister" and receive a religious tract, but the woman said nothing more. We sat in silence for a long moment, gazing at the painting. I squelched an urge to tell her what I thought about prayer, that it was useful for some people, but that others could pray and pray and pray and still things wound up in ruins. I still believed in God, but he was remote, sitting in His distant heaven, not terribly interested in anything Marjorie Corrigan had to say.

Eventually I broke the silence. "I could see how you might get that impression, from the way her face looks."

But the woman had vanished. I was once again alone in the gallery. I shivered. Who was she?

As I stood to leave, an object thudded softly to the floor. I picked it up—a small, pocket-sized Bible with a black cover. The friendly stranger must have left it behind. I opened the front cover, hoping to see the owner's name written there. But there was only a reference, scripted in an elegant hand: 1 Peter 5:6-7. Curious, I flipped through the book until I found it and read, "Humble yourselves therefore under the mighty hand of God, that he may exalt you in due time; casting all your care upon him; for he careth for you."

I gazed at the face of the girl in the painting. Maybe it was silly to think she was waiting for her lover. More likely she was just listening to a lark's tuneful song, as the artist described. After all, he was the artist, he should know.

But what if the girl was praying? I peered more closely. What if she was casting her cares? What if she was sick and tired of her situation, and was looking expectantly toward God to see if He might have something else in store for her—if He might look down from His mighty perch and observe the mess she'd gotten herself into and decide that something must be done?

At this point, anything seemed possible. I slid the Bible into my handbag, intending to leave it at the Lost and Found desk on my way out, but before I'd even reached the exit, it had slipped my mind.

By the time I telephoned Richard that evening, I'd calmed down enough to speak civilly.

"So what did the doctor say?"

"You know very well what the doctor said. You called him and discussed my case behind my back."

"Well, sure I did, sweetheart," he said, as if he'd done nothing objectionable. "I wanted to talk to him doctor-to-doctor. It's my job to look out for you, you know."

"Doesn't your medical code of ethics, or whatever it is, say you're supposed to keep private things private?"

"Now darling, don't be angry. I only wanted to make sure you were getting the best care possible."

"The best psychoanalysis, you mean."

Silence hung heavy. Clearly Richard had not expected Dr. Cragin to share *all* the details of their conversation. After a moment he spoke. "Sweetie, it's obvious you've been under a strain. I didn't think you'd mind if—"

"That's right," I snapped. "You didn't think."

"I'm sorry, Marjorie," he said, not sounding sorry at all. "There's no need to get all riled up over it."

"I'm not riled up. I would simply prefer to handle my own private business from now on."

"Fine."

Before the conversation escalated into a full-blown argument, we said a cool good-night.

Early the next morning I packed my bag and dressed in my traveling suit and Darling Yellow Hat. I bid good-bye to Miss Brownlee and Miss Jessop with a heavy heart, not because I would miss them but because leaving their home meant leaving Chicago, the city I'd grown to love in just a few short days. When Miss Brownlee said she was looking forward to the wedding, I felt like a fraud, struggling to maintain the beaming smile of the happy bride.

Lugging my suitcase on the streetcar was an unappealing prospect, so I splurged on a taxicab to the station. As it crawled through downtown traffic, I lowered the dingy window and watched the stenographers and shop girls rush to work in their stylish hats, knee-length skirts, and modern lace-up brogues, wishing I were among them. They looked so free and unconcerned about other people's expectations. Once the bell rang at five o'clock, their evenings and weekends would be their own. These energetic single girls were free to do anything they chose.

I desperately needed some guidance, yet I couldn't think of anyone I could trust who'd give me reliable advice, untainted by their own expectations. The memory of the lady in the art gallery, what she'd said about prayer, kept popping into my mind. Did I dare to ask God for guidance and trust Him to give it? Prayer hadn't worked out so well for me in the past. Was I willing to give it another go?

The cab pulled up at the station. When I reached into my bag to pay the driver, my hand brushed against the Bible I'd forgotten to turn in to the Lost and Found. I'd have to mail it back to the Art Institute from home, in case the owner came back looking for it. The verse written inside floated through my brain: "Cast all your care upon him; for he careth for you." He careth. Nice to know somebody did.

I paid the driver and entered the terminal, struggling like a salmon swimming upstream against the tide of commuters pouring out to begin the workday. Above me the waiting-room ceiling arched high above over rows of wooden pew-like benches, giving the cavernous room a churchly quality. I took a seat in the vast waiting room, settled my suitcase at my feet, and bowed my head.

Then I finally did what I should have been doing all along. I prayed.

Dear Lord, I began. Then my mind went blank.

I'd been steering clear of God for so long, my praying mechanism was rusty. As it creaked to life, I pictured Helen and how she talked to God as easily as she talked to me. I used to have that easy sort of trust, long ago. I wanted it again. I closed my eyes, oblivious to the bustling travelers around me, then silently cast my cares in the general direction of heaven.

Dear Lord, I'm sorry for neglecting You for so long. I grew distant from You, but I was the one who moved. You didn't move. I drew in a deep breath. *I'm sorry for blaming You for everything, because I didn't trust. Well, I'm trusting You now. Thank You that I'm healthy and strong.*

The longer I prayed, the easier the words seemed to flow. *And now, Lord, about this tangled mess. I don't know what to do. I miss Jack so much. Am I still in love with his memory? What about Richard? Under the circumstances, should I break our engagement, or will that make a bad situation worse? Should I stay in Chicago or go home to Kerryville? Either way, I'm scared of what the future holds. If it is Your will for me to marry Richard, then Your will be done. But if You have another plan for me, then please make it clear to me. I'm turning this whole situation over to You. Please, dear Jesus, show me the way.*

That was as good a prayer as I could muster up. But I recalled what the Bible said about the Holy Spirit doing our groaning for us when we can't find the words, and felt a tingling warmth inside.

A strange peace settled over me. Nothing about my situation had changed, but there was something comforting and right about handing the reins over to God. My heart expanded as I turned to Him after so many years of running the other way.

When it was time to board the train, I trudged along the platform and up the steps on leaden legs. As the conductor bellowed, "All aboard," I settled into a seat and stared out the window at the bustling platform.

Suddenly all the breath whooshed out of my body in a single breathless cry.

"Jack!"

There on the platform, looking very much alive, stood Jack Lund.

CHAPTER TEN

I bolted down the aisle. Passengers glared as my suitcase banged against their seats. "Sorry, sorry," I murmured, desperate to reach the sliding doors.

The conductor blocked my exit. "Miss, please take a seat. The train is leaving."

"I'm so sorry," I pleaded. "I made a huge mistake. Please open the doors and let me off. Please!"

"Crazy dame," the conductor muttered. He pushed a button and the doors slid open. I lurched off the train, shaking with anxiety. *Where is he? Where's Jack?* I'd lost sight of him in the swirling mass of humanity.

The train slowly puffed and clanged out of the station, toward Kerryville, without me. I never looked back.

Panic seized my throat. *Which way did he go?* Was my mind playing tricks? But there was no mistaking that face.

Suddenly there he was, trudging up the broad marble staircase. I lumbered after him, my heavy suitcase beating against my legs.

"Jack! Jack Lund!"

The man didn't respond. Clearly he couldn't hear me over the echoing din. Outside the station, he paused to buy a newspaper. I caught up to him, wheezing from the frantic climb up the stairs. Then I saw the scar—a thick, jagged line that ran like a lightning bolt up the left side of his face. I gulped.

"Jack Lund?" I could barely wheeze out the words. "Is . . . that . . . you?"

The man stared at me, a quizzical look on his face. At least I think it was quizzical. I couldn't see clearly through watery eyes.

"Jack?" I breathed, voice quavering. "Jack? It's me. Marjorie."

His face blanched, but otherwise his expression did not change. "I'm sorry, miss. I'm afraid you have me confused with someone else."

His voice. Was it Jack's voice? It seemed deeper than I remembered. But of course, he'd be older now. My brain tumbled frantically to remember details.

He turned to go. "Wait." Part of me—the miniscule part that remained clear-minded—suspected he was telling the truth. Jack Lund was dead, his broken body lying somewhere in France. But other, wilder thoughts kept swirling around in my head and heart. What if the army had made a mistake? What if they'd lost Jack, or gotten him confused with someone else? What if he was really alive, and had somehow made his way back and was now standing right in front of me on a busy Chicago sidewalk?

I couldn't think. In a sharply tailored suit, crisp shirt, and silver cufflinks, the man looked like he'd just stepped out of a newspaper ad, one of those sketches of an impeccably groomed fellow leaning against a shiny Pierce-Arrow. Jack had been more the flannel-shirt-and-work-boots type. I didn't think he even owned cufflinks. A discreet nametag on the man's lapel bearing the name "P. A. Bachmann" seemed to confirm this was, indeed, not Jack.

But his face sparked an electric shock straight through my body. Even with the rugged scar, he had the same close-cropped brown wavy hair, the same hazel eyes. He looked incredibly like Jack, if Jack were a few years older and a few thousand dollars richer. Who *wouldn't* look older after all these years, especially after enduring a war? Charlie certainly didn't look the same after months of trench warfare.

My mind exploded with possibilities. Maybe "P. A. Bachmann" was an alias. Maybe he had amnesia on account of the injury that had caused the scar and didn't even remember his real name. I'd seen that happen once in a movie. Or maybe God had heard my prayer and was working out some sort of miracle.

I could not tear my gaze away from the man's bewildered face as I stammered, "You're not Jack Lund? But . . . are you *sure*?"

If the gentleman had wondered if I were deranged, that question removed all doubt. However, he had the grace to smile, or perhaps grimace. "Sorry, miss. I was sure when I woke up this morning. Now if you'll excuse me . . ."

My vision blurred with fresh tears. Could I be any more of an idiot?

Maybe I was dreaming, the kind of dream I'd had off and on since the war. I'd dream Jack was alive and whole and laughing his crinkly-eyed laugh. Then I'd wake up and soak my pillow with tears at the realization it wasn't true. I hadn't had the dream in ages, not since Richard came into my life and pulled me down a different path. Still, at any moment I could wake up and realize this encounter was a mere figment of my imagination.

"I'm so sorry," I blabbered. "The—the resemblance is uncanny." I fumbled in my handbag for a handkerchief and did my best to sound like a reasonable human being. "Are you any relation at all to the Lund family? Of Kerryville? A cousin, perhaps?"

The poor soul gave a puzzled frown. "Where's Kerryville?"

"It's a small town west of here—oh, never mind." I gave up on finding a handkerchief and forced myself to smile as if this were all a jolly misunderstanding. "You just look a lot like someone I used to know."

"Do I?" he said gently. He pulled a clean handkerchief from his pocket and handed it to me.

"You're very kind." If I were him, I'd be running away as fast as my legs could carry me. Yet here he stood, offering assistance. He must have decided I was the non-threatening sort of lunatic. He smiled a little and my insides melted. In an instant his smile gave way to concern.

"Miss? Miss, are you ill? Perhaps you should sit down." He took hold of my elbow and steered me toward a nearby bench.

For a figment of my imagination, he had a mighty firm grip.

"I'm all right," I insisted. The waves of shock flooding my body were ebbing to ripples of embarrassment. "I'm sorry to have bothered you. Here." I offered up his soggy handkerchief.

"Keep it. It's no bother. Are you sure you don't want me to telephone someone?"

"No, thanks. I'll be fine in a minute."

We stared at each other for an awkward moment as commuters brushed past us, too wrapped up in their own concerns to take notice of a puffy-eyed girl and a bewildered man who probably wished he'd taken an earlier train. Finally he said, "Well. All right then. I really must be going. Good luck to you." And he turned and strode off down the street.

I watched his retreating back. *He's not Jack, not Jack, not Jack,* my brain hammered. *Jack is gone. He's dead.* This P. A. Bachmann, or whoever he was, was not Jack, wavy hair and hazel eyes to the contrary.

Then one split second before the stranger moved out of sight, he reached up and rubbed the back of his neck. I'd have known that gesture anywhere.

And then he was gone.

Still lugging that confounded suitcase, I hurried in the direction he'd gone, but the crowds had swallowed him whole. Numb with disappointment and disbelief, I returned to the bench.

Marjorie, get a hold of yourself. I wanted to burst into tears, to cry for joy, to grieve and wail and shout hallelujah, all at once—and all over a complete stranger I'd known for three minutes, tops.

Was this the sign from God I'd been waiting for? Or was Richard correct, and I was slowly losing my mind?

One thing was certain: I couldn't leave Chicago before I knew for sure whether or not the man was Jack. But how was I going to do that? He'd just walked down the street and out of my life.

I sat on the bench for a long time, taking stock of my situation. How could I stay all alone in the city? At the same time, how could I leave, knowing Jack might be out there somewhere? Even if I wanted to leave, there wouldn't be another train to Kerryville until the following day.

My mind tumbled to formulate a plan. Since the man had arrived on a train, perhaps he commuted to the city every day. If I showed up again at the station during rush hour, I was bound to run into him again, and we could straighten this whole mess out. Or rather, *I* could straighten it out. Surely he didn't realize there was any mess in need of straightening.

And what if he did turn out to be Jack? Then what?

I'd worry about that when the time came.

I opened my purse and counted its meager contents. Where would I sleep? I couldn't show up on Miss Brownlee's doorstep again like some sort of stray animal. *Please, God. Show me what You want me to do.*

As I fumbled through my purse, my fingers brushed against my unused train ticket. I jumped up and hurried back into the train station, where I gave a stern-faced clerk a breathless song and dance, one moment winsome, one moment quivering on the edge of tears—Helen would have been proud of my acting chops—about why I needed to cancel my trip. Finally he relented and refunded my fare—just enough for a cheap lodging and a few bowls of soup. No matter. The excitement of seeing Jack had driven my appetite clean away.

With fresh resolve I straightened my shoulders and strode to consult that oracle of all knowledge, the Traveler's Aid lady, about where to go next.

CHAPTER ELEVEN

The Traveler's Aid lady directed me to the Young Women's Christian Association. The plain truth was, I couldn't leave the city until I knew for sure, *truly* for sure, that P. A. Bachmann was not Jack Lund. And who knew how long that would take? But I'd have to think of something; my traveling money was dwindling fast.

The first thing I did was call Richard, so he wouldn't be waiting for me at the train station. I found a public telephone in the lobby and asked the operator to connect me with Kerryville General. Richard was busy with a patient, so I left a message, secretly relieved that I didn't have to speak to him directly yet. I needed more time to plan out what I'd say—not a lie, but something easier to swallow than the bald truth that I was chasing down the ghost of a past lover.

The Y seemed like a pleasant-enough place, a buzzing beehive of young working women—stenographers, shop girls, factory workers. I started to hoist my suitcase up a flight of stairs when a woman wearing a light blue uniform and a hairnet zoomed past me.

"Wait there, Millie," she called over the railing to her friend. "I'll be ready in a jiffy."

"Hurry up," her friend replied. "I'm starving."

"Think about where to eat," Hairnet yelled as she rounded the landing.

"Where do we *always* eat on payday?" the friend replied in a snippy tone. I sympathized. Hunger made me snappish, too.

Wait. *Payday.*

All at once I knew what to do. I hurried up the stairs, glanced around the tiny, spartan room assigned to me, flung my suitcase on the floor and my hat on the bureau, and raced back downstairs.

In the lobby, I tapped my foot and tried to catch the heavily shadowed eye of the bottle-blonde now hogging the sole telephone.

"So I says to him, I says, 'Just how do you expect me to do that?' And he says to me—get this, Myra—he says, 'I dunno, you figure it out, you're supposed to be the smart one." So I says to him—hold on a sec, Myra." The blonde placed her hand over the mouthpiece and glared at me. "You want something, sister?"

"Yes, the telephone. Are you almost through?"

"Hold your horses." She turned her back toward me and continued her conversation. "So, Myra, as I was saying . . ."

My temples pounded. At long last she replaced the receiver. "It's all yours. Let's see how you like talking with somebody breathing down your neck and listening in on your every word."

I mumbled an insincere "Sorry," dropped some coins in the box, and gave the number for Corrigan's Dry Goods to the operator.

To my relief, Charlie answered.

"What's up, sis? Thought you'd be on your way home by now."

"Charlie, listen," I hissed, my hand cupping the mouthpiece, even though nobody at my end had any reason to eavesdrop. "Where's Pop? Are you alone?"

"He's out front with a customer. What's gives? Are you all right?"

I took a deep breath. "I need you to do me a huge favor. I need to stay in Chicago for a couple of days. Yesterday was payday—can you wire me my pay?"

He sounded confused. "Sure, but—"

I exhaled with relief. "Oh, thank you."

"But why? Do Pop and Frances know you're not coming home?"

"Not yet. I'll—I'll call them next."

"Is something the matter?"

I hesitated, then said slowly, "Charlie, I think I've seen Jack."

"Who?"

"Jack. I think I saw him, here in Chicago. Although he's going by a different name. I don't think he remembers who he is."

"What are you talking about? Jack who? *Your* Jack?"

"Yes. My Jack. I saw him at the train station. He said he wasn't Jack, but . . ." I lowered my voice even further. "I think he has amnesia."

Charlie's voice went flat. "Marjorie, are you joking? If so, it's not funny."

"I know it sounds crazy, Charlie, but I swear—"

"Darn right, it sounds crazy," my brother said, forgetting to be quiet. "You're mistaken, that's all. Lots of people resemble other people."

"I know, Charlie, but I swear, this man—"

"You listen to me," he interrupted. "No matter what you think you saw, that man wasn't Jack. Jack is dead. I know you've been under a strain, but you have to stop this nonsense here and now."

"But, Charlie—"

"I mean it, sis." His voice lowered to a growl. "Look, I didn't want to say anything, but Frances has been telling Pop she thinks you're having some kind of nervous breakdown or something."

"Me?" I snorted. "You're kidding, right?"

"I'm dead serious. Pop doesn't think so, but Frances has her suspicions. She keeps saying stuff like she can't imagine how anyone in her right mind could abandon everything right before her wedding and run off to Chicago."

I groaned. "First of all, it's not 'right before my wedding.' That's four months away. And I didn't 'run off.' For heaven's sake, she practically put me on the train herself."

"Don't shoot the messenger," Charlie said. "I just thought you should know. She may have even discussed it with Richard. She was on the horn with him for a long time the other evening."

"Oh, my goodness." So Frances and Richard agreed that I was becoming unhinged. Naturally he'd discussed my mental state with my parents as well as with Dr. Cragin. Why not just stand up and ask Pastor Rooney to announce it from the pulpit?

"Yeah. So for Pete's sake, don't throw gasoline on the flame by talking about seeing ghosts."

"But if you could *see* this man—"

"Marjorie. No."

I bit my lower lip. "But you'll still send the money?"

"I'll send the money. But you're going to have to talk to Pop." He raised his voice. "Pop, it's Marjorie."

"Wait. Charlie—" *Oh, boy.*

I heard some shuffling, and then my father's deep voice came over the line. "Marjorie?"

"Hi, Pop." I choked up a little at the sound of his voice. Maybe he would be more reasonable than everybody else and see the commonsense genius of my plan.

"What did the doctor say?"

"I'm right as rain." In my elation over seeing Jack, I'd forgotten all about the reason I'd come to Chicago in the first place. "No explanation for the dizzy spells, and anyway, they've stopped."

"That's fine. You did the right thing to get yourself checked out. By the way, Frances told me you wanted to stay in the city. That you don't want to come home."

"Oh, Pop. It's not that I don't want to come home, exactly." How could I make him understand? "I just—I really love it here, and I feel like it's important for me to have some freedom before I get tied down." I thought it best not to mention the real reason . . . that somewhere in the vast metropolis existed a man who might be the long-dead Jack Lund, and that I aimed to find him. Charlie's reaction convinced me to keep this incredible news to myself, for now.

"Tied down, eh." My father grew quiet. I pictured him rubbing his chin, as he did whenever he mulled something over. "Honey, tell me the truth. Are you having second thoughts about marrying Richard?"

"I—I have some things to think over," I admitted. "I don't really care to discuss it over the telephone."

"I see. Do you need me to come there?"

"No, I'm fine. Really."

He cleared his throat. "So how long are you thinking of staying?"

"I don't know." Mentally I calculated how far my paycheck would stretch. I also had a small savings account at Kerryville National Bank that I could tap if absolutely necessary. "Maybe a week or two?"

My father paused again. "You know, your mother loved the city."

"She did? I didn't know that." Goosebumps rose on my arms. Pop spoke about my mother rarely, if at all. He had taken her death hard. So hard that, in my less charitable moments, I suspected he may have jumped into marriage with Frances without giving the matter enough careful consideration.

"Yes. She was a city girl when I met her. Minneapolis born and bred. She would have loved to have visited Chicago more often, but

I always . . . well, things were always so busy, and now I wish—" He broke off for a moment, then said briskly, "Are you still at Richard's great-aunt's house?"

"No, I've taken a room at the Young Women's Christian Association," I said, with an emphasis on the "Christian" to ease his mind.

"Well . . ." he said finally, "if you want to stay awhile, I have no objection. But I won't be able to send you any spending money. After all, I have a wedding to pay for."

Great day in the morning! "Oh, Pop, thank you. But what about the store? Can you and Charlie manage all right without me for a while?"

"Now, don't you worry about the store," Pop said. "We'll be fine. Helen's been nagging me to give her a summer job. Business slows down in summer anyway, as you know. We'll miss you, of course, but I think maybe you're right—a change will do you good." His voice took on a more serious, resolved tone. "I want you to use this time to really think things over, Marjorie. Marriage is a mighty big step. Be absolutely clear in your mind about what you want to do with your life, and how you feel about Richard. You don't want to rush into anything, like—like some people do."

"Oh, Pop. You're the bee's knees." I could hardly breathe, my heart felt so full.

"Take care of my girl." He cleared this throat. "And no more long-distance calls. Too expensive."

"Gee, thanks, Pop. I love you."

I hung up after telling Pop where to have Charlie wire the money, settled up with the operator, and trailed a chattering flock of women up the stairs. Pop had been swell. But everyone else in my family, including Richard, was doubting my sanity. As for me, I was starting to doubt *everything*—my sanity, my eyesight in seeing Jack, and my judgment in marrying Richard. Pop's words echoed in my head. *Be absolutely clear in your mind, Marjorie.* Did I dare to ask Richard, yet again, to postpone our wedding? Did I dare call the whole thing off? I needed to be sure. Because once the decision had been made, I knew there'd be no going back.

CHAPTER TWELVE

Early the next morning I took extra care getting dressed, then positioned myself strategically at the train station. If Mr. P. A. Bachmann passed by, I was sure to see him. The terminal seemed remarkably empty. Then I realized it was Sunday morning—no commuters. I abandoned the quest and spent the rest of the day exploring the lakefront and the park.

On Monday I returned to the station, but still didn't see P. A., which was probably just as well. What would I say to him? *Hello. I think you might have amnesia.* Or *Excuse me, but do you recall that you and I were in love at one time?* The longer I went with no sign of Jack—or P. A.—the more I suspected I was badly mistaken. Still, I couldn't give up that glimmer of hope that Jack was alive.

I went to the Western Union office to collect the money Charlie had wired, then stopped in a used-book store and bought a battered old book that turned out to be *Robinson Crusoe.* I returned to the YWCA and arranged to stay a few more nights. Upstairs in my room, I sat on the bed, opened *Robinson Crusoe,* and carefully clipped out a section of the middle with a pair of manicure scissors. I placed my remaining cash in the hole, closed the book, and slid it back into my suitcase, safe from prying eyes. Who would suspect that dog-eared copy of *Robinson Crusoe* was actually my piggy bank? And now, how to fatten him up?

It occurred to me that, with the busy tourist season coming on, some shops might be hiring extra help. With a temporary job, I could extend my stay even longer. I could hardly expect Charlie to keep sending me money I wasn't earning at Corrigan's.

I headed for the State Street shopping district and started inquiring about jobs. My experience clerking at Corrigan's should have counted for something, but nobody seemed to be hiring.

In the late afternoon I trudged back to the Y, bone-weary and sweating. While it was nice to be around younger people after the dreariness of Miss Brownlee's house, the hall outside my tiny room held a steady stream of laughing, chattering women. Not only was it impossible to get a moment's quiet, but the wait for bathroom time was interminable.

At last, on Thursday morning my efforts paid off. I spotted P. A. Bachmann emerging from Union Station, newspaper under his arm. Heart fluttering, I followed him at a discreet distance for several blocks. He turned in at a side entrance to the stately Marshall Field building, smiling a greeting to the doorman, who let him in even though the store was not yet open for business. Did he work at Field's? I was determined to find out.

As soon as the doors were unlocked to customers, I launched my search. I zigzagged up and down every floor of the enormous store, but did not spot him. Perhaps he worked somewhere out of the public eye, in administrative offices or the stockroom. This was going to be harder than I thought.

"Excuse me," I finally said to the clerk at the information desk on the first floor. "I'm looking for Mr. P. A. Bachmann. I believe he might be employed here."

The clerk flipped through a directory, then pointed to a page. "Here it is. Mr. Bachmann works in the Store for Men." She picked up a telephone receiver. "Whom shall I say is calling?"

All at once my mouth went dry. What would I say to him? That I'd trailed him from the train station like some sort of lady spy? Marjorie Corrigan, Girl Detective.

"I'd prefer to speak to him in person," I said. "Where can I find the Store for Men?"

The clerk directed me to an annex across the street, accessed by an underground tunnel. I scurried through the tunnel and located the Store for Men.

This section had a woodsy, leathery feel to it, quite unlike the more feminine atmosphere of the rest of the store. My pulse raced as I spotted P. A. Bachmann across the sales floor, one hand holding up a suit jacket, the other gesturing to the lining as he pointed out some feature to a customer. I slipped behind a rack of shirts, a safe vantage point from which to study him unobserved.

P. A. Bachmann certainly had Jack's coloring and height, although he seemed slimmer than I remembered. Slimmer in the waist, broader in the shoulders. Of course there was the jagged scar—Jack hadn't had that, but for pity's sake, he'd fought in a war. Had Jack had that small cleft in his chin? One would think I'd remember something like that. I'd have to pull out an old photograph to check, and of course all the albums were back home in Kerryville. It had been ten years, after all. I couldn't quite recall every—

"May I help you, miss?"

I whipped around and faced the cordial smile of a young male clerk. In desperation I grabbed a random shirt from the rack and stammered, "I'm wondering if you have this shirt in green."

The clerk's forehead creased. "That *is* green, miss."

I looked at the shirt for the first time. "So it is. I'm afraid I dislike green. Thank you for your help." I thrust the shirt into his hapless hands and rushed off before P. A. Bachmann could glance over and see me. Once safely out of sight, I leaned against a wall to catch my breath. My full investigation would have to wait for another time. But when? I couldn't keep lurking around the Store for Men forever, feigning an interest in tab collars and cuff links.

Still, I'd found him. I walked back through the tunnel to the main store and celebrated this accomplishment with a small bag of pistachios.

On Thursdays the Art Institute stayed open later to accommodate working people, and admission was free. So rather than spend the evening sitting around in my cell at the Y, I boarded a streetcar for Michigan Avenue. I passed the bronze lions of the Art Institute, and on impulse found the part of the building where classes were held. I'd intended to inquire about the adult classes I'd read about on the brochure, but found the registration office dark and locked, even though the hallway bustled with students. I'd have to come back another day. Meanwhile, I wandered down the hall, peeking into doorways.

"Say, that hat is the last gasp," said a friendly voice beside me. I turned to see a dark-haired woman wearing what looked like a flowered silk kimono and slippers. The ensemble struck me as avant-garde, but I reminded myself that my fashion sense had been formed in Kerryville and was not to be trusted.

The woman's face and voice seemed familiar. It took me a moment to recall where I'd seen the glossy dark hair and rouged cheeks. Then it hit me.

"You work at Marshall Field. In the millinery department." I touched the brim of the Darling Yellow Hat. "You sold me this hat. Remember?"

She laughed. "Why, sure, doll." She walked around me, admiring the hat from all angles. "I do know how to pick 'em, if I do say so myself." She snapped her fingers. "Say, you're the girl who's getting married soon, right? The one I tried to talk into cutting her hair." She lifted a skeptical eyebrow. "I see you haven't taken my advice."

"I'm—still thinking about it."

She extended a hand, showing exquisitely lacquered blood-red fingernails. "I don't believe we've properly met. I'm Dorothy Rodgers. Everyone calls me Dot. As in polka."

I shook her hand. "Marjorie Corrigan."

"Say, are you here for a class?"

"Oh, no. I'm just exploring. I wanted to get some information, but…" I shrugged and gestured to the locked office door.

"Since you're here, why don't you pick a class to sit in on and observe? They encourage prospective students to do that."

A thrill shimmered up my spine. "I am kind of interested in Textiles."

"Down the hall and to your right." Dot pointed. "Say, you seem like a good egg. You all alone in the city?"

I nodded.

"Why don't we get together tonight after class? I know a little place where we can grab a drink and get acquainted. Meet you at the front entrance right after class, all right?"

"I'd like that," I said. "But I have to warn you, I don't drink anything stronger than coffee."

"Pity. Well, coffee it is, then." Students began filing into their studios. "Duty calls." Dot turned toward a doorway marked Life Drawing.

"So you're taking Life Drawing," I said, thinking this was an interesting choice for a milliner.

"Goodness no." Dot laughed over her shoulder. "I'm the model."

"You have to disrobe?" I exclaimed to Dot later that evening as we sat in a nearby coffee shop. "I would feel so humiliated, being naked in front of all those strangers."

"We prefer to call it 'unclothed,'" Dot said, glancing at the menu. "It's not as bad as you think. The art students don't see you . . . you know, *that* way. They're more interested in learning how to draw the way your ribcage connects to your hipbone and all that."

I frowned. "The ribcage doesn't connect to the hipbone."

"You know what I mean. What I'm trying to say is, they don't view you as a *woman*. You're more like an anatomical specimen. Why, it's practically *medical*." She snapped the menu shut. "Let's talk about something else. How did you like the Textiles class?"

"I loved it. I just don't think I could keep up. I don't have any real background, you know. Just an interest."

"That was an advanced class. You don't have to have experience for the beginner classes," Dot said. "That's why they call them 'beginner.' Let's eat, I'm starved."

Over grilled cheese sandwiches and iced tea, I learned that Dot had moved to Chicago from a small town in Indiana, and that although she scraped together an income by selling hats at Field's during the day and posing at the art school at night, her real ambition was to sing professionally. To that end she sang with a band on the weekends, at an Italian restaurant called Louie's Villa Italiana.

"It's a members-only kind of place," she said, "but I'm sure Louie will let you in, if you want to come and listen."

"Members only? Sounds like a speakeasy. At least, what I know about speakeasies from the movies, which isn't much."

She shrugged. "If you want to call it that. Say, are you one of those crusaders?" One side of her mouth quirked up into a half-smile, half-smirk.

Stiffly I said, "No. I just don't like it. Not to mention buying alcohol is illegal."

"Prohibition is a farce," she said. "What makes anything more attractive than saying you can't have it? If they decided to outlaw candy bars, we'd all have rings of chocolate around our mouths. Besides, it's plain cruel to separate a working man from his beer."

"Not when the beer wreaks havoc with his life," I said, thinking of Charlie and his struggle with the bottle.

"Well, as a matter of fact, I don't drink much myself. Maybe an occasional cocktail. Anything stronger makes me forget the words to the songs."

I ought to have been put off by the fact that my new friend sang at a gin joint, but under the dazzle of the city lights it all sounded quite sophisticated. And her friendly smile warmed my heart like a cozy quilt on a chilly night. I hadn't realized how lonely I'd been feeling. For my part, I told her a bit about Kerryville and Richard and my plan to spend some time in the city before my wedding. I left out the parts about premarital jitters, reputed nervous breakdowns, and childhood sweethearts risen from the dead. No sense in spilling all my secrets right away.

At one point I did, however, venture to ask whether, while working at Field's, she'd made the acquaintance of one Mr. P. A. Bachmann of the men's department.

She shook her head. "The name sounds familiar, but I can't place it. Why?"

"No reason."

Suddenly I had an idea. "I need to make some money. Do you think you could help me get a job there? You know, put in a good word for me?"

"At Field's? I don't see why not. Usually they're desperate for summer help—all the tourists and whatnot pouring through the doors. I'll bet they'll hire you like that"—she snapped her fingers—"with your retail experience and all." She pushed aside her half-eaten sandwich and stretched like a cat. "It's getting late. Where did you say you were staying?"

"At the YWCA."

Dot made a face. "Oh, you don't want to stay *there*," she sneered. "I lived there for a while and they have far too many oppressive rules. No men in the rooms and whatnot." She brightened. "Say, why don't you come and spend the night at my place? Then we'll go to Field's first thing in the morning and see about getting you a job."

Disappointed, I said, "Thanks, but all my belongings are at the Y."

"Well, you can't very well fetch them tonight," she replied. "I'll lend you a nightgown, and you can collect your things tomorrow."

The taxi dropped us off in a leafy North Side neighborhood in front of a modest brick apartment building. Dot ushered me up two flights of stairs and opened a door off a dim hallway. She switched on a lamp to reveal a narrow living room with scarred wooden floors and a small window-lined alcove at one end. There wasn't much furniture, just a sofa, a couple of mismatched chairs, and an end table with a lamp on it. Dot hastened to pick up the several pieces of clothing strewn about.

"Sorry. I wasn't expecting company," she breezed. "I had a terrible time deciding what to wear this morning."

The room contained a fireplace, apparently unused, flanked by bookshelves holding little in the way of books. Instead they held several framed photographs, mostly of Dot herself, posed alongside various other carefree-looking people. Dot on the beach. Dot on a sailboat. Dot in an evening gown.

She showed me the extra bedroom—not much more than a large closet with a narrow cot in it—but it was cozy and safe, and heaps quieter than the YWCA.

"What a lovely place," I remarked with a touch of envy. "A sweet little nest, all to yourself."

"Yeah," she agreed, glancing around. "It's pretty nice. The landlady's a dear. Better than being cooped up in the Y with a zillion other women, don't you think? Say, my former roommate moved out recently and I could really use some help with the rent. You could move in here. What do you say?"

All at once a terrific roar shook the building. Tinkling glasses shivered together in a cabinet and the picture frames wobbled on their shelves. Then in a moment, it was over.

"What on earth was that?" I said, grabbing the doorframe for support.

"What? Oh, that's the El. The elevated train. It runs right past the building. After a while, you don't notice it anymore."

As my heartbeat slowed to its normal pace, I said, "Gee, it's tempting to move in here, but I'm only in town temporarily. I'm getting married in September, as you know." *Maybe*, came a thought from out of nowhere.

"Yes, that's too bad," she said cheerfully. "But from where I sit, a summer's worth of rent is better than nothing. And as I said, I'm a busy gal. I'm hardly ever home. You'll practically have the place all to yourself."

I sighed. "We're putting the cart before the horse. I need a job first."

"Don't you worry about that," she said confidently. "We'll take care of that little matter first thing tomorrow."

I shivered deliciously. *Yes. And then I can spy on P. A. Bachman and discover his true identity.*

"Do you think they might put me in Millinery with you?"

"Not Millinery, I'm afraid," she said with regret, as if Millinery were the highest of aspirations. "That takes special training. But plenty of other sections need help. Don't worry, they'll find a place for you." She yawned.

I glanced at my wristwatch, a Christmas gift from Richard. With a pang of guilt I realized that, in my excitement, I'd neglected to consider what he might think of all this upheaval. What would he think of my taking a job at Field's? More to the point, did I really care what he thought?

Dot disappeared into her bedroom and emerged with bedding, a towel, and a nightgown—a slinky apricot satin number that would have done Theda Bara proud. "Here, you can wear this. And first thing in the morning we'll go down to Field's and see what we can do about getting you a job." She yawned again. "And now, I'm off to bed. I've been out late every night this week and I'm absolutely done in."

After she retired, I took a bath in the claw-footed tub in the tiny bathroom. It felt like heaven to enjoy a leisurely soak uninterrupted by a long line of other girls pounding on the door, or Miss Jessop complaining that I used too much hot water. As I relaxed into the steaming tub, I daydreamed about my new job. I saw myself gliding sylphlike through the store, helping some grateful customer select a becoming dress or smart accessory. That I'd never in my life glided sylphlike was entirely beside the point.

Best of all, working at Field's would put me into close proximity to P. A. Bachmann, thus making it easier to find out who he really was. If he turned out not to be Jack, then no harm done. But what if he did turn out to be Jack, after all? What would I do then? I decided to worry about that later.

I toweled off and attempted to squeeze myself into the peach satin nightgown, but it wouldn't even slide over my hips. Grudgingly I put my own petticoat back on, slipped my cardigan over it, and padded out to the galley kitchen, where I scrounged the makings for a cup of tea. Then I made up my bed and crawled into it.

Just as I was drifting off, the roar of the El shook me from my slumber. I hauled myself out of bed to the bathroom, where I took two cotton balls from Dot's stash and stuffed them in my ears. Back in bed, I punched the pillow and threw off the covers. I didn't think I'd sleep a wink, but the next thing I knew, early morning sunlight was streaming through the little window and Dot, wrapped in the sort of fluffy aqua peignoir that Greta Garbo might wear, was standing over me, saying, "Wake up, sleepyhead. Time to go to work."

CHAPTER THIRTEEN

I followed Dot through the heavy revolving door of Marshall Field & Company. She propelled me toward the elevator. "Go on up to Eight and find the Personnel department," she ordered. "You'll have to fill out a bunch of paperwork. I'll clock in first, then I'll meet you up there as soon as I can. Now scoot." She gave me a little shove and trotted off. I strode toward the elevator with a quick glance around, yearning for a glimpse of P. A. Bachmann. No such luck.

"Eight, please," I told the elevator operator.

"Shopping today?" he asked in a friendly manner.

"Not today. I'm hoping to get a job."

"So you're headed up to Personnel?"

"Yes."

"When they ask you, say 'Candy.'"

"Pardon me?"

The operator glanced at me over his fringed epaulet. "Tell them you want to work in the Candy section. Clerk just quit yesterday, and they need to hire somebody quick."

"I see. Candy. Thanks." Frankly I'd been hoping for something more glamorous, like Evening Wear or Fine Jewelry. But a girl had to start somewhere. I was determined to land a job, even if it meant scooping jellybeans while wearing an unfashionable hairnet. "Any other advice?"

"Just be yourself. You look like the classy kind of girl that Field's goes for."

A warm glow of pleasure spread across my face. The doors slid open and the operator called out, "Eight." He pointed to a frosted glass door marked Personnel. "There you go, miss. Good luck to you."

I stepped out of the elevator and stood for a moment, rooted to the spot by my jumbled feelings. I dipped into a restroom to check my outfit. Having not yet retrieved my belongings from the Y, I still wore the previous day's dove-gray skirt and matching blouse, brightened by a fresh floral-print scarf and rosy lipstick thoughtfully provided by Dot. I took a deep breath, pulled my Darling Yellow Hat firmly down on my forehead, and marched resolutely into the personnel office.

The room was long and rectangular, lined with benches and crowded with people of all ages. A perky brunette in a blue smock handed me an application form and a pencil. I sat on a bench and used my handbag on my lap as a writing surface.

At long last the brunette called my number and I followed her into the office of Mrs. Carlson, a tweed-clad woman of about forty. She motioned for me to sit down. Several moments of silence ensued while she glanced over my application, expressionless. Finally she jotted something in the corner of the application.

"Your experience appears limited to clerking a small-town dry goods store," she began. "I'm not sure that—"

All at once, a familiar voice caroled from the doorway, "Oh, Mrs. Carlson!"

We both turned to see Dot's smiling face poking around the doorframe. Behind her, the brunette woman gestured wildly. Dot ignored her.

"Mrs. Carlson, how did your husband like that hat you purchased last week?" she purred. "The one with that cunning little feather?"

Mrs. Carlson's face brightened. "Oh, it's perfect, Miss Rodgers. You were so right about paying attention to which way the feather points. It makes all the difference." She nodded to her assistant, who backed off.

"I must say, you have the perfect face for that sort of hat, Mrs. Carlson. Not everyone can pull off such a sophisticated style. Well, I won't keep you, I see you have company—" Dot glanced at me in feigned surprise, eyes wide and mouth forming an O. "Mercy me. Is that Miss Corrigan? Miss *Marjorie* Corrigan?"

Mrs. Carlson's glance slid from Dot to me and back again.

"Um—oh, uh, good morning, Dot. M-Miss Rodgers," I stammered, not at all sure what game we were playing.

"Are *you* applying to work *here*? Oh, what great good luck." Dot clapped her hands as if she'd just won a prize. "Mrs. Carlson, don't let this one get away. Marjorie Corrigan is a darling, and she is a genius at retail. Simply a *genius*."

"She is?" Mrs. Carlson turned to me with fresh interest.

Dot winked at me. "Please excuse me. I must get back to Millinery. Big rush on summer *chapeaux* in this warm weather. Mrs. Carlson, do stop by and take a peek at our new broad-brims."

"I'll do that, Miss Rodgers. Thank you." Dot vanished and Mrs. Carlson peered at me over the top of her spectacles. "Now, Miss Corrigan, you were saying . . ."

I told her about my work at Corrigan's Dry Goods, and the plans I had for displays and possibly bringing in a ready-to-wear-section.

"I see," Mrs. Carlson said slowly. "But if you already have a job, then why do you want to work at Field's?"

"To broaden my knowledge of retailing in the world's finest department store." *And to spy on the handsome man in menswear*, I thought, but of course she didn't need to know that part.

"Well, as it happens, we do have a temporary opening, just for the summer."

"That sounds perfect."

And a few minutes later, I was Marshall Field & Company's newest employee in Ladies' Nightwear.

"You may start on Monday. Nine-thirty sharp." Mrs. Carlson's glance swept me from head to toe. "Dark colors only, please. Black or navy." She handed me a form to sign. "As I said, it's only for the summer. Six days a week, Sundays off. By signing this form, you commit to work until Labor Day."

I gulped. That meant I'd be going home just a couple of weeks before the wedding. How would I ever explain this to Richard and my family? But I couldn't quit now. I needed the money, not to mention the close proximity to P. A. Bachmann. I signed.

We discussed a few more details, then I floated to the elevator, breathing a prayer of gratitude. My mind drifted back to the words of the elevator operator. He'd called me a classy girl. A real Field's kind of girl. As for explaining it to my family and Richard . . . well, I'd figure that out somehow.

I left Field's and went to the Y to fetch my suitcase and take it over to Dot's place. I figured anyone who'd go to bat for me like that must be a good egg. Before checking out, I telephoned Richard. When the operator connected us and he answered, I said, "Hi, Richard. It's me."

A slight pause. "Marjorie?"

"Of course. Who else would it be?"

"I don't know. You just sound—different. That's all."

"Do I?" The change in attitude I was already feeling must have started showing in my voice.

"Have you forgiven me yet for speaking to Dr. Cragin?"

"I suppose so." So much had happened since then. "That's not really what I'm calling to talk to you about." I inhaled deeply, then blurted in a rush, "I'm calling to say I've decided to spend the rest of the summer here in Chicago and I've taken a job until Labor Day."

A pause. Then, "You're joking."

"I'm not."

"A job. What kind of a job?"

I tried to sound confident. "You're speaking to the newest salesclerk at Marshall Field & Company." Silence. "In Ladies' Nightwear." More silence. "Richard? Are you still there? Hello?"

"A salesclerk," he said finally, to nobody in particular. "My fiancée has become a salesclerk."

"What's wrong with that?" I reasoned. "I've been a salesclerk for years, in Pop's store."

"Exactly. In your father's store, surrounded by your family. Not miles away in a strange city." He sounded weary. "Marjorie, what in blazes is the matter with you? You don't sound like yourself. You're talking nonsense, and you have me worried. Me and your whole family."

I fiddled with the telephone cord. "I'm *not* talking nonsense. I'm merely telling you I've taken a summer job. For heaven's sake, lots of girls do it."

"You're not lots of girls. You're *my* girl. And in a department store, of all places."

My throat tightened. "My goodness, you make it sound like a den of iniquity. I thought you'd be proud of me."

"Proud of you?" he sputtered. "Proud that my future wife is ped-dling who-knows-what to who-knows-who in downtown Chicago?"

"I'm not peddling. I'm serving a distinguished clientele," I said, parroting Mrs. Carlson. I recited the list of advantages I'd practiced in advance. "It's not forever, just for the summer. I'm earning money that can go toward the wedding and setting up our new home. And I'm not *just* a salesclerk." I warmed to my topic. "I'm learning retail-ing procedures and techniques that Charlie and I can use at Corrig-an's. It's sort of like a professional training program."

So maybe "professional training program" was a bit of a stretch. But I could not even begin to explain the real magnet that drew me to Field's, the real reason I didn't want to come home—a mysterious salesman who bore a remarkable resemblance to the man I'd loved long before Richard came on the scene.

He snorted. "Training program? Be serious. Besides, I thought you were going to stop working at Corrigan's to devote yourself to your duties at home."

"*You* thought that. I didn't think that."

"I earn an excellent salary, Marjorie. I don't need my wife selling underwear to support herself."

"Nightwear. And I know you'll be able to support us, but right now there's also the apartment to pay for."

"Your *apartment*?" he sputtered.

Oops.

I hurriedly explained about Dot's offer of hospitality, carefully sidestepping the artist's-model and speakeasy-singer bits.

I pictured that little vein in his temple starting to throb.

"See here, Marjorie," he blurted. "I don't know what game you're playing, but I'm tired of it. Either come home, or else."

My face burned. "Or else what?"

He inhaled audibly. "Listen, I've got to go," he said. "Think about what I've said." The line went silent.

I sat for a moment, staring at the telephone. Richard, too, had his limits. I couldn't put off a decision about our marriage, one way or another, much longer. I'd never thought I was the sort of girl to break up with a man long-distance. But I had to admit, the idea had its merits.

CHAPTER FOURTEEN

My first morning as a Field's employee sped past in a blur of instructions about cash versus charge versus cash-on-delivery, sales slips in triplicate, pink copy here, yellow copy there, this form and that form, and a dizzying array of numbers: employee number, time card number, locker number, section number, department number. I despaired of ever remembering it all. The manager for Ladies' Nightwear was a Mrs. Cross—a diminutive, white-haired woman with ramrod posture whose name echoed her temperament, as she seemed permanently out of sorts.

After a polite but frosty greeting, Mrs. Cross grilled me about my experience. When I told her about my job at Corrigan's Dry Goods and Sundries, she seemed less than impressed. "Let's hope you know a thing or two about fabrics," she said in a tone that indicated she harbored no such hope. She introduced me to a few other salesladies who, in the haziness of that first day, all had the same name. I could have sworn Mrs. Cross introduced them as Miss Ryan, Miss Ryan, and Miss Ryan. They looked enough alike in their plain black dresses and tidy chin-length bobs that I assumed they were sisters and wondered how on earth I'd learn to tell them apart. Only much later did I discover they weren't at all related, and their names were actually Miss Ryan, Miss Bryant, and Miss O'Brien.

My new habitat, Ladies' Nightwear, was the boreal forest of nightgowns—acres and acres of them. I despaired of ever learning my way around, but Miss Ryan (or was it Miss Bryant?) told me I wasn't expected to sell anything that first week. I was only to watch, listen, and learn. That much I figured I could handle.

"Our store stocks only the highest-quality merchandise, and we must treat every item like a jewel." Mrs. Cross propelled me through the labyrinth of gowns and robes and described styles, colors, sizes, and fabrics in a rapid-fire delivery that left me dazed, along with a whole new vocabulary. *Peignoirs. Chemisettes.*

"You will be expected to have a complete understanding of each garment and its selling points," Mrs. Cross stated crisply. "Neatness is a must at all times, in our personal appearance and the appearance of our section. In the early days, when Marshall Field himself was in charge, a supervisor made the rounds to make sure we were dressed appropriately."

Just when I thought my head would explode from all the facts I was required to remember, a tall, stately older woman entered the department, and I was mercifully abandoned as Mrs. Cross hurried to wait on her. I overheard her greet the customer in a silken, honeyed tone nearly unrecognizable from the no-nonsense bray she'd been using with me.

The customer looked familiar. I struggled to figure out where I'd seen her before.

Miss O'Brien drifted up to me. "Don't stare," she said under her breath.

"What?"

"Don't stare at the customers. It's vulgar."

"I'm not staring, I'm just . . . I think I know her from somewhere."

"From the society pages, no doubt," she stage-whispered. "Don't you know who that is?"

"No. Who?"

Her eyes widened in disbelief at my naiveté. "That's Evangeline Dunsworthy, of the North Central Bank Dunsworthys. Rich as Croesus. Of course, she was a Chadwick before she married."

I nodded as if I understood what she was talking about, although I hadn't the faintest clue.

"Looks like Mrs. Cross is putting her in Dressing Room One," she said. "Mrs. Dunsworthy is an exacting customer. Usually nobody waits on her but Mrs. Cross herself. But you should remain on standby at all times, at a discreet distance, in case she needs you to fetch something. And *please* pay attention. Mrs. Dunsworthy is a *very* important customer."

Cowed by this speech, I dreaded being called in to help. Thankfully Mrs. Cross managed fine without me.

When lunchtime rolled around, I'd half expected the other salesgirls to invite me to join them, but none did. The thought of navigating the employee dining room alone made my palms sweat. I contemplated heading down the street to Walgreens when Dot swooped past and collected me. In the crowded employee dining room, I followed her through the line, selecting a tuna sandwich and a glass of Ovaltine, and we pushed our way to an empty table, raising our voices above the din. We were joined by a curly-haired girl whom Dot introduced as Agnes-in-Books, and a hearty, stalwart young woman with a rosy complexion called Ruthie-in-Stationery.

As soon as I sat down, I realized how tired I was. My back ached and my shoes clamped like torture devices onto my swollen, throbbing feet. I'd better make some conversation or I'd start groaning out loud, right there at the table.

"Ruthie, how long have you worked at Field's?"

She chomped down on a carrot stick. "Two years. Say, has anybody talked to you about the food drive?"

"Food drive?"

Her face took on an earnest expression. "Field's encourages its employees to get involved in some sort of community service. The food drive is just one example. Employees donate canned food and things for the needy. It then gets distributed to charitable institutions around the city. Will you help us?"

"Gee." I faltered. "This is only my first day, and . . ."

"Ruthie's out to save the world," Agnes said. "Don't let her twist your arm."

Ruthie jabbed her with her elbow.

"I see. Well, it sounds like a good cause, and I'd like to help, but . . ."

Before I could formulate an answer, Agnes lifted her arm and shouted, "Hey, Betty Boop. Over here."

We were joined by yet another young woman. "This is Marjorie in Ladies' Nightwear," Dot said by way of introduction, a description that made me blush, but nobody else seemed to think anything of it. "It's her first day," Dot added, as if that weren't glaringly obvious.

"Welcome. I'm Betty Hendricks. Hosiery." The newcomer squeezed in on the other side of Ruthie. The women were all in high spirits, chatting between bites about the upcoming holiday.

Betty glanced at me. "Lucky girl. A holiday during your first week."

"Holiday?"

"Wednesday is Memorial Day," Dot said. "The store closes so we can all attend the parade. You'll come too, won't you?"

My heart sank. "No, I don't think I will. Thanks for asking, though."

Every year I tried to forget Memorial Day. Without Jack's grave to visit, the day always felt hollow and incomplete, although in Kerryville I did usually attend the local festivities for Charlie's sake. Here in Chicago, I saw no reason to force myself to go through the motions.

Thankfully, Agnes changed the subject. "So, Marjorie, what do you think of Old Rugged?"

"Who?"

"Mrs. Cross. That's what your predecessor used to call her. You'll have to keep on your toes with that one."

"Why? What's wrong with her?"

"Mrs. Cross is one of the oldest employees at Field's," Agnes said. "She's been working here since the dawn of time, when the original Marshall Field was still in charge. A fact she's eager to tell all and sundry at the drop of a hat."

"*Back in my day . . .*" crowed Betty in a voice that sounded uncannily like Mrs. Cross.

Agnes giggled. Then she snatched up her water glass and took a sip as a blond man in a blue uniform sidled up to the table.

"Hello, ladies," he said. "Lovely day, isn't it?"

Agnes blushed. "It's a million degrees in the shade, Kurt. What's so lovely about it?"

The man leaned over and gazed straight into Agnes's eyes. "It's all in your attitude, doll face." She glanced toward the ceiling in mock disdain, but her face was glowing. While it was clear she relished the attention, this Kurt fellow struck me as overly cocky and sure of himself.

He turned his gleaming smile on Dot. "How's our little canary today? Been doing much chirping these days?"

"Sure thing," Dot said. "I'm still singing at Louie's Villa Italiana on weekends, ten until two. You should come."

"You girls ever hear this one sing?" Kurt said. "She's got pipes like an angel. Her boyfriend kind of scares me, though. He's one of those menacing types."

"Aw, go on," Dot said, but I could tell she was pleased.

He beamed his grin my way. "And who's this?"

"Marjorie, meet Kurt Steuben," Dot said. "Kurt's one of our esteemed store security guards. Kurt, meet Marjorie. It's her first day. She's in Ladies' Nightwear."

"Oh, if only," Kurt said, looking me up and down in a way that made me squirm inside. *Fresh!* Then abruptly he said, "Excuse me, ladies. There's someone over there I need to talk to."

After he'd sauntered away, Agnes breathed, "That man is so dreamy."

"Kurt Steuben?" Betty said, wide-eyed. "Ugh. He's slick as snake oil. Gives me the heebie-jeebies."

Privately I had to agree.

"Not Kurt, silly." Agnes pointed across the room. "That man he's talking to."

We all turned to look, and immediately I broke out into a cold sweat. Kurt Steuben was talking to none other than P. A. Bachmann.

"That's the new manager in Menswear," Betty said. "Only just started. Name's Peter Bachmann."

Peter. His name is Peter.

"Catch me, I'm swooning," Ruthie said. I couldn't tell if she was serious or just making fun of Agnes.

"Marjorie, weren't you asking me something the other day about somebody named Bachmann?" Dot said.

"Uh, different fellow," I mumbled when I regained the power of speech. I watched as Peter raised an arm and rubbed the back of his neck.

Betty continued, "I heard he transferred here from some big store in New York City. Macy's or Gimbel's, something like that. Made a few people plenty sore, let me tell you, bringing in a manager from the outside instead of promoting somebody who's already here."

"New York? Are you sure?" If he was from New York, then he couldn't be Jack.

Betty looked at me. "That's what I heard. Why?"

Thankfully, Dot interrupted. "Wonder where he got that doozy of a scar."

Betty adopted a soulful gaze and mouthed, "The war."

Agnes shook her head. "Betty, how do find out the dirt on everyone so quickly? I swear. The man's been here two minutes and you already practically know his hat size."

Betty shrugged. "I'm highly motivated by a chiseled jaw."

Dot leaned over the table. "Keep your hats on, girls. If that's the new manager, then it's all over the moccasin trail that he's a real sheik with the ladies. Be on your guard."

"All over the what?" I asked.

"The moccasin trail," Ruthie explained. "Field's version of a grapevine."

"Looks like he's working on a conquest right now."

I stole another glance at the mysterious Mr. Bachmann, who was chatting up a statuesque redhead. The "sheik" description sounded nothing like the Jack I remembered, who'd been shy around girls. Now as I watched Peter Bachmann share a laugh with Kurt and the beautiful redhead, the green-eyed monster wrapped its ugly tentacles around my heart. I couldn't deny my attraction to this man. If he was Jack, clearly he had no recollection of ever knowing me before. And if he wasn't Jack, then there was no way he'd ever give me a second glance. Not with all these glamorous city women around. All at once I wished fervently that I looked and acted more like Dot and less like a milkmaid fresh from the farm.

"*You* don't need to worry about him, of course," Dot said to me with a conspiratorial wink, interrupting my thoughts. "You're already spoken for."

"You are?" Agnes lifted one neatly penciled eyebrow.

"Marjorie here has a hometown honey," Dot explained. "She's engaged to be married. To a *doctor*, no less."

"Oh, how exciting," Betty squealed. "When's the wedding?"

"Not until September." No longer hungry, I stood and hoisted my lunch tray. "Sorry, girls, I have to scram. I can't be late getting back on my first day, or Mrs. Cross will tan my hide."

"Food drive meeting next Wednesday," Ruthie said. "See you there."

I nodded. I didn't remember saying yes, but now was not the time to argue. I had more important things to think about.

I scanned the room once more for Peter Bachmann, but he had gone. As I loaded my tray onto the conveyor belt, I shot up a quick prayer that God would make it clear once and for all who Peter Bachmann really was. If he was Jack, I prayed he'd remember me, and that he once loved me. On the other hand, if he really was Peter Bachmann, I could abandon this pointless quest and resume my normal life. If I indeed *wanted* to resume my normal life.

And I tossed in a quick prayer for forgiveness, for feeling unaccountably annoyed with Dot for telling everyone I was off the market. Which was, after all, the truth, regardless of how I might feel about it.

CHAPTER FIFTEEN

If there was one thing I hated, it was running late. My anxiety peaked as the packed streetcar inched along State Street. Arriving tardy the second day on the job would hardly earn points with Mrs. Cross, who'd made it clear that, "As old Mr. Field used to say," punctuality was of vital importance for a clerk under her supervision.

When we'd boarded the streetcar, a fellow commuter had taken one look at Dot, tipped his hat, and offered her his seat—the last one available—so I clung to the overhead strap and leaned as far as possible from the odiferous man standing next to me. My blouse grew damp and I longed for a breath of fresh air, but with a thunderstorm slashing furiously against the sides of the vehicle, the chance of someone opening a window was unlikely. I could practically feel my hair turning to frizz in the early June humidity, springing out of a hastily gathered bun. I hadn't had much time to style it, thanks to Dot's hogging of the bathroom. *She* looked just dandy, though, reading a newspaper with her legs daintily crossed and tossing an occasional dimpled smile to the gentleman who'd given up his seat.

Finally the streetcar belched to a stop, disgorging us near the employee entrance. I scurried into the locker room, shoved my raincoat and hat into a locker, and punched the time clock with seconds to spare. When I reached Ladies' Nightwear, Mrs. Cross made a point of consulting her wristwatch. Within minutes I was too busy to think about Peter or anything else that wasn't made of organdy or silk charmeuse. All morning long, the department buzzed with customers, mostly busy society ladies stocking up on nightwear for trips to Europe and their summer homes. We also had a steady parade of spring and summer brides purchasing honeymoon attire. I enjoyed helping them, but I felt indifferent about choosing items for my own trousseau. I knew I needed to break off the engagement, or at least postpone the wedding, until I could sort out my feelings. I'd started many letters, but hadn't gotten much beyond "Dear Richard" before tearing them up.

I spent the morning scampering between the dressing room and the sales floor, my arms filled with silks and chiffons and my ears filled with the critical tones of Mrs. Cross.

"Miss Corrigan, *do* hurry up. Mr. Field always said that time is money."

"I asked for a size *eight*, Miss Corrigan. See here that you've brought us a *ten*."

"As Mr. Field used to say, the customer is always right. Our motto is 'Give the lady what she wants.'"

Around lunchtime we finally had a lull in customers as ladies revived their spirits at the Walnut Room or the Tea Shoppe. With sore feet and a growling stomach, I was looking forward to my own break when Mrs. Cross assigned me to straighten the fitting rooms, retrieving garments discarded helter-skelter by customers, and replacing them neatly on their hangers. Much as I longed for a rest, putting things back in order helped me organize my thoughts, and was a relatively peaceful task, free from Mrs. Cross's prying eyes and her endless quoting of the sainted Mr. Field.

Because I ended up taking lunch later than usual, I had to brave the lunchroom without my friends. Nibbling at my lonely sandwich, I glimpsed a copy of the *Chicago Tribune* someone had left lying around on a nearby table and stood to grab it. Maybe catching up on the comic-strip adventures of Winnie Winkle over lunch would distract me from my own pathetic life.

"Excuse me," said a polite male voice. "I believe that's my newspaper."

"Oh, sorry, I thought this table was unocc . . ." I glanced up, and something like electricity shot up my arms as I found myself gazing straight into the astonishing eyes of Peter Bachmann. Lashes that long were wasted on a fellow. "Unoccupied," I finished in a weak voice.

He blinked like a startled owl. "Oh. It's you. The girl from the train station."

"Yes."

We stared at each other for a brief moment, then he averted his gaze. "You seemed rather upset that day," he said evenly as he set down his lunch tray and took a seat. "I hope things are looking brighter for you now."

My face grew hot. "Yes. Sorry. I—I mistook you for someone I knew a long time ago." In truth, I was not yet convinced I was mistaken, but thought it best to let him think so for the time being. "I felt as if I'd seen a—a ghost."

"A friendly ghost, I hope."

"Oh, yes." I grinned and fervently hoped there was no lettuce in my teeth. I waited for him to invite me to join him, but he didn't.

Instead he said, "I didn't know you worked here." He unfolded his napkin and placed it on his lap, something Jack Lund would never have thought to do unless prompted.

"I didn't," I faltered. "I mean, I didn't at the time, anyway, when we met. Not that we *met*, exactly. . . ."

He extended his hand. "Might as well make it official. Peter Bachmann. Store for Men." His smile seemed friendly enough, but his glance darted around as if locating the nearest exit. Was I that threatening?

"Marjorie Corrigan. Ladies' Nightwear." I wished desperately that I could say something more suitable for mixed company, like Books or Leather Goods.

"Corrigan, eh?" A flicker of hope lit my spirit. Did my name sound familiar to him? Trigger a memory of the girl he once loved? But he said nothing, and simply tugged at one impeccable cuff. That was another difference between this man and Jack. Jack had gone around perpetually rumpled, not caring much about clothes and things. I'd been forever straightening his collar. Peter looked as if he had a personal valet standing by at all times. For untidy Jack to turn into a fastidious man seemed unlikely, but maybe military discipline instilled orderliness in a man.

I realized he was waiting for an answer. "I like it fine," I said. "Busy. Lots to learn, and so many special occasions this month. Weddings and honeymoons and . . . you know." *Ugh.* Why did I have to bring up honeymoons, of all things?

"I do know. It's the same in the Store for Men. Graduations, Father's Day. There's always a big run on silver cufflinks and bay rum this time of year. Sometimes I think every male in Chicago ends up with either cufflinks or a bottle of bay rum, or both, on every possible gift-giving occasion. The bathroom shelves of America are groaning under the weight of bay rum bottles."

"Really? I thought importing bay rum was off-limits since Prohibition took effect." Not for nothing was I the stepdaughter of a WCTU chapter president.

He shrugged. "It's legal as long as it's blended into something undrinkable, or if it's for medicinal purposes." He stirred his coffee. "At any rate, I'm sure your father would appreciate receiving something else. Or your husband."

"Oh, I'm not married." I felt my face turn crimson and silently cursed how easily my pale skin gave my feelings away. I wished I could banter easily like the other women, but once again I couldn't think of anything clever to say. The word "husband" felt like an indictment. I wasn't being disloyal to Richard just by talking to this man, was I? Not technically. After all, this was a workday, and he was just a coworker. Just a friendly chat between colleagues. That's all this was, despite the butterflies flapping around my midsection.

"Not married?" He held my gaze for a second, then glanced away. "I guess I assumed—"

"I'm engaged," I blurted. "Engaged to be married." Honesty was the best policy. Wasn't it?

His expression shifted. "I see. Well, I guess I should eat up and get back before there's a mutiny at the cufflink counter. Nice seeing you again." He picked up his coffee cup with one hand and the *Tribune* with the other. Desperate to prolong our conversation, I stood rooted to the spot. He glanced up, saw I wasn't leaving, and extended the newspaper toward me. "Please, take it."

"Oh, no, it's yours," I said hastily. "You keep it."

"All right." He returned to reading the headlines as he sipped his coffee.

My mind scrambled for something to say

"Mr. Bachmann, there's something I've been wanting to ask you."

A sharp sidelong glance. "What is it?"

Holy mackerel. Think of something, Marjorie!

"You see—"

"Yes?" Impatience frosted his tone.

"I know you're probably really busy and everything—That is, if you have the time . . ."

That's it. Time. I need to spend time with you, to get to know you. Once I know you, I can satisfy myself that you're not really Jack and stop all this nonsense.

In a rush I blurted, "I'm wondering if anyone has talked to you about—about the employee food drive." *Ugh. Did I really say that?*

"Food drive?" His expression froze, then his lips curved into a smile. "What do you need? Donations of canned food or something?" He gave a shaky laugh, as if relieved. Gracious, what did he think I was about to ask?

"I thought you might consider serving on the committee. With me." *So that we could get to know each other, working side by side for hours on end, getting acquainted.* "And several other people, of course," I added hastily so he wouldn't think I was suggesting we'd work together à deux . . . appealing as that option might seem, to me at least.

He dabbed at his mouth with the napkin. "I'm afraid my schedule won't allow me to take on any additional commitments at this time. But thank you for asking." He smiled gently. "It's good that you're getting involved, though. Field's likes that in an employee."

"So I've heard."

"You know, from the moment I met you, I said to myself, 'Now, *she* looks like just the sort of girl who does good works.'"

I cringed, thinking of Ruthie's earnest face and no-nonsense demeanor and doubting that that was the kind of compliment he gave to his statuesque redheaded friend.

"Now if you'll excuse me. . ." He lifted his sandwich.

"Oh. Sure." I backed away.

Good works, indeed. I returned to my table and stared glumly at my half-eaten sandwich. Who wants to be thought of as the sort of girl who does good works?

CHAPTER SIXTEEN

"If you'd bob your hair like I've told you, this sort of thing wouldn't happen," Dot scolded without sympathy when I told her about Peter's "good works" remark. I immediately regretted telling her anything. We were seated at the kitchen table in front of the electric fan. I wore a fresh cotton nightgown, newly purchased from Field's using my employee discount. Before Dot had waltzed in, I'd been perfectly content, sipping iced tea and reading a detective novel while my freshly washed hair hung down my back to dry. Now Dot was giving my long locks the evil eye.

"Pardon my saying so, but with your hair always up in a bun, you look positively Victorian. Why wouldn't a fellow take you for the earnest do-gooder type, too heavenly minded to follow fashion?"

"Who cares what Peter Bachmann thinks?"

"*You* care. Otherwise why bring it up?"

"I just didn't think it was a very flattering comment, that's all. It doesn't matter who said it."

"Oh, I think it does," Dot said knowingly. "You have to admit, Peter Bachmann is some real date bait. But he goes for the smooth modern type of girl."

Like that redhead. I stared unseeing at the book in my lap. "I don't care about date bait. I'm engaged. Remember?"

"Yes, I know, to a man who thinks you're a loon. I don't know why you're still thinking of marrying him after the whole Dr. Cragin fiasco."

I wasn't sure either, except for some high-minded yet fuzzy ideals like duty and honor and keeping my promises, and not embarrassing myself or my family with a broken engagement.

"I don't take my commitments lightly. I'm sure he meant well. No doubt he'll apologize. In any case, he always says a woman's hair is her crowning glory."

Dot winked at me. "Do you take it down when you two are together? Pull the pins out and let it tumble dramatically around your shoulders, and wrap it around yourself like Lady Godiva?"

The kitchen grew even hotter. "No, of course not. How silly."

She snickered. "Then what difference does it make whether it's long or short, if you always wear it all squished up in that bun?" She stepped over to the icebox. "Want a refill on your tea, or can I entice you to try my ginger lemonade?"

"Neither, thanks." Dot's signature secret-recipe ginger lemonade contained, of all things, bootleg gin she'd obtained from Louie. No doubt refreshing, if you liked that sort of thing. Still, she knew I didn't approve, which is why she kept it in its own pitcher at the back of the icebox, well away from my innocent iced tea.

I drew my hair over one shoulder and stroked it protectively. "Richard says there are more important qualities than beauty. He thinks women should look natural."

"Natural, my foot," Dot scoffed. "That may be what he says, but deep inside, every man is a sheik in search of a glamorous sheba. Oh, come on, Marjie. Just give it a try. You'll love it—I know you will. Bobbed hair makes you feel so—free. Untethered. Ready to take on the world." She made some sweeping Isadora Duncan-style moves around the tiny kitchen, then plopped down in a chair. "Tell you what. I'll march you up to the salon myself on Monday and introduce you to my favorite hairdresser. She works wonders with even the most difficult hair." She eyed my locks with pity.

"Are you listening to me? I said I don't want to have it bobbed."

"Now don't get in a lather. It's up to you." Dot shrugged. "But to be honest, doll, you do look *miles* behind the times. You could at least put on a spot of rouge and a little lipstick. Try my shade, High Society Red. The world won't end if you shorten your skirts or roll your stockings. You're young, live a little. Give Richard something to look at besides his medical charts." She slid me a sidelong smirk. "Or maybe it's not *Richard's* eye you're worried about catching."

I avoided her gaze. "Nonsense. I'm not worried about catching anyone's eye."

"Oh, I don't know about that," she purred. "You seemed pretty riled up a minute ago that Peter Bachmann complimented you on your do-gooderism instead of . . . whatever it was you were hoping for."

"You're crazy," I mumbled, embarrassed at how defensive I sounded. "I'm extremely loyal to Richard."

"I never said you weren't. But didn't you say Peter reminds you of your old beau?"

"Yes. The resemblance to Jack is remarkable."

Dot's dark eyes sparkled. "Maybe he really *is* Jack. Maybe the government faked his death and has him working incognito as a spy at Marshall Field & Company. I read something like that in a novel once."

"Now you're just being silly," I said with forced laughter—as if that weren't exactly what I'd been thinking all along.

"Just be careful," she said. "As I told the girls, I hear he has quite the reputation. I've even spotted him around Louie's a time or two, and not for the spaghetti, if you know what I mean. And if you're interested in him—not saying you are, but if you were—Peter Bachmann definitely goes for the glamorous type." She glanced at the clock. "Well, I should get ready for the club. Have you finished in the bath?"

After she'd gone, I settled in my chair, spread my hair out across my back to dry, and picked up the mystery novel. I tried to concentrate as the hardboiled detective grilled the not-so-grieving widow, but in my mind's eye the detective looked like Peter Bachmann and the widow looked like . . . well, it was too hot to read, anyway. I threw the book on the table, walked over to the cracked mirror, and wondered how strenuously Richard would object if my lips bore just the slightest hint of High Society Red. And tried to ignore the fact that I really cared less and less what Richard thought.

On Friday evening, pushed along by the sea of employees exiting the store, Dot and I quite literally bumped into Peter Bachmann. My pulse fluttered.

"Ladies." He touched the brim of his hat. "A few of us are going over to the Green Mill this evening to hear some jazz. Care to join us?"

"The Green Mill?" Anxiety coursed through my veins at the mention of the famous gin joint. It billed itself as a restaurant, but everybody knew what it was, even the cops who turned a blind eye. Jack, a staunch teetotaler, would never have suggested an outing to the Green Mill. But then again, war changed people. Maybe a soldier *had* to take up drinking, just to survive the horrors of battle.

While I cast about for some reply, Dot turned her sparkling smile on Peter. "Thanks ever so much, Mr. Bachmann, but our friend here doesn't enter such establishments. And I'm afraid I'm working at Louie's tonight."

"Is that true, Miss Corrigan?" he said with a little grin. "'Lips that touch liquor shall never touch mine' and all that?"

Embarrassment started at my toes and worked its way upward. Why did Dot have to make me sound like such a goody two-shoes?

To Dot he said, "Say, Miss Rodgers, maybe we'll swing by Louie's later and give you a listen." His eyes met mine. "You're sure you won't come with us? We could discuss the food drive."

"I'm sure," I said. I would have loved to discuss the food drive, or anything else, with him, but not at a speakeasy. "Thanks anyway for the invitation."

"All right, then. Have a pleasant evening, ladies." As he walked up the street with Kurt Steuben and a few other friends, I watched with sinking heart as the tall redhead linked her arm through his. I wheeled on Dot, hands on hips.

"Why did you have to go and tell him I wouldn't go to the Green Mill?"

She gaped at me in surprise. "Because you wouldn't. Would you?"

"No. Of course not."

"Marjorie, you've told me over and over how you don't approve of speakeasies. That's been your excuse for never coming to Louie's place to hear me sing."

"I know, but when you said it, you made me sound so . . . so prudish."

She stopped short of saying "If the shoe fits," but her expression said exactly that.

"It's true I don't like such places," I said. "They're against the law, for one thing. And you know I don't drink. But that's beside the point."

"What is the point, then?"

I had to admit, I had no idea. Sometimes being a good girl was no fun at all.

On the streetcar, I relayed to Dot my most recent frustrating telephone conversation with Richard. She listened with growing impatience, then blurted, "For goodness' sake, Marjorie. How long are you going to keep waffling?"

That stung. "Who's waffling? This is my future we're talking about. I don't want to make a decision I'll regret."

Dot sighed. "I hate to say it, but I think you're going to have to schedule a visit home to Kerryville."

"Whatever for?"

"Oh, Marjorie, men are such insecure creatures. Go home. Hash everything out with him. Patch things up. Or not. Work out in your own heart how you feel. But whatever you do, don't lead him on. Don't let him go on thinking you love him if you really don't." She gave me that sidelong glance that always made me squirm, as if she could see everything going on inside my head. I'd never considered that I might be leading Richard on. What an awful thought.

I stared unseeing out the window. After nearly three weeks in Chicago, I still had no desire to go to Kerryville. Yes, a part of me missed Helen, Charlie, Pop, and even Frances a little. I was tired of always feeling like the new girl, the fish out of water here in Chicago. On the other hand, the prospect of spending a weekend with Frances and her wedding chatter filled me with dread. And Richard . . . I didn't know what to think about Richard. I ought to miss him, to long to see him, but it was hard to conjure up any feeling at all.

On impulse I blurted, "I'll go if you come with me."

"What?"

"Come with me to Kerryville. You can meet my family. See the place I come from. Get out of the city for a couple of days. Breathe the fresh country air." As if on cue, a truck idling next to the open windows of the streetcar belched black fumes.

"I don't know . . ." Dot gasped through the sooty haze. Doubt shadowed her face. "It sounds like fun, but I don't know if I can get a weekend off from the club. Besides, Louie might not like it." Louie not only owned the speakeasy where Dot sang; he was also the current object of her affections, although whether he returned those feelings wasn't entirely clear—a situation which seemed only to increase Dot's fascination with him. The more indifferently he treated her, the more she seemed to want him. It made no sense. Dot could have had any man she wanted.

"Oh, please try," I begged. "It would be so much more fun if you were there. Besides, it wouldn't hurt Louie any to see what it's like to get along without you for a weekend."

She thought for a moment, then broke into a grin. "All right. When do you want to go?"

"I'm so new on the job, I don't think Mrs. Cross will let me take a Saturday off, but I'll ask her. And oh, there's one more thing."

"What is it?"

I drew a deep breath, thinking of the redhead's possessive grasp on Peter's arm. *Peter Bachmann goes for the glamorous type.* "Before I go home, I want to get my hair bobbed." If I were going home a changed woman, I'd change all the way.

"Hallelujah." Dot threw her hands in the air, startling a man who was standing in the aisle. He moved a few steps away for his own protection. "I knew you'd come around. Hey, wait a minute. I thought Prince Richard was insisting that you keep your Rapunzel locks. Has he changed his mind?"

I shrugged. "Richard doesn't get to decide everything."

Dot's eyes widened. "That's the ticket. Ladies and gentlemen, Miss Marjorie Corrigan makes a daring decision all by herself," she announced to the entire streetcar. I sank in my seat. "Miss Lenore in the salon will do wonders with your hair. She really knows her onions. You'll see. We'll march right up there tomorrow and get it all arranged. Richard will love it!"

CHAPTER SEVENTEEN

Richard will hate it. That was my first thought, as Miss Lenore whirled the chair around and I faced the mirror for the first time. My very next thought was, *But maybe Peter will like it.* Gone was my prim bun. In its place was a riot of curls springing out around my head, like the head of a cherub whose halo had shorted out in a shower of sparks. What on earth had I done?

"Oh, it's *darling*," Dot squealed, clapping her hands. "Who knew you had such glorious curls? Miss Lenore, you're a wonder." The hairdresser beamed. "Oh, Marjie, don't you just love it?"

I blinked at my reflection. "It's . . . different."

Miss Lenore frowned. "You no like?" she growled in a vaguely European accent. I suspected her to be a born-and-bred Chicagoan adopting an accent for glamorous effect. Clearly she'd never worked at Madge's Cut 'n' Curl, where Madge called everyone "honey." Still, I didn't want to offend Miss Lenore, who'd stayed late to accommodate me.

"Oh, it's—um—I think I just need some time to get used to it." I touched my newly revealed neck, which looked bare and vulnerable. I did look modern. I just wasn't convinced that modern suited me all that well. Maybe Richard would hate it, and Frances would surely blow her stack. But the real concern was, would it suit Peter?

"Oh, Marjorie. It's perfect," Dot breathed. "Come on. Let's settle up and get out of here. I can't wait to fix the rest of you."

"What's wrong with the rest of me?"

Plenty, apparently. Back at the apartment, Dot sat me down and went to work on my face with her pots and pencils. When she finished I looked like a cross between Mata Hari and the Witch of Endor—kohl-lined eyes peering out from under a mop of fluffy curls, and with a cupid's-bow mouth colored High Society Red.

Then she said, "We've got to get you out of those dull sweaters and skirts." She ducked into her closet and emerged with a short, floaty sleeveless dress, a type I would never have considered wearing, until now.

"My cousin works as a garment cutter on the West Side and she sent me this sample," Dot explained. "It's miles too big on me, but should fit you fine."

Although the observation about my size stung a little, I humbly accepted the dress and slipped it over my head, yanking at the hem where it hovered above my knees.

"It's too short."

"Nonsense. It's perfect."

"I feel naked." I hunched over, crossing my arms, as if it were my first day changing clothes for gymnastics class.

"Oh, for heaven's sake."

"No, really. I can't wear this in public."

"Well, no. Not if you're going to skulk around like the Hunchback of Notre Dame. Stand up straight."

Apparently being glamorous required enduring both a cold neck and exposed kneecaps. But even I had to admit that if shorter hair, vampy makeup, and a fashionable dress didn't capture certain masculine attention, nothing would.

"What do you think?" Dot said. "Will Richard swoon when he sees you?"

"Well," I said finally, "maybe if he's distracted by the hemline, he won't mind as much about the hair."

My hunch was correct. When I requested time off to visit Kerryville, Mrs. Cross turned me down flat, saying she couldn't possibly do without me until the end of June. I didn't know whether to feel disappointed or relieved. In any case, I didn't have time to brood about it. With strong encouragement from Dot, I finally got myself registered for the evening Introduction to Textiles class at the Art Institute. Whether on account of my snappy new appearance, or simply the fact that the other students were all beginners like me, I felt much more confident at my first class than I had when I'd visited the more advanced class. The teacher, Miss Smith, was a gentle soul who removed any last traces of intimidation. I could hardly wait to get started.

A week passed before I saw Peter Bachmann again, even though I watched for him every day in the cafeteria. I wanted him to see the changes to my appearance, so he'd know I wasn't hopelessly old-fashioned even though I didn't go to speakeasies. I'd show him I could be a modern girl. A modern, chic girl. A modern, chic girl with a chilly neck and kneecaps.

I also needed to find out more about him, to reassure myself once and for all that he wasn't some new version of Jack Lund.

Eventually I lost patience and casually strolled over to the men's section, trying to look for him without looking like I was looking. Sensing his presence before I actually saw him, I carefully scrutinized a silk necktie.

"Miss Corrigan?"

I glanced up, feigning surprise. "Why, good afternoon, Mr. Bachmann." My insides did a jig.

"I almost didn't recognize you." He gave a low whistle that made me blush. "Nice haircut." Self-conscious, I touched the back of my neck. He cocked his head. "You look so different. I wouldn't have pegged you for a short-hair kind of girl."

My cheeks burned. "Is that so?" I teased. "What, pray tell, is a short-hair kind of girl?"

"Oh, you know," he said. "All sleek and modern, on-the-go, devil-may-care . . ."

I crossed my unsleek arms over my chest. "Sounds like a race-horse, 'Two bucks on Devil-May-Care in the ninth.'"

He laughed. "I'd bet on you any day." Then he cleared his throat and gestured to the rack. "These are our finest ties. One hundred percent silk." He paused. "Are you shopping for a present? A gift for your fiancé, perhaps?"

"No." I blushed again. Why did I have to be so darn quick to tell him I was engaged? "I mean, yes, it is a present. For my, um, father."

"Of course. Father's Day."

"Yes. That's it," I blurted, startling both of us. Why hadn't I thought of that before? What a perfect excuse—I mean, reason—to look for a gift for Pop.

Peter flashed a dimple. *Jack had a dimple. Didn't he?* "Your father is a lucky man. Let me help you make a selection. What color suit does he normally wear?"

Suddenly I had trouble recollecting Pop wearing anything other than his scruffy dressing gown or his tattered flannel hedge-trimming shirt. Even while working at the store he tended to fidget with his tie, whisking it off at the first opportunity. I fingered a silk foulard. "Maybe a necktie isn't the best choice for him after all." *Don't you remember my Pop?* I longed to say. *If you're really Jack, you'll remember him.* I watched Peter's face for any flicker of recognition, but he only nodded.

"Perhaps I could recommend a nice men's cologne then. We've a wide selection over here."

"Not bay rum, I hope." The joking reference to our earlier conversation fell flat. Seeing his blank expression, I decided it was safer not to say anything more for the time being and busied myself with sniffing cologne testers.

A few other shoppers drifted into view. "I'll be right with you," Peter called to them, reminding me that both he and I were supposed to be working.

"I mustn't take up any more of your time." I thrust one of the bottles at him. "I'll take this one."

"A fine choice. Your father will be pleased."

I watched his hands as he wrote up the sales slip. He had nicely groomed hands, for a man. As I recalled, Jack's hands had always been rough and a little grimy under the nails. Mechanic's hands.

When I saw the figure Peter had written on the slip, I gasped a little. It hadn't occurred to me to check the price. I swallowed hard. "Does—does that include my employee discount?"

"Yes, it does."

"Oh. Uh, don't you need to have the manager to approve an employee sale?"

"I am the manager."

"Oh. Well, all right." I pulled some bills from my purse and wracked my brain for something brilliant to say to hold his attention. "Hot weather we're having."

So much for brilliant.

"Yes. You must enjoy having shorter hair." He paused and glanced up. "It really does look sensational. You could be one of those fashion models on Six."

A tingle swept up my bare neck. A girl could practically live on a compliment like that. He slipped the tissue-wrapped bottle into a little dark-green bag and handed it to me. His fingers lingered on mine an extra moment. Or maybe I just hoped they did.

As I floated back to Ladies' Nightwear, even Mrs. Cross's pointed stares at her wristwatch didn't bother me in the least. Nonetheless, early the next morning, well before Peter's shift was due to begin, I discreetly returned the bottle of cologne to the men's department and got my money back.

CHAPTER EIGHTEEN

"Come on, Marjie," Dot said, pulling on her gloves. "Let's grab a bite on the way to class."

"No can do." I gestured to a rack filled with wrinkled nightgowns. "This shipment arrived late in the day, and I promised Old Rugged I'd get them out on the floor tonight."

Dot made a face. "Can't you do it tomorrow?"

I shook my head. "There's no refusing her. Believe me, I spend enough time on her bad side as it is."

Dot shrugged. "Suit yourself. If it were me, though, I'd tell the old bat to—oh, never mind." She didn't bother to finish her thought. I was not Dot, and we both knew it. "Guess I'll see you later."

I turned back to my task, steaming the wrinkles out with a portable steam contraption that hissed and gurgled like a mythical sea monster. In spite of the machine's ominous appearance, I found the task of steaming to be calming, soothing work. It felt gratifying to take a wrinkled mess and let the steam ease the creases out, ending up with a smooth, flowing length of batiste or dimity. I wished life were like that—you could just steam the problems away.

The gowns were of thinnest cotton in a lovely lawn-green shade, sleeveless, with a dropped waist and delicate embroidery around the neckline, almost too pretty to wear only to bed. I held one up to myself and looked in the mirror, but even with the torturous bodice-flattening undergarment Dot had encouraged me to buy, I simply couldn't pull off the look. With a sigh, I placed the gown back on the rack. It was the wrong moment in fashion history to have an hourglass figure. Clothes cut on the straight and narrow were unforgiving on curves like mine.

The gown made me think of a garden party. As if I ever went to garden parties, much less wore a nightgown to one. Still, I loved the whole idea. Green lawns. Banks of flowers. A string quartet playing Mozart under a white lattice gazebo.

Suddenly a burst of inspiration seized me. What Ladies' Nightwear needed was a display. Not just a nightgown hanging on a mannequin, but the kind of fanciful, colorful vignette I'd been yearning to create in the front window of Corrigan's Dry Goods Store, if only Pop didn't have so many objections to what he called "that artsy stuff."

Soon I was scampering all over the store, collecting a white wrought-iron table and chair from House Furnishings and a porcelain teacup from China and Glassware and brilliant artificial flowers from Fancy Goods. Since the store was closed and most of the staff had gone home, I left a hastily scribbled note in each department, explaining about the borrowed merchandise. Surely no one could object to such a worthy use of the items.

An hour later I had created a charming tableau at the entrance to Ladies' Nightwear. A delicate china teacup sat on the wrought-iron table. Next to the table, artfully draped over a matching chair, was the green cotton nightie. In Millinery I found the perfect summery hat to position near the gown, with a pair of delicate satin slippers. Then I set the artificial flowers in clusters all around, until Ladies' Nightwear bloomed like the Garfield Park Conservatory.

I stepped back and looked at my work with satisfaction. If that rendering didn't scream, "Garden party," nothing would. You could almost smell the fragrant tea and the freshly mown grass, and hear the tinkling of teacups and the murmur of well-modulated voices, and the delicate strains of a sonata carried on the breeze. The display said, "Summer." It said, "Beauty." When shoppers saw this display, the green gowns would simply fly out of the store, I was sure of it. Mrs. Cross couldn't possibly have any objections. In fact, I reckoned she'd be impressed by my ingenuity and creativity.

I was mentally practicing the modest and humble response with which I'd accept Mrs. Cross's exuberant praise when I happened to glance at my watch and realized I was late for class. I tore down to the locker room, grabbed my handbag and sketch pad, and high-tailed it out to the street.

By the time I hurtled into the Art Institute wheezing like a plow horse, class had already started and the other students were hard at work on the evening's assignment, a small wall-hanging woven on a tabletop loom. My heart sank a little. Surely it would be tedious, weaving all that yarn. I tiptoed in, made my way to the supply shelves, and began selecting my yarn. Miss Smith walked over to greet me.

"I'm sorry I'm late," I said. "I was stuck at work."

"That's all right, Miss Corrigan. I'm glad you're here." As she showed me how to get started on the project, she commented, "You have a natural eye for color and texture. I will be teaching a more advanced-level textiles class in the fall. I encourage you to continue developing your talent." She smiled at me with a twinkle in her eye. "And I don't usually compliment so freely." Indeed, she didn't.

"Thank you," I said. "I'm flattered."

"Of course if money is an issue, there are scholarships . . ."

"You're kind. I'll think about it."

But of course there was nothing to think about. At the end of the summer, I'd have to go home to Kerryville, where the closest thing to textile design would be sewing silk rosettes onto my wedding veil.

Unless I could figure out a way to stay.

Unless I broke my promise to marry Richard.

"I'll be watching for your name on the fall roster," Miss Smith said, and moved off to examine another student's work.

With renewed energy, I selected some brilliant yarn, knotted it onto the loom, and launched my creation, weaving a new life for myself with every pass of the shuttle.

By the next morning I'd nearly forgotten my garden-party display, until I walked into Ladies' Nightwear to greet the unsmiling face of Mrs. Cross. Standing next to her was Mrs. DiRosa from China and Glassware, wringing her plump hands.

"There you are, Miss Corrigan," Mrs. Cross said. "What is the meaning of this?" She pointed to the rack of wrinkled nightgowns still out on the sales floor where customers could see them—a cardinal sin at Field's. "Did I not tell you to finish steaming and hanging those gowns last night?"

My stomach knotted. "Oh, dear. I'm so sorry, Mrs. Cross. I must have forgotten. I got—distracted."

"Distracted by creating this little theater set, I presume." She stormed over to my garden-party tableau. "Miss Corrigan, we are a department store, not center stage at the Lyric Opera."

"No, of course not. I just thought—"

"In all my years here, we have never needed such nonsensical props to sell our merchandise. When a display is needed, I create it." She pointed to an uninspired-looking mannequin draped in a brown crepe hostess set. "A proper display is simple, elegant, and to the point," she continued. "It does not need to be improved upon by inexperienced junior clerks trying to be clever. And as for stealing merchandise from other departments, why, Mrs. DiRosa here is absolutely livid, and rightly so."

"Oh, I wouldn't say *livid*, exactly . . ." interjected the timid Mrs. DiRosa.

"Poor Mrs. DiRosa has been *sick* with worry. A precious artifact, gone missing. Only to find out one of my own employees was the thief."

"I'm not a thief," I said. "I left a note. Didn't you see my note, Mrs. DiRosa?"

"Yes, I did, but—"

"We have procedures here, Miss Corrigan," snapped Mrs. Cross. "Procedures."

"I didn't think anybody would mind my borrowing this stuff," I said. "Not when they knew where it was."

Mrs. Cross pinched the bridge of her nose. "It is not *stuff*, Miss Corrigan. It is *merchandise*. And absconding with it willy-nilly is *not* following procedure."

Mrs. DiRosa looked at me with sympathy. "You're supposed to fill out an F-22."

"A what?"

"An F-22," she said, almost apologetically. "You probably didn't know this, because you're new, but when one department borrows merchandise from another department, you have to fill out Form F-22. In triplicate. It needs to be signed by the section manager and the head supervisor and the—"

"I'm sorry. I didn't know."

Mrs. Cross broke in. "That's no excuse, Miss Corrigan. As an employee of Marshall Field & Company, it is your business to find out what's expected of you."

I lifted my hands in defeat. "I understand. I'm sorry, Mrs. DiRosa. I should not have acted so impulsively." I picked up the offending teacup and thrust it at her. "Here. Take it back. Please."

She took it from me with a sheepish expression. "I'm sorry for the confusion. For what it's worth, I think your display is very pretty."

"Pretty vulgar is more like it," sniffed Mrs. Cross. "Miss Corrigan, you will return *all* of the items to their respective departments immediately. And you will never again—"

"Excuse me. What is going on here?" interrupted a sharp male voice. We turned our heads to see a slim, well-dressed older man with a quizzical expression. "What are all these flowers for? Who is responsible for this?"

"I'm so sorry, sir." Mrs. Cross fluttered. "A misguided employee put it up, and she's just about to take it down."

"Now, now. Let's not be hasty." The man paced around the display, hands clasped behind his back. He peered at it, tilting his balding head. He glanced at Mrs. DiRosa, standing frozen in place with her teacup. "Are you the person who assembled this display?"

"No, sir. She did it." The teacup trembled as she pointed to me.

The gentleman lifted an eyebrow in my direction. "And you are—?"

"Marjorie Corrigan. Sir."

He gave a brisk nod. "Leave it up. I like it."

"You *like* it, sir?" Mrs. Cross sounded dumbfounded.

Suddenly he smiled. "Well done, Miss Corrigan. Have you had experience working as a trimmer?"

"A trimmer?"

"A decorator. You know, for store windows and the like."

"She certainly is *not* a trimmer," Mrs. Cross answered for me. "She is merely a clerk."

"I sometimes dress the windows of my father's dry goods store," I stammered. "At least as much as he permits."

The man turned back to the display and examined it.

"I like it, and so will the customers, which is the important thing. Of course, you need to add signage. Small discreet signs, telling customers where to find the table and chair, and where to find the flowers, and so forth. The merchandising department can help you there. Tell them I sent you and they'll see you get what you need." He gave me a look of respect. "Cross-promotion, my dear. An innovative practice in retailing these days. Harry Selfridge will be bringing his staff for a visit soon, and they'll surely be interested to see what's possible. Carry on." And with that he was gone.

Mrs. DiRosa quickly replaced the teacup on the wrought-iron table. "I will take care of the forms," she mumbled, and scurried off. Mrs. Cross looked dazed.

"Who was that?" I said. "And who is Harry Selfridge?"

She looked as if she might topple over. "That, my dear, was Mr. Simpson, the company president. And Harry Selfridge is . . . well, Harry Selfridge." She sounded flustered.

My knees weakened in wonder. "The company president likes my display?"

Mrs. Cross recovered her cool demeanor. "I'm amazed he approves of your little tableau. Simply amazed. It's so . . . amateur." She sighed. "Of course, things have been different since he took over the store. He's nothing like the old Mr. Marshall Field. Now there was a *real* gentlemen. Why, I remember . . ."

"Mrs. Cross," I interrupted gently, before she got wound up in another meandering memory. "I apologize. I should have asked your permission before making changes to the department. Would you like me to take down the display?"

"Oh, well, if Mr. Simpson likes it, I guess it can stay for now." She gestured to the rack of wrinkled nightgowns. "But you must finish putting out this shipment immediately. Please take them in back to steam them. We mustn't subject the customers to our half-done housekeeping."

"Yes, ma'am." I wheeled the rack and steamer into the stockroom and set to work on the nightgowns, mulling over what Mr. Simpson had said. He liked my display! If he liked that one, then I had plenty of other ideas. Maybe someday I could work on displays full-time. And then Peter Bachmann would say, "Who created all these clever displays?" and someone would say, "Why, it's the work of that talented Marjorie Corrigan," and then he would beg me to create a display in the men's section, and I'd graciously agree with a modest blush, and he and I would work together, side by side, and then—

"Yeow!" A burning pain shot through my hand as I absentmindedly moved it too close to the steaming machine.

Miss Ryan poked her head around the door.

"Miss Corrigan. Are you all right?"

"I think so," I said through clenched teeth, clutching my hand. "I just wasn't paying attention."

"Be careful what you're doing," she warned, "or you're liable to get hurt."

Too late, I thought, staring as an angry red blotch appeared on my hand.

My left hand.

The hand wearing an engagement ring given to me by a man I did not love, who was expecting me to show up at the altar on September fifteenth.

Something had to be done. And I'd have to be the one to do it.

CHAPTER NINETEEN

Later that morning, the onerous steaming chore finished, I emerged from the stockroom with an armload of nightgowns on hangers.

"Will you assist me, please?" said a distinguished voice. I spun around to see Mrs. Dunsworthy holding a green silk gown. "I'd like to try this on."

"Certainly, ma'am. I'll be right with you." I flung the gowns I was holding on the nearest rack—I could display them properly later—and composed a smile. My insides fluttered as I recalled Miss O'Brien's warning that nobody but Mrs. Cross herself was to wait on the regal Mrs. Dunsworthy. Quickly I scanned the sales floor, but Mrs. Cross was nowhere to be seen. I could hardly leave the customer just standing there in the aisle. I took the gown and led her to a fitting room.

"Oh!" A woman in a skivvy glared at me as I flung open the door.

"Oh, my. So sorry." I backed out and banged the door shut. Meekly I knocked on the next door. Finding it unoccupied, I ushered in Mrs. Dunsworthy, hung the gown on a hook, and turned to exit the cubicle. "If you need anything, I'll be right outside."

She stood still and raised an eyebrow. "Aren't you going to assist me?"

"Ma'am?" I cocked my head. Then it dawned on me that a woman of her station was accustomed to having a lady's maid. She was waiting for me to help her change clothes.

This wasn't how things were done in Kerryville. Still, I rose to the occasion, having had plenty of experience wrestling my sister in and out of her clothing when she was younger. I unbuttoned Mrs. Dunsworthy's sleeves at the wrist and pulled the gown upwards over her head. So far, so good.

Then, to my great dismay, the garment got stuck. I gave it a yank.

"Ouch!" cried Mrs. Dunsworthy, her voice muffled within the folds of silk, now covering her entire face.

"Sorry." I gave the gown another yank. "It seems to be caught on something."

"Well, don't pull on it." The woman's arms flailed. "What are you doing? I can't breathe."

Suddenly the door opened and in flew Mrs. Cross. "What is going on here?" She gasped. "Mrs. Dunsworthy! What in the world—! Step aside, Miss Corrigan."

Pushing me away, she took over. "Oh, dear, oh, dear," she muttered, as Mrs. Dunsworthy continued to grunt and flail. "Please hold still, Mrs. Dunsworthy. It appears a fastener is caught on your necklace. Just a moment while I unhook you."

With a final yank, the gown came up over the matron's head.

"My word." Mrs. Dunsworthy regained her composure and patted her hair. Uttering profuse apologies, Mrs. Cross shoved the dress at me with a glare. Meekly I turned it right side out and started to place it on a hanger, until Mrs. Cross snatched it from my grasp.

"Mrs. Dunsworthy, on behalf of Miss Corrigan here, I cannot apologize enough."

"No harm done," said the customer, with what I thought was incredible generosity of spirit considering I'd nearly suffocated her. "Let's try again, shall we?"

Mrs. Cross slid the silken nightgown over Mrs. Dunsworthy's head and tugged it over her hips.

"There," she said, adjusting the skirt. "Now isn't that simply lovely."

Mrs. Dunsworthy and I stared into the three-way mirror.

The nightgown, done up in a shade called "Eau de Nile" but reminiscent of pond slime, looked anything but lovely.

"Are you certain this gown looks well on me?" Mrs. Dunsworthy asked with a skeptical eye on her reflection.

"Oh, yes, madam," Mrs. Cross breathed. "It fits perfectly, and that shade is divine against your complexion."

I blinked in astonishment. Was she blind? The dull hue made Mrs. Dunsworthy appear slightly seasick—as it did nearly everyone, which is why the store had a large inventory of these gowns still in stock.

Mrs. Dunsworthy's eyes caught mine in the mirror. Embarrassed, I quickly glanced away and busied myself by brushing invisible lint from my navy blouse, hoping my expression had not betrayed my distaste.

"What do *you* think, Miss . . . Corrigan, is it?" she said.

I glanced up. She was still looking at me in the mirror.

"Oh. Um . . ." I said with my usual aplomb.

"Miss Corrigan is in training," Mrs. Cross said with a forced smile. "I assure you, this garment is most becoming to you."

"Mrs. Cross," Mrs. Dunsworthy said, "I believe I'd like to try on that little red number you showed me last week, with the dolman sleeves. Do you remember the one?"

"Yes, madam, right away," Mrs. Cross turned to me. "Miss Corrigan, please go and fetch—"

"Miss Corrigan will stay and help me change out of this one," Mrs. Dunsworthy said firmly. "She could use the practice."

"As you wish." Mrs. Cross lifted an eyebrow, but she could hardly argue with the truth of that statement. She shot me a warning glance and scurried out to the sales floor.

Mrs. Dunsworthy smiled at my reflection in the mirror. "You seem like a busy young woman. Tell me, do you still find time to visit *The Song of the Lark*?"

"Excuse me?" Then all at once I remembered where I'd seen her. "Why, you're the lady from the Art Institute."

The silver-haired woman laughed, a musical, tinkling laugh. "I volunteer there as a docent. I almost didn't recognize you. You've changed your hair. That style is becoming on you."

"Thank you."

She smiled gently. "I remember you looked so lost that day we spoke. Like a little lost sheep. Have you made your decision yet?"

Amazed that she remembered our conversation, I shook my head. "No, I'm afraid I haven't."

She turned to me and with a gentle smile said, "Remember what we talked about, dear. Keep your face turned toward heaven. The Lord will guide you."

Her words jostled my memory. "Oh, I think I have your Bible. You left it behind on the bench that day. It's in my handbag, which is down in the locker room. If you don't mind waiting, I'll just—"

She held up a hand. "I left it behind on purpose," she said. "For you."

"For me? But—"

"Never mind. I have plenty of Bibles."

"I see." I envisioned her handing out Bibles to distraught young women all over the city. "Well, thank you."

She extended her hand. "I don't believe I've properly introduced myself. I'm Mrs. Theodore Dunsworthy."

I grasped her hand. "Marjorie Corrigan. I'm delighted to meet you."

Mrs. Dunsworthy cast a glance toward the doorway, then back to the mirror. "Tell me the truth, Miss Corrigan. Does this gown do a thing for me?"

I knew Mrs. Cross would kill me, but I had to come clean. "To be perfectly honest, I'm afraid not, Mrs. Dunsworthy. The cut is not bad, but the color is all wrong. In fact, if you're fond of green, we have a new model in a pale celery shade that would be much more flattering to your complexion."

She laughed. "That's what I thought." She lifted up her arms so I could pull the offending garment over her head. "Please bring it here so I can try it on."

"I'll be glad to." This time I was able to extricate her from the gown without a hitch. As I left the dressing room, I brushed against Mrs. Cross on her way in.

"Mrs. Cross," Mrs. Dunsworthy said, "Miss Corrigan here will assist me today. It turns out that she and I have similar taste." She smiled sweetly. "I'm sure you don't mind."

"Oh. Well. I suppose that's all right." Mrs. Cross hesitated. "Of course, she's a mere trainee."

"Then she may practice on me. A well-developed fashion sense can't be taught. Miss Corrigan here appears to be a natural." Mrs. Dunsworthy shot me a wink in the mirror.

"Of course." Mrs. Cross's expression said, *We can't possibly be talking about the same person.* I shrugged and scurried off to fetch a pale celery nightgown for my new friend.

After Mrs. Dunsworthy left, I ran into Ruthie from Stationery in the ladies' restroom.

"Are you feeling all right, Marjorie?" she said. "You look like death warmed over."

I glanced at the mirror over the sinks. Puffy cheeks and two dark-ringed eyes stared back at me. "I'm all right. I just haven't been sleeping too well." I whipped out my compact to repair the damage.

In reality, I'd slept, but my sleep was haunted by dreams about Peter Bachmann. But then Richard's face would pop up, and I'd wake up with a start. This went on all night, resulting in my tired and haggard appearance. But I didn't need to explain all that to Ruthie. Ruthie was the wholesome type of girl who wouldn't ever get herself into predicaments like this, much less understand them.

"I'm sorry to hear that," she said. "Is there something I can pray about for you?"

"Um, no, that's all right," I mumbled, startled at her offer. While I appreciated the gesture, and hadn't known Ruthie to gossip, I barely knew her and couldn't risk my personal troubles becoming fodder for the moccasin trail.

"I'm so glad I ran into you," Ruthie continued. "I've been meaning to ask you—would you like to go to church with me sometime?"

"Church?"

"Yeah," she said. "I thought being new to the city, you might not have had a chance to find a good church yet."

"Oh. Um, well—" The truth was, I hadn't been to church even once since coming to Chicago. I'd been meaning to, but the weeks had slipped past, and Sunday was my only morning to sleep in, and Dot never went, and with one thing and another . . . I knew I should go to church if I meant what I'd said to God that day in Union Station.

"Or maybe you have already," she said at my hesitation. "Found a church, I mean."

I couldn't lie. "No, I haven't," I admitted. "I'll be happy to go with you. Sometime. Just to visit. You're very kind to ask me." Which she was, despite my heathenish waffling.

"Glad to hear it. How about this Sunday?" she pressed.

"Oh. I guess so. All right."

She told me which streetcar to take to the church. "I look forward to seeing you there."

I smiled and nodded as she exited the lounge. Sunday was a long way off.

I turned to the mirror, sighed at the devastation, went to work with my powder puff and lipstick, and didn't give Ruthie or church another thought.

Betty intercepted me as I walked back to Ladies' Nightwear. "Say, there's a new John Gilbert movie playing at the Oriental. Want to go?"

At the name of my favorite actor, my day brightened considerably. "Sure. Why not?"

"Swell. Meet me at the Randolph Street entrance after closing. Maybe we can make the early show and grab a bite afterwards."

The movie, called *The Cossacks*, paired John Gilbert with Renée Adorée, his *Big Parade* costar. We settled happily into our seats, but first we had to sit through the newsreel. In the lead story, images of federal agents hacking open crates of bootleg liquor in some warehouse flickered across the screen. The agents then smashed the bottles inside, creating an ankle-deep flood of liquor. Beside me, Betty shook her head.

"All that gorgeous hooch, going straight down the drain. Can you imagine? Prohibition is such a waste."

I shuddered. "It doesn't look so gorgeous to me," I said, thinking of Charlie. "Alcohol causes all sorts of problems. People are better off without it, don't you think?"

"What I think is that the Feds should mind their own business."

"But I've never seen you take a drink."

"That's because you've never come out with us to the speakeasies. Why should I pay for my own liquor when some fellow will buy it for me?" Betty glanced at me in the dark. "By the way, why haven't you?"

"What? Hit up a fellow for a drink?"

"No, silly. Why haven't you come out to the speaks with us? We have so much fun. You should come with us sometime, at least to hear Dot sing. I know she'd appreciate it, and frankly, you'd seem like less of a wet blanket."

That stung. I was not a wet blanket. Some people thought I was a lot of fun. Didn't they?

I shrugged. "I haven't had a lot of free time . . . certainly not to spend in disreputable gin joints." I didn't want to compound my wet-blanket status by adding that I was scared to death to set foot in a speakeasy, although that was the truth. Not only was Kerryville dry as the proverbial bone, but since Frances was head of the local chapter of the Women's Christian Temperance Union, our tabletops were always littered with anti-saloon propaganda. Any tiny leanings we might have had toward taking that first illicit sip would have been squashed hard and fast. It had almost killed her when Charlie took to the bottle. But all the anti-liquor crusading in the world hadn't prevented him from finding plenty to drink.

As if reading my thoughts, Betty opined, "Prohibition is a waste because it doesn't work. It forces perfectly upright citizens to become scofflaws."

"What do you mean, it doesn't work?" I gestured to the screen, where the agents continued to hack away at barrels of booze. "Look at all the people who will be saved from the evils of alcohol."

"You're such an innocent," she countered. "Bootlegging is the biggest racket around. Why, haven't you heard the rumors going around the moccasin trail that some Field's employees are involved in it?" Her eyes widened. "Some say it even starts at the top, with Mr. Simpson himself."

"Really?"

"Yep. I've also heard the name of that new manager in the Store for Men bandied about."

My mouth went dry. "Peter Bachmann?"

"Yeah. It's rumored he's a bootlegger himself, that he's running a racket with Mr. Simpson."

The blood drained from my head. "I don't believe it."

"Oh, yes. You'd be surprised to learn who does what around that place."

The newsreel came to a close and we settled back to watch the feature. *The Cossacks* was probably an exciting movie, because later I recalled hearing the audience gasp, but I didn't remember much else, I was so distracted by the whirl of thoughts and emotions swirling through me.

Peter Bachmann, a bootlegger. That rumor couldn't possibly be true. Could it?

Jack would never in a million years traffic in liquor. On the other hand, war could change a man. And a person could change a lot in ten years.

I raked back over my few conversations with Peter. The one that stood out in my mind was when he'd invited Dot and me to join him and his friends at the Green Mill. He'd said he wanted to hear jazz, but now I wondered if it was the booze he was most interested in.

But he seemed like such an upstanding citizen. The rumor couldn't be true.

But what if it was? Just my luck to fall for a bootlegger, of all people, when I had a perfectly fine, straight arrow of a man waiting for me at home—a man I could learn to love, if I'd just make an effort. Thank goodness things hadn't progressed any further with Peter.

When I got back to Dot's apartment, I did penance by writing a long, chatty letter to Richard. I regaled him with stories about life at Field's, my classes at the Art Institute, and what I remembered of the plot of *The Cossacks*. I inquired about his work and his health and his family. When I was finished, I blotted the ink, folded the pages neatly in thirds, and tore them up into tiny, tiny pieces.

CHAPTER TWENTY

On Saturday night I couldn't get a wink of sleep. An oppressive heat wave blanketing the city didn't help. The open windows let in all the noise of the city streets, including the occasional bone-shattering rumble of the Elevated, but not a whiff of a breeze. I sat at the tiny kitchen table, sipping a glass of ice water and reading a detective novel, until Dot came home from her singing gig. She sank wearily into the chair opposite me and kicked off her satin pumps.

"How'd it go?" I asked.

"Hot as Hades." She fanned her pretty face with a magazine. She looked luminous, being one of those women who glowed fetchingly in the heat. I merely sweated. "Especially when the place is as packed as tonight," she continued, "with every sheik and sheba from Lake Forest to South Shore. We've begged and begged Louie to put in one of those new air-cooling machines, like the movie theaters have, but he's too darn cheap." She ran her fingers through her hair, fanning it up off her neck. "What are you still doing up? Can't sleep?"

I shook my head.

"You really should try my ginger lemonade," she urged as she poured herself a glass from the icebox. "It will put you right out."

I sighed. "I'm just thinking about things."

She reached over, patted my arm, and said with an exaggerated pout, "Poor baby. Man trouble?"

"Sort of."

"Never mind, doll. Men are like buses. If you miss one, another one will come along soon enough."

"That's true for you," I said. "If you wanted to, you could change boyfriends as often as you change hats."

"Why would I want to? Louie's enough for any girl." Her face brightened. "Speaking of hats, you wouldn't believe how many ladies were asking today about that little straw number, after seeing it on your darling display. We've taken to calling it 'the garden-party hat,' because that's what the customers keep asking for. 'Can you show me that garden-party hat?' they say." She giggled.

"I wish somebody would say so to Mrs. Cross," I said. "She still hasn't warmed up to it, although she doesn't dare take it down since Mr. Simpson said he likes it."

"Aw, she's just jealous." Dot yawned and stretched. "Guess I'd better hit the hay. Got any plans for tomorrow? Or should I say, later today?"

"I told Ruthie I'd go to church with her," I said. "Care to join us?"

"Church?" She gave a harsh laugh. "You're joking, right?"

"Oh, come on. It'll be lots more fun if you're there. I'll even treat you to lunch afterwards."

"First of all," she said, "have you ever known me to get up before noon on a Sunday?"

I had to admit that I hadn't.

"And second, I was a preacher's kid all through my growing-up years. I did enough of that religion stuff to last me a lifetime."

"A preacher's kid? You?" I caught the note of disbelief in my voice and hoped she wasn't offended.

She chuckled. "I know. I don't fit the mold, do I? Well, you should have seen me. I was the perfect pastor's daughter. Obedient, quiet, helpful. My sisters and I sang together in church every Sunday, in our giant hair bows and patent leather Mary Janes. 'Those Rodgers girls,' people called us. 'They sing like the angels.' We were angels, all right. Good as gold during the week, and in church every Sunday, without fail." She shook her head as if she, herself, couldn't quite believe it.

"What happened?"

She shrugged. "Oh, you know. Everybody thought my father was this fine, upstanding preacher-man, and he was—in public. But at home it was another story. He had a demon of a temper, helped along by the secret bottle of scotch he always kept stashed in his desk drawer. He terrorized us girls. We never knew when he was going to explode and give one or the other of us the strap. Made life a living hell for my mother. He was such a hypocrite." A shadow crossed her delicate features. "As I grew older, we argued all the time, he and I. He hated my clothes, my hair, my friends. I was always being invited to sing in school musicals and such, but he forbade any singing outside of the church. He thought my desire to have a singing career was shameful and evil. Home felt like a prison, there were so many rules and regulations."

"Oh, Dot. I'm sorry," was all I could say.

She drew in a deep breath. "Anyway, to make a long story short, the final straw came when I figured out he was seeing some woman on the side. Guess he took the passage about 'loving thy neighbor' a little too literally. For my mother's sake, I never told anyone, but I could never trust my father again. The minute I finished high school, I packed my bag and headed up here. Never looked back. Now I'm living the life *I* want to live. At least I *will* be, when I get my big break."

I swirled the melting ice cubes in the bottom of the glass. "Do your sisters ever come to visit you?"

Dot looked away. "No. He's forbidden them to come. I'm a bad influence, dontcha know." She stood up and stretched. "And now after that invigorating walk down memory lane, I'm off to bed. Have a fun time with Ruthie tomorrow. Good night."

"G'night." I sat in the kitchen a while longer. *This is what I don't understand, Lord. Why didn't You help Dot? How could You let a pastor, of all people, cause so much suffering? You want people to trust You, but then You pull the rug out from underneath them. Help me understand.*

I doused the light and trudged off to bed. The thought of getting up for church in just a few hours no longer appealed. I briefly considered skipping it and sleeping in. But Ruthie was expecting me, and I couldn't let her down.

Lying in my stifling room, I continued railing at God. *First You took away my mother, then Jack. And then I thought You'd given Jack back to me, but You were just playing a trick. You replaced Jack with a lookalike gangster. A gangster whom I now have feelings for.*

I blinked at the ceiling as the truth settled over my heart. *Yes, I have feelings for him. For Peter. Even now that I know he's not Jack. And even though I barely know him. And You knew the whole time I would. How could You let this happen? Why, oh why, can't You make me feel this way about the man I've promised to marry? It would make everything so much simpler.*

I turned my face to the wall, knowing it was wrong to accuse God of being out to hurt me. But at least He and I were back on speaking terms. By now I'd thoroughly talked myself out of wanting to go to church. But I would go. Ruthie was counting on me. And if nothing else, I was a woman of my word.

The morning light made everything seem more hopeful. In spite of my irrepressible yawns, I enjoyed visiting Ruthie's church. The steeple rose above the squat tenements and dingy alleyways of the West Side neighborhood like a beacon of hope. The pastor preached with vigor on the story of the prodigal son.

"And he wasted his substance with riotous living . . ." he quoted from the Scriptures.

Chagrined, I recalled how I'd been tempted to visit a speakeasy solely in order to spend an evening with Peter. Sinful behavior was a slippery slope. If I didn't get a grip on my wayward heart, I'd soon find myself wasting my substance with riotous living, right alongside Mr. Prodigal.

"Son, thou art ever with me, and all I have is thine," Pastor Higgins thundered from the pulpit. "It is meet that we should make merry, and be glad; for this thy brother was dead, and is alive again; and was lost, and is found."

Surely a person could make merry and be glad in a way that didn't involve gin mills.

In a strange way it felt good to be back in church. Familiar and comfortable, like visiting the home of an old friend. I vowed to be less of a lazybones and join Ruthie more often on Sundays. As she and I exited the sanctuary, she paused to shake the pastor's hand and introduce me.

"It's a pleasure to meet you, Miss Corrigan," Pastor Higgins said. "I hope you'll join us again."

"I'm looking forward to it." I said. I meant it, too.

He smiled at Ruthie. "Miss Gardner, tell me, how are things going down at the settlement house?"

"Fine, Pastor. We're getting ready for the big Fourth of July concert in Grant Park. I hope you and Mrs. Higgins will be able to come."

"We wouldn't miss it," the pastor said. "It's a great opportunity for the children. You've been working wonders with them."

Ruthie blushed. "Not me, Pastor. It's all the Lord's doing."

"The Lord works through His people. Well done, Miss Gardner."

While we waited for the streetcar, Ruthie filled me in. "The church supports a settlement house on the Southwest Side. I help out there as a volunteer, teaching music and directing the choir."

"You're a music teacher?" This girl had more layers than an onion.

"Not a trained one," she said. "I just love music and sort of fell into the job."

"What was Pastor Higgins saying about the Fourth of July?"

Ruthie's eyes sparkled. "Every year the city picks a children's choir to sing at the big Independence Day celebration in Grant Park. This year our little choir was selected."

"Gee, that's impressive. They must be good."

"We've been blessed with an abundance of good singing voices. But it's still a lot of work." All at once the sparkle in her eyes spread to her whole face. "Say, Marjorie, we could really use some help. A few of our regular volunteers are out of town and we're even more short-staffed than usual. Would you consider lending us a hand?"

"Me?" I choked out a laugh. "What on earth could I do at a concert? I dread getting up in front of people, and I can't carry a tune in a bucket."

"Oh, we don't need you to perform, or even sing," Ruthie said. "We really need help with costumes and staging. You're so creative— everyone simply loves what you did with the display down in Ladies' Nightwear."

Word traveled fast. Clearly the moccasin trail was up and running.

"Thanks." I fidgeted with the collar of my dress, which suddenly felt snug. "I don't know . . . I haven't ever worked with children before."

"Nonsense. You've mentioned doing things with your little sister. This is pretty much just like that." I had my doubts, but her eyes were pleading. "Please? This concert will help attract donations, and it means so much to the children. You'd be doing them—and me—an enormous favor."

"Well. . . ." Against my better judgment I heard myself say, "All right. I guess I could help out. Just this once." Flattery will get me to say anything. Plus, I rather liked the idea of devising costumes, free from the stifling influence of Mrs. Cross.

"Oh, thank you. You're an answer to prayer." Ruthie clapped her hands.

My insides warmed. Never before had I been called someone's answer to prayer.

Then Peter's throwaway comment scrolled across my mind. *You look like the kind of girl who does good works.*

What exactly had I just gotten myself into?

CHAPTER TWENTY-ONE

On Monday morning I ran myself ragged, assisting a June bride who grew increasingly fractious and demanding as the day wore on, like a toddler in need of a nap. Or maybe it was my own attitude that needed refreshment, along with my sore feet. However, being busy helped me keep my mind off other things. Once again I'd lain awake most of the night, wondering what on earth I was doing marrying Richard while having feelings for Peter. My mind ran through scenarios of breaking off my engagement, of the pain of telling Richard there was someone else. But there *wasn't* someone else—not as long as Peter was a scofflaw who, in any case, was squiring a gorgeous redhead around town.

These mental gymnastics kept me from sleeping, making me groggy and mistake-prone at work. Mrs. Cross criticized more than usual, maybe because of my listless demeanor and the dark circles under my eyes. In spite of my success with customers, she kept me busy in the back, doing maintenance tasks, like checking inventory and re-pressing a shipment of white linen robes too wrinkled for her liking. I didn't really mind these jobs. Being sequestered behind the scenes gave me time to think.

Mrs. Cross came back to check on my progress. "When you've finished, Miss Corrigan, put them out on the rack next to the ecru peignoirs." She noted my expression. "Is there a problem?"

I had nothing to lose by being frank. "Please come with me, Mrs. Cross. I want to show you something." I picked up the garment and we walked out onto the sales floor. I held the white robe next to the ecru peignoirs. "See? The pale beige looks dingy next to the white, and the white just washes out. And white linen is a hard sell. It wrinkles like crazy. See?" I crushed a handful of fabric, causing it to dissolve into wrinkles.

"I'm aware of what linen does," Mrs. Cross said.

"Of course. But easy wrinkling deters customers from buying. If we want these robes to sell, we'll have to do something creative with them."

"I suppose you have a better idea."

I thought for a moment. "The trouble is, we're thinking of them as bathrobes."

Mrs. Cross blinked. "They are bathrobes."

A spark of an idea floated up through my exhausted brain. I examined the robes with a critical eye. "How about we do a display with a nautical theme?"

"Nautical?" Mrs. Cross frowned. "You mean boats?"

"White, navy, and red," I pronounced. "Crisp and clean. Sails snapping in the breeze. You know. *Nautical.*"

Mrs. Cross looked skeptical. "Who wears a bathrobe on a boat?"

"Not bathrobes," I said. "Beach cover-ups. What woman wouldn't appreciate a cool white linen robe to wear over her swimming costume?"

I forgot all about being tired.

"Picture it," I continued, framing the imaginary display with my hands. "White linen robe. Navy swimming costume underneath. A daring red sandal. All displayed against a contrasting background of fluid, airy fabric." Miss Smith's words from art class came back to me. "Blue fabric. A cheerful blue, like Lake Michigan sparkling in the midday sun. And we'll need a metallic touch. Gold jewelry—a necklace, a bracelet. The effect will mimic the shining brass hardware on a—on a yacht." I made a mental note to hunt down the sailor hat that Dot had pronounced "perfect for yachting."

Mrs. Cross pursed her lips. "Oh, for heaven's sake. Brass hardware, indeed. And what on earth do you know about yachts?"

"We need to paint a picture for the customer. Help them imagine the possibilities."

"Yachting, indeed." But she didn't say no.

"We want to sell the robes, don't we?" I coaxed. "I think it's worth a try."

"It sounds like so much nonsense to me," she said, "but I don't suppose it will do any harm to let you try. And with those bigwigs from Selfridge's coming soon for a tour, we want to look our best."

She shook an admonishing finger. "Mind you submit the proper paperwork this time. I don't need to have the other managers storming Ladies' Nightwear, chasing after their merchandise."

Later that afternoon, as I worked on the display, Peter came by the department. He gave a low whistle as he perused my handiwork.

"That's some snazzy stuff," he said with admiration. "Say, kid, you've got talent. Have you considered becoming a trimmer?"

My insides melted at his compliment. Or maybe just at him. "Oh, I couldn't. I haven't had any training."

He shrugged. "I think you should consider it. Don't sell yourself short. When a position opens up on the design team, you should apply for it."

"Do you really think so?"

"Definitely."

"That's kind of you to say."

"I'm not just saying it. It's true. You're really good at this."

I thought my heart would burst. Peter was the first person since Jack to encourage my dreams.

"I don't know . . ." I demurred, but my mind started conjuring up images of what I could do inside Field's enormous plate glass display windows lined up along State Street. What fun it would be, coming to work every day from my fashionable penthouse apartment, dressing the mannequins while passersby whispered to each other, "Isn't that Marjorie Corrigan, the famous window designer?"

Peter's next remark shook me out of my reverie. "I came by to ask whether you'd like to grab a bite to eat this evening."

A shadow of disappointment passed over me. "I'm sorry. I already have plans." This wasn't a manufactured excuse—I'd arranged to meet Ruthie at the settlement house.

He shrugged. "That's all right. Short notice and all. How about tomorrow night?

I winced. "Sorry. Art class on Tuesdays."

Wednesday. Ask me about Wednesday, I pleaded inwardly. I didn't want to appear overeager, but neither did I want him to think I was putting him off. I smiled my biggest, most encouraging smile. But he only said, "All right. Maybe another time," and walked away.

As I rode to meet Ruthie after work, the scene outside the street-car window turned from downtown office buildings and stores to ramshackle tenements and shabby storefronts. The sharply dressed office workers seated around me gave way to women in headscarves and men in shirtsleeves and suspenders. When I reached my destination, a cacophony of languages hit my ears: Italian, Yiddish, Polish. Everyone talked at once: gossiping, bargaining, arguing. Automobile horns honked and horses whinnied. An unfamiliar smell pervaded the air, like a mixture of cabbage, raw meat, garlic, factory smoke, and unwashed bodies. Swarms of children dodged traffic, skipped rope, or gathered in doorways, many of them dressed in rags. I felt overdressed in my smart navy frock and straw hat—proudly purchased with my first paycheck—and wished I'd worn what Frances called a "washday dress."

The settlement house had seen better days as a private home, back when the neighborhood had been more prosperous. But though dilapidated, its stately facade stood out from the rest of the buildings on the street. As I stepped inside I could feel energy and excitement pulsing through the hallways. Young people swarmed everywhere: running up and down the stairs, chattering, yelling, pushing, shoving. I stood in the front hall, feeling at loose ends, until Ruthie emerged from the melee.

"Marjorie, there you are," she said. "We're just getting started. Come with me."

I followed her through the house into a large room that had been a ballroom at one time, but now served as a makeshift gymnasium, with basketball hoops at either end and stripes painted on the scratched wooden floor. At one end stood a rickety set of risers, on which a dozen or more children of varying ages and sizes fidgeted, squirmed, and tried to push each other off. Ruthie clapped her hands sharply.

"All right, children. Settle down. This is Miss Corrigan. She is going to help us with our program. So give her your full attention and mind what she says."

A dozen pairs of curious eyes turned my way, evaluating me. A couple of the older girls whispered to each other and giggled. What on earth was I doing here?

When the rehearsal got underway, though, things went more smoothly. A surprising number of the smudgy-faced urchins had angelic voices.

When a husky, black-haired man walked into the room, some of the boys started hollering.

"Hey, Mister Joe. Wanna play some dodgeball?"

"Mister Joe, do we hafta sing this stupid song? Singing is for girls."

Ruthie rapped a ruler on the podium. "Children, children, come to order."

"She's right, boys," the man named Joe said good-naturedly. "There will be time enough for dodgeball when your rehearsal is over. Pay attention now."

"Aw, nuts," said Tommy O'Malley, who appeared to be the ring-leader of the boys. But despite his scowl, he joined the others in singing "Columbia, the Gem of the Ocean," in a clear high soprano that belied his tough-guy image.

My main job, besides helping to keep some semblance of order, was to help with the costumes. I already had a simple idea in mind: patriotic striped pinafores and hair ribbons for the girls and matching vests and bow ties for the boys, provided I could find some appropriate fabric at a decent price. I wondered if the store might donate some and made a mental note to ask.

Next the little angels tackled "The Star-Spangled Banner."

"Oh, say, can you *seeee*, by the dawn's early *liiight*, o'er the *red* parts we *waaashed* by the twilight's last gleeea-ming. . . ."

Ruthie rapped her ruler. "*Ramparts*, children. *Ramparts.* O'er the *ramparts* we *watched*." She sighed and pointed to a boy who waved his hand. "Yes, Frankie?"

"What's a rampart?"

Just then a slim, dark-haired woman came up beside me, shaking her head as she watched the choir. "Francis Scott Key is spinning in his grave right now," she murmured. I'd noticed her earlier, standing next to Joe. Wife? Girlfriend?

I laughed. "You're probably right. But I'm awfully glad the boy didn't ask *me* what a rampart is, because I don't think I know." I held out my hand. "Marjorie Corrigan. I'm a friend of Ruthie's."

"Oh, yes, Ruthie told us you'd be coming." She shook my hand warmly. "Thank you so much. We need all the help we can get. I'm Annamarie Manelli. And that's my husband, Joe."

"Nice to meet you." I gestured to the youngsters squirming on the risers. "Do you work with the children, too?"

"Oh, no," she said. "That's Joe's department. I'm just here to pick up my nephew. He's the one over there on the end, crossing his eyes." She cupped her hands around her mouth and yelled, "Paulie, stop that. Do you want them to stay that way?" She sighed. "He's here under protest because Joe said the choir was short on boys. Paulie'd do anything for Joe."

"The children sure do seem to like him."

"And he sure likes them," Annamarie agreed. "We grew up in this neighborhood, and by helping out here, Joe feels he's giving something back. Making it a better place to grow up, you know? Besides, he genuinely enjoys the children. Some of them are orphans. Others are just youngsters from the neighborhood who come here after school and on weekends. During the summertime, they practically live here. Most of their parents are at work in the factories all day, and there's nobody at home. We do what we can to keep them off the streets."

"That's admirable."

"But it's a drop in the bucket compared to what they really need." Annamarie shook her head. "An afternoon of singing and dodgeball won't keep them safe from the local gangsters."

"Gangsters?" I shivered, thinking of my streetcar ride home after dark.

"Bootleggers. Smugglers. They try to entice the children into drinking liquor and get them involved in running errands for them. Joe has seen too many boys and girls end up on the wrong side of the law for making friends with those crooks. Especially this one man— Luigi Braccio." She practically spat the name. "He's the worst. A real menacing sort of fellow, but he's got this tough, powerful swagger about him, and too many of the neighborhood boys think he's worthy of respect."

Luigi Braccio. The name rang a bell, maybe from the newspaper. I started to say, "Tell me more," but the rehearsal had ended and the children were running and shouting, loosed from their constraints. Annamarie excused herself and went to corral her nephew.

I helped Ruthie and Joe clear away the bleachers to make room for dodgeball. Most of the older girls siphoned off into giggling groups, but one girl stood off to the side, by herself. I'd noticed during the singing that she had one of the clearest, sweetest voices in the bunch. With uncombed hair and a patched dress, she looked to be about Helen's age. I walked over to her and held out my hand.

"How do you do," I said. "My name is Miss Corrigan. What's yours?"

"Gabriella," she said, looking down at her scuffed shoes. "Gabriella Grimaldi."

"That's a pretty name."

The girl smiled but didn't meet my eyes.

"How old are you, Gabriella?"

"Sixteen."

"I have a sister your age," I said. "Her name's Helen. She loves to sing."

"So do I." She brightened. "It's my favorite thing."

"Well, you certainly have a lovely voice."

"Thank you."

After that brief exchange, Gabriella became my shadow, trailing me around the gymnasium and helping me take the children's measurements.

The evening flew past. As Ruthie and I said our good-byes at the streetcar stop, she said, "What do you think? Will you come back?"

"Yes, I'll definitely be back," I said. "I knew I'd be helping a worthy cause, but I never knew I'd have so much fun."

I also realized, with a shock, that I hadn't given a single thought to my own problems during the entire evening.

CHAPTER TWENTY-TWO

On Friday Mrs. Cross was all aflutter, making sure that Ladies' Nightwear was shipshape to host a distinguished visitor. Mr. Harry Selfridge was something of a legend, having launched his career at Field's in the early days, working his way up from errand boy to executive. Then some twenty years ago he'd moved to London and opened his own elegant department store there. Now he was coming back for a visit, bringing his top executives with him. They were to tour the store that day, and a fancy reception in their honor was scheduled for Friday night at the tony South Shore Country Club, to which all section managers were invited, including Mrs. Cross, who was blazing with determination that Mr. Selfridge would not find so much as a ruffle out of place.

"Everything must be perfect. We must show Mr. Selfridge that Marshall Field & Company is still the world's greatest store, second to none." She stood on a stepstool, using a feather duster to brush an imaginary cobweb from a lighting fixture, lest the Selfridge crew find Ladies' Nightwear not up to snuff. "Miss Corrigan, please make sure all the glass cases are free of fingerprints."

As I turned my back to polish the cases, Miss Ryan sidled up to me and whispered, "Methinks she carries a torch."

"What?"

Her eyes glinted with intrigue. "Mr. Selfridge and Old Rugged. Moccasin trail says they had eyes for each other when she was a young clerk and he was a rising star. But then he married Rosalie—"

Crash! We wheeled around to see the stepstool upended and Mrs. Cross lying on the ground, still clutching her feather duster.

"My ankle! My ankle!"

I dropped the polishing cloth and rushed to her side. Already her ankle was swelling. I loosened her boot. A small crowd gathered and Miss Ryan telephoned down to the infirmary. Before the floor walker and an elevator operator hoisted her off on a stretcher, she reached out and clutched my forearm. "Miss Corrigan," she rasped, "you'll need to go in my place tonight."

"What? To the reception? But shouldn't Miss Ryan go? She's been here the longest—besides you, of course."

"This is not a merit award, Miss Corrigan," she hissed through gritted teeth. "We need someone who is best able to represent Ladies' Nightwear in a good light. That's you. Mr. Simpson already likes your work. Miss Ryan is too mousy to make a good impression."

I cringed and glanced around, hoping Miss Ryan was out of earshot and relieved to see her engaged in conversation with Gladys from Hosiery—gossiping, no doubt.

"You'll find the invitation in my reticule," Mrs. Cross continued. "You'll need it to gain admittance."

I decided that the pain must have gone to her head, but I was secretly thrilled to comply.

That evening, as the taxi glided up to the grand entrance to the South Shore Country Club, my stomach did the Charleston and my palms sweated inside the silk evening gloves I'd borrowed from Dot. The grandeur of the place had my insides churning, never mind that I was going to an impressive formal event with store bigwigs after less than a month on the job. I stepped out of the taxi and gazed up at the club, an imposing Mediterranean Revival structure, the largest building for blocks. Lights glowed from dozens of windows, and the gentle music of a string quartet floated across the lawn as day slipped into evening.

As I followed a queue of fashionably dressed guests into the Grand Promenade, I became painfully conscious of my own simple frock, the same one I'd worn to the hospital auxiliary tea. Though I'd desperately wished I could have purchased something new, my budget wouldn't allow it. At the last minute, however, I'd adorned the dress by plucking a small bunch of daisies from the landlady's modest flowerbed and tucking them into the sash—an embellishment I'd spotted on a mannequin at the store. I thought the daisies added a perky touch, and besides, the landlady, Mrs. Moran, would never miss them.

A uniformed butler ushered me and several others into a large reception room. I spotted a row of enormous palmetto plants which sparked uncomfortable memories of the hospital auxiliary tea at Mrs. Cavendish's. Had that dismal event been my first clue that Richard might not be the match for me? That I'd never fit into his world? I thought of how Mrs. Cavendish and her cronies would gape at the splendor of the South Shore Country Club. If only they could see me now.

Beyond the reception room, a series of French doors opened out onto a large terrace with sweeping views of the lawn. Soft breezes gently billowed the tall gauzy curtains, beckoning me to step outside. As I stepped toward the door, I heard my name.

"Miss Corrigan. I didn't expect to see you here."

My heart skipped a beat as Peter approached me. I hadn't considered that he'd be here, although it made sense since he was a manager. I doubly wished I were wearing a sophisticated slinky gown—the type of gown Dot would wear—but nonetheless I saw unmistakable admiration in his eyes. He appeared as his usual impeccable self in evening clothes, his brown waves tamed with brilliantine. Even the scar on his face lent him a dashing air, like a man who had led an adventurous life.

"It's more pleasant outside. Shall we?" He touched my elbow and gently steered me through the throng of guests to the stone terrace. The first stars were just beginning to twinkle in the purple sky as the sun's golden rays disappeared in the west. A waiter passed around frosty glasses of iced tea and lemonade, perfect refreshment on the warm, humid evening.

"Beautiful night," I said between sips, gazing out at the sloping lawn, conscious of Peter's nearness.

"Beautiful," he agreed, but from the way he said it, I don't think he meant the view alone. Thank goodness the fading light hid my flushed face.

"I'm awfully glad you're here, Peter. Otherwise I wouldn't know a soul."

"I'm glad, too." He set his glass on the stone railing and turned to face me. "Listen, Marjorie, I—"

"Yoo hoo! Peter Bachmann, there you are. Come and say hello." A trilling voice cut through the starry twilight, jarring me back to my senses. I took a hasty swig of lemonade to steady my nerves while Peter turned to see who'd called him. Then he led me across the terrace to a small knot of department heads and introduced me. I mostly stayed silent and let him talk shop to his cronies. Once they had me pegged as a mere clerk in Ladies' Nightwear, they didn't appear interested in knowing me further. I didn't mind. I let my attention wander to the stately pillars flanking the terrace, graced with flowering vines, and the reflecting pool and gardens beyond, shimmering pale and fragrant in the moonlight, all the while wondering how on earth I'd landed here.

Eventually Mr. Simpson himself walked up to our little group. He greeted us and introduced his wife. When the introductions came around to me, he said, "Why, you're the young lady who brought cross-promotion to the Nightwear section. Well done, my dear."

Peter grinned at me, and I'm sure I blushed. The other managers eyed me with fresh interest. I stood a little taller, relieved he didn't question how a lowly clerk had managed to sneak into a reception meant for upper-level staff.

"Thank you so much." I turned to Mrs. Simpson. "This is a lovely place."

"I'm glad you like it," she said. "So many of the old guard—our neighbors, that is, or their children—are abandoning the South Shore and building rather vulgar new houses, way out in the back of beyond, in places like Lake Forest." She shuddered slightly, as if the thought of being exiled to such a remote outpost was inconceivable. "I suppose I can't blame them. The neighborhood is changing. Why, the next street over is gradually transforming into a series of motorcar showrooms. And just a few doors down from our home, one of the finest old houses has been turned into a psychiatric hospital for ladies. Can you imagine?"

I returned her smile, thinking that if Richard and my family continued to insist I was mentally unstable, she and I might well end up as neighbors.

"Even so," she continued, "I have no desire to leave my familiar home for the so-called fashionable places."

After the host and hostess had moved on to greet other guests, one of the people standing in our cluster—a tall, striking woman with red hair, the one I'd seen flirting with Peter on occasion—commented, "Well, well. You seem to have made quite an impression on the old man."

"Oh, it's nothing, really," I said, my face hot. "He just happened to like a display I created."

"Congratulations," she purred. "It's not every day that a clerk gets noticed by the president of the store. You must be quite special. Isn't she special, Peter?"

Her words seemed friendly enough, but something in her tone caught me off guard. As I struggled for a suitable response, Peter took the empty glass from my hand.

"Yes, she is," he said. To me he murmured, "Will you excuse me while I track down a waiter? Chitchatting with the big boss is thirsty work." He headed off into the crowd, the redhead slinking along in his wake.

Without Peter and bored by shop-talk, I thought it best to distance myself from the managers and seek sanctuary elsewhere. I excused myself, strolled back into the reception room, and admired a few of the oil paintings on the walls. They were obviously museum-quality, or close to it.

An older man with a salt-and-pepper beard came up beside me. "Ah, a fellow art *aficionado*." He lowered his voice. "Just between us, I detest these abominable receptions. So much meaningless small talk with people you've been stuck laboring alongside all the day. But I do savor the chance to survey the club's splendid art collection." He gestured toward the paintings.

"Tell me," he said, "which one do you like best?"

"This one, with the gypsy girl." I pointed. "It reminds me a little of *The Song of the Lark* at the Art Institute. Do you know it?"

"Do you, now?" He nodded. "I know it well."

Grateful to have someone friendly to talk to, I seized the topic. "See how she's gazing upward in that dreamy way. And I love the colors, the ochre and bronze and that deep, deep red." I stopped suddenly in mid-blather, embarrassed, but the man just smiled.

"It's always refreshing to meet a Field's employee who knows something about design and color," he said, shaking his head. "So many have no appreciation for it whatsoever."

"Oh, I love art," I said. "I'm studying textiles at the Art Institute. Well, taking one class, at least."

"Is that so? Well, that's a bit of cheerful news," he said heartily. "What is your name?"

"Marjorie Corrigan."

"And tell me, Miss Corrigan, which section do you work in at Field's?"

But before I could answer, another guest called, "There you are, sir," and hustled him away. I watched him leave, sorry to have lost an interesting person to talk to.

I figured I should go back to the terrace in case Peter had returned with my refilled drink, but first I needed to answer the call of nature. A maid directed me to what she called the "ladies' dressing room," which turned out to be an elegantly appointed sitting room with comfortable sofas and chairs. Ladies powdered their faces at a long mirrored table, like actresses backstage at a theater. At the back of the room, the necessaries were ensconced discreetly in separate stalls.

From behind a stall door, I heard the outer door opening and closing as ladies left the sitting room and others came in.

"My word, it's a steamy evening," a voice said. "I'm positively *roasting*. May I borrow some of your face powder, dear?"

"Of course, darling. Here you go. You really should come out onto the terrace. It's much more pleasant out there."

Some rustling noises took place in front of the large mirrors, and then the first voice said, "I wonder who she is, really."

"You heard her. Just some little clerk," the second voice said in a dismissive tone.

My ears perked up. Surely of all the guests present at this event, only I qualified as "just a clerk." I held my breath, unwilling to hear more, but equally unwilling to make my presence known.

"Did you see what she's wearing?" the first voice said. "It looks like a made-over dress from some country barn dance."

I glanced down at my frock in dismay.

"And that little spray of daisies must have cost all of ten cents from a street vendor," the first voice continued.

"Or free, if she plucked them from a public park," the second voice said with a snort. "Daisies. Did you *ever*?"

The two women cackled gleefully as my face burned and the skin on the back of my neck prickled. I'd been found out. Worst of all, I was a laughingstock. I wanted to run away, but I couldn't make myself leave the stall.

"Do you think he's seeing her?" the first voice said.

"I don't think so. I'm certain he arrived alone," the second voice said. "But even if he is, you know Peter. Women buzz around him like flies, although this one doesn't seem like his type. I give her a week before he moves on to someone else."

"But he always winds up back with you, doesn't he?" her friend said. They both chuckled, and then the second one said, "Come on, let's go. It's stuffy in here."

She was right about that. I could barely take in a breath.

I knew that voice. It belonged to the red-haired woman.

A murmur of voices rose and fell as the outer door opened and closed. As soon as I'd gathered my shredded dignity, I knew I needed to find Peter and learn the identity of this woman who clearly thought she owned him. And then I needed to go home and stuff my dress into the incinerator.

I quietly opened the stall door and, seeing the sitting room empty, crept back into the party, trying to escape anyone's notice. If I were lucky, I'd be able to locate Peter quickly and let him know I was leaving, in case he cared. If he'd brought his roadster, maybe he'd even be willing to drive me home. Then he'd be out of the clutches of That Woman, at least for the evening.

I found him in a hallway near a butler's pantry, with his back to me. Before I could tap him on the shoulder, I heard him whisper *sotto voce* to one of the waiters, "Say, don't you fellows have anything stronger on hand to spice up this lemonade? It's pretty tame stuff."

"No, sir," the waiter murmured back. "Not here. Mr. Simpson's strict on that account. Teetotaler, you know. But if you're interested, I know of a place—"

He stopped short when he caught sight of me. Peter turned around and smiled broadly.

"There you are, Marjorie," he said a little too brightly, holding out a glass of lemonade. "Having a good time?"

So the rumors were true. Peter, asking about liquor, was probably trying to drum up business for his bootlegging operation. At the very least, he was a drinker and a hooligan with no respect for the law.

The magical evening rapidly spun into a whorl of disappointment.

"I'm going home. Just wanted to let you know." I said coldly. He raised his eyebrows.

"You look flushed. Aren't you feeling well?" He reached out to touch my cheek, but I pushed his hand away.

"Not particularly."

A frown of concern crossed his face. "Let me drive you." He handed our glasses to the waiter. "We've put in our appearance, anyway. We won't miss anything, except for Mr. Simpson's long-winded toast to the Selfridge people."

"No, thank you." I could taste the disappointment in the back of my throat. It no longer mattered to me who the red-haired woman was. She could have him. If Peter was a bootlegger, he was not the man for me. Furthermore, he was a liar for telling me I looked pretty in my homemade dress that was obviously a sartorial disaster. Both a liar *and* a drunkard. So much for my taste in men.

I hurried to the entrance off the Grand Promenade, where a valet signaled for a taxi. As we sped northward, I thought, *Why, Peter Bachmann doesn't bear the least resemblance to Jack Lund. Not in the slightest.* I couldn't imagine why I ever thought he did.

When I got home, I brushed off Dot's inquiries about the evening and shut the door to my room. I got ready for bed and then immediately wrote a long letter to Richard, and this time I didn't tear it up.

CHAPTER TWENTY-THREE

On Saturday I skipped lunch to avoid running into Peter. It was better that way. Miss Ryan told me he'd stopped by and asked for me mid-morning, but when she told him I was working in the stockroom, he merely said he was glad I must be feeling better. I told myself I was disappointed in him, but really I was disappointed in myself for being a poor judge of character. I had come perilously close to throwing over a perfectly good fiancé for a scofflaw and liar.

On the other hand, I could not deny that Richard had never aroused in me the sort of feelings that Jack had so long ago—or, frankly, as Peter did now. I knew in my heart it was wrong to go through with the wedding. Richard deserved to marry a woman who felt as crazy about him as I had felt about Jack. Alas, that woman wasn't me. I just had to figure out how to break the news. And then I could go forth as a spinster and forget about men and marriage altogether. I'd work until I was as old as Mrs. Cross, and then I'd retire to a small cottage in Michigan City with geraniums in the window and a cat on my lap.

In the end, it was Dot who decided there was no time like the present to make a visit to Kerryville.

"You've been stuck at that old settlement house every night this week, except for Tuesday's art class," she said in her don't-argue-with-me voice. "You haven't had a minute's rest."

"Our concert is next week," I moaned.

"They're just *children*," she said. "Give them a little break, for pity's sake."

I had to agree. We could all use a breather—me, Ruthie, and Annamarie, too.

"And we have to settle this Richard-versus-Peter question once and for all," Dot continued, "which can only be done if you talk to the man face-to-face."

"There's no question to settle," I protested. "Clearly Peter is a disaster in the making, and Richard—well, everyone agrees he and I were meant to be together."

"I don't care about what 'everyone' thinks," Dot said. "I care about what *you* think. So we'll go to Kerryville and figure it all out."

Her motives weren't entirely altruistic. A big part of the reason she wanted to get out of town was that she'd had yet another spat with Louie and wanted him to miss her and realize he couldn't live without her. In my opinion, he'd already made it clear he could, but she didn't want to see it, and she didn't want to hear it from me. But I agreed a change of scenery and a few days at home with my family would be a welcome break to help me clear my head. Who knew? Maybe seeing Richard again would reignite my feelings for him and knock a certain wavy-haired gangster right out of my head. On the other hand, I could have a relapse of fainting spells. Either way, the weekend promised not to be dull.

Dot arranged to take time off from Millinery, and in a rare moment of sympathy—or perhaps simply annoyance at my listless demeanor after yet another sleepless night—Mrs. Cross allowed me to take a few days off as well. A wicked heat wave brought along a slowdown in customer traffic, assuring me Ladies' Nightwear would not be overburdened with clientele on the few days I'd be away.

When we stepped off the train at the Kerryville depot, my joy surged at coming home, seeing familiar sights. The very air smelled pure and fresh after the smog of the city. Charlie was there to meet the train. He welcomed me with a big hug and said, "It's great to have you home, kid." Then he grasped my shoulders and held me at arm's length. He let out a low whistle. "Hey, sis. Don't you look swell. New duds?"

"You like?" I patted my Darling Yellow Hat and stepped back to include Dot in our little circle. "Dot, this is my brother, Charlie. Charlie, this is my roommate, Miss Dorothy Rodgers."

"Please call me Dot." She extended an elegant gloved hand toward Charlie. It amused me to see my outgoing, talkative brother turn tongue-tied, rendered mute by the full-wattage smile that Dot reserved for men she found appealing. From the top of her fashionable cloche to the tips of her stylish pumps, Dot looked like nothing

Kerryville had ever seen, outside of the Orpheum's silver screen. They gazed at each other like two forest creatures sniffing each other out.

"Charlie? Where's the car?" I said, breaking the spell.

"Oh. Uh, this way," Charlie mumbled, taking Dot's valise in his good hand and leaving me to hoist mine along behind them.

When we reached the house, Helen shouted, "They're here." She bounced off the porch and ran toward us across the lawn, braids flying.

"I thought you would never get here." She nearly knocked the wind out of me. "Oh, Marjie. You've bobbed your hair. Oh, it's precious. Turn around. Oh. It's exactly what I—" She stopped and stared, star-struck, at Dot, who tended to have that effect on people.

"Dot Rodgers, this is my sister, Helen."

"How do you do, Miss Rodgers," Helen murmured, eyes round. She bobbed a little curtsy, just as we'd been taught at Mercy Gilligan's School of Dance and Deportment. In addition to teaching us the fox trot and the waltz, Mercy Gilligan's grand mission in life was to prepare generations of Kerryville girls to be presented at court, should the need arise, even though the only courts we were ever likely to see involved a white ball and a net.

Dot smiled and extended her hand. "It's a pleasure to meet you, Helen."

Helen linked arms with Dot and me as we continued to the house. Frances greeted us as we entered the hall. Her eyes swept Dot from her Louise Brooks hair to her shiny satin pumps. But her eyes really popped when she caught sight of me. She gaped as if I'd grown a third eyeball.

"Marjorie, what have you done to your hair?"

"Golly, Frances," Helen said. "Doesn't she look like a movie star?"

"Don't say 'golly,' Helen. It's vulgar." Frances quickly recovered, since one of her ironclad rules is "Make No Scene with Company Present." Nevertheless, her disapproval of Dot's and my appearance was so apparent I could almost touch it.

But Dot didn't seem to take any notice. She simply smiled and said, "How do you do, Mrs. Corrigan. I've been so looking forward to meeting you."

"If you ladies will excuse me, I need to be getting back to the store," Charlie broke in. He grinned at Dot and then said to me, "Dinner's at seven, right, sis?"

"Right."

Earlier, over the telephone, Charlie had been frankly unenthusiastic about being pressed into service to escort my roommate to dinner. However, meeting her had clearly brought about a change of heart. I reckoned he'd be stopping in at the barber for a shave and haircut on his way back to the store.

After showing Dot around and getting her settled in my room, we gathered back on the front porch, grateful for the slightest breeze on the warm afternoon. Ever the meticulous hostess, Frances made polite conversation as she poured lemonade into tall glasses.

"Miss Rodgers, Marjorie tells us you're from Indiana."

"Yes, ma'am."

"What do you do in Chicago?"

Dot said, "I'm a singer," at the same instant that I said, "She sells hats." She looked at me quizzically as I elaborated. "She's an associate in the millinery department at Marshall Field & Company." Now was not the time to raise the topic of singing jazz in cabarets. Not with Frances Corrigan, president of the Women's Christian Temperance Union, Kerryville chapter.

Dot lifted an eyebrow, but went along. "Yes, that's right, Mrs. Corrigan. I sell hats."

"Oh, I see," Frances said. "I suppose you helped Marjorie find that . . . yellow hat."

She didn't say *ridiculous* yellow hat, but I mentally filled in the adjective, knowing that's what she meant.

"Selling hats sounds like such fun," said Helen, sprawled in a wicker rocker. "I bet you get to see all the latest styles before anyone else does."

"Oh, yes, Field's is the last word on what's fashionable," Dot said. "In fact, we currently have a jaunty red beret I think would look quite fetching on you."

"It would?" Helen's eyes shone.

"You have plenty of hats, don't you, Helen? Please sit up straight, dear," Frances said, effectively ending that line of conversation.

"Not a red one," Helen grumbled.

We all sat up a little straighter and sipped our lemonade.

"My word, it's hot today," I eventually said, for lack of any wittier observation. Murmurs of agreement all around. When in doubt, fall back on the weather.

Dot beamed at Frances. "When will I get to meet Mr. Corrigan?"

"Before you girls leave for dinner, I hope," Frances said, "if he gets home in time."

"Pop just brought in the niftiest red tartan plaid at the store," Helen piped up. "Marjorie, will you make me a skirt for school? With pleats?" She heaved a dreamy sigh. "It would look just darling with a red beret."

"Oh, for heaven's sake, Helen." Frances cut me a glance. "Your sister has no time to sew a skirt. She has more than enough wedding chores she's been neglecting."

Helen leaned back in the wicker chair and said sweetly, "That's all right. I don't really need it until the weather turns, anyway."

I reached over and patted her knee. "I'll look at the material. Plaid can be tricky, especially with pleats. But I'll see what I can do." I still felt terrible about breaking my promise to her about the Spring Fling and wanted to make it up to her, even if it meant sewing plaid with pleats.

"Applesauce," she scoffed. "Pleats won't be a problem for you. You can sew anything."

Dot glanced at me in surprise. "You sew, Marjie? I didn't know that."

I shrugged. "A little, I guess."

"Don't let her fool you, Miss Rodgers," Helen said. "She's the best seamstress in Kerryville. She's even going to sew her own wedding dress."

"If she ever gets around to it," Frances muttered under her breath.

Dot's face lit up. "Say, how are you with alterations? I have this one costume that needs a little something."

Frances lifted an eyebrow. "Costume? What sort of costume?"

"An evening gown. It's gorgeous, maroon satin with sequins, but it sags a bit in the bust, and I—"

"A sequined evening gown." Helen sighed. "It sounds heavenly. What kinds of places do you wear it?"

Before we could travel further down that conversational road, I interrupted. "Frances, did Richard happen to say what time he'd be picking us up?"

Her hand flew to her mouth. "Oh, I forgot. Richard telephoned earlier. He said he's tied up at the hospital and will meet you at the restaurant."

"I simply can't *wait* to meet the famous Richard." Dot nudged me and giggled.

"You must be so eager to see him after all these weeks," Frances said.

"Of course." I nodded vigorously.

"First thing tomorrow, Marjorie, we need to go over the guest list and make some firm decisions about the invitations. *Tempus fugit.*" Frances turned to Dot. "Honestly, I've never known a bride to take less interest in her own wedding preparations."

"That's not true," I said, a bit too loudly. "I've just been busy, that's all."

"Busy with a lot of nonsense, if you ask me," Frances sputtered, but then she apparently remembered Rule Number One and pressed her mouth into a thin line.

Dot tactfully cleared her throat. "I think I'll go and wash up before dinner, if I may."

"Of course, Miss Rodgers." Frances started to stand, but Dot motioned for her to sit.

"I'm sure I'll find my way. You and Marjorie sit and catch up."

Frances smiled stiffly. "Upstairs on the left. You'll find some nice clean towels on the edge of the sink."

Dot went into the house, trailed by Helen, whose offer of help no doubt coincided with her desire to explore Dot's cosmetics case. Frances banged empty glasses onto a tray.

"Honestly, Marjorie. Art classes," she sputtered. "Clerking in a department store. And now you come prancing home with short hair and rouge on your face, looking like a—like a—"

"Like what?" I challenged.

"People are already whispering about you, and you're just pouring gasoline on the fire. I'm sorry we ever let you go to that city."

"*Let* me? You practically pushed me out the door."

"To see the doctor, Marjorie. Not to transform yourself into the Vamp of Kerryville." Frances shook her head sadly. "I dread to think what your father will say."

"Frances, it's just a haircut," I said, struggling to remain calm. "It's just a little rouge."

"And you had such beautiful hair." She sounded on the verge of tears.

"It will grow back. It's just hair. For goodness' sake, no one has died."

But somewhere deep inside, I felt a little as if someone *had* died—the old, compliant, mousy Marjorie. She was gradually being ousted by a new, different Marjorie, who wore High Society Red and spoke her mind. Most of the time I barely recognized this new Marjorie. And to tell the truth, sometimes she scared me half to death.

CHAPTER TWENTY-FOUR

In spite of Frances's hand-wringing, in the end Richard said only, "I see you cut your hair." This, after giving me a rather perfunctory kiss in the vestibule of the Tick-Tock Café, where we met to have dinner with Dot and Charlie. It was hardly the type of greeting a girl would expect after being away for six weeks, but it was Richard's way of letting me know he was still angry that I wasn't ready to come home for good. Then again, he was never one to make grand displays of affection in a public place. Or anywhere else, for that matter.

I had to admit, he looked handsome. I could tell Dot thought so, too. His hair was freshly cut and he wore a new suit. I understood why any girl would feel lucky to marry him. Any girl except me. I needed to come clean, and soon, but I didn't know how.

As we were shown to our table, Dot looked around. "Oh, isn't this just adorable? I love small-town restaurants. So quaint."

Charlie looked deflated. "Kerryville must seem pretty unsophisticated compared to what you're used to in the big city."

Dot laughed. "Honey, Kerryville is the Big Apple compared to where I came from."

"Which is . . . ?"

"A tiny burg in Indiana. Nothing more than a crossroads, really." She peered at the menu, then glanced sideways at Charlie, showing off her coquettish dimples. "So, Charlie. You must bring girls here all the time. What do you recommend?"

He puffed up a little. "I rather like the steak, myself."

I flashed a bright smile at Richard, hoping to dislodge the coolness between us. "What do you feel like eating tonight, darling?"

"I'm not terribly hungry, sweetheart," he replied stiffly. We sounded like two actors reciting lines in a play. "I ate a big lunch at the hospital."

Dot perked up. "Oh, I can't wait to hear all about your work at the hospital, Dr. Brownlee," she gushed. "It must be terribly fascinating."

"I don't know about fascinating, but I find it interesting," he replied. I waited for him to say, "Please, call me Richard," or some other friendly comment, but he said nothing further, and scanned the menu as if choosing his entree was suddenly of the utmost importance.

In a corner of the room, a dance band warmed up their instruments. I recognized Mr. Tyler, the high school band director, on saxophone.

"Since when does the Tick-Tock Café have a dance band?"

"Since the Lilac Lodge over in Harley hired an accordionist," Charlie said. "They wanted to stay ahead of the competition. The band's not too bad, if you don't get too sick of 'Yes, We Have No Bananas.' They play that one at least three times a night. But they're building their repertoire," he added quickly, lest Dot think we were a town full of uncultured rubes.

"Oh, I love that song," she assured him.

Live music helped fill in the conversational lulls. But I needn't have worried about lulls with Dot around. When she failed to get any useful conversation out of Richard, she turned her long-lashed gaze back to Charlie.

"Tell me all about what *you* do, Charlie," she purred.

My brother sat up straighter. "Well, I work down at the dry goods store with Po—with my father. And with Marjorie here. Of course, I'm the one in charge." He gave a little grimace to signify the gravity of his weighty responsibilities.

Dot looked duly impressed. "You are?"

"Well, Pop is the big gun. He founded the place. But I'm really the one who keeps things humming down there, with Pop being out on the road so much."

"Oh, and I suppose I'm just there for decoration," I joked.

"Well, you haven't been of much use there lately, have you?"

Touché.

By the time the waiter had taken our order, Charlie had pretty much established himself in Dot's eyes as the dry goods king of the greater Middle West. Over dinner he described his efficient new system for inventory management in excruciating detail. Dot hung on his every word, as if the inner workings of the store held the universal secret to happiness. Meanwhile, Richard and I sat in near silence, like a couple of chaperones. I was dying to have it out with him, to make a clean break and clear the tension hanging so heavy between us, but that was impossible with so many people around.

I was prepared to head straight home after dessert and coffee, but Charlie had other ideas.

"Let's stay and listen to the band for a while. They sound pretty good, for Kerryville." Kept from dancing on account of his bum leg, he sat back and casually slung an arm over the banquette behind Dot.

Richard extended a hand to me. "Shall we?" We stepped out onto the dance floor. Being in his arms again felt nice—comforting, in a way. Why couldn't I feel this contented with him all the time? I leaned close to murmur in his ear.

"Hi."

"Hi." His response was cool.

What next? "I've missed you."

"Have you? Whose fault is that?"

Step-together-step. Change of topic.

"So? What do you think of her?"

"Of who?"

"Of *Dot*, silly." *Step-together-step.* "Don't you think she's lovely?"

"She looks sort of . . . fast. She sticks out in a crowd, and not necessarily in a good way."

I shrugged. "She does have a different attitude toward life than most people we know. You'd never know her father's a preacher."

Step-pivot. "He is? No, you'd never guess."

"But she's been a good friend to me."

"I don't think she's a good influence."

"Richard, you don't even know her. Can't you at least try to be nice?"

Step-step-glide-spin.

We danced past the table where Charlie and Dot were billing and cooing like a pair of doves. I flashed a brilliant aren't-we-having-fun smile, even though they weren't looking at me.

"When are you heading back?" Richard said.

"Sunday evening."

Step-together-step. "Don't go."

"Why not?"

"Marjorie, I don't want you to go back to Chicago. You know that. You should send Dot back by herself, and stay here in Kerryville where you belong." *Step-step-clunk.* "Ow."

I'd lost my footing and come down hard on his shiny black oxford.

"Sorry," I said. "But I'm going back." *Glide-glide-turn.*

His voice chilled even further. "Look at what the city is doing to you. You've already changed so much, I hardly recognize you."

"Is that what this is about?" I said. "I may *look* different, Richard, but I'm still the same girl on the inside." Even as I said the words, I knew they were false. "Anyway, I'm obligated to stay in Chicago until the end of the summer. I just . . ." Peter's sweet, crooked smile flashed unbidden through my mind. "I need some time."

"Time for *what*, Marjorie? For selling bathrobes and running around with . . . who knows who? Good grief, girl, you have obligations. Your place is here with your family. And with me."

Suddenly I found it hard to catch my breath. "Can we sit down, please? I'm getting winded."

We returned to the table.

"Richard," I started to say, then thought better of it. If I was going to call off our wedding, I needed to do it in private, not in the middle of the Tick-Tock Cafe with Charlie and Dot as witnesses. We didn't talk much more after that. There didn't seem to be anything left to say.

Later, when we were getting ready for bed, Dot said, "Is everything all right between you and Richard? You didn't seem like yourself tonight."

"Didn't I?" I tried to sound nonchalant, but suspected I was failing. I was tired of people telling me I didn't seem like myself. I didn't even seem like myself to *myself.*

Dot put her hand on my arm. "Doll, I hope I'm not speaking out
of turn, but you and Richard seem so . . ." She groped for words. "I
don't know. Mismatched, somehow." She slipped her arms through
the sleeves of her filmy peignoir. For once I was glad we were the sort
of household that got fully dressed before going down to breakfast.
"Where did you two meet, anyway?"

"At the hospital," I said. "Helen fell on the sidewalk while roll-
er skating and needed stitches in her lip. Richard was the attending
physician and, well, I suppose one thing led to another."

She kicked off her feathery mules and slipped under the covers.
"I don't think he approves of me."

"Who? Richard?"

"Who else?"

"Oh, take no notice of him. He's just miffed at me about—about
everything." Eager to focus on somebody else's love life instead
of mine, I said, "You and Charlie really seem to be hitting on all
cylinders."

"He's sweet."

"Looks like he feels the same about you."

In the mirror I swear I saw her blush, which startled me. Dot
wasn't the blushing type. But she quickly reverted to her usual insou-
ciant attitude. "Oh, he's just being gentlemanly toward his sister's
houseguest. Surely he has a nice little sweetheart hidden somewhere."

"You don't know Charlie," I said. "True, he used to be sort of a
big-man-on-campus type at our high school. But he hasn't shown
any real interest in any particular woman since he came back from
the war." *Since Catherine gave him the heave-ho*, I added silently.

Although it amused me that Charlie and Dot seemed to be hitting it off, I had to admit to a few misgivings. How suitable was it for
a man who needed to steer clear of alcohol to take up with a woman
who spent every weekend singing in a gin mill? A gin mill owned
by her boyfriend? A boyfriend with a reputation for being, as Kurt
Steuben had said, menacing?

But they weren't necessarily "taking up," I reminded myself sternly. They were simply two people enjoying each other's company on a
summer weekend, and there was certainly nothing wrong with that.

CHAPTER TWENTY-FIVE

"You'd better get to work on that wedding dress, Marjorie," Frances urged on Saturday morning. "September is fast approaching."

I touched the bolt of heavy white satin with listless fingers. I dreaded telling Frances about my change of heart concerning the wedding, and wouldn't dream of telling her before I'd told Richard himself. Although when I would work up the nerve to do that, I did not know.

"It's too hot today for sewing," I said. "I can't bear to handle heavy satin on a day like this. I'll just take the fabric back to the city with me."

"You were the one who chose satin," Frances reminded me. "I thought it was a mistake from the start. Well, maybe you can hire one of the seamstresses at your fancy department store to help you. They'd probably finish it faster on their modern machines, anyway."

After lunch Frances and I ran some errands, and then Frances wanted to go over the guest list. To keep Dot from being bored, Charlie offered to leave work early and take her to the movies. Helen begged to go with them, but he brushed her off. By dinnertime, they still hadn't returned.

After dinner I lingered on the porch with a glass of iced tea, trying to sort things out in my head. If I went ahead with the wedding, I'd be marrying a man I didn't love. I'd be living a lie, even if he promised me a safe, secure life as a doctor's wife. The man I thought I might love—or was mighty attracted to, anyway—was back in Chicago, selling neckties and moonshine. I couldn't see living out the rest of my life as a gangster's moll, either, or pining away for a man locked up in prison, if he ever got caught. What should I do?

A familiar honk sounded from the street. I looked up to see Richard's sedan pulling up to the curb. He stepped out, slammed the door, and walked up the sidewalk.

Now, Marjorie, do it now, said an inner voice that I took to be an answer to prayer. *Tell him you can't marry him.*

I stood up. *You don't waste time, do you Lord? You didn't even give me time to rehearse what to say. Oh, well. Here goes.*

Richard strode up the porch steps. "Hi, sweetheart." He leaned in to kiss me. I turned my head and his kiss landed on my cheek.

"Richard, we have to talk."

"I know." He pushed up his spectacles. "That's why I'm here."

I looked at him in amazement. "You know?"

He took both my hands in his and looked earnestly into my eyes. "Sure. You're still mad at me about last night."

"What?"

"I know I acted like a jerk last night, Marjorie, and I'm sorry." He gave a sheepish shrug. "I've just been feeling so lost without having you here."

"Richard, don't—"

"I worry all the time about your living on your own in the city, whether you're safe or whether you're lonely. And then you act as if you don't want to come home. You talk about your exciting job and your art class and your new friends . . . it's like you don't miss me and our life together at all."

I swallowed hard. "Richard—"

He dropped my hands and walked to the edge of the porch. "And then you finally come home, and I can't wait to see you, but you look so different. You even talk different."

"I do?"

He turned back and faced me. "So I came over to apologize. I'm really sorry, Marjorie. I have no excuse for acting the way I did last night. Will you forgive me?"

My heart started to crumble. This was going all wrong. "Oh, Richard. That's not what I wanted to talk to you about."

Just then Frances opened the screen door and poked her head out. "Richard! I thought I heard your voice. Won't you join us for some cake?"

Richard glanced at his wristwatch. "Thanks, Frances, but I'm on break from the hospital and have to get back. I just came by to tell Marjorie something."

"Well, then, you'll join us for dinner after church tomorrow, won't you?" Frances said.

"I'd love to." Frances went back inside, and Richard held out his arms for an embrace. I breathed in his familiar scent and an ache formed in the back of my throat.

"Thanks, Marjorie. I knew you'd understand."

"But—"

He bounded to his sedan and drove off, leaving me standing on the porch, my unspoken farewell speech dangling from my lips. I'd have to tell him tomorrow. No more dillydallying.

A short time later, Dot and Charlie returned from the movies, and the three of us sat out on the porch, drinking in the peaceful summer evening.

"How was the movie?" I ventured.

"It was all right," Charlie said, looking at Dot. "Not much of a plot."

"The lead resembled Peter Bachmann a little," Dot said. She turned to Charlie. "Did Marjorie ever tell you that there's a fellow at work who looks just like her old boyfriend, Jack?"

Charlie looked at me. "Yes, she did. As a matter of fact, she thought she was seeing a ghost."

I felt my face redden. "Don't remind me. I know for sure now that Peter is not Jack. I don't know what I was thinking."

"How do you know for sure?" Dot pressed. "What was the clue?"

"Doesn't matter," I said. "The important thing is, he's not Jack."

"Now aren't you glad I told you not to tell anyone else your suspicions?" Charlie said. "Anyone besides me would think you're a nutcase. Me, I already *know* that you are."

"Ha ha."

"He's right," said Dot. "Imagine if Richard had heard you talking about some other fellow."

"Speaking of, where is the dear doctor tonight?" Charlie said.

"On call at the hospital." I was dying to talk to them about what was going on, to spill the whole story about me and Richard and Peter and Chicago and everything. Dot already knew bits of it anyway . . . the bits I'd chosen to tell her. But now didn't seem like the time. I sensed an odd tension in the air between them.

Dot took a cigarette out of her bag but stopped short of lighting it. Later, after Charlie had gone inside to listen to the news with Pop, I found her out in the backyard, cigarette in hand.

"Everything all right?" I asked.

"Sure. Just enjoying this good clean country air."

"You'd enjoy it a lot more if you didn't cloud it up with that thing," I teased, waving away the smoke.

She gave me a smirk, but dropped the cigarette and ground it into the grass with the toe of her shoe. Then she leaned against the picnic table and looked up at the sky.

"There sure are a lot of stars out here," she said. "A lot more than you can see in the city."

"The city has just as many stars. You can just see them better here because it's so dark."

The night was clear and still. Crickets chirped, and lightning bugs flashed in the hedges.

"Did something happen at the movies? You've been quiet since you got back."

She crossed her arms. "It's nothing. Charlie said some things that made me think. That's all."

"I think he really likes you."

"Yeah. He's a nice kid."

"Kid?" I laughed. "He's older than you are."

"Well, I *feel* older. He's very different from Louie." She shook her head as if to clear it. "Your whole family's nice. Even your stepmother."

Heat rose in my chest. "No, she's not. She's been just horrible, making rude judgments about you based on the way you look."

Dot didn't take her eyes off the stars. "Maybe she's right."

"She's not."

She looked down at the grass. "I suppose I am a floozy, by the standards of Kerryville, anyway."

"Don't say that. We all admire you. We think you're independent and glamorous."

"Glamorous," she spat, and turned to face me. "I'm just doing what I have to do to survive, Marjorie. It's important to me that you know that."

"What do you mean? Working at Field's? Modeling? Singing at the club? Dating Louie?"

"Everything." She looked away again.

I tried to choose my words carefully. "Dot, I know you need to make a living, but you don't need to take off your clothes at an art school to do it," I said. "And you don't need to break the law by working in a speakeasy. And you *certainly* don't need to lower your standards and stay with a man who treats you as shabbily as Louie does."

"My standards," she said with a harsh laugh. "It's all I know."

"No, it's not," I argued. "You were raised in a Christian home. You *know* there's another way."

Dot snorted. "If that's the only other way, then no, thank you."

Lord, give me the right words to say. "Look, Dot, I know your home life wasn't perfect. But just because your father let you down doesn't mean God will do the same. He has something better for you—I know He does—if you'll just put your trust in Him. He's in control."

Dot gazed up at the night sky. "Is He? I wonder."

"Of course He is. God orchestrated the entire universe. He put every single one of those stars in place. If He did that, He most certainly cares about Dot Rodgers." *And Marjorie Corrigan,* I added silently.

She didn't reply. A moment later, a shadow filled the yellow square of light from the kitchen door and Helen's voice called out, "Hey, you two. Come inside and have some cake."

"You know nothing about it," Dot murmured to me in a chilly tone. But by the time we walked into the warm kitchen, her sparkling smile was back in place.

Charlie said, "What were you two doing out there?"

"Oh, nothing," she said lightly. "Just looking at the stars."

On the kitchen table Frances had set out a pot of coffee and a delicious caramel cake. Pop took his serving and headed for the living room, where he could read the evening newspaper in peace. The rest of us gathered around the table, laughing and joking. Helen peppered Dot with questions about the latest fashions. Charlie sat quietly, but I caught him sneaking frequent glances at Dot.

Finally Frances said, "After we clear the dishes, let's get back to work on the guest list, Marjorie. We need to finish it up so we can order the invitations."

"I'm so pooped, Frances," I protested. "Can't we do that tomorrow? Anyway, we have company."

"Oh, I don't mind," Dot said. "I'll even help. I'll read off the list of names and you can tell me stories about all the good citizens of Kerryville."

Helen giggled. "That will take all night."

"I'll go change, and then we can begin." Frances headed for the stairs. Dot and I cleared the table, then went to join Pop in the living room, leaving Helen and Charlie to wash the dishes. Pop puffed his pipe and scanned the evening paper. Idly Dot picked up one of the sections he'd discarded. "The *Daily News*?" she said. "You get the Chicago papers all the way out here?"

"It's the only way to get any real news," he muttered around his pipe stem. "The local paper is pretty worthless."

"Unless you're interested in who's vacationing in the Dells, and what kind of sandwiches were served at the ladies' bridge tournament," I added.

"Well, *I* think it all sounds charming," Dot said. "And I adore bridge. At least the Kerryville newspaper is not all about gangsters and shootings. Do you mind if I take a peek at the entertainment section?" Pop handed it to her. "I want to see if that new Pola Negri movie is—oh, my word." A look of dismay came over her face as she stared at the paper.

"What is it?" I craned my neck to peer over her shoulder.

Her eyes looked enormous against her pale skin. "It's—oh, it's nothing. Just something silly," she said, with a nervous giggle. She folded the paper and handed it back to Pop. "The movie must not be out yet. I think I'll go see about helping with those dishes."

As she left the room, Pop and I looked at each other. I opened the paper and scanned the page she'd been looking at, but saw nothing unusual, just a smattering of movie reviews and notices about upcoming concerts and other entertainment coming to town: a circus, a religious revival meeting, a flower show. Shrugging, I handed the page to Pop. Then I seized the moment.

"Say, Pop, while we've got a few minutes alone, I wanted to talk to you. I've made a decision."

"Hmm? A decision? About what?"

"About the wedding, and . . . everything."

With her usual impeccable timing, Frances chose that moment to come back downstairs.

"There you are, my dear." Pop set down his pipe. "I was just thinking, what do you say to a round of bridge to entertain our guest?"

"Oh, Melvin." Frances sounded exasperated. "You know Marjorie and I need to work on that guest list."

"We can work on it later," I said, desperate to avoid all things wedding-related.

Pop stood up. "Let's show Miss Rodgers a good time, Kerryville-style."

Frances set her mouth in a line, but she acquiesced. "Oh, you two. All right, I'll get the cards."

As she left the room, Pop turned to me. "What is it you were going to tell me?"

I smiled. "Nothing, Pop. It can wait." But deep in my heart, I knew it couldn't.

CHAPTER TWENTY-SIX

On Sunday I attended church with the family, letting Dot sleep in.

"Why, Marjorie Corrigan, just look at you," exclaimed Mrs. Varney, my former teacher. "I almost didn't recognize you. It's good to have you back."

She welcomed me with a hug. A few women gathered in little whispering clumps, but I chose to take no notice. If I'd earned a reputation as that crazy Corrigan girl who ran off to the city, then so be it.

In the stifling church, the back of my pale blue dotted Swiss clung damply to the pew. I fanned myself with the bulletin, as did so many others that the congregation looked like a flock of flapping seagulls preparing to take off.

Richard joined us in our pew. My heart twisted as I thought of what I was going to do him—to us—right after supper. No waffling. No second thoughts.

Then first thing in the morning, Dot and I would go back to Chicago, where I'd track down Peter and I'd say . . . why, I'd march right up to him and say . . .

Well, I could figure out that part later.

In place of the regular pastor, a guest speaker delivered the sermon. A church elder beamed as he introduced C. Herbert Lemmon, renowned lecturer on the Chautauqua circuit. Clearly the Lord had His eye fixed firmly on me—the scarlet woman ready to hand her heart over to a bootlegger—because C. Herbert's chosen topic was the evils of alcohol.

"After all is said that can be said upon the liquor traffic," the speaker boomed, "its influence is degrading upon the individual, the family, politics and business, and upon everything that you touch in this old world. For the time has long gone by when there is any ground for arguments as to its ill effects."

I glanced over at Frances, who was nodding her head in vigorous agreement. She would have lifted her hands in the air and shouted

"Hallelujah," if ours had been the sort of church where things like that were done.

"I go to a family and it is broken up, and I say, 'What caused this?' Drink!" the speaker continued. "I step up to a young man on the scaffold and say, 'What brought you here?' Drink! Whence all the misery and sorrow and corruption? Invariably it is drink."

I squirmed. The man I loved apparently made a tidy profit from liquor. Obviously the Lord—or at least C. Herbert Lemmon—was warning me that to have any further dealings with Peter would be a grave mistake. But would it really? Would it really help him if I turned my back on him?

As C. Herbert continued his blustery speech, my gaze drifted to the stained-glass window, etched with the words, "And the greatest of these is love."

Suddenly I knew. Rays of sunshine shone on me from a heavenly realm. Somewhere an angel chorus sang. Because all at once I saw the light.

Love was the answer. I needed to love Peter, not turn my back on him. I'd never be his sweetheart—not as long as he was a boot-legger—but maybe I could be his friend. But first, I had to make a clean break with Richard, and inform my family that no wedding would take place on September fifteenth, after all. I looked again at the comforting stained-glass face of Jesus and silently poured out my heart. I was going to need all the help I could get.

Like most men over the age of ten, Pop was utterly charmed by Dot. Over Sunday dinner he listened keenly to her stories of city life and the goings-on at Field's, even looking impressed when she told him about my merchandise displays and the praise they'd received from Mr. Simpson. Only Frances and Richard remained thin-lipped and silent on the topic of my Chicago experiences.

Pop helped himself to another serving of green beans. "I'm glad you're having such a good time in the city, Marjorie. But I hope you're not planning to make a lifelong career of working at Marshall Field."

"Probably not, but why do you say that?"

"I've always expected you'll take over Corrigan's one day. You and Charlie."

"You can count on me, Pop," Charlie said. "You know that."

"You can count on me, too." I said, shooting Charlie a look. He wasn't Pop's only loyal offspring. "But don't you think that the experience I'm picking up at Field's will be useful in the future when—"

Richard interrupted me. "Melvin," he said to my father, "I know you've been counting on Marjorie's help. But she and I have been discussing it, and we've determined she will be too busy running our home and social calendar to be of much use to you in the store."

I nearly choked on my iced tea. "What? When did we say that?"

"Right before you left for Chicago."

Pop set down his fork. "Is that true, Marjorie? You're quitting the store for good?"

My face grew hot. "No, I'm not."

"Of course she is," Frances interjected. "A new bride has her hands full just learning to run a household. Besides, Marjorie will be moving in a different social circle, and will have many obligations in the community that perhaps she isn't aware of yet."

"Hello, I'm right here. I can speak for myself." My glare traveled from her to Richard to my father, back to Richard. "What Richard means to say, Pop, is that we've *discussed* it, but we haven't *decided*. Not definitely."

Richard returned my glare. "Sweetheart, I thought you agreed running our home was the most important priority."

"Of course it's important, but so is Corrigan's. And so is Field's." *And so is Peter*, I added silently. How had I gotten myself into such a pickle?

Richard faced my father. "Of course, Melvin, I know she's a great asset to you, and I have no objection to her helping you out when the store is especially busy. At Christmastime, say."

"You have no *objection*?" I sputtered. "Believe me, Pop, if I move back to Kerryville—"

"If?" Helen exclaimed. "What do you mean, *if*?"

Suddenly everyone started talking at once.

"But, sweetheart, we *talked* about this—"

"Why wouldn't you be coming back?"

"You've gotta come back, sis. I can't run the store all by myself."

"Enough." Pop held up his hand, effectively declaring a cease-fire. "I'm sure Marjorie will do whatever it is she needs to do." A strained silence fell over the table while he dabbed his mouth with a napkin. "Please excuse us, Miss Rodgers," he continued. "Obviously we have a few family issues to sort out, but it's not worth upsetting our digestion over. Delicious dinner, Frances."

Obediently we picked up our forks. When the interminable meal had ended, I volunteered Richard and myself for clean-up duty and shooed everyone else out of the kitchen. When we were alone, I tied on an apron and filled the sink with hot soapy water as Richard cleared the table.

"What got into you back there?" I stage-whispered. "If anyone is going to tell Pop I'm quitting, it needs to be me. Nothing has been set in stone yet."

"Nothing? What about our marriage? Is that still open for discussion, too?"

"Now that you've brought it up. . ." I took a deep breath. "Listen, Richard. I think it's time we both admitted this simply isn't going to work out."

"Of course it isn't," he said firmly. My mouth fell open.

"What?" I shut off the tap.

"I'm glad you're finally seeing it too," he continued. "It's not working out, this Chicago business, with you living so far away. That's why you need to quit your art class and your job at Field's and move home."

I sighed. "That's not what I meant. I meant *us*. *We're* not working out."

"Us?"

"Yes."

His head flinched back slightly. "Why do you say that?"

"Well, for one thing, we don't have much in common." I absent-mindedly rubbed at a plate. Keeping my hands busy helped quell my nervousness. "You don't share any of my interests."

"What interests are those?"

The fact that he had to ask spoke volumes, but I pressed on.

"Like the movies, for instance. When is the last time you went to the movies with me?"

"I don't enjoy the movies," he said. "They bore me, and I think they're a waste of time. "

"I know that, but I like them. So instead of trying to talk me out of going to the Orpheum, maybe if you came with me once in a while, you might even surprise yourself by enjoying one or two. I don't mean all the time, just now and then. And if you don't want to come, then fine, but don't try to stop me from going."

I expected him to argue, but he didn't say anything, just continued calmly wiping the dishes. He didn't look angry or upset, either. To my amazement, he seemed to be thoughtfully listening to what I was saying.

"Is that what this is about?" he said. "Movies?"

"Not just movies. There's my art class. You know I love art, and you know I want to finish this class. But because you don't see the value in it, you keep pressuring me to drop out. You treat it as if it doesn't even matter, just because you don't happen to share my interest in art."

"I see."

"And my job at Field's." I warmed to my topic. "You don't respect what I do there at all. And then there's the children."

He blinked rapidly. "What children?"

"At the settlement house, Richard. Where I've been volunteering. We're doing a big concert in the park on the Fourth of July. Remember, I told you all about it."

"Yes, I suppose you did." He cleared his throat. Quietly he stacked the clean plates on the drain board. When he finally spoke, his voice was calm. "I think I see what you mean, Marjorie. You're saying I don't care about the things you care about. You think we're a mismatch."

"Oh, Richard," I said, tears stinging my eyes. "I don't *think* so. I *know* so."

Reaching into the dishwater, he lifted out both my hands and turned me to face him. "Sweetheart. I'm sorry I seem so uncaring. I get so caught up in my work at the hospital that I—I guess I forget you have a life to live, too."

What? No argument? No reasoned explanation about how he's right and I'm wrong?

"Oh, Richard. I know you work hard, and I'm sorry. I just—" *Say it, Marjorie. Say it.* "You see, I just—we're not—"

"You don't have to say anything, Marjorie," he said, looking deeply into my watery eyes. "I get it."

"You do?"

"Yes." His voice sounded thick. "You think we're too different to make a good marriage. You think we're making a big mistake."

I exhaled in a rush. "Oh, Richard. You *do* understand."

"Of course I do. I should have seen it coming." His shoulders slumped a little. "I guess I just didn't *want* to see it."

I scrutinized his face. *So that's it? No dramatic scenes? No recriminations or rash promises to make everything better?*

His expression, though otherwise unreadable, bore no trace of anger. Now that the issue seemed settled, my heart softened. Or was it breaking?

I struggled to speak. "Oh, Richard, I'm sorry."

"No need to be sorry, sweetheart. Much as it pains me to admit it, you're absolutely right."

"I am?"

I practically slumped with relief. He was being so reasonable about the whole thing. A true gentleman.

I worked up a wobbly smile. "Thank you, Richard. Thank you for understanding. I think in time we'll see this is the right decision, for both of us."

We stood there next to the sink, looking at each other.

"So that's it?" he said.

"So that's it." A strange blend of relief and sorrow washed over me. He would always hold a special place in my heart, and I prayed that one day, only fond memories would remain.

He released my hands and drew in a deep breath. "Well, that's settled. I guess we should tell your family."

"Do we have to tell them? Right now?"

All at once, I shuddered at the thought of Frances's reaction. I had hoped to break the news quietly at some other time, like, say, several years from now.

"No time like the present." He called out, "Frances! Melvin! Will you come into the kitchen, please?"

My parents appeared in the doorway. My heart appeared in my tonsils.

"Marjorie and I have been talking," he announced, "and we think it's best for all concerned if I move to Chicago."

What?

I wheeled around and gasped, "Move to Chicago! That's not—that's not—!" My brain couldn't get my mouth to form the words fast enough.

At the same time, my father was saying, "Well, this is a surprise," and Frances was screeching, "What are you talking about? And give up your job at the hospital?" and Helen was shouting from another room, "What's going on in there?"

Richard beamed, obviously pleased with himself. "Marjorie was telling me how much she loves her new life in the city, and that I haven't appreciated how much she enjoys it. She's right, I haven't. So I got to thinking, why not? I can get a position at one of the city hospitals, say, Northwestern or Michael Reese or—"

My stomach rolled. "No, Richard. That's not what I—"

He patted my shoulder. "Now, Marjorie. No arguments. You know this is what you want. I've made up my mind. Even better, I'm going to come to Chicago for the Fourth of July."

"What?"

"To prove to you I *do* care about the things you care about, I'm going to come to hear your little concert in the park. Afterward I can stick around for a day or two, maybe schedule some interviews. I can stay with my great-aunt. I owe her a visit anyway."

"Well, I certainly didn't see this coming," my father said. He wasn't the only one.

How could we have misunderstood each other so terribly? I collapsed onto a chair and struggled to catch my breath.

"Look at that," Pop said. "Now you've made her cry, she's so happy."

Frances sputtered, "But what about—"

"Come, Frances. Let's leave the lovebirds alone." He ushered her out of the kitchen.

Richard rested his hand on my shaking shoulder.

"You must always feel you can come to me with whatever's bothering you," he said. "I know I'm preoccupied sometimes, but I don't mean to be a boor. I do love you, you know."

I needed to set things straight, but I couldn't think clearly. I could barely think at all.

"Don't cry, Marjorie. It will be all right. You'll see. I know I've behaved foolishly, but you won't regret giving me another chance. This is just the beginning of a wonderful new life together." Calmly he walked over to the sink and picked up the dishrag.

All at once I understood. He hadn't heard me. He never heard me, not really. He was never *going* to hear me. He simply decided what he wanted to hear, and that's what he heard. And that was never going to change. My entire being sagged. Suddenly it all seemed so clear. What had I been waffling about?

"Gosh, Marjorie," he said, polishing a serving bowl. "I wish I'd realized sooner what was bothering you. It would have saved me a whole lot of worrying. I knew you were acting distant, but I didn't know why." He chuckled. "And here I was thinking that you might have met somebody else."

In a barely audible voice I said, "I have."

"Hm?"

I got to my feet and said, a little more loudly, "I have, Richard. I have met someone else. Or rather, gotten reacquainted."

He stared at me. His face reddened, then paled. "Who is it?"

"Myself. The woman I think God made me to be."

"This makes no sense," he muttered.

"It makes perfect sense. Hear me. I don't want you to move to Chicago. And I don't want to move back here." Gently I removed the ring from my left hand and laid it on the table between us.

In the end, I was surprised at just how easily it slipped off my finger.

CHAPTER TWENTY-SEVEN

That night I slept better than I had in weeks. Early in the morning, Charlie and Helen drove us to the train station.

"What do you mean, you're not staying for the Fourth of July?" Helen wailed as we waited on the platform. Dot and Charlie were holding their own low-pitched conversation in the shadow of the depot. "What about the fireworks? And the band concert in Kerryville Park? You're going to miss *everything*."

"They have fireworks in Chicago, too, silly," I said. "Good ones, I've heard. Besides, I'm helping out with a special program at the settlement house where I volunteer."

She tugged on the end of her braid. "I still don't get what that is."

"It's a place in the city where people can come and—well, get settled," I said. "People who are new to this country, who are poor and might need help learning the language, or being trained for jobs, or learning how to cook and sew—all sorts of things." I realized Helen had never seen an impoverished immigrant neighborhood in her life, just as I hadn't until recently." We'd led sheltered lives.

"Is that what you do there?" Helen said. "Teach cooking and sewing?"

"No, I'm just helping out with this one event, with costumes and things. It's important that I be there."

"Oh."

"But Marjorie and I have a surprise for you," Dot said as she joined us.

"What surprise?" Helen jutted her chin. She hadn't been too keen on most of my recent surprises.

Dot placed a gloved hand on Helen's arm. "We were thinking you could come to Chicago for the Fourth. We'll watch the fireworks together, and you can stay with us at our apartment. Would you like that?"

"Me, come to Chicago? Boy, would I ever!" Helen shouted over the noise of the train chugging into the station.

"Maybe we can even go shopping on State Street. We'll look for a new dress for school."

I glanced sharply at Dot. It was a fine thing to offer for "us" to take Helen shopping when she never seemed to have an extra nickel to her name. But I let it go.

"You can help me with the children," I added. "And see the settlement house for yourself."

Helen's eyes danced with excitement. "Gee, that'd be swell."

"I left money for a train ticket with Frances," I called back as we boarded. "I've already cleared it with her, so be sure to thank her politely. And it wouldn't hurt to be especially helpful around the house."

Waving to her and Charlie through the grimy window, I suddenly couldn't wait to get back to Chicago. Helen had given me a new idea to consider. Maybe the settlement house could use a sewing teacher. I'd mention the idea to Ruthie. But first we had to make it through the Fourth of July.

I also ached to see Peter. Things between us had ended on a sour note after the reception at the country club. I longed to make things right—and to set in motion my plan to convince him to stop his bootlegging activities. But on my first day back at work, I spotted him sitting at a corner table in the employee dining room, canoodling with that snooty redhead. Well, maybe not canoodling, exactly, but certainly speaking *tête-à-tête*. Why would he even consider giving up bootlegging for me when he had someone so stunning to cozy up to?

Dot followed my gaze. "Wipe that moony look off your face, doll."

"I'm not mooning."

"Yes, you are. Need I remind you, you brushed him off? What's he supposed to do now, become a monk?"

I sipped my chocolate milk without tasting it. "Who is she, exactly?"

"Stella Davenport. Fine Jewelry."

I sighed. "It figures."

"What?"

"Nothing."

But Stella—I dimly remembered from high-school Latin class—meant "star." Why couldn't she be named something ordinary, like Mary or Gladys?

At that moment, Stella laughed and touched Peter's arm. I forced myself to look away.

Stella, Stella, stole my fella.

Saving him from a life of crime was going to be harder than I thought.

Helen arrived on July third. Leaping off the train at Union Station, she nearly knocked the wind out of me, chattering ninety miles an hour. "Can I get my hair bobbed while I'm here? Yours looks so adorable. Frances says I'm not old enough, but she can't do anything about it if I come home with it already bobbed. And rouge."

"No rouge. How was the train ride? Were you nervous, riding all by yourself?"

"Fine. I'm not a baby, you know. Besides, Frances asked the conductor to look out for me. He was ever so nice. He said he'd never heard somebody talk quite as much as I do. Is that popcorn? Let's get some. I've never seen so many people. Oh! Will you look at that? Just look!"

The sight of the skyscrapers rendered her uncharacteristically speechless as we exited the station. I seized the moment to explain the evening's activities.

"First we'll drop off your things at home, but then we have to leave right away for the settlement house. Tomorrow's our big performance. Tonight's the dress rehearsal and there's so much to do. You can help us get everything ready to go."

Helen found her tongue. "Can I? It will be so much fun. I can't wait to meet everybody. Oh! Are we going to take the *Elevated*?"

Dot wasn't home when we stopped in at the apartment. I showed Helen where to stash her belongings and change clothes. I changed into my oldest skirt and blouse, as if suiting up for battle. I'd learned the hard way that the settlement house was no place for delicate clothes; best to wear a sturdy outfit that could be yanked on, spilled on, and wrapped into enthusiastic, sticky-fingered hugs without harm.

When I returned to the front room, Helen was peering at the photographs of Dot and her friends that lined the bookshelf.

"She's so photogenic," she sighed. "She looks just like Louise Brooks. I wish I could look like that."

"You look fine." I flung open the door. "Come on, we have to go."

At the settlement house, I made a point of introducing Helen to young Gabriella. As I expected, they hit it off right away, and both were a big help in corralling the younger children.

Pandemonium reigned. The children forgot the words to the songs, squirmed and scuffled, and attacked each other with swords fashioned from the small American flags they'd been given to carry.

"Please, children. Treat the Stars and Stripes with dignity," I pleaded, to no avail.

"You know the saying," said Annamarie as she helped me make last-minute adjustments to little colonial-style vests and pinafores. "Bad dress rehearsal, good performance."

"Who said that?" I said around a mouthful of pins.

"I don't know," she admitted, "but I hope he was a prophet."

"Hey, where's Joe? We could use the voice of masculine authority."

The expression in her dark eyes clouded. "There was some trouble in the neighborhood last night. Some sort of liquor raid. Three of the local boys got arrested. Joe's down at the station now, talking to the police on their behalf." She shook her head. "That's always the way it goes. The gang leaders make all the big money and let the naive young boys take the fall. Those gangsters get away with murder—literally."

When Joe eventually showed up, his presence had a miraculous effect on the children in the choir, especially the boys. With breathtaking speed they whipped into shape, even holding their flags with all the dignity of a Marine color-guard regiment, and at last Ruthie was able to successfully run the choir through its paces. Their clear, sweet harmonies made my heart swell. As I watched their fresh, innocent faces, I was sickened by the thought of even a single one of them being lured by thugs into a life of crime. But for too many of them, the bleak gates of reform school or prison, or worse, loomed large. I thanked God for people like Ruthie and Joe, who dedicated their lives to rewriting the endings of so many stories.

The Fourth of July dawned clear and hot. Dot won Helen's heart by pinning up her long hair in a convincing imitation of a bob, without cutting off any length. My sister was equally thrilled with both the sophisticated new look and the prospect of giving Frances apoplexy.

"Won't she be fooled!" Helen crowed. "I won't even tell her that it's not really bobbed until she's done screaming six ways to Sunday."

"That's not nice, Helen," I said. "Especially not after she let you spend the holiday in the city."

"I suppose you're right," she sighed. "It would be awfully funny, though, to see her pop a gasket."

"Not fun for Frances," I said, though imagining the appalled look on our stepmother's face did make me smile just a little.

Helen and I rode a streetcar to Grant Park. Dot promised to catch up with us later, after meeting with Louie over lunch.

"I think I'm going to call it off with Louie," she confided. "I don't know where things might go between me and Charlie. Maybe nowhere. But ever since I met him, I know a girl deserves something better in a fellow than what Louie has to offer."

I told her I thought she was making the right decision, and hoped I was right. Who was I to be handing out advice on romantic matters?

At Grant Park, white sailboats bobbed in the sapphire waves of Lake Michigan. Flags festooned the grassy park, from giant ones snapping in the stiff breeze overhead to small ones clutched in the hands of children wearing sailor suits and ruffled dresses. Vendors noisily hawked lemonade and hot dogs and cotton candy, while trombones and tubas played stirring tunes honoring God and country.

Helen and I located our gang at the designated meeting spot and did a thorough inspection of the children's costumes, retying a bow here and a shoelace there. The official festivities kicked off with the ringing of church bells throughout the city, followed by a parade on Michigan Boulevard.

I tried to relax and enjoy the fun, but between worrying about the concert and keeping an eye on the overexcited children, I was too distracted to feel very patriotic.

Chicago Mayor Thompson spoke next. Then the band returned to their chairs. That was the signal for our little group to take our place on stage.

The choir performed "You're a Grand Old Flag," looking sweet as could be in their tricorne hats and mob caps, waving their little flags. The audience applauded with enthusiasm. At the opening strains of "The Star-Spangled Banner," the entire crowd rose to their feet. My throat tightened with pride and gratitude as children with roots in the Old Country sang loudly of their new home, the land of the free and the home of the brave.

Afterward, once all the settlement children had been praised profusely and delivered to the safe hands of their families to enjoy the rest of the festivities, Ruthie, Helen, and I gulped down cups of iced lemonade.

"Bravo. Bravo," boomed a masculine voice behind us. "That was a mighty stirring performance."

We spun around to find two familiar faces grinning at us.

"Kurt Steuben!" Ruthie said, all smiles. "Peter Bachmann!"

Peter. My heart lurched at the sight of him. Quickly I glanced beyond him, but saw no sign of the redhead.

"We had to see what you two have been working on so feverishly," Kurt said, smiling at Ruthie. "Those little scamps did a great job."

"All thanks to Ruthie," I said. "She was the one who pulled this whole thing together."

"And you, too," Ruthie insisted. "I shudder to think what those costumes would have ended up looking like if you hadn't stepped in to rescue me."

"In any case, it was magnificent," Kurt said. "Made me want to stand up and salute Old Glory, right then and there. You've done yourselves proud. And now you must be starving. Would you ladies care to join us for a bite to eat?"

"That sounds divine, but I'm afraid I'll have to pass," Ruthie said. "I'm supposed to meet up with my cousins for a picnic. They're around here somewhere."

Kurt looked genuinely disappointed. Clearly he'd wanted to spend time with Ruthie, but I was better than nothing. "Marjorie? What do you say? Care to grab some Italian food with Pete and me on this most American of holidays?"

I glanced at Peter, who smiled but said nothing.

"That's kind of you," I said, "but my sister and I were just going to take a little rest in the shade." I had no intention of introducing Helen to a bootlegger—not before I'd managed to reform him.

"Speak for yourself," Helen said, eyes sparkling. "I'm not the least bit tired."

"Helen," I chided, but my conviction wavered. I didn't really feel like resting, either, and after all, it had been awfully sweet of them to come to our concert. Surely even a bootlegger wouldn't try to do anything unsuitably lawless in the middle of Grant Park on the Fourth of July.

"Please, Marjorie," Peter said quietly. "I'd like you to come."

He would? Maybe this would be our chance to clear the air. "All right. We'll be happy to join you for dinner." I introduced my sister to the two men. By her glowing face I could tell she found Kurt to be, in the lingo of her social set, a "real he-man."

The gentlemen escorted us to an Italian restaurant just a few blocks' walk from the park, so we could easily return to watch the fireworks display.

The restaurant was practically empty, a refreshing oasis away from the noisy crowds. Over plates heaped with spaghetti, Peter visibly relaxed. We chatted and laughed while Helen regaled us with uncanny imitations of silent-screen stars. I'd always known she was a bit of a ham, but now I realized she had a real gift for entertaining. Peter and Kurt teased and kidded with her just the way Charlie did at home, and she thrived on being the center of attention. Grateful for the amusing distraction she provided, I shoved all thoughts of bootlegging and leggy redheads to the back of my mind.

In the ladies' room she startled me by saying, "Don't you think Mr. Bachmann looks an awful lot like Jack?"

I gaped in surprise. "Jack Lund? Charlie's old friend?"

She nodded. I shrugged, held my voice steady. "Maybe a little bit. But I wouldn't mistake them for twins or anything." I prayed she'd never learn of my outrageous behavior at the train station that first day.

"Really?" she said, eyes wide. "I think they look so much alike, it's almost spooky."

"I'm surprised you even remember Jack. You were such a little thing when he used to come by the house."

"I've seen that picture of him that you keep in your sewing basket." Before I could question what she was doing in my sewing basket, she added, "Of course, he isn't *really* Jack, although he is rather good-looking. But I think Kurt is much better looking, don't you?"

"You mean Mr. Steuben."

"He told me to call him Kurt."

"Did he? Well, never mind what *Kurt* looks like. He's too old for you."

"I know that, silly. My goodness, he's practically as old as *you* are. But it's still fun to *pretend* like I'm older, just for today."

I patted some powder on my prehistoric nose. "As long as it's just pretending."

Back at the table we finished up our spumoni ice cream, then strolled back to the park. We found a spot near the lakeshore to spread a blanket which Kurt had thoughtfully provided. Helen spotted an excursion boat offering rides up and down the shoreline. "Come on, Marjie. Let's go for a ride," she begged.

"Not me," I said, patting my middle. "After that enormous dinner, I don't think a boat ride on the lake is such a good idea."

"Aw. I think it would be the cat's whiskers."

"Come on, kid, I'll take you," Kurt offered. "I feel like stretching my legs anyway."

Helen's face lit up. "You will?"

Kurt glanced at me. "Do you mind?"

"No, I guess not," I said. "Just make sure to be back in time for the fireworks."

After they'd gone, Peter and I sat quietly for a while. He seemed tense, moody, constantly scanning the crowd as if looking for someone.

"Are you all right?" I said.

"Too many people here." His voice sounded strained. "I don't much care for crowds."

"I'm glad you and Kurt came."

"It was his idea. I'm just along for the ride."

"Oh." His lack of enthusiasm stung a little. "I'm sure Kurt appreciates it. It sounded like he wanted to see more of Ruthie today."

Peter shrugged. "Just as well she had other plans. He thinks she's cute, but she's not his type."

"What is his type?"

He shrugged again. "Not her. Not someone who goes to church and does charity work. He likes a challenge, that's all, and Ruthie's a challenge. If she ever agrees to go out with him, *boom*, he'll be on to the next."

"I don't think she will," I said. "The girls talk about how slick he is."

He said, "To be honest, Marjorie, I didn't come here to keep Kurt company. I've been wanting to talk to you."

A sudden breeze swept up off the darkening lake, making me shiver. "We *are* talking."

"That's not what I meant." He reached for his jacket and settled it around my shoulders. "I think you might have the wrong idea about me."

"How so?" I said, pulling the jacket around me.

"You've been avoiding me."

"I've just been busy. You know how it is. And then I took Dot on a visit to Kerryville."

"Ah, yes," he said, resting back on his elbows. "Getting ready for the wedding, I suppose."

I plucked at the cuff of his jacket. "There isn't going to be a wedding, after all."

He sat up. "What? You mean—" The way his eyes lit up made my heart leap.

"We've called off the engagement."

"Oh. I'm sorry," he said, not sounding the least bit sorry.

I shrugged. "Nothing to be sorry about. It was for the best."

Neither of us said anything for a long time. Then he spoke, not looking at me, his gaze directed out over the water.

"I feel as if something went wrong between us the night of the reception at the South Shore. I know you said you weren't feeling well, but it seemed like more than that—like it had something to do with me, something I did or said. I've replayed that evening over and over in my mind and can't think of what might have gone wrong."

I drew a deep breath. "Look, Peter, I'll be honest. It isn't that I don't like you. I do. I like you very much. But I know you—you drink liquor."

He frowned and pulled at a clump of grass. "Why would you think that? Have you seen me take so much as a sip of liquor?"

"No," I admitted, "but at the party with the Selfridge people I overheard you ask the waiter where to find some. That's your own business, of course, but I've vowed never to date a man who drinks alcohol." *Not to mention a man who makes money off it*, I added silently. I didn't mention that part, though, as the bootlegging bit was still just a rumor.

He lifted his eyebrows. "You vowed never to date—? But we're not dating. We're just friends. Friends and colleagues. Right?"

"Right. Of course," I said, with a desperate hope that the shadows hid how deeply I was blushing. Clearly his heart already belonged to that stuck-up redhead in Fine Jewelry. How could I forget?

"I mean, you're engaged. You *were* engaged. Back then, I mean. When we saw each other at the party." It was unlike him to stumble over his words. Usually he was so poised.

"Yes, of course." Me and my big mouth. "All I meant was, I don't feel comfortable around people who drink. My brother developed a real problem with it after the war, and I saw firsthand how it can ruin lives. I mean, I suspect Dot may take a sip or two of demon rum when she's at the club, but she avoids it around me. Mostly," I added, remembering the perpetual pitcher of "ginger lemonade" sitting in our icebox.

"I see." He was silent for a moment. Then he said, "I wish you'd said something earlier. About the drinking."

"I don't know why I didn't," I admitted. "I guess I was disappointed, that's all. I didn't take you for that kind of man."

"What kind of man?"

"Someone who . . . skirts the law."

"I see. Well, I admire a woman who stands by the strength of her convictions."

"Thank you," I said, wishing fervently that convictions didn't always come at such a high price.

We sat in silence for a while, watching the lake turn a shimmering purple and gold. Our shadows lengthened as the sun set behind us. Finally he said, "Marjorie, may I ask you something rather personal?"

"Of course."

But the question never came, because just then Helen and Kurt returned from their ride on the excursion boat, accompanied by Dot, who'd managed to spot them in the crowd. Helen flopped down beside me.

"Have fun?" I said.

"It was cold," was all she said. I suspected she was regretting taking a boat ride after such a big meal, as I'd warned. I opened my arms to her and together we snuggled under Peter's jacket.

After sundown we were treated to a spectacular illumination of naval vessels anchored in the harbor. Then fireworks exploded across an appropriately star-spangled sky, reflected in the black waves below. My heart pounded from the nearness of Peter as much as from the thundering skyrockets. But when I glanced over at him, hoping to see my feelings reflected in his eyes, his face was tight, his expression tense. After the first few starbursts, he stood abruptly.

"I'm sorry. I have to leave." His breath came hard, as if he were angry.

"But why? Peter—Wait, your jacket."

"Keep it," he said gruffly. And he was gone.

Afterward Kurt drove us home in his jalopy. He, too, seemed mystified about where Peter had gone so suddenly. Helen remained uncharacteristically quiet during the drive, so after settling her onto the sofa, I gave her some tea and bicarbonate of soda to settle her tummy. Then I climbed into my own bed and lay awake, staring at the ceiling. Why had Peter left so abruptly, apparently in anger? Had I said something wrong? Driven him away with my accusations? He hadn't admitted to drinking, but he didn't deny it, either. How was I going to convince him to give it up forever, if I didn't even know for sure that he was doing it?

Why did he leave? Where did he go?

And what "personal" question had he been about to ask me?

Over the next few days Helen regained her usual pep. She perked up considerably when Dot and I took her on the promised shopping trip, including, of course, a visit to the venerable Marshall Field & Company.

"Is Kurt Steuben here today?" she asked in a carefully modulated voice as we toured the elegant main floor.

"I don't think so," I said. "This is normally his day off."

"Oh." She visibly relaxed and began *ooh*ing and *aah*ing over the store's palatial splendor. Apparently she'd gotten over her brief infatuation with the handsome security guard and possibly felt embarrassed. Or maybe she was mortified that she'd gotten seasick in his presence. A teasing remark sat on the tip of my tongue, but I thought the better of it.

CHAPTER TWENTY-EIGHT

When Dot and I put Helen on the train for home on Saturday morning, with a new red plaid skirt and matching beret in her suitcase, she seemed back to her old chipper self. Even though the ensemble had severely depleted my budget, it was worth every penny to atone for letting her down at Spring Fling. From the glow on her face as she waved good-bye, I knew I'd succeeded.

Mrs. Cross was back at work, her injured ankle nearly completely healed. The enforced rest must have renewed her energy, because she surveyed Ladies' Nightwear with a gimlet eye and declared a state of emergency. "Goodness, ladies, what has happened here? It's time for an update." And the next thing I knew, we were rearranging Ladies' Nightwear "from stem to stern," to use one of her favorite phrases.

"Would you mind staying late this evening, Miss Corrigan?" she asked. "I could use your keen design eye. And as we work, you must tell me all about the Selfridge's reception."

I readily agreed. First, I was amazed that she *asked* me about staying late instead of *telling* me, and second, that she acknowledged I might have the merest smidge of talent. Had I passed some sort of unspoken test in her eyes?

Together with the Misses Bryant, O'Brien, and Ryan, we worked late into the evening, moving racks of gowns and stacks of folded garments from one end of the department to the other to make a more pleasing arrangement.

Sometime around ten o'clock, Mrs. Cross dispatched me to check on a delivery of lace peignoirs that was supposed to have arrived earlier that day.

"Check down at the loading dock," she instructed. "Sometimes shipments linger down there in limbo."

I had to take the stairs since the elevator was no longer running at that time of night. When I reached the ground floor, something seemed odd. There were a great many men loading cartons onto

Marshall Field & Company delivery trucks. From where I stood, it looked like all of the cartons had the words "Old Jamaica Hair Tonic" printed on them. Who would have ordered such a massive quantity of hair tonic?

"Hey, you! Where do you think you're going?" shouted a stern male voice behind me. I whipped around to see Kurt Steuben, the security guard, stomping up to me. He looked startled to see me. "Marjorie? What in blazes are you doing down here this time of night?"

I explained my mission to locate the missing shipment of peignoirs. With experience, I was becoming more matter-of-fact about discussing things like peignoirs with gentlemen, without blushing. Kurt grimaced and firmly put his hands on my shoulders to steer me around toward the stairs. "Say, you'd better scram, Marjorie. Nobody's on duty in receiving at this hour. Try again on Monday."

"But Mrs. Cross said the carton might have been left on the—"

"Mrs. Cross is all wet," he snapped. Then, more calmly, "Besides, if something got left out on the dock that shouldn't be there, we would have noticed it by now."

I glanced at the loading dock. "Do they always load the trucks so late at night?"

"All the time," he shot back. "We've got a huge shipment going out first thing in the morning. Now beat it."

"But tomorrow is Sunday."

"It's for the . . . the big charity drive. You know. Gotta get all this stuff out to the nursing homes and whatnot, get it outta the way outside of regular working hours."

"Hair tonic? For nursing homes?" I said, but he was already hurrying back toward the trucks. I pondered that as I trudged back upstairs. Goodness, how much hair tonic did old folks need? How many of them even had hair anymore?

When I arrived back at Ladies' Nightwear, panting and sweating from the climb, someone had sent out for sandwiches and coffee from an all-night deli. We ate a quick meal and then worked through our tiredness, excited about the improvements we were making to the department. I reported on the missing peignoirs, and we shared a chuckle over the old people's hair tonic.

One by one, the other clerks went home, until the only ones left were Mrs. Cross and me. Sometime after midnight, although she hadn't complained, I noticed she looked fatigued and remembered she was still recovering from her injury. I suggested a rest break.

We settled into chairs near the fitting room, the ones normally occupied by fidgety husbands. Mrs. Cross glanced around the department and nodded her head. "I think even Mr. Simpson will be pleased with this new arrangement."

"Has he complained?"

"Not in so many words," she said, "but we must show him we aren't stuck in our ways. New and different—that's what he wants to see, especially after meeting with the Selfridge's people."

So this upheaval was all for Mr. Simpson's benefit. We sat quietly for a few minutes. Then she said, "It's time for me to retire."

I nodded. "Yes, a good night's sleep will do us both a world of good."

She shook her head. "No, I mean *retire*. For good."

With this revelation, my tired brain snapped back into gear. "Retire? You?" I blinked. "I don't believe it."

"It's true," she sighed. "I've been working at Field's for a long, long time. Longer than most of you youngsters have been alive."

I thought she was going to launch into one of her "in my day" reminiscences. But she startled me by saying, "I know you younger women think I'm a dinosaur."

I gulped. What had she heard? I began to protest, but she silenced me.

"Now, don't patronize me, Miss Corrigan. I still have my eyes and ears. I see the looks you girls exchange. I overhear your whispered remarks. 'Old Rugged,' indeed." Her lips pressed into a thin line.

A hot wave of shame washed over me as I remembered all the times I'd complained about her behind her back. "Oh, Mrs. Cross. Please forgive me. We were just—why, that was just silly nonsense. Ladies' Nightwear simply wouldn't be the same without you. Everyone knows that."

"Hmm." She sat silent for a while, staring off into space.

Thinking our conversation had drawn to a close, I started to stand up. "Well, I guess I'll start picking up the—"

"I didn't always work in Ladies' Nightwear, you know," she said suddenly. I sat back down. "When I first started working here, straight out of high school, I was assigned to the candy counter. I was hired as temporary help, just for the Christmas season."

"Really?" My eyes widened as I struggled to picture the aging woman before me as a young slip of a girl, parceling out licorice and peanut brittle.

She nodded. "At the end of the Christmas season, Mr. Field told me I was doing a fine job, and asked me to stay on. Even after I married Mr. Cross, may he rest in peace, I kept my job. Field's was a marvelous place to work."

I briefly wondered if Mr. Cross had known about her alleged feelings for Mr. Selfridge, then firmly decided that was none of my business.

"That's interesting," I said, and I meant it, too. "Did you enjoy working in Candy?"

"Oh, yes." She looked surprisingly pretty when she smiled. I wished she'd do it more often. "Old Mr. Field had a real sweet tooth. He'd stop by the candy counter when I was the only one there, and ask me to give him a sample of something, of licorice or jelly beans or coconut clusters—usually something we were starting to run low on. With a little wink, he'd declare them to be stale and instruct me to take the remaining stock home to my family, free of charge. 'Otherwise they'll just have to go in the trash,' he'd say. Then he'd tell me not to tell anyone else. And I never did." She smiled at me. "Until now. But I guess he wouldn't mind my coming clean, after all these years."

I chuckled. "Sounds like he was a real character."

"Oh, he was. To some of us, he was like a kindly uncle." Her eyes took on that dreamy look again. "I remember his funeral like it was yesterday." She got up from her chair, walked over to a cabinet where we kept supplies. She reached into a drawer and pulled out a bit of ribbon, once a deep lavender color, now faded to a mottled pink, with a portrait of Mr. Marshall Field encircled by a medallion. "They gave these out to all the employees," she said. "When we received news of his death, the store closed for several days. On the day of his funeral, people lined the streets to watch the procession of carriages to Graceland Cemetery. It was wintertime, and pouring down sleet, but nobody seemed to care. They had a special memorial service just for employees, at the Auditorium Theater. The place was packed. Oh, how we missed him."

She carefully set the ribbon back in the drawer. "After Mr. Field died, Mr. Shedd took over, and now we have Mr. Simpson," Her voice took on a thin layer of frost. "With him, everything must be new, new, new. He has no use for the old ways." She glanced around the rearranged department one more time, as if remembering where she was. "I think we can call it a night, Miss Corrigan," she said. "We can finish up on Monday."

We walked down the many flights of stairs together, which triggered my memory of the unusual hair tonic shipment.

"Don't you think it's odd, shipping hair tonic in the middle of the night to old people's homes?"

She didn't seem alarmed. "Well, if they're shipping it, then surely the people must need it. Field's has always been generous with what people need. And they're probably working in the middle of the night for the same reason we are—because they simply couldn't get everything done during the day."

When we reached the street, she asked me where I lived and suggested we share a taxi since she was headed in the same direction. She signaled for a cab, gazed out the window as we rode in silence for several blocks. Then she said, "I know you think I'm tough on you, Marjorie."

Leather is less tough than you, I thought, though I mumbled out of politeness, "You're not *that* tough."

She brushed my comment aside. "The reason I hold you to a high standard, Marjorie, is that I can see what you're capable of. You're bright, you're creative, and you have a pleasing way with the customers. The other clerks do a good-enough job, but they will always be clerks. If you stay at Field's, pay your dues, and put in your time, I predict your career will flourish."

The taxi stopped in front of her building and we said our goodbyes. I rode the remaining few blocks to Dot's place with my face at the open window, breathing in the cool night air and marveling at what Mrs. Cross had said.

It was the first time she'd ever called me Marjorie.

CHAPTER TWENTY-NINE

The next morning I dragged myself to church with Ruthie, but all tiredness vanished when I spotted a familiar head several rows ahead of us.

"What's he doing here?" I whispered to Ruthie.

"Who?"

"Peter Bachmann." I pointed discreetly.

"I've seen him here before. Not every week, but fairly often. Why?"

"No reason."

After the service I pushed my way up the aisle like salmon swimming upstream.

"Peter, I didn't expect to see you here. What are you doing?"

He raised an eyebrow. "What I do every Sunday. Attending church."

"I can see that. What I mean is, this is the first time I've seen you here." I didn't mean to sound shocked, but—a churchgoing bootlegger? This man grew more intriguing all the time.

"It's a big church," was all he said.

"I was worried about you when you vanished the other night. We all were. Where did you go?"

His eyes scanned the departing congregation. "Can you come out for a drive?"

"Now? I suppose so."

I said good-bye to Ruthie, not knowing whether to feel apprehensive or delighted at this unexpected invitation. I leaned toward the latter.

Peter and I walked down the block and slid into his shiny roadster. It wasn't the sort of automobile one would expect a shirt salesman to drive. But then, I supposed he hadn't paid for it out of his Marshall Field's paycheck.

"Let's grab a bite to eat. Someplace where we can talk."

He drove to a restaurant near Montrose Harbor that boasted a terrace overlooking the water. The waiter showed us to a table and soon returned with our drinks. We sat for a while and people-watched. Considering Peter had requested this outing, he seemed awfully tongue-tied. Some prompting was in order.

"So? Are you going to tell me why you left so abruptly the other night?"

"I couldn't take it."

"Take what?"

"Fireworks. Booming. Explosions." He set his glass on the table, and I could see his hands were trembling. "Ever since the war, I can't watch fireworks. Crazy, huh?"

"No. Not crazy at all." I could feel waves of loneliness shimmer off him like heat. "Where did you serve?"

"France."

The same area where Jack and Charlie had been stationed. My heart melted at the terrible things he must have seen. Everything in me yearned to soothe those memories away, but I knew I couldn't. All I could do was reach over the table and touch his hand.

"I'm sorry."

He inhaled. "I don't know. It's like there's something wrong with my head. I know fireworks are just pretend, just for show, but—" He ran a hand through his hair and gazed through the window at the lake. "It's been ten years. You think I'd be over it by now."

I leaned toward him and put my hand on his forearm. "I understand. Truly I do. My brother, Charlie, had some problems when he came back. Nightmares and things."

"And then there was your boyfriend who was killed."

I sat back. "Yes."

"I was thinking about him the other day."

"Jack? Why?"

He cleared his throat. "Well, I was just curious. Remember the first day we met, in the train station? When you said you thought you saw a ghost?"

I cringed. "How could I forget? It was not one of my finer moments."

"Do you still think I look like him?"

I chuckled. "Yes, you surely do. Even Helen thinks so."

Peter smiled and adjusted his necktie. "So, he was a handsome devil, eh?"

Ice cubes clinked as I stirred the straw in my glass. "Yes, if you must know. But of course, the resemblance is purely superficial. Turns out you're quite different, under the surface."

"How so?"

"Well, for one thing, Jack didn't drink liquor."

"That you know of."

I lifted my chin. "I knew him. He didn't."

Peter's voice grew quiet. "Did you love him very much?"

"Yes. Very much." The words seemed to dance between us on the breezy air. "I was young, not even allowed to go steady with any one boy, but we still managed to spend a lot of time together. As my brother's best friend, he was always at our house, and my parents permitted group outings, hayrides and the like. One day I looked at him and knew he was the one."

"But it sounds like you didn't spend much time alone together."

I shrugged. "True. But we managed here and there, sneaking into the warming hut at skating parties, or lagging behind the others on hikes."

He lifted an eyebrow. "You had to sneak around? That doesn't sound like you."

"Well, you see, my stepmother didn't think . . ." My voice trailed off. He didn't need to hear all the gory details. "Anyway, we had an understanding. By the time he got out of the service, I'd be eighteen, and we'd be married."

"And you loved him? More than you loved that Richard fellow?"

I hesitated. "That was different. For one thing, I was older when I met Richard, and . . ." My voice grew thick. "It's not a fair comparison. You see, Jack—Jack was my first love. And I suppose I've never quite gotten over him. It's as if, when he died, a piece of me died, too. So I guess I just didn't have enough love left to offer Richard."

A shadow of compassion passed over Peter's face. His hand covered mine. "I'm sorry, Marjorie," he said in a hoarse voice. "Truly I am."

I swallowed hard. "So you see, when I saw you in the train station that day—well—"

He pressed my hand in his, warm and strong. I wished he'd never let go.

"Wherever Jack is, I'm sure he knows that you loved him."

I forced a laugh, tried to lighten the mood. "I doubt that men sit around in heaven thinking about old girlfriends."

"He knows, Marjorie," Peter insisted. "He wants you to live a happy life, whether it's with Richard or—or somebody else."

I tried to read his expression. Did he mean—? But my reverie was broken with a *thunk*. Because at that moment, as he turned to signal the waiter, his jacket flapped opened a bit, just enough for me to catch the unmistakable glint of gunmetal strapped to his side.

He was armed. Armed and dangerous, as they said on those detective radio shows.

A soggy disappointment washed over me. Of course he was armed. What did I expect of a gangster? My appetite evaporated. What was I doing here? I pushed back my chair. "I think we should leave now. All this talking is giving me a headache."

He looked mystified. "But what about lunch?"

"I'm sorry. I really need to get back."

We left the restaurant and climbed into the roadster, but he didn't start the engine. "Marjorie," he said, slinging his arm around the back of the seat. "I wish I could—look, you know I care about you. But there are things about me that are hard to explain. I'm not free to be as open with you as I'd like to be."

"Please don't." As long as he didn't tell me, then I could pretend I didn't know.

I kept my gaze fixed straight ahead, knowing that if I looked into those eyes, I'd be a goner.

He lapsed into a tense silence. Then he switched on the ignition and pulled away from the curb. On the quiet ride home, I longed to beg him to pull over, to fling my arms around his neck and tell him it didn't matter what sorts of underworld activities he engaged in, I would follow him anywhere. This, I realized, was how good girls got into deep trouble with bad boys. Because they were so darned attractive.

When we reached the apartment, he killed the engine. Looking straight ahead through the windshield instead of at me, he said, "Marjorie, you must know I have feelings for you. If I'm not mistaken, you have feelings for me, too. But to get mixed up with a fellow like me—well, you don't know what you'd be getting into. There are a hundred fellows out there who'd be better for you than me."

I could hear the struggle in his voice. My defenses melted. I took his chin in my hand and gently turned his face toward me. Made him look me in the eye.

"I don't want a hundred fellows. Just one. The one who makes me happy." My throat felt thick.

Before I knew what was happening, he took me in his arms and held me against him. He bent his face to mine. Our noses bumped, but our lips met tenderly, clumsily, then hungrily. I hadn't had a kiss like that since . . . well, since I was seventeen years old.

When we came up for air, I said weakly, "I-I should go in. It's the middle of the day. The neighbors—"

His eyes searched mine. "Forget the neighbors."

I could feel his breath on my cheek. All sensible thought swirled out of my mind. The very nearness of him made it impossible to think clearly. I couldn't bear to say good-bye, to watch him drive out of my life and back into the arms of Stella Davenport. The heat of his kisses laced around my heart. I was playing with fire and I knew it.

I pulled away slightly to catch my breath. "Would . . . would you like to come in for a minute? Dot should be awake by now, and there's some fresh lemonade in the icebox. And I can return your jacket—the one you loaned me the other night at the lakefront."

A smile played at the corners of his mouth. "You are one hard girl to figure out. One minute you act like you never want to see me again, then the next minute . . ." He gently twirled a lock of my hair in his fingers. "Well, under the circumstances, I'd be crazy not to accept."

Arm in arm, we climbed through the insufferably hot stairwell. I made a mental note to excuse myself and powder my nose the minute we got upstairs, since I was no doubt a sweaty mess. That would give us both a moment to cool off, to get our heads on straight. And then we'd calmly sit on the sofa, and sip lemonade, and talk this whole business out like two rational adults.

I turned the key in the lock and pushed open the door.

"There you are," Dot said in an overly bright voice. Her wide smile looked stiff as she glanced toward the kitchen. "Where have you been? You'll never guess who's here."

I followed her gaze. There, in the kitchen doorway, stood Richard.

CHAPTER THIRTY

"Richard! What are you doing here?"

"Hello, Marjorie. I'm happy to see you, too." Richard stepped forward. "So this must be my competition." Behind his spectacles, his eyes glittered. The sight was most unsettling; Richard wasn't the glittering type. He extended a stiff handshake to Peter, giving him the once-over. "Richard Brownlee. Miss Corrigan's fiancé."

"Former fiancé," I corrected.

Peter shook Richard's hand as calmly as if he'd fully expected to find him standing in my front room. "Peter Bachmann. Marj—er, Miss Corrigan and I work together."

"Ah, yes, at the department store." In Richard's mouth the term "department store" sounded vaguely disreputable.

"Richard, why are you here?" I said. "Is everything all right in Kerryville?"

He wheeled on me. "No, everything is not all right in Kerryville. If everything were all right in Kerryville, would I be here now? Everyone's talking about how you left me high and dry. Cavendish even pulled me aside to say he hoped my personal troubles wouldn't affect my work." He threw up his hands in frustration. "I can't have personal troubles. I'm Dr. Richard Brownlee!"

His speech sounded oddly disjointed, like the words were too big for his tongue. His eyes shone with an unnatural brightness. He listed slightly to the right and I touched his arm.

"You're talking nonsense. What's the matter? Don't you feel well? Maybe you should sit down."

He yanked his arm away. "I don't wanna siddown. I've been sitting down all day with whatshername over there." He waved a thumb toward Dot, whose face still bore a fixed marionette smile. "I expected you home from church hours ago. Where have you been?"

Poor Dot had been forced to entertain Richard all afternoon. No wonder she looked wrung out. "Sorry," I mouthed silently. She gave a helpless shrug.

"You haven't answered any of my letters," Richard said. "The family is concerned and asked me to check on you."

I doubted very much that "the family" had asked him to check on me and was about to say so when a horrific tremor shook the floor and the walls and rattled the glassware. Richard staggered and nearly toppled over, grabbing the arm of the sofa for support. "What in blazes—"

"The El," Dot and I shouted in unison.

When the train had rumbled past, Richard regained his balance, cleared his throat, adjusted his tie, and turned back to me.

"Whereja say you were?"

I folded my arms. "I don't see how that's—"

"She was with me," Peter interrupted, square-jawed. He took a step toward Richard.

"That's obvious, isn't it." Richard drew himself up to his full height and then some.

"Stop it, both of you," I said, stepping between them. "Peter, you don't have to explain anything to him. I can speak for myself." I wheeled around. "Richard, you don't need to know where I've been, what I've been doing, or with whom."

The men backed off, glaring at each other. Peter's concealed revolver was never far from my thoughts. Who knew what would happen if a fight broke out? Visions of tomorrow's headline flew through my mind. *Gangster Shoots Country Doctor.*

This man was not the gentle, dignified Richard I knew. His smile had an unfamiliar coldness about it. And if I was not mistaken, his breath carried a whiff of liquor.

"Richard, have you been drinking?"

"Of course not. Never touch the stuff. Although your friend here was kind enough to serve me ginger lemonade on this hot afternoon." He made a wobbly half-bow toward Dot. "Thank you. It was delissssciouss." He blinked. "Say, did anybody ever tell you you look just like Louise Brooks?"

Alarm bells rang in my head. "You've been drinking Dot's ginger lemonade? All afternoon?"

Oh, boy. No wonder he was acting strange. He was plastered.

I gaped at Dot, who mumbled something about having letters to write and vanished into her bedroom.

Mortified, I turned to Peter, still standing tall and silent by the door, his jaw set. "Peter, your jacket's hanging on the hook right there. I'm sorry you had to see this. You can leave. I'll be all right."

"I'm not going anywhere." He didn't take his eyes off Richard.

Wearily I said, "For the last time, Richard, what are you doing here?"

His face broke into a sloppy grin. "I came to take you to the opera."

"The opera? You hate opera."

"Yes, I know, but you said you wanted to see the opera, so . . ." With a flourish he produced two tickets from his breast pocket. "Pavilion seats at Ravinia Park. They're doing—" he glanced at the tickets—"Lamoray duh . . . tray ray," he sounded out with great violence to the Italian language. "Sounds interesting. Wonder if it's one of those noisy numbers with sopranos dying of tuberculosis and all that. Of course there was terrible sanitation in those days, and—"

"It's not," I broke in. *Ravinia Park. Shoot.* I'd been longing to go there, the summer home of the Chicago Symphony, located well outside the city. Music under the stars. *Shoot and double shoot.* "I'm not going to the opera, or anywhere else, with you."

"Look, you said you wanted me to share your interests." He waved the tickets in my face. "Here. I'm sharing."

I sighed. "It's too late, Richard. It's over between us."

He flung the tickets on the end table and reached for his hat. "Then I think it's best we just go home."

"Yes, I think you'd better."

"I said *we*."

"We? I'm not going anywhere."

"Yesshh, you are," he said. "Get your things."

"I will not."

"Come on, Marjorie," he pleaded. "Your family is worried about you. You don't want them to worry, do you?"

"If they're so worried, they can get in touch with me themselves. They don't need you to act as a go-between."

He switched to a whiny tone. "But you ignored my letters. That's not like you. I don't even know if you've gotten them."

"I've gotten them."

He leaned his face close to mine. "Well, thassa relief. I got to thinking maybe these people were hiding them from you on purpose."

I wrinkled my nose and swatted him away. "For heaven's sake. Of course no one's hiding my mail. Who would do such a thing? But, no, I didn't answer them. It seems pointless to keep having the same conversation, over and over again. We're over. Done. You're free." I flapped my hands like bird wings.

He clasped a firm hand around my upper arm. "I don't want to be free. And neither do you, deep in your heart."

I shook off his grip. "What do you know about my heart? You never listen to me."

He shook a wobbly finger in my face. "You're not thinking straight, Marjorie. You're caught up in a bad situation. These people—they could be dope fiends, for all you know. For your own safety, I've come to take you home."

"Stop calling them 'these people.' They're my friends. And I *am* home."

"But—but I *forgive* you." He lunged toward me. I dodged out of the way and fended off his clumsy embrace. "Look, Richard. I'm glad that you've forgiven me for whatever hurt I've caused you. I would like to part on good terms. But continuing to badger me and call me crazy hardly qualify as good terms."

"Oh, Marjorie. What's happened to us?" He looked as if he were about to cry. Then his gaze hardened into a glare. "You'll be ssssorry."

"You should go."

I'd nearly forgotten about Peter until he stepped forward and placed a gentle hand on Richard's shoulder.

"Say, buddy. How about I give you a lift to the station?"

Richard shrugged him off. "I'm d-driving. My car's downstairs."

"No, you're not. I'm gonna take you to a hotel where you can sleep it off."

"Sssleep what off?"

"The headache you're gonna have real soon. Let's go."

Richard removed his spectacles and rubbed his eyes. "Come to think of it, I do feel a bit woozy. Musta picked up some kind of virus at the hospital."

"That must be it. Come on, big guy." Peter guided him to the door, then turned back and gave me the thumbs-up. My heart flipped over from the way he looked at me. Such a kind, thoughtful man.

"Thank you," I whispered.

He quirked an eyebrow as he snatched his jacket off the coat-hook. "Ginger lemonade?"

I felt myself blush. "It's . . . it's Dot's special recipe."

He tried to look stern but fell short. "We'll have a chat about that later."

With tremendous weariness I closed the door behind them.

He probably wanted Dot's recipe. Heck, he probably wanted her business.

CHAPTER THIRTY-ONE

The next day, Peter drew me aside in the employee dining room. His hand on my arm sent an electric charge through my skin, but he merely said, "Look, I'm sorry about what happened yesterday."

Which part, exactly, was he sorry for? In the cool light of morning, was he having second thoughts? I knew I was. Not that I didn't feel a powerful attraction to him, but . . .

"It's none of my business, but I have to say, I think you did the right thing, breaking off your engagement. Richard's not the right fellow for you."

No, you're *the right fellow,* my heart longed to say. But he wasn't, and I knew it. What kind of life would I have with Peter? Always on the run, hiding from the law, pretending I didn't know about his secret double life? He must have known it, too, because he walked away with nothing more intimate than a brotherly squeeze to my shoulder. Not that there was much opportunity to do anything else, in a lunchroom crowded with coworkers eager for a scrap of gossip to fling down the moccasin trail.

In spite of my misgivings, I couldn't sweep away the memory of his kiss, the feel of his strong arms around me, his lips on mine. I begged God to scrub my brain clean of those thoughts, lest I be lured down the primrose path. But I needn't have worried. Peter didn't suggest I join him for lunch, much less any more interesting activities, and I couldn't conjure up a plausible excuse to casually glide past the Store for Men. At home I drifted around, brooding over my future as a lovelorn spinster, wondering if, at eighty, I'd still be cherishing the memory of my brief but passionate fling with the underworld.

A few nights later, Dot woke me when she returned from the club. "That's enough of that," she proclaimed, flicking on the overhead light and bouncing on the end of the bed. "No more moping. Now, who's your favorite friend in the whole wide world?"

I rubbed my sleep-filled eyes. "Um . . . you?"

"That's right, doll." Her smile practically blinded me. "Look what I have." She waved some bits of cardstock in front of my face.

"Tickets?" I groaned and fell back on my pillow. "Please don't tell me those are for the opera."

"Not just any tickets. Look."

I peered as instructed. "The Aragon Ballroom? Ritzy. Some sort of dance?"

She snatched them back. "They're only the hardest-to-get invitations to the swankiest party of the year," she cried. "The studio bigwigs at Balaban and Katz are putting on a huge shindig, and guess who's going."

"Who?"

Her dark eyes grew enormous. "You . . . and me . . . and . . . John Gilbert."

I flung off the covers, all sleepiness forgotten. "John Gilbert? John *Gilbert*?"

Dot tossed the tickets on the bed and grabbed my hands. "Isn't that fantastic? He's coming to town to meet with the studio people, and they're throwing this bash, and *we're going*."

We squealed and jumped around like schoolgirls until a firm *rap-rap-rap* came up through the floor—Mrs. Moran banging on her ceiling with a broom handle. When I caught my breath I said, "How on earth did you finagle us an invitation?"

"Don't thank me, thank Louie," she said. "Somehow he wedged his way into the deal between the studio and John Gilbert—some sort of favor he did. I don't really understand it all—but anyway, he got the invitations and *we're going*!"

I paused. "Wait a sec—Louie? But I thought you and Louie were on the outs, and that you and Charlie—"

She cut me off. "These tickets are Louie's way of apologizing for being such a cad lately. Isn't that the sweetest thing?" She didn't mention Charlie at all. That should have troubled me, knowing how much Charlie liked her, but in the moment excitement clouded my thinking. Even Cinderella could not have been more thrilled on her way to the ball. I was going to be in the same room with John Gilbert. I might even speak to him. I might even *dance* with him.

And like Cinderella, my very next thought was *I haven't a thing to wear.*

Dot put a red-lacquered finger to her lips. "There's just one een-sy-teensy little catch."

"What is it? We'll have to ride in a pumpkin pulled by four white mice?"

She jabbed my arm. "Don't be a dope. You simply have to allow one of Louie's friends to escort you."

My skin prickled. "Oh, Dot. Not a friend of Louie's." If I'd wanted to date a gangster, I had one of my own in mind.

"You don't have to kiss him, silly. You just have to, you know, be nice to him, dance a little, laugh at his jokes. It's a small price to pay for meeting John Gilbert, don't you think?"

At lunchtime on Thursday, Dot and I scurried up to the dress department on the sixth floor. We had a mere forty-five minutes to find a gown worthy of John Gilbert and the Aragon Ballroom.

"If you're going to cavort with movie stars, you can't stroll in looking like Little Bo Peep," she said, referring no doubt to my home-made party dress and its makeshift corsage of pilfered daisies.

While I wrestled in and out of gowns in the fitting room, Dot shuttled back and forth to the sales racks like a frantic fairy god-mother. "What about this one?" She passed a flashy gold number with a double-dip front and cut-out back over the dressing room door. I pictured my father clutching his chest and passed it back.

"How about this? It's more covered up." She handed me a white dotted Swiss with a pink crepe sash.

I wrinkled my nose. "That reminds me of Daisy Calloway's graduation dress."

"What?"

"Never mind. Isn't there something else?"

She passed me an emerald bias-cut gown, something Garbo might wear. I'd stepped out of the cubicle and was scrutinizing the effect in a three-way mirror, cursing my freckles, when a sales clerk stopped and gave me the once-over. "Hmm," she appraised. "You'll need a bit stronger girdle with that one, dear."

Inside I fumed. *The nerve.*

"Oh, don't listen to her," Dot said. "She's just annoyed because I'm helping you instead of letting her do it. Fretting about her commission, I suppose. But this is serious business. No time to dilly-dally."

I sucked in my stomach and had to admit, the gown instantly looked ten times better if I avoided breathing. Since an entire evening without oxygen was out of the question, reluctantly I returned it to the hanger.

"Time's up," Dot said. Our lunch break was nearly over, with me no closer to looking waltz-worthy for John Gilbert. "Don't worry. There's still tomorrow. You'll find something."

"It can't just be 'something,'" I moaned. "It has to be magnificent." Magnificent on a salesgirl's wages—no mean trick.

On our way back down to reality, we treated ourselves to a stroll through the haute-couture salon, where the most exquisite gowns were displayed. Thick, lush carpets silenced our footsteps. Hushed voices crooned flattering words to customers perched on silk-upholstered sofas, watching models glide past in fashions straight from Paris and Milan. No pawing through overstuffed racks here in search of a bargain. Each garment hung on its own stand, like a precious artifact in a museum. For a few moments we amused ourselves, ogling the dresses and giggling nervously at the price tags.

I should have known better than to wander among the finest dresses when I was feeling vulnerable. Because suddenly there it was.

The Dress.

Deep-blue satin with delicate embroidery on the skirt, swirling fabulously on a slim, golden-haired model in front of a society matron who was far too lumpy to do it justice. In an instant I knew it was the gown for me. With "a bit stronger girdle," of course.

Dot's gaze moved from my face to The Dress and back again.

"You could have it, you know," she whispered, a snake in a chiffon-and-taffeta garden.

I stared at her. "You're nuts. It's way out of my league. I can't possibly afford it, even with my employee discount, not to mention shoes, bag, hosiery . . ."

"You don't have to *buy* it, silly."

"Huh?"

"You could just *borrow* it."

"What are you saying?"

She leaned in closer. "Just—you know—*borrow* it. Buy it, wear it Friday night, return it on Saturday, and get your money back."

"What?" I blurted. "I can't do that. That's—that's not right."

"Shhh!" Dot glanced around. "Don't be such a ninny. Everybody does it. You don't think I actually buy all those gowns I sing in, do you?"

I recoiled. "No. I won't do it."

She shrugged. "Have it your way . . . but you'd look like an angel in it. Come on, we're late."

My first instinct was disgust, not wanting to believe that my friend found such a shady practice acceptable. Returning a worn garment, indeed.

And yet.

I couldn't get The Dress out of my mind. That night as I lay in bed, I imagined how stunning I'd look in that swirl of blue satin. Maybe Dot was right. Maybe this is what everyone did. The sales people probably didn't even care. They probably even expected it to happen. Just part of doing business. Try before you buy, that sort of thing.

I should have stopped the minute I started rationalizing. I should have prayed for strength to resist. I should have been appalled that my friend thought doing such a sneaky thing was no big deal.

I didn't do any of that.

Instead, in the moments just before sleep, I hatched my plan. I'd buy the dress, fair and square, and then return it in flawless condition. I'd say it didn't quite suit me, which was sort of true. It didn't suit my budget, that's for sure, and it didn't suit my life. But it might suit John Gilbert.

I would be extremely careful.

I would not eat.

I would not drink.

I would not sweat.

No one would ever know.

On Friday morning I emptied *Robinson Crusoe* of its contents which, combined with my paycheck, would cover the secret purchase until I could return it and get my money back. At lunchtime I took my break early, making some excuse to Dot. I didn't want her involved, lest I chicken out. I sneaked up to the sixth floor and tried on The Dress, half hoping it would need alterations. As there was no time for alterations, I would be off the hook.

It fit perfectly. Darn it.

Hands trembling, I bought it, along with a new girdle and stockings, and stashed the package under my raincoat in the employee locker room. I hated keeping the secret from Dot, but she'd find out soon enough. She'd get a big kick out of it when I showed her, when we were safely away from the store. We'd share a good laugh over it, like the sophisticated women-about-town we were.

And John Gilbert, the celebrated actor, would be dazzled beyond belief.

CHAPTER THIRTY-TWO

Louie and his buddy Frank arrived at the apartment at a quarter past eight. By the time they rang the buzzer, my palms were sweating. Although I'd heard a great deal about Louie from Dot, I'd never met him in person. I could immediately see why Dot was attracted to him. He epitomized the classic description "tall, dark, and handsome," with a commanding air about him. Frank, pressed into service as my escort for the evening, was shorter and not as good-looking, but seemed friendly enough. I just hoped he could dance without tromping on my feet, which were already aching in a pair of dainty silver slippers borrowed from Dot that were at least a size too small. She'd been thrilled to see me in the blue gown and had insisted I not ruin the effect with clunky shoes. I pushed aside the guilt of knowing I didn't plan to keep The Dress, convincing myself it was worth the deception.

Frank handed me a gardenia wrist corsage. I thanked him, relieved that I wouldn't risk putting pinholes in The Dress. Already I despaired of returning it to Field's in flawless condition but it was too late to worry about that now.

"Ready to go?" Frank placed a sparkly silver evening wrap, also borrowed from Dot, around my shoulders. The four of us headed downstairs and out to Louie's shiny roadster.

The Aragon Ballroom, modeled after a Moorish palace, was a wonderland of crystal chandeliers, mosaic tiles, romantic archways, and a midnight-blue terra-cotta ceiling sprinkled with twinkling stars and drifting clouds. From the stage at one end of the vast ballroom, a saxophonist led the orchestra in "Sahara Rose" as couples dipped and twirled around the parquet floor.

I scanned the room for any sign of John Gilbert. Apparently he hadn't shown up yet. Meanwhile, masses of well-dressed people were hailing Louie as if *he* were a celebrity.

"Hey, Louie, nice to see you."

"Good evening, Mr. Braccio."

Louie waved and smiled and shook hands. The name *Braccio* tweaked my ears. It was a streetwise name, tough and swaggering, like *bravado* and *macho* rolled into one.

"Do people always treat him like this?" I whispered to Dot.

"Yes, isn't it a scream? This happens all the time when we're out together. Louie has important business connections all over the city."

"I see." My heart went out to my poor brother Charlie in his quest for Dot's affection. Next to Braccio's glittering empire, Corrigan's Dry Goods didn't offer much allure.

The band swung into "My Baby Just Cares for Me" and Frank swept me into a fox trot. He turned out to be an excellent dancer. I hoped the lessons I'd taken at Mercy Gilligan's School of Dance and Deportment were paying off. Twirling around the ballroom was so mesmerizing, I barely noticed my feet aching in the too-small shoes.

"You like this joint?" Frank shouted over the music.

I nodded vigorously, too breathless to respond. The lively dance threatened my no-sweating rule, but I was having too much fun to care. Next I danced with Louie, and then with a man Dot introduced to me as a "gaffer" at the movie studio.

I was about to ask him what a gaffer did when a commotion took place near the entrance. Flashbulbs popped, the crowd murmured, and in walked my idol, flanked by a cluster of women and a few tux-edo-clad men. I'd have recognized his face anywhere.

Frank found me and propelled me toward the cluster. I saw Louie shake John Gilbert's hand and introduce a radiant Dot. When we reached the star, Louie introduced Frank and me. John Gilbert smiled graciously, took my hand, and bowed a little. When I gazed into those unforgettable dark eyes I'd so admired on the silver screen, I thought I'd swoon, but by some miracle stayed upright. I made some inane comment about *The Big Parade,* and he smiled. Then, in a flash, it was over. Mr. Gilbert's entourage moved on and Frank led me back to the dance floor.

I'm afraid I didn't pay much attention to poor Frank as he steered me around beneath the twinkling lights. I spent the rest of the evening craning my neck to see what John Gilbert and his party were up to. Not once did the screen idol make the slightest glance in my direction, surrounded as he was by stunning women in gowns far more attention-grabbing than mine. The magical gown on which I'd pinned all my confidence was turning out to be nothing more than a few artfully stitched panels of blue satin and some embroidery floss.

All too soon, the event drew to a close. Louie called for his motorcar. He helped Dot into the front seat while Frank and I slid into the back. My big John Gilbert moment had turned out to be nothing more than a fleeting smile, and my feet were throbbing. Yet I didn't feel a bit tired, so I agreed when Frank suggested we stop somewhere for a bite to eat.

"How about Chinatown?" he said. "I know a chop suey joint that's open late."

My mouth watered at the thought of chop suey, which I'd grown to like at a neighborhood place called the Orange Garden. But Louie scoffed.

"Why Chinatown? We'll go to my place."

His place. The speakeasy.

"Whatever you say, boss," Frank said.

In spite of my growling stomach, I murmured, "I don't know . . . it's getting rather late."

"Oh, Marjorie, staying out late just this once won't kill you," Dot cajoled. She twisted around in the front seat and gave me a pleading look.

"You got something against spaghetti and meatballs?" Louie's glance caught mine in the rearview mirror, and his dark eyes crinkled in amusement. Dot must have told him about my aversion to speakeasies. I imagined them sharing a hearty chuckle over it and felt both embarrassed and annoyed. "Besides, you girls will be interested to know that a very special guest will be joining us for a late supper."

"Who?" Dot turned toward Louie.

"None other than John Gilbert himself." Louie flashed a grin as Dot gave a whoop and nearly levitated out of her seat. "He assured me that he and his companions will join us as soon as they can get away." He reached over and patted her knee. "He specifically said he would like to hear you sing, babyface."

"He said *that*?" She swiveled around again to face me. "Oh, Marjie, you can't say no. You just can't."

Indeed I couldn't. *Just this once*, I told myself, *for Dot's sake. Don't be a wet blanket. John Gilbert will be there.*

With the car's collapsible top down, we cruised through the sultry night. The breeze blew my hair around and cooled my flushed face, even as my conscience nagged that I was once again doing something I knew to be wrong. First The Dress, and now a speakeasy. But I couldn't spoil Dot's chance to sing for John Gilbert. Maybe this would be her big moment of discovery. So once again I shoved the nagging thoughts to the back of my brain and shored up my courage by reciting silently, *John Gilbert. John Gilbert. John Gilbert.* Who knew—maybe he'd notice me and my fabulous blue dress when there weren't so many other people around.

We snaked through the city streets, ending up in Little Italy, just a block or two from the settlement house. I imagined the children there, accustomed to seeing me in my scruffy workaday clothes, gaping at me all dolled up in my fine gown. For some reason the vision did not bring me the pleasure I thought it would.

Louie parked the roadster in front of a small neighborhood restaurant. It looked harmless enough. The air smelled rich with oregano and garlic. Ravenous, I also knew the narrow cut of my dress wouldn't accommodate much spaghetti. I vowed to nibble like a lady and not gorge myself, and above all, avoid stray spatters of tomato sauce. Maybe spaghetti wasn't such a good idea, after all.

The headwaiter greeted Louie and they exchanged a few words in Italian.

"What are they saying?" I whispered to Dot.

"I don't know, but doesn't it sound romantic?"

Our dates escorted us through the crowded, smoky dining room toward the back of the building. The place was packed. I didn't see a single empty table. Louie opened a door, and for a moment I wondered if we were going to eat in the kitchen. But the door led to a narrow stairwell.

"Is there another dining room downstairs?" I said, staring dubiously down the dark staircase.

"Something like that," Frank said.

Louie led the way. At the bottom of the stairs, he knocked on another door stenciled "cleaning supplies." I heard the click of locks.

When the door eased open a crack, he leaned forward and said something to a faceless figure on the other side. The door opened wider, revealing another large, smoky room filled with tables, and a sea of tuxedos and sequins.

Soon we found ourselves jammed around a table with several of Frank and Louie's friends: a boisterous, red-faced man they called Duke, a quiet man with sad dark eyes called Bobby, and two flashy women named Charlotte and Veronica. Veronica had an angelic face that called to mind a Renaissance Madonna, were it not for the cigarette dangling from her mouth. Of course I'd seen Dot light up here and there, but still found it disconcerting to see so many women, sparkling in fringe and beads, smoking right alongside the men.

Everyone was talking at once, loud and animated, greeting us heartily as Louie made introductions. Frank went to fetch drinks.

"What'll you have?" he said.

"A Coke, please," I shouted over the din. "I'm parched."

Louie escorted Dot toward the small stage where a jazz band blared, leaving me alone with the tableful of strangers. A crush of dancers careened and collided on the dance floor. The air was thick with the nauseating stench of cigarettes and whiskey and perfume. My desire to be anywhere else but a gin mill battled my determination not to appear like an unsophisticated rube from the sticks. I desperately wished we were back at the Aragon, swaying gently under the fake scudding clouds.

Frank returned and set a glass of fruit punch in front of me.

"This okay? They're out of Coke."

The liquid sparkled fetchingly in the glass. I thanked him and took a sip. I could detect pineapple juice and orange juice, along with some other flavors I didn't quite recognize. It tasted exotic and tropical, and its iciness felt cool and refreshing on my parched tongue.

"This is delicious. What's in it?"

Frank shrugged. "Beats me. The bartender calls it Planter's Punch."

I took a bigger sip. It tasted delicious, fruity and sweet.

Frank slid his arm around my shoulder and leaned close, shouting over the racket.

"Hey, baby. This joint's crazy loud. What say you and I make like trees and leave?"

"No, thank you." I stiffened my posture and forced a smile. In truth, I wanted nothing more than to leave. But with Frank growing increasingly amorous as the evening wore on, I didn't want to be alone with him. Besides, Dot was getting ready to sing, which was the whole point of being here—so Dot could sing for John Gilbert. Who as far as I could see, hadn't yet made his appearance.

I was not going to be a country mouse and demand to be taken home like a silly schoolgirl. This was the big city, after all, and I was a city girl now. Right? And who was I to judge? Didn't the Bible say not to judge people? So I might as well sit back and enjoy the refreshing fruit punch. When I drained the glass, another appeared to take its place.

I mimicked the way Charlotte held her glass, wanting to appear as urbane and sophisticated as she did. I noticed how she blew smoke rings, pulling her painted Cupid's-bow mouth to the side in a comical way. I gave a little snort.

"What's so funny?" Charlotte said, exhaling smoke in my face.

"Nothing," I coughed. I took another fruity sip of punch. And another. Soon the glass was empty again, but it didn't stay that way for long.

I started to relax, feeling calm and excited at the same time. I tapped my foot to the beat and watched the dancers shimmy across the floor, beads flying. Duke cracked a joke and I exploded into laughter along with everyone else. Why, these people were the bee's knees! So friendly and witty. Whatever had I been afraid of?

A waiter set a plate of spaghetti on the table before me. I took a bite, but my appetite had withered to nothing. Frank said something, sounding like he was underwater. He refilled my glass again and again as the evening wore on. *What time is it, anyway? Where is that John Gilbert? Oh, who cares.*

On the small stage, Dot was crooning "You're the Cream in My Coffee," sounding every bit as good as Ruth Etting. Why, she was marvelous! Why hadn't I ever come to hear her before?

"Lissen!" I hissed to Veronica, pointing sloppily toward the stage. My tongue felt too big to fit in my mouth. "Thass my friend. Thass my friend."

All at once a buzz snapped through the crowd. The band faltered. Dot's voice drifted to silence. Someone shouted, "Cheese it! It's the cops."

The table rocked as everyone stood up at once. The plate of spaghetti overturned, spilling its contents onto my lap in a scarlet river. I leaped up in horror, knocking Frank's whiskey glass from his hand. Amber liquid splashed across my bodice.

The door burst open and blue-uniformed police officers scattered throughout the room, batons raised. What happened next was sheer pandemonium: a melee of screams, shouts, breaking glass, overturned tables, and panicked customers scattering like cockroaches, every man for himself. Frank took off without a backward glance. Out of nowhere Dot materialized and yanked my arm. "Come with me," she said through clenched teeth. "Ladies' room."

A wildly inappropriate time for a comfort stop. But I soon understood her plan. She dragged me through a claustrophobic storeroom stacked high with crates and up some rickety and cobweb-strewn steps. The top step opened onto a dim upstairs hallway and a door marked Ladies. Locking the restroom door, she climbed onto the radiator, boosted herself up on the window ledge, and tried to open the casement window. It wouldn't budge. She banged into it with her shoulder and then hammered against the frame with one satin dancing pump. Finally it creaked open. Like a serpent she slithered through, then turned back and reached out her hand to me.

I gasped. "I can't possibly fit through that little window."

"Marjorie, don't be an idiot. Come on." Someone pounded on the locked door. I sucked in a deep breath, gathered my skirt, willed myself to be as small as possible, and crawled through the opening. I got through as far as my waist when I felt a tug on my skirt. It was stuck on something—a nail, maybe. Dot grabbed me under the arms and yanked. Hearing a loud *riiiiiip* as my skirt released from whatever it was caught on, I hurtled headlong the rest of the way through the opening, knocking Dot flat. We found ourselves on a narrow roof on the back side of the building. On hands and knees we crawled to the edge, where a tree's thick foliage partially hid us from the view of the police and patrons swarming on the ground below. We huddled there for a few minutes, motionless and panting, listening while the police took names and addresses and loaded people into police wagons destined for the city jail. Not one of them, of course, was John Gilbert.

"You two! Stay right where you are."

A policeman's head poked out of the ladies' room window.

"Follow me," Dot shouted. She clambered through the tree branches and shimmied down the trunk.

I groaned. Shock, fear, and fruit punch collided in my gut. Behind me, the policeman was squeezing his bulk through the window. Swaying woozily, I kicked off the silver slippers and followed her, the sharp branches doing further violence to The Dress. I hadn't climbed a tree since third grade, but this rusty skill didn't fail me as I made my way to the ground.

Dot spotted Louie's auto idling in the alley and shouted "Run for it!" As we made a mad dash around the corner, I collided with a man wearing a business suit. At least it wasn't a cop.

"'Scuse me,'" I slurred, stumbling around him.

"Marjorie? Is that you?" I lifted my head to see a familiar face. A shocked and horrified face, staring straight at me.

"*Peter?*"

In that moment I became excruciatingly aware of how I must appear, wobbling barefoot in my ripped dress, with a blood-red stain splashed across the front and reeking to high heaven of whiskey and cigarettes.

There was no time to say anything more. Dot yelled my name. Within seconds Frank grabbed me and shoved me into the backseat of Louie's roadster and we roared off into the night.

CHAPTER THIRTY-THREE

On Saturday morning, my first thought was that I was dying of some exotic disease. My head throbbed. My stomach churned. My mouth tasted as if I'd been chewing the contents of a carpet sweeper.

Every single cringe-inducing detail of the previous evening socked me in the ribs, along with the aftereffects of Planter's Punch—Planter's Poison, more accurately. Behaving like a complete . . . a complete . . .

I buried my face in the pillow. Why did Hollywood only show the glamorous side of drinking? Why didn't they show the other side . . . the morning-after side? In my misery I vowed to personally never touch an alcoholic beverage again as long as I lived.

Much as I tried to block them out, images of the previous night reeled through my mind. The shocked look on Peter's face. Wobbling along in Dot's too-small shoes, clinging to Frank's arm for dear life. Some kind of messy good-bye scene in Louie's roadster. Dot and I pitching ourselves up the stairs in the dark, making plenty of noise to alert the neighbors that the drunken floozies were home.

Dimly I realized it was a workday. *Get up*, I told myself sternly. If I could only get up, I could make things right. Life would return to normal and I could forget about ever setting foot in a speakeasy. But it was still early. I'd close my eyes for a few more minutes, just a few, and then I'd go. I'd get up, scrub off the wickedness, put on fresh clothes, and go to work, one foot in front of the other. Just a few more minutes.

Sometime later I sensed Dot standing over me, holding a glass and an aspirin bottle.

"Up and at 'em," she said. "Poor kid. Here, take a sip of ginger lemonade." She held the glass next to my lips. One whiff of the gin-laced concoction made my stomach heave. I waved her away so violently that I nearly knocked the glass out of her hand.

"What are you doing?" I croaked.

"The best cure for a hangover is the hair of the dog that bit you," she said matter-of-factly. "Well, try to swallow the aspirin, at least. I'll tell Old Rugged you're sick."

I fell back on the pillow. "Why bother? I'm never going back."

"Yes, you are, and you'll do it quickly if you want to keep your job."

"I don't care."

"We'll talk about it later."

I turned my face to the wall. I didn't want to talk about it later. I was quitting Field's. This whole Chicago business had been a terrible mistake. I wasn't cut out for city life. Furthermore, the possibility of running into Peter, after the disgraceful spectacle I'd made of myself, was unthinkable. True, he had been at the speakeasy too. But he was a bootlegger—that was his job. For all I knew, he'd been among the many hauled off to jail. Me, I had no excuse. I shuddered to consider what he must think of me. After all my lofty speeches about avoiding alcohol, he'd seen me as I truly was. Surely he felt as disgusted by me as I was by myself.

When I did finally get up, I stumbled over the blue dress crumpled in a heap on the floor. The fabric was torn, mottled and discolored. Panic squeezed my chest as I realized I'd squandered all my money on a dress I could neither return to Field's nor ever wear again. How was I even going to cough up my share of this month's rent? In disgust I wadded up the ruined garment and shoved it into the bottom drawer of the dresser.

I threw on a robe and padded through the empty apartment to the kitchen, where I chased two aspirin with a glass of water. With any luck, Dot would go straight to Louie's after work and we could skip all the talking.

Louie. The name made my gut roil. Without him and his so-called connections, we would have never gotten into this mess. We had only wanted to see John Gilbert. Was that too much to ask?

But a ray of reason sliced through my foggy brain. None of this was Louie's fault. At any point I could have backed out, said no, hailed a taxi. Still, I wished I'd never heard the name Louie Braccio.

Slowly a clammy chill settled over my heart.

Louie Braccio. *Luigi* Braccio. The gangster Annamarie had warned me about. The terror of the neighborhood around the settlement house. A fearsome gangster who was, oh by the way, dating my roommate.

A fresh wave of nausea swept over me. I'd just spent an evening with one of the most notorious criminals in the city, blinded by his flashy connections and eager to impress his friends—and a no-show movie star—with my worldly sophistication.

Some sophistication.

Sick with remorse, I shuffled back to my room and got on my knees. *Oh, Lord,* I sobbed. No words came. Deep inside, I knew that God had no use for someone like me. I so longed to start over, to make things right. The trouble was, I had no idea how.

I must have dozed off, because suddenly I jerked awake, a phrase running through my mind.

Thou art ever with me.

I glanced around to see who had spoken, but I was alone. Still, I heard Pastor Higgins's voice echo in my head. *Thou art ever with me.*

Then I knew. I could do nothing to make things right with God. But there was Someone who could. I just needed to trust Him.

Feeling slightly stronger, I took a long bath, put on a fresh nightgown, fixed myself a supper of tea and crackers, and curled up on the sofa. Then I picked up the little Bible Mrs. Dunsworthy had given me and flipped through it until I found the phrase, nestled in the familiar story of the prodigal son, who ran away from home, spent all his money in riotous living, then returned home humiliated.

Son, the kindly father said to the disgruntled older brother, *thou art ever with me, and all I have is thine. It was meet that we should make merry and be glad; for this thy brother was dead, and is alive again; and was lost, and is found.*

I, too, was lost. I wanted to be found.

My eyes traveled back up the page. At his lowest point, the wayward brother knew he had done wrong, and he understood the remedy.

I will arise and go to my father.

And when he did so, his father greeted him with open arms.

All at once, I knew what I had to do. There are times when a girl needs both her Father, and her father.

First I needed God.

And then I needed Pop.

That much decided, I slept. Then, before dawn started slanting through the windows, I washed my face, got dressed, packed my bag, scribbled a brief note for Dot, and headed for the station. As the nearly empty El train rocked and rattled its way across the sleeping city, I tried to cobble together some sort of plan, but couldn't see beyond simply getting home.

With an hour to kill before boarding the Kerryville train, I settled on a bench in the station's soaring waiting room, quiet and cathedral-like on this Sunday morning. At this early hour, the only person in the waiting room besides me was a cleaning lady, swishing her mop over the tile floor.

I thought about *The Song of the Lark* and the girl with her face lifted toward the sky in hope and expectation. "Lord, why would You want to hear from someone like me? After all the terrible things I've done?"

Thou art ever with me.

I bowed my head. In my heart I told Him everything, laid out the whole sordid story. How I'd abandoned my job after spending an evening getting rip-roaring drunk in a speakeasy owned by a ruthless gangster. How, in preparation for that illustrious event, I'd purchased an expensive gown with full intention of returning it as if it had never been worn.

"It gets even worse, Lord," I said, as if He didn't already know. "I've made myself look perfectly ludicrous in the eyes of the man I want, who now will definitely never want me back, which is probably just as well because he also happens to be a bootlegger—a *bootlegger*—for whom I threw over a decent, upstanding, caring man who would have given me a secure future and a stable home. And after all that, Peter isn't even Jack!"

I paused to gather my thoughts, then plunged ahead.

"Lord, I've made such a shambles of things. I know I've said this before, but I mean it this time. I'm turning the reins of my life over to You. From now on, I'm out of the driver's seat, and You're in it. Whatever You say, I'll do. Amen."

In the hush of the station, as a strange sort of peace settled over my aching heart, I thought I heard the swoosh of wings. An angel? But when I opened my eyes, the only soul around was the cleaning lady, her mop making a gentle *swish-swish* as she washed away the grime.

I arrived at Kerryville toward midday. Since I'd told no one I was coming, naturally no one met my train. I could have telephoned Pop or Charlie for a ride, but preferred to walk home, passing familiar and reassuring landmarks of my life B.C.—Before Chicago. The gray stone bulk of the high school. The grocery store. The Tick-Tock Cafe.

When I reached Corrigan's Dry Goods, I stopped and peered in the window, noting how clean and orderly the store looked. Clearly Helen was doing an excellent job, running the front counter in my stead. Maybe I hadn't even been missed.

I took my time, practicing a speech for my family. By the time I reached home, they were just sitting down for Sunday dinner.

"Hello, everybody," I said, dropping my train case on the linoleum. With a cry, Helen leaped up and threw herself at me. Over her blond head I announced in a quivering voice, "I've come home. For good." After that my speech flew out the window. I simply sobbed.

The whole family gathered around me. Once they'd ascertained I was not mortally wounded, no one pressed me for details on what had taken place.

"There'll be time enough for talking," Pop said when Frances tried to launch an interrogation. To her credit, she closed her mouth and opened her arms. Then she went upstairs and drew me a hot bath, and later brought a tray up to my room. After a while I slept, and when I awoke, sunshine was streaming through the curtains. I was back where I belonged.

CHAPTER THIRTY-FOUR

My days fell into the once confining, now comforting routines of Kerryville life. I helped in the kitchen and the garden—whatever I could do that didn't involve seeing people. I sensed I was the hottest topic since Mercy Gilligan performed a scandalous *Scheherazade* at an Odd Fellows' fund-raiser. News of my broken engagement had spread like wildfire, and from what I could tell, most people had thought Richard dodged a bullet. After all, I was the crazy Corrigan girl who'd—depending on whom you asked— left town in a hurry to hide an unwed pregnancy, a mysterious illness, or a nervous breakdown. And now I'd come back from the big city, a failure.

I longed to confide in Charlie all the details about what had taken place at the speakeasy, about Dot and Louie's involvement, but didn't want to sound like I was blaming anyone for my poor decisions. When he told me he'd started corresponding with Dot again, I simply told him to tread carefully, that her old boyfriend could cause trouble. Beyond that I backed off of giving advice.

I telephoned the Art Institute to say I wouldn't be back to finish the textiles class, explaining only that I'd needed to leave the city quite suddenly. In reply I received a kind note from Miss Smith, praising my work and encouraging me to enroll again when circumstances allowed. Enclosed in the envelope was a refund. I didn't foresee ever taking another class, but I kept the letter to remind me of what might have been.

As the weeks went by and summer dwindled into fall, I settled back into my old job at Pop's store and regained my strength. Helen stayed on until school started, and then worked after school and on Saturdays. She and I had a lot of fun working together, unpacking the fall fabrics and figuring out creative ways to display them. I'd picked up a trick or two during my weeks at Field's. Pop, finally seeing the necessity to keep up with the other Main Street merchants, stopped complaining about too much "razzle-dazzle" and gave me free rein to spiff up the store.

Seeing Richard around town with this or that girl brought a pang, a sense of the path not taken. As time passed, memories of our quarrels faded, and my firm conviction that I'd done the right thing to break our engagement started to waver. Could my heart have learned to love him if I hadn't been so eager to seek adventure? Would I eventually have gotten over my strange attacks of nerves over the idea of marrying him? I'd never know.

On the third Saturday in September, as Helen and I unwrapped bolts of woolen fabric, I realized with a start that, under other circumstances, this would have been my wedding day. The uncut length of satin intended for my gown now sat on the markdown table. Seeing it made me feel a little melancholy, but mostly relieved. Still, I wondered if God had a plan more interesting for me than a lifetime of selling dry goods to Kerryville homemakers. I hoped so. But if He didn't, I determined I would be content. Wasn't that what the apostle Paul said? "Be content in all things"? I'd had my little taste of excitement and adventure, and wrecked everything in the process. Now it was time to settle down to real life.

Helen's voice broke my reverie. "Marjie, doesn't it bother you when people say mean things about you? It makes me livid."

I had to think a moment before I answered. "I won't lie and say the gossip doesn't hurt, sweetie, because it does. But if there's one thing I've learned, it's that you can't stop people from talking when they want to talk. All you can do is hold your head up and cling to God for strength."

"I guess so. But I can't help wishing God would smite some people in the head."

"Helen."

"Imprecatory prayer," she added, drawing out the syllables of the unfamiliar word. "Mrs. Varney told us all about it. It's biblical."

"'Love your enemies' is also biblical," I said. "I think that's a more suitable idea in this case, don't you?"

"Oh, all right," she muttered. "But loving your enemies is a whole lot harder than letting them have one good smite." Suddenly she

perked up. "I almost forgot to tell you. I need next Saturday afternoon off."

"I suppose I can limp along without you. Why?"

"It's Jeannie King's birthday, and her father's taking a bunch of us
out on the river in his runabout."

"Sounds fun," I said, "but go easy on the cake and ice cream.
Remember what happened the last time you rode on a boat with a
full stomach."

Her brow wrinkled. "When?"

"The Fourth of July. Remember? You and Kurt Steuben went out
on Lake Michigan on that excursion boat right after lunch, and you
were sick for the rest of the evening. Poor thing."

She looked down, her face as red as her sweater. "That's not what
made me sick, Marjie," she said slowly. "I was just fine until that Kurt
fellow tried to kiss me. *That's* what made me sick—his dirty paws all
over my dress. Not the boat."

My blood ran hot and then cold. "Kurt Steuben made a pass at
you? Why, he's old enough to be your—your—" I couldn't think.
"Why in the world didn't you say anything?"

"Because I knew you'd blow a fuse—just like you're doing now,"
she said. "I didn't want everyone to think I was a baby."

"But you *are* a baby," I wailed. "Oh, the nerve of that creep. If I
ever get my hands on him—"

"It's all right, Marjie," she soothed. "I socked him good in the
solar plexus, and he left me alone after that." She gave a wry grin. "I
smote him."

I gathered her into a shaky hug. "I'm so, so sorry, Helen. I feel
responsible. I gave you permission to go with him."

"Marjie, it's all right," she repeated. "It's not your fault. How were
you supposed to know he was a creep? Besides, I begged and begged
to go on that boat ride."

"Have you told Pop and Frances?"

A look of horror crossed her face. "Oh, Marjie, please don't tell.
Pop will blow his stack, and Frances will never let me leave the house
ever again. I'm fine, really I am."

"Oh, sweetie," I said, dismayed that my own poor choices had
such far-reaching consequences.

Unable to sleep, I prayed late into the night. The next evening after supper I sought out Pop in the front room.

"I need to go back to Chicago."

He folded his newspaper. "To collect the rest of your things?"

"No, I mean . . . go back."

"I had a feeling this was coming." He removed his spectacles and polished them with a handkerchief. "I wondered if it would be hard for you to live in the same town as Richard, after everything that's happened."

"It's not that," I said. "I see now that in coming back to Kerryville, I was trying to run away from my problems. I'd made such a mess of things, I just wanted to start over. But I can't run away, can I? I have to finish things, to tie up loose ends."

Pop nodded. "I see. How long do you think you'll be gone this time?"

"I'm not sure. Probably not long, as I no longer have a job there. When I called to explain my absence, the lady in Personnel told me my services were no longer needed."

"That seems overly harsh."

"She said rules are rules."

"You'll always have a job at Corrigan's, you know."

"I know, Pop. Thanks." My heart swelled. "Can you manage without me for a while? I hate to leave you in the lurch."

"Don't worry about the store." Pop patted my hand. "I wish you'd stay here forever, of course, but maybe God has something else in mind for you. And if it takes going back to Chicago to find out, then I'll drive you to the station myself."

He did, in time for me to catch the earliest train the next morning. I didn't have a clear plan in mind of what I'd do when I got to Chicago. I just knew I had to finish what I'd started. I had to see Peter one more time. And I couldn't let Kurt Steuben get away with what he'd done.

CHAPTER THIRTY-FIVE

As I emerged from Union Station, the smell of exhaust fumes evoked images richer than any Paris perfume. How I'd missed Chicago— the energy and vitality, and the independent woman I'd been when I lived here. I'd come here once to have my heart healed. Now I sought heart-healing of a different sort.

First, I needed to return the extra key to Dot's place that was tucked away in my handbag. I rode the streetcar to the apartment, climbed the musty stairs, and knocked timidly on the apartment door, half hoping she wouldn't be home so I could just let myself in and leave the key on the table. I didn't know what kind of reception I'd get. Although I knew she'd been in contact with Charlie, she and I hadn't spoken directly since that terrible night at the speakeasy.

She opened the door in response to the buzzer.

"Dot?"

I almost didn't recognize her. She wore a simple skirt and sweater, minus the sparkly dresses, jangly jewelry, and kohl-rimmed eyes. She looked as beautiful as ever—in my opinion, even more without all the glitter and rouge—and younger somehow.

"Marjorie." Her dark eyes reflected my surprise.

"I hope you don't mind my dropping in out of the blue. I just wanted to return this." I held out the key. She looked at it but didn't take it. She slouched against the door, twisting the doorknob in her hand.

"I'm glad you've come, Marjie. Come in." She stepped aside and motioned me toward the sofa. "I've been wanting to talk to you ever since—since that night. I've wanted to telephone, but Charlie said it was probably better to leave you alone for the time being. How are you?"

"I'm well," I said. "Really well." I chose my next words carefully. "I know you and Charlie have gotten together. So Louie's out of the picture?"

"Completely." Her voice trembled. "There are so many things I've wanted to say to you."

I shook my head. "You don't owe me any explanations."

"Please let me talk." Her pretty face crumpled. "Oh, Marjorie, I've been feeling so horrible. The entire fiasco was a terrible mistake, and it was all my fault. Can you ever forgive me?"

My heart melted as I embraced her. "Dot, it wasn't your fault. I chose to do what I did that night. I was the one who drank too much, who practically stole a dress, who disgraced my family and myself, and worst of all, God. It was the best thing for everyone that I just go back home where I belong. I've only come here to finish up some business and return your key. I'm staying at the Y."

"Don't be ridiculous." She straightened and dabbed her eyes with a handkerchief. "You're staying right here. Your room is waiting for you, exactly how you left it. I haven't touched a thing."

I took off my hat. We could sort out the lodging question later. By the time she'd made us both some tea, I'd worked up the nerve to talk openly about the night at the speakeasy.

"It was terrible of me to sneak out on you like that," I confessed. "I just felt so humiliated, I didn't want to see or talk to anyone, not even you."

"And I felt so rotten, too. After all, I was the one who got us into that mess in the first place." She sipped her tea. "I've made a few changes."

"I can see that. New duds?"

She nodded. "Yes, but more important, I'm not seeing Louie anymore. Not singing at the club, either. No cigarettes, no booze. That life is over for me."

"I'm glad. But why?"

Her slender shoulders drooped. "There was something about that night," she said, shaking her head. "Seeing you, sweet little Marjorie Corrigan, dangling from a tree branch, one step ahead of the cops—" She winced.

"That must have been a sight to behold."

"Well, it made me realize that's no kind of place for you," she continued. "Or for me. You helped me see I deserve something better."

"But what about your singing career?"

She shrugged. "I love to sing. But in the end, the fame, the glitter . . . it's not worth it," she said. "Not if you have to sell your soul to get it. You showed me that. You and Charlie. You both made me want to change, to be the kind of girl you'd both be proud of."

"Dot, you don't have to change for us."

"Yes, I do. I want to." Her mouth tilted into a smile. "I really admire you, you know. Beneath that Pollyanna exterior, you're a genuinely good person."

"I'm not. I've never felt less good in my entire life."

"Yes, you are. And I want what you have."

"The only thing I have, Dot, is faith in God. He's all any of us ever needs. Including you."

She gave a harsh laugh. "What does your Bible say about a girl like me? Nothing good, I imagine."

"Oh, Dot. There's nothing good in *any* of us. That's why we need a Savior."

She glanced away. "You really believe that stuff, don't you?"

"With all my heart."

"Yeah. So does Charlie."

"Yes. And so can you."

After a pause she said, "I don't know, Marjorie."

"Just promise me you'll think about it."

"I will." She sat up straighter. "There's something I do know for sure, though. No more singing in nightclubs for me. From now on I'm just a plain old clerk selling hats in a department store."

"You're neither plain nor old. And you're *not* just a hat girl in a department store." Echoing Mrs. Cross, I said, "You're a purveyor of elegant headwear at Marshall Field & Company. And nobody does it better than you."

The next afternoon I took the streetcar to Field's, fighting every urge to walk straight up to the Store for Men to find Peter and beg his forgiveness, but first things first. Instead I stomped down to the loading dock and asked around until I located Kurt Steuben. I found him on his break, smoking a cigarette in the alley with a couple of other men.

"Excuse me, gentlemen," I said. "May I speak to Kurt alone?" The men exchanged glances, then stubbed out their cigarettes and went back inside the dock. I stood as straight and tall as I could.

"So you're back?" Kurt drawled. "I thought you were gone for good."

"I'm back," I said. I read him the riot act for making a pass at Helen on the Fourth of July.

"What on earth were you thinking?" I seethed. "She's sixteen years old."

"I should have known she'd be a cold fish like her sister."

The next thing I knew, I'd slapped him right across the face. Hard.

"Hey!" he shouted, rubbing his face, which bore an expression of shock. I may have looked like I wasn't tough enough to squash a spider, but I had a pretty strong right hook when provoked.

"I have a good mind to tell your supervisor what you've done," I threatened. Inside I knew I probably wouldn't bring up such a personal matter at the workplace. Helen wouldn't have wanted me to. But I would if I had to—if Kurt pushed me hard enough. Surely Marshall Field & Company wouldn't want to keep such a lecherous fiend on the payroll, if they knew what he tried to do with young girls.

Kurt's eyes narrowed. "You say one word to anybody, about anything, and you'll be sorry."

"You don't scare me," I said. I turned on my heel and strode away. But once I was out of his sight, it took quite a while before I was able to stop shaking.

When I'd calmed down, I went to Ladies' Nightwear to say hello to Mrs. Cross and to ask her forgiveness for running out on my job and leaving her in the lurch. But when I got there, Mrs. Cross was nowhere to be found.

"She retired at the end of August," Miss Ryan told me. "I'm in charge of the department now."

"I see."

"I hope you're not here to try to get your old job back," she said. "You may have been Mrs. Cross's favorite, but you certainly weren't mine. Field's doesn't look kindly on employees who quit without notice."

"I'm not here for a job. I just wanted to say hello to Mrs. Cross." I'd been her favorite? I never would have guessed.

My determination to face Peter wavered. Maybe another day would be better. I headed to the main floor and was almost out the door when I heard my name.

"Miss Corrigan, is it?" I glanced up to see a bearded man, who extended his hand. "Arthur Fraser. I made your acquaintance at the Selfridge reception."

All at once I recalled the friendly man.

"Why, yes. We had a discussion about paintings, if I remember correctly."

"That's right. You're a hard person to track down."

"I no longer work here."

"So I'm told. The only address the Personnel Department had was for the YWCA, but when they inquired they were told you no longer lived there."

"You've been looking for me?"

"The display department is desperately short-staffed, and we've had a terrible time finding a qualified person. Mr. Simpson commended your display work, and I believe you told me you had an interest in becoming a trimmer."

"Yes?"

"I'm wondering if you'd consider working for me as an apprentice window dresser."

He continued talking, something about hard work and long hours, but I barely heard him through the ringing in my ears. Me. An apprentice window dresser at Marshall Field & Company. It was enough to make a girl faint.

But not this girl. I simply drew myself up, smiled, and said with great confidence, "Yes, Mr. Fraser. I'd be happy to discuss the position with you."

CHAPTER THIRTY-SIX

The next morning I met with Mr. Fraser, who outlined the terms of the job. "Miss Corrigan, I'm eager to add a trained artistic eye to my team. You'll have to start at the bottom, of course, and gain more experience. Long hours, hard work. But I have no doubt that, with your talent, you'll rise through the ranks quickly."

I knew working on Arthur Fraser's team would mean working with the best in the business. But was I prepared to work at Field's again? "It's a very tempting offer, Mr. Fraser. I promise to think about it."

"Don't think about it too long, Miss Corrigan," he said. "Soon we'll need to start on the Christmas windows."

As I was leaving the store, I ran into Ruthie.

"Marjorie, I'm so glad to see you. I heard you were coming back." The moccasin trail had certainly wasted no time.

I explained the new job, adding, "I haven't decided whether to accept it yet."

"Why not? Sounds like the work is right up your alley, and you can resume helping at the settlement house."

I shook my head. "No, Ruthie, I don't think so."

"Why not?"

"It's a long story," I said, not knowing how detailed a version Ruthie had heard. The truth was, I didn't think a girl like me had any right to be working with impressionable children. But she wouldn't take no for an answer.

"Everyone's been asking about you since the Fourth of July. We've started working on a Christmas concert. After our stirring performance on the Fourth, we've been invited to sing at Orchestra Hall during the holidays."

"Ruthie, that's so exciting!"

"So we need help. Loads of help. Oh, Marjorie, please think about it. The children adore you, you know. We start rehearsing tonight."

I agreed to think about it. I should have remembered that, in Ruthie's view, "thinking about it" was tantamount to saying yes.

Sure enough, I found myself back at the settlement house that evening, brainstorming costume ideas. I delighted in seeing the children again, and my young friend Gabriella latched on to me as if I'd never been gone.

"I'm to sing a solo," she announced with pride.

"That's quite an honor," I said. "I'm sure you'll sing beautifully."

"I hope so. I'm a little nervous."

"That's natural. Just do your best. Sing your heart out as you normally do, and you'll do fine."

"I only wish I had a pretty dress to wear to the concert," she said. "Not some old patched hand-me-down of my sister's."

In Gabriella's family, spending money on a new dress was out of the question. "Never mind, sweetie. What matters is that you sing your very best. That's what the audience wants to hear. Whether or not you have the perfect dress won't matter, in the long run."

Hearing myself, I cringed. Where had that little gem of wisdom been when I needed it most?

Gabriella nodded. "I know. 'The Lord looks on the heart.'" Parroting a verse I'd repeated often to the children, she looked at me wistfully. "But still."

"I know." Pretty dresses were important to young girls, and it was no use trying to convince them otherwise. Older girls, too. Even though I had little extra money to buy her a new dress, I vowed to ferret through the clearance racks in Field's basement to see if I could find a suitable bargain.

I telephoned Pop and Frances about Mr. Fraser's job offer and received their blessing in return. Now that my engagement to Richard was no more, there was nothing to tether me to Kerryville except my job at Corrigan's Dry Goods, and Pop was the first to encourage me in my new position.

Working for Mr. Fraser turned out to be tough but rewarding. We "trimmers" did a lot of our work after hours, in order to not mess up the sales floor during the shopping day. So I frequently found myself working a different schedule than most of the staff, which suited me fine. Even during normal hours I was sequestered in a basement workshop, not out on the selling floor. I saw less of my friends, but the longer I could put off running into Peter Bachmann, the better. My heart longed to see him, but my head knew better. I had no idea what I'd say to him.

Meanwhile, despite scouring the racks in Field's basement and other discount retailers, I'd had no luck finding a suitable dress for Gabriella that I could afford. One evening in October, after a particularly trying concert rehearsal, I came home and ranted to Dot about it.

"She's such a sweet girl, and I know she'll look beautiful in whatever she wears," I said, "but she's growing so fast that it's hard for her mother to keep her supplied with everyday clothes, much less a special-occasion frock she'll wear maybe once or twice. Still, it would mean so much to her. I'd love to buy her one, but I'm strapped."

Dot nodded. "When I stopped singing at Louie's, I gave all my costumes away to charity," she said sadly. "They held such bad memories, I didn't want them around anymore. But now I regret not saving even one. With your skill with a needle and thread, I'm sure you could have made it over for your young friend."

I thought of the violet dress I'd refashioned for Helen for Spring Fling. I wondered if it might fit Gabriella, and whether Helen would be willing to lend it for the occasion. It was really a springtime dress, not particularly suitable for Christmas. Still, if I could only—

A lightning bolt flashed through my brain. I snapped my fingers. "Dot, you're brilliant."

"What'd I say?"

All at once I knew what to do. I went into my bedroom, rummaged through the bottom drawer of the dresser, and pulled out a length of crumpled blue satin.

Working backstage at Field's freed me from some of the strictest rules regarding my appearance. Likely as not to be covered in paint and sawdust by the end of my shift, I was able to let my guard down somewhat—to wear older clothes and not worry so much about making a polished appearance to impress a supervisor or anyone else.

I relished this new freedom, sometimes not even bothering to apply powder or lipstick. So it shouldn't have surprised me that—on a Saturday afternoon when I had not only let my grooming standards slip, but had flung them forcibly to the ground and stomped on them—I ran smack into Peter Bachmann in the employee lounge.

"Marjorie!" he said with delight. "I'd heard you were back. Congratulations on the new position. I know you'll make a terrific success of it."

Heart thumping, I thanked him and tried to slink away, hoping he wouldn't notice my arms were blue to the elbows from painting a night-sky backdrop for the Christmas windows.

"Can I convince you to have dinner with me tonight?" he said, as if he'd never seen me standing in a torn dress outside a speakeasy, liquor on my breath, like some sort of floozy, especially after my self-righteous anti-liquor proclamation. While I would have preferred for the earth to crack open and swallow me whole, resistance to his endearing crinkly-eyed smile was futile.

"All right, but I'll need to freshen up first."

"We could go to that German place you like so much. I hear they're running some Oktoberfest specials."

At closing time I did my best to repair my appearance. We walked over to the Berghoff, chatting of inconsequential things. It wasn't until after we'd ordered that he pinned me under his gaze.

"How have you been, Marjorie?"

"All right, I guess."

"And your family?"

"They're fine."

He leaned toward me across the table. "I've missed you. You have no idea how much."

A delicious shiver touched my spine. I broke our gaze and looked down at my wrist, where a faint line of blue pigment showed above the hem of my glove. *Don't*, I pleaded silently. *Don't be kind. One kind word and I'll fall hopelessly in love with you, and we both know that's a mistake.*

Safer to stick to business. "How are things going in the Store for Men?"

He sat back. "It's been a hard day. I need to send a huge order of silk neckties to a sports team on the West Coast. The coach wants them for his players to wear at some big promotional event. Unfortunately the shipment can't go out until Monday, which cuts it really close."

"Why can't they ship it tomorrow?"

He twisted his mouth. "No shipments on Sundays."

"Sure there are," I said. I told him about seeing trucks being loaded with cartons of hair tonic late on a Saturday night. "I'm sure Kurt said they had to do it then, because the shipment needed to go out early on Sunday morning. So it's not out of the question. You should talk to the shipping manager and see if he'll make an exception for you."

"Hair tonic?" Peter snorted. "You mean to tell me that some customer was having a hair tonic emergency?"

"Some *huge* customer," I said. "Truckloads of the stuff. Kurt said it was part of the charity drive."

"Charity drive?" He grinned. "I think you were just dreaming. Or delirious, after too much time around glue and paint fumes."

"I know what I saw," I said, secretly miffed he didn't believe me. "Besides, this happened pre-fumes. I was still working in Ladies' Nightwear."

Something in his expression shifted. "Hair tonic." He rubbed his chin. "Lots of it, you say?"

"Cases and cases."

"Do you remember anyone else who was there, besides Kurt?"

I named off a couple of other fellows I'd recognized. "But most of them I didn't know."

He leaned forward. "Who else have you told about this?"

"No one except Mrs. Cross. She said Field's was just being generous to the needy."

"I see." He stood up and threw some money on the table. "If you'll excuse me, Marjorie, I'm going to take your advice about talking to the shipping manager. With any luck I can catch him before he goes home. Can we postpone dinner? Say, tomorrow night instead?"

"Sure."

"Aw, you're swell. Pick you up at six." Without warning, he bent down and kissed me soundly on the forehead, and was gone.

My hand shook as I lifted my coffee cup. I struggled to put two thoughts together. I hadn't even had a chance to tell Peter how terrible I felt about that night at the speakeasy. Maybe he'd forgotten all about it, unlikely as that was. But what about that gorgeous redhead? And—oh, yeah—the bootlegging? But now the only thing that seemed to matter was the feel of his lips against my forehead. The man was poison and I knew it. And the worst thing was, I didn't care.

On Sunday afternoon after church, I sat cross-legged on the apartment floor, surrounded by a sea of blue satin, carefully cutting around the stains on the skirt of what was to become Gabriella's dress. After being wadded up in a drawer and forgotten, the garment had needed a thorough cleaning, and was still ruined in several places. Fortunately Gabriella had the petite figure of a fairy sprite and there would be plenty of fabric left to fit her.

The door-buzzer sounded. Dot tossed aside her magazine and stood to answer it.

"Oh, dear," I said, glancing at my wristwatch. "That must be Peter. We're supposed to have dinner together, but either I completely lost track of the time or he's awfully early."

But instead of Peter, the voice that floated up through the speaking tube was Charlie's. Moments later he stood in the doorway, a bouquet of flowers clutched in his hand.

Dot lit up like a firefly and kissed him on the cheek. "Charlie! This is a surprise. What are you doing in the city?" She blushed like a schoolgirl as he handed her the flowers.

"I guess you're not here to see your old sister." I rose stiffly on my cramped legs and gave my brother a hug.

"I'm here for several reasons, not the least of which is to make sure my old sister's all right. The folks at home are a bit worried about how you're making out."

"I'm fine. Coming back here was the right thing to do."

"That's good." He ruffled my hair as if I were ten, then smiled at Dot, who looked positively demure in a sweater and skirt. "I was also hoping to take my best girl out to dinner. You don't have to work tonight, do you?"

"Nosiree. As I told you, I'm through with all of that. Louie, the club, everything. I really mean it this time. I'd love to go out with you." She winked at me. "If we wait just a little while, you can meet the mysterious Peter Bachmann. Maybe we can double-date for dinner. What do you say, Marjie?"

"Who's Peter Bachmann?" Charlie said.

"Richard's replacement," Dot said.

"Oh, yeah?" He grinned. Concerning my broken engagement, Charlie was every bit as relieved as Frances was appalled.

"He's not replacing anybody," I said. "Peter and I are just friends."

"*Special* friends," Dot said, making me regret I'd confided to her about the kiss in a moment of roommately weakness.

"We wouldn't want to intrude on your evening." I scooped up pieces of blue satin from the floor.

"You won't be intruding. Right, Charlie?"

"Of course not. I should probably meet this guy, anyway, if he has designs on my sister."

"Nobody has any designs on anybody," I said.

"Oh, I don't know about that," Charlie countered, gazing meaningfully at Dot. She giggled. I rolled my eyes.

"Then I guess I'd better change."

"You run along and get prettied up," Dot said. "I'll put these flowers in a vase, and we'll just sit here and visit until you're ready."

Sensing they wanted some time alone, I took my time in the tub. The glorious hot water soothed my tired back after a long afternoon bent over my sewing. I smiled inside when I realized that remarkably little talking was taking place in the front room. I dawdled about fixing my hair and choosing an outfit.

When the buzzer sounded, I called, "I'll be right out," and wrestled with the hook and eye on the back of my dress. I heard Dot speak into the tube. "Peter, come on up. There's somebody here who's just dying to meet you."

I emerged from the bedroom just as Peter appeared in the door-way. At the sight of him, Charlie's face drained of all color, then flushed a deep red. The two men stared at each other for a long moment.

"Charlie, I'd like you to meet—"

But before Dot could say another word, Charlie hauled back his good arm and decked Peter straight across the jaw.

CHAPTER THIRTY-SEVEN

"Jack Lund! You moron! We all thought you were dead," Charlie shouted. Peter sat on the floor with a stunned look on his face and worked his jaw, apparently knocked speechless. "Ten years without a word to anybody? You don't let anybody know you're alive? You never heard of a telephone? Or Western Union?"

Dot gave a little yelp.

"Charlie, stop it," I cried. "That's not Jack." I put a hand on his arm and he shook it off.

"Whaddya mean?" Charlie pointed a shaking finger at the hapless Peter. "That there is Jack Lund, as sure as I'm standing here."

"No, it's not. Look, I thought so too, but it's not Jack. Really. It's Peter Bachmann, from the store."

Charlie rubbed his fist against his shirt, breathing hard. His eyes were bright with unshed tears as he stared at Peter.

"Charlie, it's the fellow I told you I thought was Jack. Remember that?"

Charlie ran his hand roughly across his mouth. "You mean that time I said you had a screw loose?"

"Yes. But he's not, I tell you."

"Well, I'll be . . . gosh, he sure had me fooled." Sheepishly Charlie extended a hand to Peter, helped him up off the floor, and retrieved his hat from where it had fallen. "Sorry about that, fella. Gave me sort of a shock there. You look exactly like an old friend of mine."

"I know. I've been told." Peter rubbed his tender jaw. "Quite a hook you got there. If that's how you treat your old friends, I'd hate to see what you do to your enemies."

"I'm really sorry." Charlie reached out for a handshake. "Gosh. Let's start over. I'm Charlie Corrigan. Marjorie's brother."

"Peter Bachmann. Marjorie's . . . friend."

"Well, good thing that's settled." Dot eyed the three of us warily. After an awkward pause she said, "Peter, Charlie and I were just on our way out to dinner. Won't you two join us?"

"I'm afraid not," Peter said.

Charlie scrubbed a hand over his face. "Hey, buddy, it'll be my treat. It's the least I can do to make up for practically busting your jaw."

"I appreciate the offer, Charlie, but it's not that." He turned to me. "Marjorie, I apologize. I just came by to tell you I have to break our plans this evening. Something—well, something's come up."

"Sure, Peter. That's all right." It didn't really feel all right, but who could blame the man? I sure wouldn't want to go out with someone whose brother had just socked me in the face.

"We'll do it real soon," Peter promised, and off he went.

"Gee, sis. I don't know what to say." Charlie shook his head. "I really thought he was Jack for a moment there. I'm sorry I doubted you before. I thought you were just—you know, dreaming. Now I know why you thought—"

"I know." I cut him off, weary of the topic. "I'm just relieved you now know I wasn't crazy. Let's just forget the whole thing, shall we?"

Dot linked her arm through mine. "You'll still come out to dinner with us, even without Peter, right, Marjie? I'm starving. What do you say we drown our sorrows in sweet-and-sour sauce?"

We drove to the Orange Garden in Charlie's car. Over chow mein and egg rolls, I told him everything I knew about Peter, which turned out to be not all that much. Charlie mostly listened, interjecting every so often with an incredulous, "It's the darndest thing."

As we waited for the check, Dot slid her arm through Charlie's. "It's so sweet of you to come all the way to the city to see us. Where should we go next?"

Charlie squirmed. "Well, to be honest, there is another reason I came here tonight."

"What's that?"

"Now don't get steamed," he warned. Dot shot him a wary glance. "I'm going to the revival meeting at the Coliseum tonight." He checked his wristwatch. "In fact, I need to leave soon." His voice turned pleading. "And I'm asking you one last time to come with me. But, with or without you, I'm going."

"Oh, Charlie. No." Dot's eyes glittered. "I *told* you. Reverend Barker is nothing but a big con man. Why, he has no more healing powers than a magical toad in a fairy tale. Don't be a fool."

"What are you two talking about?" I said, mystified by Dot's sudden fit of temper. "Who's Reverend Barker?"

"He's a healer. He's helped lots of others, and he can help me. I know he can," Charlie said firmly. "Dot doesn't believe it."

She lifted her chin. "Your brother thinks a traveling carnival man can perform healing miracles," she spat. "Well, you can do as you like, Charlie Corrigan. But I want no part of it." She stood up, grabbed her purse, and stormed out of the restaurant. Charlie tossed some money on the table and ran after her. I chased after Charlie. We reached the sidewalk just in time to watch Dot speed away in a taxi.

I still didn't understand. "What just happened? Why is she so upset?"

Charlie shook his head, his face pale in the glow of the restaurant's neon sign. "Haven't you been reading the papers? This Reverend Barker has been healing all kinds of people—making the crippled walk again, that sort of thing. This is his last night in town." He held up his limp arm. "Look at me, sis. My useless arm, my bum leg . . . the docs haven't been able to help me. I'm at the end of my rope. What have I got to lose?"

My heart cracked wide open. "Oh, Charlie—"

He shook his head. "I've been telling Dot for weeks that I want to see this fellow, to see for myself if he can heal me. But every time I bring it up, she won't even discuss it. She says he's just a huckster."

"Charlie. I don't know," I said, gently touching his shoulder. "Maybe she's right. If this Reverend Barker really has healing powers, why doesn't he just walk up and down the wards at Cook County Hospital, making people well? Why does he only do it in a stadium filled with thousands of people?"

"He wouldn't have this reputation if there wasn't some truth to it," Charlie reasoned. "Maybe he can't heal everybody, but even if he can help just a little—" He looked skyward as if speaking to the stars. "Look, sis, you don't know what it's like, being in pain all the time.

Always having to ask for help. Never being able to dance with your girl, to show her a good time." He walked to his roadster and opened the driver-side door. "I don't care what you say, sis. I'm going."

"Wait." I reached for the passenger door. "You're not going alone."

When we got to the Coliseum, a line had already formed outside. Mixed into the crowd were many people with visible ailments: wheelchairs, crutches, canes. The air crackled with energy as we took our places in the queue.

In the shadows against the building, a woman in an orange dress spoke animatedly with her companion. I nudged Charlie.

"See that woman over there? In the orange dress?"

"Yeah? What about her?"

"She shops at Field's. A regular. I see her all the time."

"Big deal. Probably half the women here shop at Field's."

"Maybe I should go over and say hello."

But Charlie wasn't listening. He was straining to get inside the building.

A small army of sharply dressed ushers stood at various points. Some greeted people, making friendly inquiries about their health and well-being. Others directed foot traffic, funneling people to various sections of the vast stadium.

Finally Charlie and I entered the cavernous hall. Organ music warbled over the steady hum of voices. An usher approached us.

"Good evening, folks." He reached out his right hand to shake Charlie's. In response Charlie extended his left hand. "Bum arm." He looked down. "Bum leg, too. War injuries."

"Ah. War injuries," the usher repeated. "On behalf of the Reverend Barker ministry, let me express our thanks for your service to our country." As he motioned for us to follow him down an aisle, I noticed he discreetly observed Charlie's limp. About halfway to the stage, he stopped. "Here are some seats, right here."

Charlie nodded toward the stage. "I was hoping to sit up closer to the front, closer to Reverend Barker."

"There'll be a time to come forward," the usher said. "You'll have ample time. We need to reserve the front places for the severely impaired. Now please be seated."

So we sat.

Before the great evangelist took the stage, there was about an hour of music—group singing of familiar hymns interspersed with solos by a warbling soprano and a deep, resonant baritone. Glancing around, I saw many faces glowing with anticipation and excitement, and others glazed over with fatigue, or maybe boredom.

When Reverend Barker finally took the stage, the crowd cheered. He acknowledged the cheers and then spread his arms and looked heavenward. As the audience settled down, music continued in the background, softly, enticingly.

"I have an anointing from God to heal people," he shouted. "Jesus doesn't want you to be sick."

As he spoke, his voice modulated crazily, now rapidly, now loudly, now practically a whisper. He held a Bible in his hand, but I didn't ever see him open it.

Next came a series of testimonies from people who claimed to have been healed at past meetings. A man spoke of being healed of severe headaches, another of back pain, another of an addiction to alcohol. One woman hobbled to the front, obviously in pain, but claimed to have been healed of needing a wheelchair.

After several such testimonies, Reverend Barker closed his eyes and extended his hands out toward the crowd, as if he were feeling something tangible hovering in the air.

"In the audience God is touching people right now, right here," he declared. "The Lord has just told me a muscle spasm has been healed. Hallelujah, amen. Somewhere in the audience, a sinus condition has just been healed. A neck injury has been healed. The Lord is touching many of you in this audience right here in this auditorium. Those of you listening to me on the radio at home, many of you are being healed."

I glanced over at Charlie. He stared at the stage as if hypnotized, his expression impossible to read. Was he buying this?

Reverend Barker lifted his arms. "I want you to reach into your pocket or your billfold and pull out the largest bill you have. If it's a ten-dollar bill, I want you to get that out. If it's a one-dollar bill, I want you to get that out. If it's only a quarter or a dime, get that out, too. Give God the biggest offering you can."

Ushers extended baskets on long poles down each row. Soon the baskets were filled with bills and coins, and an occasional scribbled note. When the basket came to our row, I kept my purse firmly shut, but Charlie tossed in a few bills.

After the collection, at long last the preacher said, "Those of you in need of healing, come forward."

People seated at the front began lining up near a set of stairs leading to a stage.

"I'm going up." Charlie stepped out into the aisle. An usher moved quickly to block his path.

"Sir, you can't go up there now."

"Why not? Everyone else is. He said it's time." Charlie tried to move past the man, but he was bigger than a Green Bay Packer, and just as menacing in spite of his frozen smile.

"I'm afraid the stage is too crowded just now. For your own safety, please return to your seat."

Charlie panicked. "But I need to get to the stage. I must see Reverend Barker. I've waited so long."

"Sit down, sir, or I'll have to ask you to leave."

The usher stood firm, arms crossed. Charlie scanned the gigantic hall, desperate to find another way to approach the stage.

Just then a flash of orange caught my eye. A wheelchair-bound woman passed us, propelled down the aisle by another one of the ushers. Something wasn't right. I clutched Charlie's arm.

"Charlie, see that woman? The one in the wheelchair? It's the woman in the orange dress. Look."

Charlie stared in disbelief. "But—wait a minute. What's she doing in a wheelchair? A few minutes ago, she was walking around, same as us."

We watched in horrified fascination as the chair was wheeled up the ramp. When her turn came, Reverend Barker muttered some unintelligible words, waved his arms, and commanded her to stand up, which she did. The frenzied crowd burst into cheers, whistles, and "Amens."

Charlie's profile was stoic, but his jaw worked in frustration as he stared at the preacher onstage, eyes glistening with fury and disappointment.

My heart clenched. "Come on, Charlie." I said, putting a hand on his arm. "Let's go home."

He didn't protest. We pushed our way back through the crowd, through the lobby, and out into the cool autumn air. People were still streaming in.

To our surprise, leaning against a wall in the shadows near the entrance, Dot stood watching the crowd. She spotted us and walked over, soberly assessing the expression on Charlie's face.

"You came," Charlie said.

"Yes," Dot said quietly, touching his arm. "I've been here the whole time."

"You wasted your time. Nothing to see here." His voice cracked.

Wordlessly she put her arms around him. They held on to each other for a long minute while people brushed past them. "I'm so sorry, Charlie. I'm so sorry," Dot said over and over, her voice muffled against Charlie's jacket. He didn't answer, just stood with his face buried in her hair.

"You were right, Dot," I said. "That man is a complete charlatan." A few passersby gave me dirty looks. I didn't care.

At long last Charlie lifted his head. In a choked voice that broke my heart in two he said, "I wanted to be whole, Dot. I wanted to be a whole man—for you."

"For me?" she cried, her voice raw with disbelief. She pounded his shoulders with her fists. "You idiot. Don't you know I love you, just the way you are? You're perfect in my eyes."

Charlie looked at the ground. "I should have listened to you. Pretty funny, huh? I guess you can say you told me so."

She grasped his shoulders and looked squarely into his face. "Charlie, I'd give anything to be wrong. Anything. Nothing would have given me greater joy than to be proven wrong. But he's a charlatan, Charlie. He's nothing but a fake."

He shook his head. "You're right. You were right all along." He glanced back at the entrance. "But he seems so convincing. How could you be so sure?"

Dot gave a derisive snort. "That's easy," she snarled. "Reverend Barker is my father."

CHAPTER THIRTY-EIGHT

"He's your *father*?" Charlie said for the umpteenth time, shaking his head as if he still couldn't wrap his brain around Dot's revelation. The three of us sat huddled over root beer floats in a brightly lit diner near the Coliseum. The place was crowded and hot, despite the autumn chill outside. An oscillating fan created a breeze against the nape of my neck, giving me shivers and making me temporarily regret my chic haircut.

"Barker's my real name," Dot explained. "Dorothy Barker. Rodgers was my mother's name. After I left home, I never wanted to be associated with . . . with *him*." She shook her head. "That day in Kerryville, when I saw in the paper that he was bringing his spectacle to Chicago, I couldn't believe my eyes."

"So that was it," I said. "That's what upset you in the paper that evening—the notice of the revival meeting. Pop and I were wondering."

She nodded. "Yeah, sorry. I didn't want to talk about it. I tried to ignore the whole thing. But then, Charlie, when you wrote to me that you wanted to see him, that you hoped he would heal you, I felt absolutely sick."

"I can see why," Charlie said, his face grim. "He sure took me for a fool."

"You're not a fool, Charlie," I said, touching his forearm. "You hoped, that's all. Just like I hoped that Peter was really Jack. But we both put our hopes in an illusion."

"So did I, for years and years." Dot stirred the straw around in her glass. "My father wasn't always a fraud. I believe he started out in the ministry with good intentions. But that was long before I was born. By the time I came along, he'd let his thirst for money and fame get the better of him. That's why I left home—I couldn't stand it anymore, watching good people get fleeced. And that's why I've stayed away from church for so long. Hypocrites, all of them." She glanced up at me through wet lashes. "Well, maybe not all."

"Reverend Barker may be a fraud," I said, "but not all Christians are."

"I think I know that now," Dot said. "I'm beginning to, anyway, thanks to you and Charlie." She pushed her glass aside and rested her forearms on the table. "I've done some horrible things. I was a gangster's girlfriend, for Pete's sake. I've done things that weren't honest or even moral. I've treated you so shabbily, Marjorie. I know you've already said you've forgiven me, but—"

"There's nothing to forgive. You gave me a home, and helped me get a job. If it weren't for you . . ."

Dot's voice quivered. "If it weren't for me, you wouldn't have spent your last dime on an expensive gown that got ruined."

"What gown?" Charlie broke in.

She sniffled. "Or nearly gotten arrested at the speakeasy. . ."

"Arrested? Speakeasy? *You*?" Charlie's eyes grew even wider.

"Long story," I muttered. "Tell you later."

Dot reached across the table. "Please, Marjie, say it again—you'll forgive me."

I took her hand. "Of course I forgive you, Dot. But more important, God forgives you. And he forgives me, and Charlie here, and everybody who trusts in Him."

Dot gave a cold, mirthless laugh. I shot up a silent prayer for the right thing to say. Mrs. Dunsworthy's wise words floated to mind. "Dot," I said carefully, "I wasted a lot of time feeling distant from God. Then I realized that He wasn't the one who backed off; it was me. He promises believers he will never leave us or forsake us." She looked unconvinced.

Charlie tried another approach. "Look, Dot. Your father . . . he might have been a fraud and a hypocrite. But the fact is, the church is *filled* with hypocrites. The Bible says the sick need a doctor, not the healthy."

I watched as a tear slid down her flawless cheek. "Oh, Dot. Don't you see? No matter what your father did or didn't do, Jesus loves you. Come back to Him. Don't let someone else's mistakes shake your faith forever."

Dot dabbed her eyes with a napkin. In the intensity of the moment, I noticed she even *cried* prettily. Some things in life simply weren't fair.

When she'd composed herself she said, "If it's all right with you, I think I'd like to come to church with you on Sunday, Marjie. From what you've told me, it sounds like a real church."

"Oh, Dot, I'd love it."

"No promises, though," she added quickly. "No promises about— you know. Jesus."

"I understand," I said. "You just come and listen, and learn." I turned to my brother. "And you—you mustn't give up hope either, Charlie. If it's God's will, He will heal you. In His time."

"And if He doesn't, that's all right by me." Dot grasped his hand in hers. "It's *you* I love, Charlie Corrigan. I don't care about your leg, or your arm, or whether or not you can dance the Charleston or throw a baseball. I only care about *you*."

We finished our drinks, then Charlie drove us home. He drew the roadster up to the curb and I climbed out of the back seat.

"If you don't mind, Marjie, I won't go in just yet," Dot said with a grin. "Charlie and I have some things to talk over."

"Yeah. Things," Charlie added. "I'll bet the harvest moon over the lake is really something to see."

"Well, happy moon-gazing, you two," I teased. "Don't stay out too late. Tomorrow's a work day."

"Yes, mother." Dot winked as they drove off.

I watched the taillights until they were out of sight. Thrilled as I was that Dot and my brother had found each other, their happiness punctuated my loneliness. I glanced up at the moon, glowing orange through the tree branches. Without someone special to watch it with, it was just a big old orb hanging in the sky. I thought of Peter and wondered whether he'd ever speak to me again. After Charlie's fit of temper, he'd probably had more than enough of the Corrigan family.

The wind picked up. Dried leaves whispered and scuttled across the sidewalk. I pulled my cardigan more tightly and hurried toward the steps, eager for a warm bath and a good novel.

Suddenly a figure lurched out from the shadows. My heart leaped to my throat. Instinctively I raised my handbag, ready to swat.

"Hold on," the figure protested, arms raised in self-defense. "It's only me."

When I saw who it was, I still swatted him, though not as hard as I would have otherwise. "Good grief, Peter. You frightened me out of my wits."

"Sorry, I didn't mean to."

I hugged my arms against the chill. "What are you doing here?"

"Waiting for you," he said. "There's something important I have to tell you."

I peered at him under the porch light and gasped.

"What happened to you?" His right eye was swollen and turning purple, and a thin line of blood had dried on his lip. "Charlie didn't hit you that hard, did he?"

"No. Some other guy."

"Come inside. Let's get you cleaned up."

"I can't stay. Here, let's sit down for a minute."

I sat on the top step, smoothing my skirt around my knees. He sat beside me. "I thought you should know, Field's was raided tonight."

"What do you mean, raided?"

"Liquor raid. I wanted you to hear it from me before you got to work in the morning. Lucky thing the store was closed today. Nobody got hurt. Well, not too badly." Gingerly he touched his wounded lip and winced.

"A liquor raid? At Field's?" That didn't make sense. Liquor raids happened at gin joints and back-alley barrooms, not classy department stores.

"Remember that hair tonic you saw being loaded onto trucks?" I nodded. "Bootleg Jamaican rum. Every drop of it. Gang's been using Marshall Field trucks to move liquor around the city undetected."

"Rum. I see." I shivered and hugged my knees. "And you happened to be there." On a Sunday. When the store was closed. "You saw the whole thing."

"Well . . . yeah. That's what I wanted to talk to you about."

Was Peter in on it? Was this his confession? I steeled myself for what I was about to hear. "Peter, are you in some kind of trouble? Did you have something to do with it?"

"Huh?"

I was exhausted with the effort of pretending. Suddenly the whole scene played out in my mind. The black eye, the cut lip, the torn clothes—Peter had, as they say, given them the slip. It happened all the time in detective movies. The criminal would evade the cops, stopping only to bid his best girl good-bye before running for his life. Was I Peter's best girl? In any case, if he went on the lam, I might never see him again. It was time for both of us to come clean.

"Peter," I breathed, "I know all about it."

He frowned. "You do?"

"Yes."

"How? It just happened."

"Not about the raid," I said. "About you."

"Me?" His eyes grew wide. He rubbed the back of his neck. "How did you know? Why didn't you say anything?"

"I figured it out," I whispered, lest Mrs. Moran overhear and call the cops. "I didn't say anything because I don't want you to go to jail. I care about you too much."

"Jail? What—"

"It doesn't matter now." My voice cracked. I couldn't take any more. "Oh, Peter. What will you do? Where will you go?"

"What do you mean, where will I go?"

"Now that you're on the lam. Will I ever see you again?"

"On the—what are you talking about?"

I flung my hands in despair. "I know all about it. The—the *bootlegging.*"

He looked at me curiously for a long moment, then burst out laughing. "Wait a minute. Which side do you think I'm on in this business?"

"Huh?"

"Why would I go, as you said, 'on the lam'? And who taught you to talk like that, anyway? Jimmy Cagney?"

My face burned. "You're a bootlegger, aren't you? Isn't that what this is all about?"

Several minutes passed before he was able to stop laughing enough to speak. Finally he wheezed, "Marjorie . . . sweet, funny Marjorie. I'm not a bootlegger. I'm a federal agent!"

I gasped. "You're a *what*?"

"I'm an agent. I've been working undercover at Field's for months, trying to crack this big liquor-smuggling ring. And now with your help, we've done it."

"That's wonderful, but . . . with *my* help? What did I do?"

"The hair tonic," he said. "The trucks. He only dared that risky caper once or twice, so if you hadn't tipped me off, it might have taken even longer to figure it out."

"No." Gradually the truth dawned in my thick head. "So you've been faking all this time? You're not really a menswear salesman?" He shook his head. "But you have everyone fooled. They all think you sell shirts and ties—and you're so good at it."

"I am good at it." He shrugged. "I told you, I worked at Gimbel's. That's one reason I got chosen for this assignment. I knew how to blend in."

A memory edged into my brain. "So that night at the country club, when you were asking the waiter for liquor . . ."

"Just trying to ferret out whether Mr. Simpson was in on the ring. By the way, he's not. Staunch teetotaler, all the way. He and the other executives had no idea what was going on, and are cooperating fully in the investigation."

"And the gun you wear . . ."

He winced. "You saw that? You shouldn't have. My mistake. It's agency issue."

"And that night at the speakeasy . . ."

"I was there to assist with the stakeout." He shook his head. "Boy, was I ever surprised to see you there."

"Ditto." I flinched. "Don't remind me. That was the worst night of my life."

"Glad to hear it. I thought you were keeping a secret identity of your own."

I'd had enough secrets for one night. "First Dot tells me she's Reverend Barker's daughter, and now you're telling me you're a federal agent. Next thing you know, Charlie will be telling me he's actually the Duke of Windsor, slumming among the common folk in disguise. I must admit, it bothers me you're such a good liar."

Peter flinched. "All part of the job." He rubbed his jaw. "Gotta give 'em credit, using the trucks was a clever trick. Nobody would think twice about seeing a Marshall Field's delivery truck in a wealthy neighborhood, and a lot of those mansions hide secret liquor stashes behind false walls and things like that."

"So tell me about this smuggling ring," I urged. "If the Field's bigwigs aren't in on it, who is?"

"It's a branch of an outfit based in New York. Braccio's the local thug in charge."

"Braccio? As in, Luigi Braccio? The terror of the West Side?"

"Yeah. When I saw you and Dot at his joint that night, I had to wonder if you were involved, too, but you both came up clean."

"Came up *clean*? Heavens. Well, that's good, I guess." My head started to pound. "Dot used to sing at Louie Braccio's club. They were seeing each other, too, until Dot called it off and started dating Charlie."

"Smart move on her part. Well, the good news is, Braccio's locked up. Thanks to you, most of the ring has been apprehended, but unfortunately Braccio's number two man is nowhere to be found. And it's somebody you know."

"Who?"

His jaw tightened. "Kurt Steuben."

"Kurt, the security guard? You're kidding." That snake had no limits. "But I thought you two were buddies."

"Only because we were trailing him. I hoped he'd invite me in on the operation, which would have made the whole case a lot easier to crack, but he never did."

My stomach roiled as I thought of how I'd allowed Helen to ride on the excursion boat with not only a common lecher, but a dangerous criminal. If it were up to me, she wouldn't talk to another man until she was thirty-five.

"There was another insider, too, a woman," Peter said. "Stella Davenport."

"Stella from Fine Jewelry? The redhead?" Peter nodded. My heart gave a little skip. "Is that why I kept seeing you two together? You were spying on her?"

"Yeah, just trying to get her to inadvertently spill what she knew." He glanced at me. "You noticed us together? When?"

"All the time. In the cafeteria, on the street . . . I thought you two were an item."

"That's good. That's what people were supposed to think, including her." He smiled sweetly. "But, nah. Not my type."

"Who is your type?" I blurted.

Before he could answer that shamefully bold question, the El roared overhead, rattling our bones. When it had passed, he spoke again, his voice husky.

"I think you know the answer to that. I'm crazy about you, Marjorie. Do you understand now why I couldn't tell you before? I couldn't risk blowing my cover. My line of work requires certain doors to remain closed, even to people I love."

People he loves. My breath caught in my throat. "And I couldn't risk dating a bootlegger. But in fact, that's exactly what I did. Or thought I did. Turns out I fell in love with a federal agent. If that doesn't beat all."

"Marjorie." He took both my hands in his and leaned in as if to kiss me, then backed away. "I need to be sure of one thing," he said in a low, husky voice. "Is it really me you love . . . or the ghost of Jack Lund?"

I had to think for a moment. "At first I wanted to be with you because you reminded me of Jack," I admitted. "But now I know it's you. Just you."

He grinned and leaned toward me. But before his lips touched mine, the tinkling of shattered glass sounded somewhere on the block. His expression darkened. He stood up and pulled me to my feet. "I'm dying to continue this conversation, but we'll have to pick it up later. Let's get you inside. Kurt Steuben's still at large, and we can't take any chances."

"Why would Kurt come after me?"

"According to the men in custody, apparently you and Kurt had some kind of argument recently."

"You could say that." A fresh wave of anger surged through my chest, remembering how he tried to foist himself on Helen.

"Could be revenge, could be fear you'll squeal about what you witnessed in the loading dock. Until we find him, he could be anywhere, and he might be armed. I don't want you to worry, but don't open the door to anyone except Dot or Charlie. Or me."

"I won't." A chill crept up the back of my neck as I slid my key into the lock. "But how did Kurt and Stella get away with being the inside contacts for Braccio?"

"You kidding me? He's a security guard. Everybody trusted him. Trusted her too, working with all that expensive jewelry. But it was nothing a few bribes couldn't take care of. This is Chicago, after all. I have to get back to work. We'll talk later." He held the door open for me and gave me a quick peck on the cheek, then hurried down the steps.

"Peter," I called after him. "I'm sorry I thought you were a bootlegger."

He laughed. "Not me, baby. Never touch the stuff."

"Be careful."

He stopped, turned and loped back up the steps. He cupped my face in his hands and kissed me. Hard. And then he was gone.

That was more like it! With stars swirling in my head, I climbed the inside staircase on wobbly legs, forgetting to avoid the squeakiest stairs so as not to disturb Mrs. Moran. When I opened the door to the apartment, my foot slid on something. I switched on a lamp and saw an envelope on the floor. I reached down and picked it up. It was a telegram, signed for by Mrs. Moran. I ripped open the envelope.

MARJORIE STOP
YOUR FATHER GRAVELY ILL STOP
My insides lurched. *Oh no. Not Pop.*

CHAPTER THIRTY-NINE

Hastily I packed a bag, and as soon as Charlie and Dot returned from moon-gazing, I gave them the news. Then Dot kissed us both good-bye, and Charlie and I drove like the wind toward Kerryville.

Dr. Perkins greeted us as we drove up. Pop had suffered a serious heart attack. Frances, Charlie, and I took turns sitting by his bedside at Kerryville General, fearing for the worst. After two days, the crisis abated and Pop's health stabilized—no better, no worse.

At the hospital, Richard stopped in to see us as often as he could between his rounds. I welcomed him as a comforting old friend, nothing more. He was a good man, and we were both moving on with our lives. Whatever awkwardness there'd been between us vanished in our shared concern over Pop.

A couple of weeks later, after a long afternoon at the hospital, Frances and I dodged roving gangs of costumed trick-or-treaters. As we approached the house I was surprised to see Helen sitting on the porch steps, dressed as Raggedy Ann.

"Why aren't you off bobbing for apples at the church harvest party?"

"Waiting for you. Marjorie, Charlie wants you down at the store."

I glanced at my wristwatch. "Store's closed. He'll be on his way home for supper by now."

"He said it was important and I should send you anyway."

I felt my nerves rapidly fraying. "Helen, I'm exhausted. What does he want?"

"Beats me. He just said to send you down there."

"Oh, for heaven's sake. This had better be good."

I trudged on past the house and down to Main Street. Sure enough, the store was locked and the "Closed" sign was visible. I was reaching into my handbag for my key when Charlie unlocked the door and swung it open.

"What's up? We have a telephone, you know." I rubbed my aching forehead.

Charlie looked queasy. He locked the door behind me and drew a deep breath. "You might want to sit down."

"I don't want to sit down. Tell me what's happening."

"Marjorie, listen." His voice was hoarse with emotion. "You were right. You were right all along."

"Right about what?"

"After meeting Peter at your place, I couldn't shake the image of his face out of my mind. Couldn't get over how much he looked like Jack. So I contacted the War Office for Jack's records."

"You what?"

"I thought they might have a record of where he was buried."

"Even I didn't go that far."

"I'm former military. They pushed the request through."

I braced myself. "So? What did you find out?"

"He's alive."

All at once, my knees practically melted right out from under me.

Time stopped. Earth ceased circling in its orbit.

"What?"

Charlie opened a drawer beneath the cash register and pulled out an envelope. "See for yourself."

I turned my face away. "I don't want to see."

Charlie held out the envelope. "Take it."

My hands shook as I opened the envelope. Inside was a stack of papers, but they didn't make any sense to me. They spoke of the military service, medical records, and honorable discharge of one John P. Lund, Jr.

Jack.

"I don't understand."

Just then a male voice that wasn't Charlie's said, "It's true."

Peter walked in from the stockroom. I froze in place.

"I'm Jack. Jack Lund." His voice cracked and tears glistened at the corners of his eyes. "You were right all along."

Hysteria rose in my chest, nausea in my gut. "What do you mean, I'm right?" My fingers balled into fists. "You're Peter. Peter Bachmann."

"I'm Jack."

"But you said you didn't know me. You said you didn't know Jack Lund or Kerryville, or—or anything."

"I know."

My skin turned to ice. "What game is this? What kind of sick person are you? What kind of sick, dirty, loathsome—"

All at once I was sobbing and couldn't stop. He put his arms around me and drew me close, muffling my great gulping sobs against his coat. Fury turned to joy turned to confusion turned back to fury. I pummeled his chest with my fists.

"Why are you doing this to me?"

"I'm not doing anything to you. When you calm down, I'll explain."

He guided me to a chair.

"You have to understand. I should have told you from the beginning—I wanted to tell you—but I couldn't blow my cover. And then it was just easier to be Peter Bachmann. But when Charlie got hold of my records and confronted me, I knew I had to get straight with you."

"I asked him to come here," Charlie said. "I wanted the three of us to discuss this together." He reached for his jacket and hat. "Jack and I have been talking all afternoon, sis. I'll head home now and tell them you'll be late. Leave you two to talk."

I eyed Peter uncertainly. To Charlie I said, "Don't say anything to them yet about—about all this. I'm not ready."

"I won't." He headed out into the twilight, where an autumn wind whipped the trees.

As the sky through the shop window turned blue, then purple, then black, Peter—or Jack—gently explained about being injured and left for dead on a French battlefield. About waking up in a hospital, not knowing what happened or where he was. About two years spent recovering, undergoing treatments, being shuffled from place to place around Europe.

"Somehow the army mixed up my records," he said. "One day I just up and walked out of some old chateau that had been turned into a hospital. Nobody stopped me. I just kept walking. But even though I'd pretty much recovered physically, I was in a bad way mentally. At first I had trouble finding my way, holding a job, or leading any kind of normal life. I just sort of bummed around Europe, working odd jobs. Eventually I landed in Paris and found work in a men's clothing store. After a while I earned enough to pay for passage back to the States."

"Not to Kerryville," I accused. "Not back to me."

"I couldn't stand the thought of coming back to you a broken wreck. I thought you'd be repulsed by me, or worse, stay with me out of pity, as some sort of good deed."

The kind of girl who does good deeds.

"You should know I'm not like that," I said.

"My head wasn't right for a long time," he said. "And I thought you'd run screaming if you ever saw this." He pointed to his scar.

"Oh, come on. It's not that bad," I said. "In fact, I sort of like it. It makes you look heroic and valorous."

He cocked a grin. "Valorous?"

I bumped his arm playfully. "You know what I mean. Then what happened?"

"When I got back to the States, I stayed in New York first. Got a job at Gimbel's, took a few night courses in business. Then I heard the Bureau was hiring former soldiers, so I started training for that." He glanced at me. "But I did come back to Kerryville. Once."

I stared at him. "When?"

He hesitated, then said, "I guess you might as well know everything."

"Yes. Tell me everything," I said, even though I didn't know how much more of "everything" I could handle.

"By the time I made it back to Kerryville," he continued, "my parents had died, and you were engaged to marry Richard. I heard all about how happy you were, how he could offer you this great life as a doctor's wife. And here was I, damaged goods in more ways than one." He ran a forefinger along his scar.

"When was that? When did you come back?"

"About two years ago. I was only in town for a day. Just a few hours, actually. I saw no reason to stay."

Confusion fogged my brain. "But I still don't understand. You didn't even tell Charlie that you were alive. He was your best friend. He was shattered when you died."

"Disappearing seemed like the right thing to do at the time," he said simply. "You deserved better."

"I never stopped grieving, not inwardly," I said. "I was never really able to love Richard or anyone else—not in the way I had loved you."

"I wish I'd known that," he said. "But you were still really just a kid when I left. People change so much. You're not the same girl I left behind. And I sure as heck am not the same boy who went to war. And as I said, I'd been told your life was turning out perfectly and not to interfere. And since you'd stopped answering my letters . . ."

"Letters?" I said. "What letters? I answered all your . . ." A sickening realization darkened my heart. *It couldn't be* . . . "Jack," I said slowly, "when you came back to Kerryville, who told you about me and Richard?"

He hesitated. "Does it matter?"

"It matters."

He bit his lip. "I don't think—"

I was pretty sure I knew the answer, but I needed him to say it. "Tell me."

He looked at me for a long moment, then sighed. "Frances."

Ice chilled my veins. "Frances. I should have known."

"I came by the house and she answered the door. You weren't home. She said you were blissfully happy with Richard, that you'd long gotten over me, and that it'd ruin everything if you found out the truth. At the time, I'm sorry to say, I was weak enough to believe her."

"Frances," I muttered. "She must have thrown out your letters, too." I turned to him. "Oh, Peter—I mean, Jack—I mean—" I threw up my hands. "I don't even know what to call you."

He smiled weakly. "I don't need to keep my cover identity intact anymore. But I still feel like Peter. Jack is—well, let's just consider him gone. I'm a different man now, Marjorie. And you're a different woman."

I shivered. "It's a lot to take in. I feel so—I don't know. Like everything has been a lie."

"Not everything," he said, touching my cheek. "My feelings for you are real. It's always been you for me, Marjorie." He moved his thumb along my jaw, sending tingles down my spine. "Even when I wasn't sure who *I* was, when I wasn't in my right mind, it was always you."

So many years lost. A flash of anger threatened to choke me. "I still can't believe this—that you stayed away so long, and that Frances deliberately came between us. And now that you're playing this—this—charade of being Peter Bachmann."

"I *am* Peter Bachmann," he said. "I put Jack Lund to rest a long time ago. And as for Frances, well, don't be too hard on her. She only wanted what was best for you. And in the end, she didn't succeed in keeping us apart. God wanted us together, and when God wants something, there's no stopping Him."

He shifted and leaned his face toward mine. By instinct I pulled back at first. Amid so much falsehood, how did I know this part was real? But the magnetism was too strong. Jack was back. Frances was a problem for another day. For now, we had some catching up to do.

Later, as we strolled back to my house arm-in-arm, I said, "I want to know the rest of the story. How did you end up working for the Feds?"

"Turned out my military experience, plus my lack of family ties, made me a good candidate for undercover work. And since I had retail experience—I really did work at Gimbel's for a while—the bureau assigned me to crack the smuggling ring at Field's. They sent me here from New York. I adopted an alias, and everything was fine, until you showed up."

"Yes. I showed up." I smiled through my tears, remembering the scene I made at Union Station, in what seemed like another lifetime ago.

"I almost swallowed my tongue when I first saw you," he said.

"You were one cool cat then. I thought for sure I was seeing things," I said. "How did you choose the name 'Peter Bachmann'?"

"Easy. My middle name's Peter and my mother's maiden name was Bachmann."

"So many lies."

"The bureau calls them cover stories. I wanted so badly to tell you everything, to get it all out in the open," Peter insisted, "but I couldn't risk blowing my cover. Not until the case was over, at least. To do so would have put the entire operation in jeopardy, and worse, could have put you and your family's lives at risk. The less you knew, the better."

I shivered.

"Even when the case was over, I could never rustle up the nerve to tell you. And you being engaged to Richard mixed things up even more . . ." He grimaced. "I have to warn you, Marjorie. While I'm a lot better than I was even a couple of years ago, I don't know if I'll ever be completely well. I get headaches sometimes. Nightmares. I would never want to burden you."

"You could never be a burden. And this may come as a shock to you, but I'm not perfect either."

He laughed.

I said, "Together with God we are more than a match for whatever comes our way." I snuggled against his shoulder. "So what happens now?"

"I guess that's up to you, me, and the Lord."

"Let's take our time. It's a big adjustment."

"There's no rush. We have all the time in the world."

CHAPTER FORTY

"I'm so sorry, Marjorie," Frances said tearfully, during a late-night vigil by Pop's hospital bed after I'd confronted her about interfering between Jack and me. "I never meant to cause you heartache. I truly thought you'd have a much better future with Richard. I only wanted the best for you."

"You wanted the best for *you*, Frances," I said as gently as I could under the circumstances. "You weren't looking out for anyone's interest but your own—not mine, and certainly not Richard's. Richard is a good man, a kind man. He deserves a woman who truly loves him."

I glanced at Pop, who appeared to be sound asleep, his chest rising and falling under the starched sheet and army-green blanket.

"Did Pop know, too?" I whispered. "Did he know Jack was alive?"

"No. I never told him."

"That's a relief." Tension drained from my shoulders. Somehow the sort of subterfuge that I found par for the course in Frances would have been unthinkable in Pop.

Frances's eyes glistened with tears of genuine remorse. "Can you ever forgive me?"

Gulping hard, I reached out and put my hand over hers. Holding a grudge wouldn't do anybody any good. "Of course I can, Frances. The important thing is that he's alive, and he's back. Even when we couldn't see it, God's been in charge the whole time. No matter what plans you or I make, in the end, His plans prevail. He's in control."

Frances turned her gaze to Pop's face, wan and ashen against the pillow. "He is in control, even now."

I squeezed her hand. "Yes. Even now. But from now on, let each of us live our lives the way we see fit. That goes for me, and for Helen and Charlie, too. Respect works both ways. We appreciate your advice and guidance, and we promise to listen to what you have to say. But no more schemes and manipulation."

She spoke barely above a whisper. "I'll never do anything like that again." I believed her, and felt the weight of resentment slide off my shoulders.

The following week, I was able to return to work in Chicago, coming home on the weekends. Mr. Fraser temporarily let me work a four-day week, Monday through Thursday, so I could spend Friday through Sunday in Kerryville.

"You're a good worker, Marjorie," he said. "I wish I could grant you a full leave of absence to help your family, but I desperately need your help on the Christmas windows."

I didn't mind. Pop was recovering well, and I missed my life in the city—and Peter. No longer assigned to Field's, he worked on other, smaller cases that didn't require such an elaborate ruse. We saw each other as often as we could, but our dates were mostly confined to fleeting lunches or hastily grabbed dinners. Still, we made the most of them. I loved every minute of getting to know the man he was now, no longer a ghost from the past.

With its owner in jail, Louie's Villa Italiana closed its doors (at least temporarily, until Louie found the right authority to bribe, which in Chicago would not take long). At my suggestion, Dot started filling her evenings by helping Ruthie at the settlement house. With her musical talent, she was a natural at getting everyone enthusiastic about singing, even the boys. My new schedule didn't allow me to make it to rehearsals very often, but at home I sewed two dozen angelic white robes with red collars, while continuing to work on Gabriella's new dress in secret.

Mr. Fraser wasn't kidding about the amount of work that went into preparing Field's Christmas windows. The theme that year was "The Store with the Spirit of Christmas," a splendid wonderland of dolls dressed in the native costumes of many lands, along with model trains, miniature Ferris wheels, and a lavish showcase of the finest toys money could buy. In the middle of everything, the famous aviatrix Amelia Earhart came to sign her new book at Field's book department—a momentous event I shared with Helen. Over post-book-signing sundaes in the tea room, she positively bubbled over with excitement.

"Imagine, a lady aeroplane pilot! I might do that too, someday."

But upon learning that piloting a plane required a great deal of math—not her strong suit—she announced with confidence, "Then I'll portray her on the screen," reverting to her longstanding dream of movie stardom.

I was afraid I'd have to work straight through Thanksgiving Day to get everything done, but at the last minute, Mr. Fraser let me go home for the holiday.

Pop had been released from the hospital well in time for turkey dinner. Peter drove out from the city and joined us for the holiday. Frances treated him as kindly as she had ever treated Richard, even saying how proud she was of him for cracking the smuggling ring at Field's. After dinner, he and I took a stroll around Kerryville. We passed his old house, the pond where we'd skated as youngsters, the park where he and Charlie had played baseball, the gazebo where he'd first told me he'd be going to war.

"It's strange," he mused. "Everything looks so familiar, and yet so different."

"You're a different man now," I said, squeezing his hand.

"Yes, I am," he agreed. "A better man, and a happier man, now that I have you."

We drove back to the city that night, and plunged back into work: me at the store, Peter mopping up details from the Braccio case and pursuing other booze-related cases as the season of revelry unfolded.

I continued to spend weekends in Kerryville. On the Sunday before Christmas, we all piled into Charlie's roadster for the drive to the settlement house Christmas concert—including Pop, who felt strong and eager to get out of the house. Charlie parked near the Congress Hotel, where he, Pop, and Frances would stay overnight, and we walked the short distance to Orchestra Hall. Helen would bunk with Dot and me.

While the family marveled at the elegant lobby and stashed their wraps at the coat check, I sought out Ruthie backstage amid the milling choristers.

"Marjorie!" she exclaimed, her face glowing.

"We made it." I gave her a peck on the cheek and glanced around the backstage area. "How can I help?"

"I think everything's under control. We've been so grateful for Dot's help. She's been a godsend."

"Who's a godsend?" Dot appeared, dressed in a column of ivory silk that made her look like a Grecian statue.

I hugged her. "You are. I can't thank you enough for helping out when I couldn't be here."

"The pleasure's all mine," she said, then added, "You haven't said anything to Charlie, have you? About tonight? I want him to be surprised. He's never heard me sing."

"My lips are sealed."

Next I located Gabriella and tapped her on the shoulder.

"Miss Marjorie!" she squealed, flinging her thin arms around my neck. I returned her hug, then handed her a package. She eyed it curiously.

"What is it?"

"Open it and see."

Quirking an eyebrow, she tore the paper and uttered a joyous cry as she unfolded yards of blue satin.

"For me?" she gasped, her eyes sparkling with unshed tears. "Oh, Miss Marjorie, I've never seen anything so lovely."

"Go put it on," I urged. "Let's see if it fits."

It did. No princess had ever looked more enchanting. I whispered a prayer of thanks to a God who can turn even the worst blunders into something good.

When I returned to the lobby, Frances and Helen had already taken Pop into the auditorium. Charlie paced the lobby. "Where's Dot? She should be here by now."

"I'm sure she's helping out backstage," I reassured him. "We'd better find our seats. She'll catch up with us."

Someone tapped me on the shoulder.

"Peter! You made it."

I longed to throw myself into his arms right then and there, but being in public, we simply exchanged a warm handclasp. The look in his eyes was enough to tell me that he was as happy to see me as I was to see him.

"Come on," he said. "Let's find our seats."

The concert opened with a spirited rendition of "Go Tell It On the Mountain." Everyone applauded, except for Charlie, who kept turning around to keep an anxious eye on the doorway.

"Will you stop?" I hissed. "You're disturbing people."

"She said she'd be here."

"She will be. Relax."

Ruthie, as choir director, stepped to the microphone. "Our next song will be a duet, performed by Miss Gabriella Grimaldi and Miss Dorothy Rodgers."

Charlie's eyes were riveted to the stage as the lights dimmed. A spotlight shone on the two ladies: Gabriella, shimmering in the blue satin dress, and Dot, tall and dignified in her ivory gown. Tears pricked my eyes and a lump formed in my throat as their voices soared and blended in a stirring duet arrangement of the beloved hymn.

While shepherds watched their flocks by night,

All seated on the ground,

The angel of the Lord came down,

And glory shone around.

And glory shone around.

His glory shone around all of us: me, Peter, and my family, and everyone in the auditorium. Peter took my hand in his. With the Lord in His heaven and Peter beside me, I knew that, no matter what, everything was going to turn out all right.

After the concert, we gathered in the lobby over coffee and cookies, basking in the afterglow and congratulating Dot and Gabriella on their performance. As we were collecting our coats, Helen said, "Let's all go see Marjie's windows!"

Laughing and huddling close for warmth, we all traipsed over to State Street and then the couple blocks north to Field's, easing our way into the milling crowd of package-laden shoppers gathered in front of the huge plate-glass windows. Visiting Field's brilliantly lighted Christmas windows was an annual tradition for many Chicagoans. I had to admit, under Mr. Fraser's direction, our team had outdone ourselves, creating an enchanting spectacle of gently falling snow, mannequins resplendent in velvet and taffeta, piles of shimmering presents, and festive carols piped into the frosty air. I strolled over to my father and looped my arm through his.

"What do you think, Pop? A little too heavy on the razzle-dazzle?"

He patted my gloved hand but didn't take his eyes off the window. "Magnificent," he breathed, his breath forming an icy cloud. "Well done, Marjorie. I'm very proud of you."

"We both are." With a gentle smile, Frances took my other arm and gave it a squeeze. A satisfying warmth filled my chest, and I wished I could preserve this perfect moment forever in a little crystal snowglobe.

After we'd viewed all the windows, Helen stamped her red boots in the snow and announced, "I think we should celebrate Marjorie's great accomplishment over hot cocoa. With whipped cream."

Charlie gave her a playful shove.

"Sly fox. Why not just admit you want cocoa?"

"Well, so do I," Pop said heartily.

"There's a coffee shop on the next block that's open 'til midnight," Peter said, pointing. As the family shuffled off in that direction, he pulled me away from the rest of the crowd. "Your dad looks even better than he did at Thanksgiving. How's he coming along?"

Our breath mingled, misted on the cold air.

"His health improves every day," I said. "Dr. Perkins said he should be able to start back to work in January. So very soon you'll have to put up with me being around here every weekend."

"Not soon enough for me," he said, squeezing my hand.

Ahead of us, Helen turned around. "Come on, you two slowpokes. You're lagging behind."

"Go on. We'll catch up," Peter said. Then he steered me into a doorway and kissed me. I returned his kiss. Finally he broke away. "Listen, Marjorie, we need to talk."

"Oh, dear. More secrets?" I said, half joking, but my stomach clenched. I'd heard enough profound revelations out of his mouth to last the rest of my life.

"No more secrets," he promised, swinging my gloved hands in his. "But I do need to tell you . . . now that the Field's case has closed, the bureau wants to send me on a new assignment. Back in New York."

"New York." My heart plummeted. "So far away?" I feigned interest in a holly-festooned window so he wouldn't see my expression. "Well, after all, I suppose you have to go where they send you."

"I'm not going."

"I hope they give you something more exciting than a department store. But nothing too dangerous, either. I hate to think of you out there with all those . . ."

"Are you listening?" he said, turning me to face him. "I said, I'm not going."

My heart gave a little leap. "You're not?"

"Nope. I'm staying right here."

"In Chicago?" My breath whooshed out of my body. "Oh, Peter, I'm thrilled. What's your new assignment? Or is it a secret?"

He took my hand, and we walked on a little farther. "That's the thing. The bureau said 'New York or nothing.' I had to resign."

"Oh, no."

He shrugged. "It's not so bad. I found something else."

"Already? Good for you! Where?"

A smile played around the edges of his mouth. "A department store."

"Huh?"

He stopped directly under the famous clock and turned to me. "You're looking at the newest head of security for Marshall Field & Company."

"At Field's?" I threw my arms around his neck. "That means we can still work together!"

"Work, and plenty of other things. If you'll have me." He reached into his pocket and pulled out a small velvet box. My knees turned to jelly. He opened the box. Something glittered inside, but I couldn't quite make it out through my tears. "Marjorie Corrigan," he said in a husky voice, "will you marry me?"

"Yes! A thousand times, yes."

His voice trembled. "Another man could offer you more, but nobody on earth could love you more than I do."

I brushed my fingers over his temple, scar and all.

"Any woman would be proud to have a man like you by her side."

He hugged me so tightly, I thought I would burst. Beneath the clock, oblivious to the stream of passersby, we formed a little island of two. Over his shoulder, a familiar slogan caught my eye. "Marshall Field & Company . . . Give the lady what she wants."

Thank you, Marshall Field . . . and thank You, God.

This lady could want nothing more.

AUTHOR'S NOTE

Readers have asked me how much of *You're the Cream in My Coffee* is true. It is a work of fiction, with invented characters, settings, and details. All of the primary characters and the entire plot are fictional. Marshall Field & Co. was a real place. I have a fond childhood memory of dining in the store's Walnut Room at Christmastime with my grandmother and cousins, the great shimmering tree casting a glow over the room. When I needed a suitable workplace for Marjorie, the flagship department store seemed the perfect choice. I learned as much as I could about the store in the 1920s from resources like old employee manuals, promotional material, newspaper ads, and books such as *Give the Lady What She Wants*, by Lloyd Wendt and Herbert Kogan, and *Through Charley's Door*, by Emily Kimbrough. James Simpson was president of the company during the 1920s, and Arthur Fraser, designer of the famous windows, worked there from 1895–1944. The Ladies' Nightwear department where Marjorie works, her supervisor, and all her coworkers are fictional, as is the entire plot. Marshall Field & Co. was acquired by Macy's, Inc. in 2005.

The Art Institute of Chicago is also a real place, but Marjorie's experiences there are entirely fictional.

ACKNOWLEDGMENTS

"Alone we can do so little; together we can do so much." (Helen Keller)

To God be the glory.

I offer my deepest thanks to:

My agent and fairy godmother, Ann Byle, who works tirelessly on my behalf and makes this writing journey a lot more fun;

Marcy Weydemuller, whose skilled wordsmithery worked wonders on an early draft of the manuscript;

Kathryn Davis and the talented team at Lighthouse Publishing of the Carolinas, who sculpted the manuscript into a book;

Anita Aurit, Cassandra Cridland, Terese Luikens, and Pam Webb, cherished writer friends and eagle-eyed critique group, who let no lazy adverb go unremarked;

The brilliant Blogettes of Writing North Idaho: Nancy Owens Barnes, Elizabeth Brinton, Kathy Dobbs, Anna Goodwin, Mary Jane Honegger, and Jennifer Rova;

My parents, Donald and the late Patricia Lamont, who gave me a love for books and reading, as well as their constant love and support;

And especially to my husband, Thomas Leo, who encourages me daily, greets wild schemes (like "I think I'll write a novel") with unflinching courage, and never complains, even when deadlines loom and "dinner" is popcorn and coffee.

And thanks to you, dear reader, for taking a chance on a new author. I hope you enjoyed getting to know Marjorie as much as I did. Please visit my website at http://jenniferlamontleo.com to sign up for my newsletter or drop me a line. I'd love to hear from you.

Made in the USA
San Bernardino, CA
05 November 2016